Leap of Faith

by
Amanda McCusker

May you have love to
face your fears and
always choose joy!

♡ Amanda

Balancing Tree Press
Tukwila, WA 98188

First Edition: December 2019
ISBN 978-1-7343685-0-5

Cover design by Trina Krieger

This is a work of fiction. Names, characters, places and incidents
either are the product of the author's imagination or are used
fictitiously, and any resemblance to actual persons, living or dead,
business establishments, events, or locales is entirely coincidental.

Leap of Faith

Chapter 1

I Forgot to Remember to Forget

ARIA

The sand squishes between my toes as warm salt water laps over my petite, calloused feet with the consoling tide. I enjoy this paradisiacal moment at my favorite beach in peak season, napping in the warm afternoon sun with the breeze drifting lazily along my shoulders. My long, chocolate brown hair sways as if to a beat, tickling my skin. With my eyes closed tight against the brightness, I sigh with contentment in this moment.

I shift in my lounge chair, taking in the serene and quiet of the Southern locale, the definition of a perfect day. Almost too perfect, I think vaguely as a raven caws in the distance.

The ugly shrill increases in volume as it gravitates closer toward my peaceful oasis. After only a few moments, the scream sounds right in my ear. I try to shoo away the invisible pest, but the constant piercing won't cease.

Finally, blinking my eyes open, the ideal piece of paradise shatters. The dull, beige walls remind me that I sleep in a small studio apartment in Nevada. Sadness overcomes me as I realize that I lay almost as far away from the picturesque lounge by the sea as I could possibly get.

Yet, I can still smell the salty ocean breeze of my childhood in the air. I reluctantly roll over, slamming the snooze button on the unyielding squawk intruding on my blissful dream.

I've experienced this same fantasy off and on for the last couple of weeks, ever since I found out my best friend was coming to visit. Leana is the only connection I keep from my hometown in South Carolina. I swore I would never return after my abrupt departure five years ago. I fled about as far away as I possibly could and still remain in the continental United States.

Too many demons haunt me in that corner of the world. The most tormenting one being a very loud, selfish person I reluctantly call Mother. Nonetheless, this recurring dream makes me miss my Southern home, warm afternoons lounging at the beach and a life that moved just a little bit slower.

I wish, as I have many times while living in the desert, that I could spend a relaxing day by the beach, like I'd grown up taking for granted. However, that was not going to happen today, or any day in the near future. I try my best to put it out of my mind as I stare idly at the bland ceiling, attempting to come to terms with reality.

I have a good life here in Las Vegas. I am able to write, not exactly my dream job of being a fantasy author, but writing screenplays for a variety show has its perks. I have one good friend, and know the cast of the show well enough to enjoy drinks and laugh together.

Another gem was when I found a small apartment that I can mostly afford within bus distance of the strip where I work that has a pool and very few roaches. I enjoy the excitement of Sin City; it never fails to entertain, when I remember to look at least. I have no complaints in particular, yet it feels like I'm sleepwalking through life.

In the moments between being asleep and awake, I'm increasingly getting this persistent feeling of something lacking in my life. I'm feeling it more strongly as these vivid dreams fill my nights. I am coming to accept that something is missing, but I'm still unsure what it is, or where to find it.

I moved to the other side of the country in hopes of forgetting all my problems. Ignoring my past has worked for the last five years, why can't it last forever? The small South Carolina town feels like a lifetime away and yet, it still haunts me. The freedom I felt when I dropped everything and fled, regretfully isn't holding up over time.

The ugly scenes of memories play through my head causing me to bolt out of bed. "No use for a pity party," I mumble out loud. Looking around, I realize there is not one to listen anyway.

That never made me sad before, yet today I feel disheartened after smelling the warm, salty beach air so strongly. I miss having a connection. However, I realize that with little exception, I've never had much connection anyway.

My feet drag on the worn carpet to my miniscule bathroom. I remember the elation feeling when I finally moved into this tiny apartment, my very first one. My best friend, Leana, had come all the way from Myrtle Beach to help me move in three years ago. Which was really just an excuse to see each other and the only time she's been able to visit. We spent that first night sitting on a blanket toasting with cheap champagne in plastic flutes. The blanket under us was the only furniture I had back then, at least it was soft.

I consider that a good memory as I pluck my eyebrows in the vanity mirror. It doesn't change the present though, I am no longer living the shiny Vegas dream. Anger and restlessness sent me here, which had started big and exciting. However, whatever I am seeking in my subconsciousness isn't here, and the city is becoming nothing more than a distraction to finding what that is.

I'd learned a lot in these last few years on my own in Sin City, but the most prominent thing I learned was that I want more out of life. Where am I supposed to go from here? That is the question I have not quite found an answer to.

The warm water rinses off my body as I enjoy my shower and try to still the chaos of thoughts in my head. I don't want to dream of the soft sand and waves kissing my toes in the shores of South Carolina anymore because I would not consider moving back. I do not want to go down that road again, not now, not ever.

I decide on a bright sundress and step into my makeshift kitchen to find some breakfast. Looking at my kitchen cat clock, I release an audible sigh as it ticks 7:30 am. It is so early. There are many benefits to contract work as a screenwriter, not having to wake up and keep office hours is at the top of the list. I begin to prep myself for my meeting with the theater director, though the thought of discussing upcoming projects is about as interesting as mindlessly pouring this cereal and milk into a bowl.

This meeting that drug me out of bed so early is not one I'm looking forward too. I can hear the gossip around the theater just like everyone else, and unless there is something spectacular that the powers that be are keeping to themselves, there is nothing upcoming to get too excited about. The current show has only been open for two weeks and will run through the summer. However, all the ideas they pitched so far sounds about as interesting as watching milk curdle when it comes to writing creatively. All I really want to do is to work on my own novel; however, right now that option does not pay the bills.

Before I could get depressed by my lack of options, again, my phone buzzes. Reading Leana's message jolts me awake for a few moments, *We're on our plane now! We're still on for dinner in, right? I'm always a wreck after flying.* Of course! At least seeing Leana was something to look forward to today. *I'm ordering pizza. You still like Margherita style pizza right?*

Oh yeah, perfect. Do you have wine?

A Malbec with your name on it.

You know me well. Don't forget Alicia is with me, that means no embarrassing escapades.

Like that's ever stopped us? Your sister knows us too well.

True. See you soon girlie! Only 3,000 miles to go.

It goes by before you know it. Take a nap!

I'll try! Later.

I smile into the phone, thankful that Leana is coming into town. The reoccuring somber mood these last few months is starting to worry me. Even though I'm often surrounded by people, I feel lonely. This lost in the crowd feeling is a sensation that I only recently realized. The worst part, I have no idea what to do about it. I hope Leana has some insight for me, she tends to have impressions about what will happen next.

At least I can't keep throwing myself a pity party with Leana around, she wouldn't even consider letting me brood. It's not the first time we've had to pull each other out of a pit, nor do I imagine it will be the last. Leana has been there with me through it all and I am so thankful for her. Especially after I decided to move three thousand miles away from everything I knew in a state of anger, Leana still stood by me.

Being so distant from her and her family that supported

me through my rough teenage years with an absentee mother is my one regret to such an extreme relocation. That and the feel of the warm sand under my feet sitting by the edge of the ocean on a Carolina beach. Those are the only two things I really miss about the South, and yet, it is enough to feel homesick.

Leana and I are notorious for some crazy adventures while growing up. Leana's mom, Mrs. Grace, always made sure we stayed out of trouble. This was no easy task since there was always so much going on. Their mother also didn't appreciate us corrupting Alicia so young. We good-naturedly laughed at her reprimands, but we never did anything that bad, never illegal or life threatening. We were mostly harmless, just restless teenagers in a busy town of tourists. It seems, not much has changed.

I feel a lighter mood descend upon me as I think about our youthful misadventures. I'm looking forward to seeing Leana this evening. I know I can't go back to those days, but I feel a sense of belonging that I realize I am missing now.

The theater offices are about a ten minute bus ride from my apartment. Checking the clock again, I realize I have only about five minutes to catch the bus. Dropping my bowl in the sink, I gather my purse before running out the door. These types of meetings usually don't take long, but I don't want to be late.

I don't own a car, there's really no need for one. Public transportation is available and mostly reliable. Not only do I not want to deal with the ridiculous traffic in this city, but I don't care to pay for insurance or maintenance either. No, the bus and my own two legs are good enough to get my wherever I need to go.

I wait for the bus, as I do everyday. It is easy to get around this town, all you need is a little patience. I am constantly amazed at how little patience people have. I wonder if every city is like this or just this one. I don't remember the hurry growing up in the southeast, even in the popular tourist spot of Myrtle Beach, SC. Then again, that could just be the product of being a kid. I was still a kid when I left, though I felt grown up enough.

As I step onto the bus and take a seat in my favorite spot in the back I wonder why I am reminiscing so much today. I am excited to see Leana, sure, but we talk fairly often on the phone and through social media.

I step off the bus feeling pensive and head toward Planet Hollywood, home of the V theater and the small establishment I thank for helping me pay my bills, most of the time, at least.

I wonder again as I walk up the familiar space, is life so bad for me here? It is loud, but there is no shortage of interesting people. It is tolerable, a challenge sometimes to get away from the craziness this city entices, but at the same time that is exactly why I came here. I wanted to forget the years leading up to my impromptu move. This was definitely a city to come and forget your troubles, the problem is, you forget where you are heading in the process.

When I reach the small set of offices inside the V theater, I make small talk with the receptionist. The middle age blonde, Rachel, tells me how her son just hit his first home run in the little league game last weekend. I can hear the pride in her voice and something unknown in me aches.

I wish my mom would have been proud of me growing up, but nothing was ever good enough. At the same time, I wish I had someone to be proud of as well. The loneliness surfaces again so I force my smile as I give the appropriate nods of interest, even while I try to get away from the front desk.

What is wrong with me today? I wonder as I begin to head towards my boss's office. Normally, I'm an expert at suppressing my emotions, but today is providing a challenge. It is another reminder that I am missing something, perhaps I'm not doing as well at pretending as I thought.

I didn't expect to stay with the theater as a contract based screenwriter past my first project. Now it has been three years and this last show marks my sixth screenplay. None of them were my original ideas, I wish. I might actually enjoy the work if I could create it myself. However, these are rewrites, adaptations to convert a familiar story the directors already decide on into screenplay format, sometimes with a twist. It's all gimmicks for easy marketing and to make the audience stay engaged. Some creativity is managed along the way, but nothing like the fiction I desire to create.

I have worlds in my head bursting to get out, but something always blocks them. I tend to blame my circumstances, but they don't seem to be changing. Perhaps if I'm honest, the holdup lies with me. If only I could figure out how to get out of my own way to discover my next step. I have a novel half finished on my laptop sitting in my apartment. It just sits there looking sad and discarded, kind of like I'm feeling these days.

Shaking my head, I am even less than excited about the upcoming meeting and I feel completely stalled in my role here. It solidifies my increasing desire to get out and focus on something else more creative.

I knock on the half-open door as I stick my head in my boss's office. Lead director Ken Julant looks up from a pile of papers with a smile on his face. "Aria, how are you today?"

"I'm well, thanks, and you?" I reply as I sit down in the chair across from his desk. His life is here in pictures of his family and awards for the theater.

"Oh good, yes, I'm just fine. I just wanted to touch base with you on some upcoming projects." At my nod he continues, "We have another collaboration meeting next week if you want to sit in. The next story is going to be "Bonnie and Clyde: A Romance Robbery," he explains with his arms panning the title.

He seems so excited about the idea, but I groan inside.

"That sounds very interesting," I try to fake interest, I don't want to do this project; however, I need to figure out what else I can do before I burn this bridge. "I will let you know by Friday if I will be able to work on that project. I also wanted to check and make sure that handful of edits worked out in rehearsal yesterday."

"Oh yes, they were a great improvement. The scene with Teresa and Brent flowed a lot easier. Thank you for taking the extra time on it."

"You're welcome."

We continue to talk all the while I think more and more about this afternoon when I can see Leana and less about the words exchanged. I am glad when Mr. Julant hints that he needs to address another matter now. I politely take the cue and head out to the strip without giving the interaction any more thought.

Instead, my novel blazes in my mind. I haven't checked in with the characters in a while and I find I miss them and the story they are trying to tell me. Writing is my one true love in life, the one thing that has ever set my soul on fire. Why haven't I made it more of a priority? Why can't I manage to pay the bills and still be able to write? Once again I think, what am I missing?

I yearn to finish the story, but somehow, every time I start spending time on it something else gets in the way. The last time I worked heavily on it, I was so excited because I had a little money in my pocket after finishing a screenplay. However, the show flopped. It wasn't anyone's fault in particular, it turned out not to be the kind of show Vegas desired. Any additional revenue was cut back so I had to take a second job as a bartender just to get by.

The thought of bartending made me nervous at first because though I can be outgoing, I am an introvert at heart. The experience turned out to be a good one though because that was when I got to know Mikey. He also works at the V Theater in the Audiovisual department. He hooked me up with the bartending gig and taught me everything I know.

I was thankful for the job and for a new friend. Mikey and I get along great, and bonded quickly over dysfunctional parents and trying to escape from feeling trapped in our hometown. Mikey is from Raleigh, NC, so we would often check each other to make sure our southern accents didn't sneak out.

He remains the one and only candidate for possible boyfriend material, however, we found out quickly that we are just friends. After an awkward kiss while staying up late talking one night, we looked at each other and laughed. I still consider him one of the best friends I've made here, but he's more like the brother I never wanted. We pick on each other, but it's nice to have someone to talk to in this town.

Even with the extra work and a reliable friend, I had a hard time making it. I worked around the clock for several months to design a script for the next production that Las Vegas did want. For a while, anytime I was not writing on the script or at the bar was spent sleeping.

I enjoyed the creativity they allowed me and hoped they would continue with the freedom. But no, after that they decided to go back to their regular way of doing things leaving me wondering where do I go from here.

Now, things are going well with this show, so I have a little money saved up, and amazingly some time as well. These are both good things; nonetheless, the inspiration disappeared with the influx. I find I am completely unmotivated and not writing at all these days. I feel lost and sorry for myself, two things I hate. Thankfully, it won't last long. Now that my morning responsibilities were done I could start counting down the minutes until Leana and Alicia landed in Vegas.

Chapter 2

My Old Friend

ARIA

I am dozing on the couch while watching *The Great British Baking Show* when my phone dings. I sit straight up as I read Leana's message: *Vegas baby! The plane has landed, now to find a bathroom and a taxi! I can't wait to see you girlie, go ahead and pop that cork!*

I text back, *Pop! See you soon!* I add celebrating, hearts and cheers emojis.

I order the pizza and then get up and go in the kitchen to open the wine. I try to keep my hands busy, but it only takes so long to pop a cork. I know it will still be a bit before they get here, but I feel my heart racing with anticipation.

I wish I would have gone over to the airport so I could see them when they got off the plane. We decided that since I didn't have a car, there was little need for me to go to meet them at the airport only to take a taxi back anyway. Still, I almost bussed over there just to see Leana sooner.

Before I can start pacing a trail into my carpet, I hear a knock at the door. Suddenly, I'm glad I didn't go to the airport after all because that could only be one person.

I open the door wide to reveal my best friend and her little sister. Squeals could be heard for miles as they drop everything on my doorstep and step in for hugs. It feels good to see her again, talking on the phone is good, but there is something powerful about human connection.

"You're here already!" I squeal into Leana's ear.

"Our plane landed early, so we waited to text. I wanted to surprise you."

"Well you did! Great surprise." I hug her again. "Though I did just order the pizza."

"Did you get the wine opened?"

"That I managed."

"Then we're golden." Leana replies with a smile. I let her through the door with Alicia trailing after her.

"I'm glad you could come, Alicia." I reach for her second bag and close the door behind them.

"By that you mean, thanks for keeping Leana company on the flight so she doesn't freak out going through the airport." she answers with a smile.

I look her straight in the eye, "yes."

We all burst out laughing. It is an interesting relationship we all have. Even though they are not my blood relations, I have a stronger bond with them than my own family.

Alicia is three years younger than us and always trying following us around. It was annoying at times, but also useful when we made backyard productions to cast her in a role. We generally had a fun time together. Being older, we wanted our own space, but we usually didn't mind when Alicia tagged along.

It is a joy having Alicia here, especially to celebrate her birthday, though a little late.

"Didn't you just have a very important birthday?" I ask.

She looks back at me with a wicked smile, "Maybe."

"I have a feeling I know why you wanted to come so bad. Celebrating your twenty-first birthday in Vegas is pretty exciting."

"Yeah, it is," Leana nudges her sister in the hip, "We're going to have a great time."

"Absolutely." I agree as Alicia continues to beam.

"For now, let's start with some wine." Leana puts her hand on her sister's shoulder, "which you, for once, can legally drink."

I lead the way, showing them where they can put their things in my small bedroom. We get the wine from the kitchen and relax on the couch.

Leana gushed about their flight, particularly about the handsome Army man that sat in the row across from them. Alicia complained about how early they had to get up.

I feel myself loosen up and enjoy this moment sitting in the comfortable company of friends talking about idle things. I don't get this very often, I miss the luxury. That ache lingering from my dream seems to be sedated, at least for now.

Once the pizza gets here, the real conversation begins. Apparently, Alicia is head over heels for the shortstop of the Myrtle Beach Pelicans, a Minor League baseball team.

"Cameron is handsome." Leana agrees after Alicia's digest of details.

"Does he treat you right?" I ask.

"He does. Cam's from old money down in Charleston and is following his passion. He played four years at Coastal Carolina, and is now trying to make it to the big leagues. He's working his way up. Scouts are constantly at the games, he pointed them out when I was there last week."

"Now that's exciting. Are you guys serious?" I inquire.

"Maybe, yes. We've been dating for a little over a year. I met him at one of the NCAA clubs last year." Alicia glows. I can tell that it's serious, she speaks of him so intimately.

"That makes sense." I reply. Alicia is a very competitive and plays NCAA volleyball for Coastal

Carolina. This is her senior year.

"I'm just glad one of us is happy in love," Leana says.

"Uh oh, does that mean Bill isn't the one?" I ask her sympathetically. It only takes one instant to know that the answer was incredibly not good. In the breath of his name Leana's eyes narrow and a shadow crosses her face. Even Alicia grows quiet.

Unfortunately, the haunted look was one I knew too well. When we were in our senior year of high school, Leana had a boyfriend name Graham. He was a jock and a popular guy. He seemed really nice until he beat her one night for talking to another guy. We found out then how cruel a person he really was. She was devastated by the entire ordeal and I can't blame her, he hid his cruelty extremely well.

After seeing that look in her eyes again, I immediately lean forward reaching out toward my friend, my heart breaking for her. "Why didn't you tell me?"

Leana breathes in deeply, exhaling heavily before she looks up, "It's one reason why I'm here. I needed to get away and I wanted to tell you in person. Alicia came as a bodyguard I think."

I look over at Alicia sipping her wine. She shrugs letting her sister tell her own tale.

"Of course, I didn't expect to have this be one of the first conversations." Leana smirks weakly.

"It should be. I can't be there for you if you don't tell me." I want to let her off the hook, but our friendship is too strong for such nonsense.

She takes my hand and squeezes it, a familiar gesture of shared strength. "You are right, best to get this part over and done with so we can properly enjoy this trip."

After a moment and a hearty sip of wine, she begins. "It happened a lot like Graham. Boys always like how I can charm a room until I talk to anyone else besides them. It was at a Baseball Gala in celebration of a new sponsor for his team. I had just gotten a new dress and was having a good time mingling. Everyone was so pretty. It was hard to recognize some of them, even though I knew most everyone on the team by this point.

"After a few glasses of champagne, Bill began to shut down. I could see the hard look he gave me. He was waiting for some news to see if he would move up in the league, so I figured he'd gotten his answer and didn't like it. However, when we got home Bill practically pushed me into the bedroom yelling at me because I was flirting with one of the pitchers.

"I didn't have a response. I couldn't even remember which one that was. The entire encounter came out of left field," she paused with a chuckle, "Though the pun wasn't intended, I suppose it would work."

It takes me a minute to remember Bill plays left field for the Myrtle Beach Pelicans.

"He started to reach for me with violent hands and called me a whore." She pauses with a shake of her head.

It always amazes me how someone who can give such great advice and wisdom to others has a hard time not getting herself into tough situations. I think of how strong she is now as she continues with a stern look on her face. "I will not associate with these jealous men who think they have some kind of sick control over me or who I talk to. I was so mad."

Alicia starts chuckling to herself, letting me know the punchline is close. Leana started taking self-defense classes after Graham, which let to martial arts and yoga. Now, she is a force to be reckoned with.

"What did you do miss black belt?" I ask truly curious if Bill left the room unscathed, while secretly hoping he didn't.

"I kneed him in the groin and then reached down and took my heel off and hit him upside the head with it. Knocked him out cold. I then proceeded to gather what little stuff I had at his place and left a note saying that is no way to treat a lady and if he ever comes near me again I will call the cops without asking questions first."

"Good for you." I congratulate her on her quick thinking and vow to follow her lead and never take any abuse from a man. Leana has always been strong, but now she isn't scared anymore, it has made all the difference. She's always been a spitball, it's nice to see her harness the energy. Charisma is a double edged sword, she would say, it takes finesse to know how to wield it.

As we sit in my small apartment eating pizza, drinking wine and talking about things that really matter, I am caught up in a moment of ecstasy. This is what home feels like, not the place, but these people and sharing things that are real. I think of my dream again, of the feeling of something missing, I wonder if this is it.

"What are you thinking about?" Leana asks.

"It's nothing, we should do something really fun this week so you can forget all about senseless men."

"We will," Leana says confidently, "but you were thinking of something else."

I start to deny it, but the look she gives me says I better start telling the truth. That is the problem with having friends who've known you for so long, you just can't lie to them, even about the little stuff. "It's nothing, I'm just a little out of it lately."

"Have you been dreaming about the ocean again?" Leana looks at me with a knowing eye.

I turn to her, "How did you know? I told you about it only that one time."

She points at me, "I remembered it because it matters. You're getting that look again. It's the same look you got before you moved out here. You are about to do something big, I know it."

"I don't know what. I'm just getting restless. I miss South Carolina in the spring. This place is so fake, even my shows are getting more and more ridiculous. Whatever I was looking for, it certainly isn't here."

"Did you really think it was?"

"Yes." I reply more confidently than I feel.

Even Alicia laughs at this. I can't help myself, I join in. Somehow everything seems a little more bearable with them by my side. "Why am I always the last to know?"

"I think I know you better than you know yourself."

"I wish you would give me some insight."

"Something big is about to happen, I can see in your eyes, and you are ready for it. It will be unexpected and it will move fast, trust it."

I look at her a moment, contemplating her words. Prophecy is one of Leana's gifts. So many of her words have come true over the years, I can't help but sober at the thought, suddenly nervous of the unknown.

It didn't matter that it was a Tuesday, the Las Vegas strip never stops, day or night, 365 days a year. People come for the food, the shows, and of course, the booze. Alcohol of all varieties, especially expensive fruity cocktails, are available everywhere, even on the sidewalk, which you are allowed to carry around with you since Las Vegas has no open container restrictions.

It was once exotic, but now as I have to clumsily maneuver around a lady stumbling down the sidewalk at two o'clock in the afternoon, I admit it can be a little sad. Vacation is one thing, but this is not a life.

Walking arm in arm, we spot Senor Frogs and head towards the gigantic frog sitting on the roof. As we skip along, we pass two big ships that sit in front of the entrance belonging to Treasure Island, a pirate and ocean themed resort. When I first moved here, the resort presented a big pirate show every night to draw in tourists. They don't anymore, and I was sad to see it go. I'm always in the mood for a theatrical show.

It's crazy to think I've been here long enough for things to change so much. Then again, especially in a city like Vegas, it's all about the next big thing. It makes sense that acts come and go quickly.

I follow the bridge to the entrance of the restaurant with Leana on my arm and Alicia wandering slightly behind us. Since it's her first time in Vegas, I can appreciate her yearn to take it all in. It feels like magic, the bright colors that feel larger than life. I remember when it felt like that for me.

We get to the greeter and are surprisingly able to get a table right away, there are some benefits to eating dinner in the middle of the afternoon. The biggest benefit is leaving more room for drinking and shenanigans during the evening hours.

I woke up this morning feeling better than I have in a while. It surprises me how much Leana and Alicia's being here makes me feel whole and confident in myself again, at the very least much less alone.

Maybe there really is some truth to the recent reminiscing I've been having lately. Like Leana said, it is time for a change. I'm still not sure if I'm ready to go home again, but being closer to my friend could be a life changer. I don't know what else there is left in Vegas for me. The big, bright lights that fascinates Alicia are starting to give me a headache.

As we sit down at the table, I am unable to think deep thoughts anymore as a handsome man asks us if we want drinks. "Margaritas all around," Leana exclaims.

Alicia and I nod in agreement and show our IDs. It's slightly annoying for me, but I can see the twinkle in Alicia's eyes when she shows that she is old enough to consume the beloved beverage.

We've all come a long way from the children we were dressing up and creating plays in the backyard. Leana beams as she sees another person bringing around festive hats for pictures and she grabs them up for all of us.

I love Leana's enthusiasm for the smallest things, she is one of the most charismatic people I know and attracts people with just a look or a word, sometimes even simply by being present.

Of course, this gets her in trouble as much as it is helpful, but we have a lot of stories to tell thanks to her talent. At least in this instance, we get to keep wearing the hats when they would normally take them back after explaining that we haven't gotten our drinks yet and were waiting for the perfect picture opportunity. Only Leana would get her way, which she did.

It is no surprise Leana found a career on stage as an actress. It was thanks to her that I started writing screenplays, first for ourselves as kids. Her brother hated being dragged into them, but since he was the youngest of the three, it became our chore to watch him. We made the best of it. Alicia took part willingly for the most part, she liked to be involved in what we were doing. She never minded taking the baby or little sister part. Their dog Cleo usually got to be the prince, who did as much saving as needed to being saved, usually because he ran under the house when we tried to put costumes on him.

I seemed to find myself in the damsel in distress roles, while Leana always took on the villain roles. She was good at it too, I think she likes that they were powerful roles. In traditional stories, it seems women can only be powerful if they were evil. It took me a while to realize this and that is one reason I want to write a story where the female is the powerful force of good looking to save a prince and anyone else she could.

Leana squeals as our huge margaritas came, bringing me back to the present, "This is perfect!"

We order our food and then Leana lifts her fruity cocktail for a toast, "To being together on this beautiful day, the power to overcome annoying people who only want to bring us down, new beginnings that are yet to be seen," she looks at me, "and having an awesome time in Vegas baby!"

"Here, here," Alicia and I cheer, a familiar echo to Leana's famous toasts and we drink our first sips of margaritas. We all sigh in pure contentment. Okay I have to admit, there are some great things about this city, too.

Chapter 3

Viva Las Vegas

ARIA

No matter how tiring Las Vegas becomes to live in, fun will always exist downtown, otherwise known as the Fremont Experience. After a delicious, relaxing meal, including another round of margaritas, we headed out to the one place I knew we would have a good time.

Even on a Tuesday night, the music pumps along the pedestrian streets as lights flood the dome making the sky move the the beat. I don't know what Downtown Las Vegas was like back in the day, but since they built the dome and stages, it promises an experience like no other.

I look down the street with a knowing smile creeping along my lips. Leana and Alicia stare with wide eyes and gaping mouths at the blue lights projecting onto the ceiling, reflecting in their eyes. This is the experience they are looking for and one I hope to never forget along with them.

Alicia wraps me into an enthusiastic hug and kisses my cheek. "The is amazing!" she exclaims.

"Happy birthday, Alicia." I hug her back.

"Best birthday ever," she responds with stars in her eyes.

I laugh, glad I could make her day and also giddy with a lightness that I haven't felt in years.

Alicia nudges Leana's hip, "What better place could there be to come and forget Mr. Asshole."

"Mr. Who?" Leana exclaims, "I already forgot. I'm

ready to forget why I need to forget. Time for another drink and to experience life to the fullest."

"Right this way, I know the perfect place." I take Leana's hand and dance towards the bar where I work with Mikey. I had texted him earlier to let him know we'd probably stop by. *A friend?* he'd responded, *My night just got a lot more interesting.*

Something foreign and wild in the Fremont Experience awakens the soul. It holds little back, appearing gritty, extremely opposite to the polished flamboyance of the Vegas Strip. This is where real life happens, often unexpectedly. All of it is something very different than our serene southeastern home.

Las Vegas is exciting to visit, but living here is quite different. A simple night out with friends that breaks up the monotonousness of everyday life is a godsend. I feel alive tonight. I am thankful because I haven't gone out for a night on the town in over a year. Coming here for work is so different than coming here for the experience of it. I didn't realize I needed a kick in the butt so bad to get out and do something stimulating. Oblivious of my inner qualms, Leana and Alicia both crack into excited grins and squeals of laughter as I lead them through the streets.

My comrades are overcome by the bright neon lights known for this part of town as we walk along the pedestrian-only street. I point to a local bar, the one that I work at off and on as times get tough and money needs some coaxing to enter my bank account. Though I haven't worked there for a few months now, I'm still friends with much of the staff. Mikey is working tonight, I figure he'll get a kick out of Leana in her short black shirt and lacey white top that accentuates her breasts lovely.

"Lights," shines brightly in neon lights against a blue background. Even the door shines with brilliant royal blue fluorescent. This little dive bar, almost hidden on the upper floor at the edge of downtown proper, feels comfortable to me. It's a location where I know I am safe, especially when Mikey is working. Strange that feeling comes from a bar, I suppose. This place and the people in it saved me when I thought I was down and out.

Mikey, especially, makes life fun. He is like a big kid and always makes me laugh.

I spot Mikey as we walk in. I lead my entourage toward the tall, thin man with a scruffy beard standing behind the bar talking easily with a couple of ladies.

Mikey looks away and smiles at me as we approach. He waves me over to an empty stool on the back side of the round bar. Leana and Alicia follow giggling.

The karaoke had already started and the bald man screeching out "Walk this way" as we walk around the bar was, well, he wasn't good. I try not to cringe as I make a beeline for the bar stool to put more distance between me and that noise.

"Don't you look fine tonight" Mikey hands me my go to drink, gin and tonic, and looks me over. I am suddenly very aware that I am wearing more makeup and showing more skin than usual.

"You can close your jaw now Mikey, Leana wouldn't let me leave the apartment until I rolled my skirt up two inches." I gesture over to my friend.

"Well, at least I know who to thank. Hello ladies, can I get you a drink this fine evening?"

"Absolutely." Leana answers with a wink, "I'm Leana, and this is my sister Alicia. I'll start with a gin and tonic as well. Now, how exactly do you know my best friend?"

He chuckles and turns to Alicia who nods to have the same, "We work together over at the theater. Aria writes the scripts, I man the sound booth." He shrugs and gestures around him, "and this pays the bills."

"That sounds about right. I'm an actress, I understand completely." Leana nods.

He raises his brow at that and asks. "What type of work do you do?"

She looks over at me intrigued, "I work with a small theatre company called Stage Left. I'm currently in a production of *Deathtrap*, a murder mystery that started a few weeks ago."

"That sounds captivating. Are you the murderer?" I watch as he focuses his entire attention on Leana, leaning in a little. I've seen him talked easily and flirt with women often, but I noticed a spark in his eye that is not usually there.

She leans in towards him resting her chin on the back of her hand and says in a sultry voice, "What if I am?"

Mikey's eyes look her up and down "Then I definitely want to see this show."

"You should, it's pretty good." She replies and sits up straight on her stool causing her breasts to become the focus of Mikey's attention.

"Umhmm," I catch him licking his lips as he turns his attention to make their drinks.

I lean back to catch Alicia's eye to make sure I wasn't the only one who caught that very flirty vibe. The wide eyes and smirk on Alicia's face let's me know it was definitely there. Wouldn't that be nice, I think idly.

While Mikey's back is turned, Leana looks over to me with a "he looks good" gesture. I smile back with a nod and a thumbs up.

Once Mikey turns back around and sets drinks in front of Alicia then Leana, she asks him "Is the current show you two are working on any good? Aria here didn't have a lot to say on the matter."

I huff, "I said it was good."

"I need more. I need to want to see it."

Mikey laughs with a deep baritone, "It's hilarious. The characters behind the makeup really pull off the twisted fairy tale classics that Aria masterminded. You'll never laugh so much as when you see them try to bury Snow White alive after they couldn't find the prince." Mikey answers.

"Spoilers" I scold, but start laughing as I remember the first rehearsal for that scene.

Leana turns to me exclaiming, "Much better. See, now I want to see it."

"Well if you could have stayed until Thursday night, you would have been able to" I counter.

"I know," she raises her hand, "I wish I could stay longer."

"Me too," I agree.

"Me three," Mikey chimes in with a huge grin. Leana smiles back before he turns to take care of other customers.

I watch the way Mikey easily flows between people making comfortable conversation. I enjoy talking with people, but I've never felt the effortlessness that he radiates. I much prefer being on the outside looking in, where my mind is always creating a story.

I sit quietly, letting the familiar chatter wash over me as Leana and Alicia comment on all of the lights and sounds around us. It's nice to have friends from here and from home in the same place. Sitting in this blend of companions, I feel intensely that something is about to change. This notion has been building consistently as the week goes on.

Mikey comes back to us and chats about this and that. He and Leana get along very nicely. I wink at Alicia when she leans back and points to her sister once again leaned deeply over the counter talking with Mikey. It makes me happy to see them getting along.

I enjoy the energy in this place. I could spend the entire evening sitting right here, but there is more to experience. After finishing our drinks and Leana savoring a little more flirting time with Mikey, we order a second drink and take it with us, a fun little perk of Vegas.

They have a lot left to see in Vegas if this hole-in-the-wall impresses them. I thank Mikey and wish him a good night as we take our drinks down among the lights and sounds of Old Vegas, the side where real life happens.

On this warm night in May, it does.

We dance in the streets among the many performers and find another round of drinks along the way down the pedestrian street. We eventually settle in to enjoy an unusually good 80's cover band, complete with red hats and an impressive guitarist spinning out stunning solos.

A group of four guys dance next to us for a good bit of the night. They are fun and flirty, but for the most part keep their distance and respect our girl's night out. However, there is one in the group that catches my eye.

I can't tell what it is exactly that intrigues me so much about him. Perhaps it is his muscular body swaying to the beat in a slightly awkward motion like he's trying too hard to enjoy the moment. It could be his cautious smile to his friends to assure them he's having a good time.

It is when I get a glimpse of his eyes that I know I am smitten. They are bright blue sapphires that seem to sparkle overpowering even bright lights of the city.

I keep glancing over at this tall blonde unable to deny I am intrigued. When he looks back and holds my gaze for a moment, I still. Caught in the moment, I'm not sure what to do.

He smiles and then looks away. Immediately, he glances back. A warm feeling rises in my stomach. I yearn to speak with him. In that moment the trance of the music and the closeness of my friends next to me keep me in place. I will have to remember to thank Leana for convincing me to dress up and live a little.

ROMAN

Music from the 80's flows through the air with a beat of another lifetime. I can remember listening to these songs blasting as a kid when my family was still whole and happy. My sister, Athena and I got those little red block hats and thought it was the most amazing thing ever. I am lost in another era as the memories breeze by on the waves of sound. I thought I forgot what it was like to be happy, I miss the easy smile of that time.

I try to let it all go, shunning the reminder of events long out of my control. I would much rather concentrate on the brunette to my right dancing with a couple friends that keeps stealing glances my way. She would be considered beautiful by anyone's standards, but I am curious about what causes that little gleam in her eye.

It has been a long day. The trip to get out here yesterday from Charleston took more effort than I expected and I still feel lagged by the time difference. My mentor and friend, Andrew, laughed as I complained about how off I felt because I was eating breakfast when I craved lunch.

"It's just part of the business, Roman, you will get used to the travel." Andrew told me earlier today. "There's lots to see and do in Vegas, starting looking around and you'll see. Don't worry so much, it will be a good time."

Andrew doesn't like the travel as much now because it keeps him away from his wife and three kids, but my friend's eyes lit up when we entered the city.

I have to admit, it is an impressive view of the world. I can stand at my hotel window and see Paris with New York up the street and even the fantastical land of Excalibur further still. Perhaps I need to adjust my attitude, this place is pretty cool.

Even that is harder than I expected. I've spent the last five years behind a desk with my nose in books, anything to forget, to survive. Books and the endless quest to learn more became my lifeline and I did not look up often. It is time though. I've been working at this company for almost a year and the promise of travel opportunity is a huge testament to my hard work and dedication. The supervisors decided that since Andrew didn't want to travel as much in the future he'd better train a new recruit to handle the business at conventions around the world. I'm that lucky guy.

The travel doesn't really bother me so much, though I don't have much experience. I figure with only me to worry about, there should be no problem. I might even grow to like it. I've never really gone much of anywhere. Florida to Disney World when I was a kid. We camped in the Great Smoky Mountains of Tennessee once while I was in Boy Scouts. Not a lot of adventure until my belt, but there's no time like the present. I am glad Andrew is here, he takes the lead and I follow behind trying to learn how to navigate in his footsteps.

The open container laws in Las Vegas surprised me. It seems there are lots of things allowed in this audacious city that were frowned upon in most of the country. Andrew laughed when I asked, and said, "the rules don't apply here, this is Sin City, a place with its own set of rules."

I'm still not sure how I feel about the lackadaisical atmosphere. I happen to like rules, knowing how far I can go and who blame when things go too far. I hesitate at first, feeling overpowered in this large city of lights and sounds. However, this is my second day here and after spending that time conversing about business, I'm getting the hang of how to interact with people in this sense. Turns out I'm fairly good at it. Upon realizing this I'm finally ready to relax, riding the confidence boost.

I'm not sure why I feel so hesitant in coming out tonight. Even Andrew, the most grounded person I know, thinks it is a brilliant idea. There is always something holding me back from trying new things and putting myself out there in any type of social setting. I'm beginning to wonder if it is all just in my head.

It is a beautiful spring night, in the high 80s with the temperature dropping slowly as the sun goes down. It is a different kind of warm than the humidity surrounding the lowcountry of South Carolina, but it is nice.

I read about the Fremont Experience in one of the brochures I got from the hotel. It seems like fun with live bands and a screen projection on the roof.

It feels surreal seeing a concert on a Tuesday night. Somehow it sets the entire experience apart from reality. I try not to act as overwhelmed as I feel seeing the lights and all the diversely dressed people around.

Once we got out of our taxi, we walked around taking it all in. Andrew bought me a drink and Dawson cheered our night of debauchery. We headed toward a band playing on stage in the center of the blocked off road. They are an 80's rock band and I laugh when I see them wearing little red hats.

Before they finish the first song, I spotted a group of three girls. They were dancing and laughing to the music.

Just the sight of them makes me smile, thinking they are having a good time. I should be doing the same.

The one with chestnut hair looks alive and free. I have never seen anyone so idiosyncratic and I am curious as to who she is and where she comes from. There wasn't anything in particular that stood out, but the way light beams from her eyes draws me in. It is a pure energy that feels like magic.

I'm not a lightweight, but I wonder if the alcohol is getting to me. I laugh along with the guys and sway along with the beat like most others around me. The night feels like there is a spell over it, a magic saved for this one spot in this particular moment in time.

Just before the last farewell that marks their second encore, the brunette glances my way again and our eyes lock setting butterflies free in my stomach. I grin, feeling like I am back in tenth grade smiling like an idiot just before Shirley Hugh turned me down for a date. Deciding that was a long time ago, I gather my courage and decide I need to say hello. I wonder if she is really as interesting as I picture in my mind.

Chapter 4

Magic Hours

ROMAN

A street performer takes over the entertainment where the band left off, filling the silence with well-crafted rhymes. The lyrical cadence of the performer impresses me and I almost get lost in the hypnotic performance like those around me. However, I figure this is my shot to talk to the brunette that arouses my spirit. I walk the couple steps it takes to close the distance between me and this beautiful girl before I can think too hard and chicken out of the entire interaction. Relying on the alcohol I already consumed for courage, I stand next to her and lean in close, "You look comfortable on this street."

She smiles, studying me. Her brilliant green eyes captivate me, as she considers her response, "Yeah, this is my town."

"You live here in Las Vegas?" I ask, surprised at the possibility.

She chuckles at my reaction, "I've lived here for almost five years now."

"This is where you come for fun on a Tuesday night?" I ask, gesturing to the crazy lights and sounds still surrounding us even after midnight.

"There's always fun in Fremont." she replies. "Tonight I'm showing my friends downtown."

I look to where she points out her friends who are now talking to mine. Well, that worked out nicely.

When I look back at her, a crease forms in her eyebrow. "You aren't from around here." It isn't a question, but a statement of fact.

She was not the first one to comment on my accent here, it seems that natives don't encounter a southern accent very often. I decide to play along. "Me?" She nods with a coy smile. "No, I'm not from around here. What gave it away?"

"The accent of course." She considers me a moment, "My guess is somewhere in the Southeast, maybe South Carolina?"

I smile cocking my head to the side, "You are quite good. I'm from Charleston. My accent fits right in there. It's strange to have people here have trouble understanding me."

She chuckles, "People here don't really take the time to understand anyone, no matter how they talk." I wonder about the comment as she continues. "I can understand you just fine. I grew up in Myrtle Beach, not too far from Charleston actually. I've been surrounded by that accent most of my life. It took me almost a year to lose it."

"Really?" The statement takes me by surprise. Figures, I think about how she pinpointed where I was from, it takes one to know one. "You must be quite the beach girl then."

I casually reach for her elbow to draw her closer to me. I tell myself I do it to better hear her response, but really I just enjoy the physical contact with her, like there is a warming pulse where we connect. I feel more alive where she touches my arm and leans into me slightly. I don't want to appear provocative, but she draws me in and I am helpless to resist. There is something about her that intrigues me and it is getting stronger the longer I'm near her.

"Born and raised," she purrs.

"My name is Roman." I move close to her ear. Her hair tickles my nose.

"Roman." She repeats, putting the emphasis on the "Ro" and dragging out the "a." It sounds right coming off her lips. "It's nice to meet you, I'm Aria."

"Aria" I repeat just as she did. I like the sound of that, a strong name for a spirited woman. "It's nice to meet you too."

She emits great strength and intelligence, two of my favorite qualities in a person. It is a chance encounter, but I remain eager to learn more about this one-of-a-kind girl from my home state. Strange that I had to cross the country to meet her.

A boisterous laugh gets our attention. Her friends giggle behind me by something Dawson said. Leana turns around to us and states, "These guys are great!"

Andrew turns to Aria while gesturing to me and says, "So, I see you've met Roman." In that moment, I realized that our arms intertwined a bit more than appropriate for strangers. I try to take a step back, but she holds me in place. Well, if she doesn't mind, then I won't either. The thought surprises me. I don't mind this sort of contact with my family, but I've only met her. Still, I have this warm feeling inside makes me want to hold on tight to this girl who, at least in this moment, makes me feel alive.

"Yep" she answers and I can't help but blush a little. "I'm Aria." She moves to grip Andrew's outstretched hand. I move slightly so that she can reach forward more easily. I'm dazed as she leans back firmly into my chest. I'm not sure what to do with my hands, but they naturally come to rest on her hips and her body sighs at my touch. This is dangerous territory now and I don't know quite how to navigate it. In this instant I do not want to let her go, at least not until we have a chance to talk more.

"Nice to meet you." My mentor responds and it's the first time I ever really noticed that he also has a heavy Southern accent, "I'm Andrew. This is Miguel and Dawson." I never noticed our accents before. It is normal in South Carolina, but here it stands out. I'm already learning more about the world, and find it is a good feeling.

"Nice to meet you, too." She nods to them all and then sweeps her hands towards her friends who have gotten very close with Dawson and Miguel. "You've met Leana and Alicia, I presume."

"Yes, they are fun." Dawson says.

"They sure are," She looks at her friends with a huge smile, they shrug in response. The one who Aria pointed to as Leana tips her glass to me with a wink causing me to smile.

Dawson takes Alicia's hand and pulls her over toward the street performer continuing to create verses about the people in the crowd. Leana waves at Andrew and Miguel to come with her and join them. Aria and I are left alone standing behind the crowd for the moment. I take a deep breath, appreciating the warmth of this girl in my arms. This night has taken quite a turn, I'm now far from normal.

ARIA

I am floating in a dream. The rest of the viewers become white noise, falling into the background as I watch Roman's lips move, trying to hear the words he's all but yelling in my ear. "How did you end up in Las Vegas?"

I'm confused for a moment and lean closer into him, he rests his hand on my waist. It feels right there, a strange feeling to have for someone whose name I just learned. What a name it is too, it feels comfortable on my lips. I realize that I'm getting way ahead of myself already, it must be the gin talking. I try to concentrate on what Roman is saying as he repeats his question, "You said you were from Myrtle Beach. You're a long way from home, how'd you end up out here?"

The question catches me off guard. He is paying attention to what I am saying more than I am. That is intriguing on many levels. However, my childhood was not the buzz kill to drop at that particular moment, so I decided to keep it light. "A series of misfortunate events."

Laughing, he asks, "Like the entire thirteen book series?"

That got my attention. Honestly, I didn't expect him to get the reference, but it was one of my favorite book series growing up. "Pretty much. Don't worry though, no murderous relatives."

I enjoy his laugh about as much as the feel of his hand along my waist and the heat of his breath against my cheek.

"I needed to get away and I ended up here by following a writing gig that went nowhere. Then I made a friend in a local theater who needed a screenwriter, so here I am. Still. Have you ever been to the west coast before?"

"No, this is my first trip."

"It's a different world over here. You picked Las Vegas?"

He laughs shaking his head, "My company picked Las Vegas. There's a big convention this week,"

"There's always a big convention here. What do you do?"

"I'm a Solutions Engineer for Benefitfocus. We're all here for the EMC World convention to find out more about the newest networking systems available."

"Are you finding anything good?"

He seems intrigued by my interest and leans down even

closer still to look me in the eyes, "It seems that I have."

"Well, then it was worth the trip," I smile. "I'm glad you are here tonight."

"Me, too." He smiles in a way that lights up his eyes.

I find that I am looking up into his sapphire eyes and getting lost in the moment. We subtly move to the musical rhythm of the street performer who apparently found a couple of percussionist to join him in his lyrical melody. The noise hums into a beautiful song that we sway to.

His eyes glance down to my lips causing butterflies to flutter in my stomach in eager anticipation. As he looks back up at me, I give him the permission he seeks by closing the distance and softly pressing my lips on his. It is an electrifying feeling. I want more of him, a feeling that has never come over me this strongly before. I don't know what to make of it, but I am curious to find out.

He opens his mouth in a sigh and I take the opportunity to explore, rising and falling with the music. He pulls me closer to him with his firm hands caressing my back. I want more of him, I want to feel his hands all over me.

I'm not usually in favor of one night stands. I may make an exception when a smart, seemingly generous and ridiculously sexy man comes along and makes me forget my own name with a kiss, that just doesn't happen every day. I don't want to stop, all I can think about is the warmth of his hands and the pleasure of his kiss.

The rhythm of the performer's beat changes, which tells me something is wrong. Leana stumbles over to me with Alicia leaning heavily between her and Andrew.

I know that look, I've seen that look. Hell, I've had that look. She's done, about to puke and needs to go home before she passes out on the sidewalk in the middle of downtown. I step away from Roman and reach out to Alicia to check her eyes. She's fine, just had a little too much to drink.

"Can you stand?" I ask her.

"Yeah, yeah," she answers with a slight slur. "I just tripped."

Leana laughs. "Yep, over the cup that you dropped on the ground."

"How was I supposed to know it would land under my foot?" Alicia argues, barely able to keep her head up.

"Okay, time to get you home." Leana lets her sister lean on her shoulder again.

"I'll help you, I just need one minute." I say.

"Oh, no you don't." Leana protests, "I'll get her back. You stay, seems like you're having a good time." She winks at me. I blush and look over to see Roman with his hand extended in an effort to help. The concern in his eyes for a complete stranger makes my heart melt a little. He looks to me and I turn back to Leana, "I don't want to stay if you need help."

"Come on. I've got this. Graham was a lot heavier than Alicia is." I can't help but laugh thinking of her carrying her high school boyfriend to the car, blind drunk after the homecoming post game party. I nod to her as she reaches over to pull her quickly fading sister closer to better support her. I get her drift and I trust her judgment, she wouldn't hesitate to ask for help if she actually needed it or considered the situation she was leaving me in to be questionable. I had to hand it to her, I'd found a great friend, both strong in mind and body.

"Good, it's settled. Besides, you can help me more by finishing your evening. It looks like things are just getting started."

"Are you sure you can get back okay?"

Leana looks me with an accusing glare. "This is not my first time in Las Vegas, and I can handle hailing a taxi.

We'll be fine. Go. I want details tomorrow."

I hold her eye for a moment and then agree. I hand her my apartment key, "Call me if you need anything and I'll be there. No questions asked."

"Same goes for you. Have a good night. Don't do anything I wouldn't do."

I laugh as she walks away with Alicia leaning heavily on her shoulder thinking that doesn't really narrow down many options. Andrew and Dawson follow after Leana to make sure they get a taxi safely. Roman's friends sure do make a good first impression, they seem to be pretty amazing. It bodes well for Roman, too.

There are good things about going out with a lifelong friend whom I've gotten trashed with more times than I can count, we have a long stated agreement about when to stay and when to go. It doesn't matter at all that we haven't seen each other for three years, it's something ingrained somewhere along the way. I appreciate her confidence in my choice of guy, especially since his friends have proven to be genuine. I can only hope Roman proves the same. If I had any doubts so far, I would have left with my friends. Now it is time to find out what happens next.

I turn back to Roman to find the concerned look still on his face, "Will your friend be okay?" He asks, the Southern drawl standing out. I note the genuine worry in his eyes and my heart does a little leap in my chest.

"Yeah, Leana will get her back safe. They don't have far to go. She'll text me in like 20 minutes with an okay or a S.O.S."

"Well, I hope it's an ' A-Okay.'" he exaggerates the expression with his southern accent and it sounds silly coming off his lips.

He glances back to his friends as they come back from the street and I realize they are ready to call it a night as well. I hesitate and then say, "Well, it looks like you need to go, I should probably head home anyway."

Roman turns back to me and takes my hands from where they fidget in front of me, "Actually," he looks a little nervous, "I was hoping," he pauses, "Would you like to have a drink with me back at my hotel?"

I look at him, debating his offer. "Where are you staying?"

"At the Bellagio, down on the strip. It's a taxi ride, but I don't think it's that far."

I consider the logistics briefly, but honestly it's just not that hard to get around Las Vegas. There are buses and cabs everywhere. I haven't felt pushed or uneasy all night, which makes me feel safe to say yes. I see his friends cutting up, but waiting to hear my response in support of their friend.

Is it possible that he is too good to be true? Probably, but there's only one way to find out. At least I know enough self-defense to be confident I can get away and call Leana or Mikey or even a taxi if the night goes sour.

"Okay." I answer thinking this is an opportunity that I do not want to miss. If I let him go now, I will never see him again. I know I will regret that decision.

He reaches out his hand. I take it intertwining my fingers in his as we follow his companions back to the street to hail a taxi of our own. We don't talk much, instead I listen to his buddies go on about the Fremont Experience.

Roman squeezes my hand. This is the best experience I've had, that is for sure.

We ride the familiar route back to the strip. I don't come here often, but in a city that is constantly changing, the foundation stays remarkably the same.

I listen as they talk about the music, apparently, the 80's brought up some fond memories from the good ole boys of

South Carolina. I can only imagine the exploits of their youth, I know I've had quite a few of my own.

Roman sits close to me in the back seat and holds my hand, eventually putting his arm around my shoulder. He seems nervous and that intrigues me. I get the feeling he is not one to participate in one night stands either, and yet here we are on the way back to his hotel.

We get out of the taxi at the Bellagio and I look up at the grand resort realizing that I'll never get used to the extravagance of this city. This place that I wanted to come to forget my shortcomings has become a reminder that I'm still not what I imagined I would be by now.

Roman wraps his arm around my shoulders, "Are you okay?"

I lean into his shoulder, "Yeah," I answer in truth. "I forget how majestic this place is."

"It is impressive, isn't it?" He agrees, looking up at the Chihuly glass art on the ceiling.

"Understatement." I elbow him in the ribs to lighten the moment. "I work on the strip just up the way. I used to come out here and smoke cigarettes by the fountains and pretend my life was glamorous."

I am amazed I said so much, but Roman smiles and whispers in my ear, "I think you are captivating."

I blush and lean into him as Andrew grabs Roman's attention, "Hey Roman, I wanted to let you know, the room will be empty tonight. Knock on Dawson and Miguel's door if you need anything. I'll stay over there tonight."

"Andrew," Roman starts, but Andrew cuts him off.

"You only live once man, enjoy it. Have a good night you two." He winks and leads his companions, obviously more inebriated than he, toward the hallway of elevators leading up to the hotel rooms.

Roman turns to me with an open mouth. I realize he

was not expecting that gesture. In the same way Leana gave me the wink of approval, his friend did the same.

Roman gestures to the bar inside the hotel. "Well, would you like to drink?"

I smile and offer my hand to him, "Yes, please." He takes my hand and we head to the bar.

The bartender, a slim guy with a playful smile, greets us, "What can I get you?"

Roman turns to me. I don't think about it, I just order my usual, "I'll take a gin and tonic, please."

Roman nods to the bartender and says, "I'll have the same."

When the bartender turns around, Roman nudges me. "Is that your preferred drink or are you playing it safe?"

I give him a considering eye and reply, "Both. It is my go to, comfort drink. It's hard to mess up a gin and tonic. You ordered the same. Which is it for you?"

"Totally playing it safe," he answers.

"Really?"

"Absolutely." He nods.

"What's your preferred drink?"

"Either a pinot noir or bourbon and coke."

"Well, you're speaking my language, on both accounts. Are you a wine connoisseur?"

"I don't know about connoisseur," he laughs openly, "but I do enjoy drinking it."

"Do you even like gin?" I nudge his arm.

"Yes, I like gin." He rests his hand on my leg, which makes me close this small distance between us. He leans in for a sweet kiss. "I like the way your lips taste."

"Right back at you, handsome." I tease and lean in for another, not as chaste kiss. As our drinks appear and the night wears on, I soak up his warmth and generous attention. We talk about anything and everything. I feel like

I am put under a spell. This is one moment where I don't mind so much. I find a rare comfort in letting go with him, a feeling I would love to have more of in my life.

Chapter 5

With One's Heart In One's Mouth

ARIA

Once our drinks are empty, our non stop chatter turns quiet as Roman signs our bill. He holds my hand, circling his finger in my palm. "Look," he says gently, "I don't really know how to do this."

"You don't know how to charm women?" I ask seductively.

He chuckles, a bright, good-natured sound, "I suppose not."

"Would you like to show me your baseball card collection?" I ask him in a sexy voice causing him to laugh harder, "Or maybe the inside of your briefcase?"

With some effort, as I wag my eyes at him, he manages to be serious for a moment. "I don't want you to leave. I want to wake up with you tomorrow and see your beautiful smile. That will be the perfect way to start my day."

Wow. This man may not play the game often, but he sure knows what to say. "Yes," I respond with reverence.

He kisses my hand and leads me off the bar stool and across the casino floor. The bright lights, still going even at this hour, are a blur as I feel like I'm sleepwalking in the best dream.

The path up to his room is a surreal experience. I've been all over the strip and in many of the resorts, including this one, but never to the rooms. Those elevators are guarded and you must have a room key to even get into the parlor. I suppose it is not unlike most nice hotels, but there is something majestic about the space that feels larger than life. A moment where you have to stop and think, wow, I've made something of myself to get to this spot. Then I remember that I am just a girl about to enter a fancy hotel room with a stranger. That sounds so bad, but then why do I feel so good. Right now, I feel on top of the world like I have everything I could ever want and more.

We enter his room giggling. He holds me close to him as I comment, "I can't believe you are staying here."

"I know. It's crazy, right? The company is paying for all of it." His eyes beam as he looks at me.

I glance at the door, "Are you sure they're okay?"

He looks at me saying with his eyes, 'Hey they offered and I'm not letting you go.' Out loud he says, "I'm sure they'll manage."

I think back to Leana's A-Okay text and realize this is all going a little too well. What's the catch? I look back at this man who inspires and intrigues me and I don't care.

Roman leans in then and I am eager to feel his closeness. When our lips meet, I can feel the heat and his desire. When he looks into my eyes, it seems like he really sees me, not something than many seem to take the time to do. I'm having such strong feelings from a guy I've only known a few hours.

In the back of my mind, it occurs to me that this is probably a bad idea. Knowing that SOS phone call goes both ways if I'm the one that needs to get out of a jam, I have confidence to be in the moment. Right now, it is an incredible date and I want to see where this goes. My best friend trusts me to make good decisions, maybe it's time to trust myself.

Though my mind wanders, I don't hesitate to accept and reciprocate Roman's eager kisses. He makes it easy, like a dance, a rhythm that I've known my whole life. I begin to lean into him and push away from the wall I rest against. It takes two to tango and I am ready to take the lead. He leans into my advancement and picks me up. The action surprises me causing me to gasp and lose his lips. He finds other uses for them by kissing down my jaw and then my neck. I wrap my legs around him as his lips wander to a sensitive spot right at my collar bone. His stubby beard caresses my skin sending shivers down my spine, forcing a heavy sigh to escape my lips.

I feel him grin as he sits down on the edge of the bed with me in his lap facing towards him. I arch my back, drawing my breast closer to his chest. His arms wrap around my waist hugging my hips to his. He lines kisses down the responsive space between my breasts.

As he rises up, I realize an opportunity he offers me and I pounce on it. I gently push him backward on the bed with caresses and kisses of my own. I taste the salty sweetness of his skin that makes me crave more of him. When he is far enough back for me to straddle him with my knees on the bed, I lean in for a slow, sensual kiss. Taking his plump lips in mine, I enjoy the unique flavor of him. I already know this is a scent that will stay with me. Slowly, I sway my hips towards him. My short dress rises up so that only my thin panties and his jeans lie between us.

I kiss his lips and then make my way from his jaw line toward a tender spot just behind his ear. He releases a satisfying breath as I continue my swaying motion across his lap.

My hands find the buttons to his dress shirt as I release them one by one. My lips follow my hands down his firm chest. His hands rest on my hips and unconsciously pull me closer, a sign for more.

I detangle his shirt from his body and run my hands down his skin. When I reach the waistline of his jeans, I collect the edges of my dress and pull the thin fabric over my head.

He watches my action, locking eyes with me as I settle back down. His smile is warm and comfortable. He sits up reaching his generous hands to rest sensuality on my bare hips.

I begin my swaying motion again towards him as I unclasp my bra. As he witnesses my reveal he holds his breath, then releases it in a rush of eagerness. I can feel his desire radiating from him, yet he takes his time to appreciate the moment. He leans back slightly and catches my eye. I didn't expect his movement as he reaches his arms around me to hug me close, skin on skin. Now it is my turn to breathe heavily as I enjoy the feel of his tight muscles. Being wrapped in his arms and feeling him even through his thick jeans, makes me crave for more. I am in bed with a beautiful man, how can life get any better than this?

Except, as our kiss deepens, I realize something very unromantic, but also very essential to real life. Romance novels never prepare you for the inevitability that you will have to pee just as things get hot and steamy. Unfortunately, for both of us, this wasn't going anywhere until the problem was taken care of.

Damn alcohol, I think as I pull back from the kiss, getting his attention even as he pulls my hips closer to him. Sexy, yes, but not helping my current problem. I pull back further and find his eyes.

"I'm sorry, but I really have to pee."

He chuckles a little, but smiles broadly. "I'll be waiting

right here," he says as he lets me go.

"Okay" I hop off his lap almost tripping on the bed and skip to the bathroom, not even bothering to shut the door. It takes me a minute, it's one of those I've been drinking more liquid than normal pees that feels like it will never end, especially when a beautiful man without a shirt on is in the next room waiting on me. Finally, I finish. I don't bother to put my panties back on. After flushing the toilet, I rinse my hands off and wipe them on a towel.

Even with my extended pee and clean hygiene, I was out of the room for approximately three minutes. What I find when I return to the room stops me in my tracks and makes me silently laugh.

Roman is laying down on the bed in the exact spot he was sitting, legs still hanging off the bed, fast asleep. I take a mental picture and file it away for a good laugh later. This has been a very interesting night indeed.

I walk back in the bathroom and get a drink of water from the faucet in glass sitting on a tray on the counter. I slip my panties back on and then collect his dress shirt and button it on myself.

I gently touch Roman on the leg and whisper, "Roman, come on. Let's go to bed."

He stirs a little and I repeat myself quietly as he continues to stir awake. He smiles up at me, his eyes unfocused from exhaustion and alcohol. I take his hand and pull him up, leading him to the left side of the bed. I don't know which side his preference is, but this feels natural. I turn down the covers and he almost gracefully falls into bed.

Thankfully, at some point I was unaware of, he took his shoes off. I left his jeans on and I have his shirt so he'll have to deal with that tomorrow. I cover him with the blanket and he reaches for my hand. "Thank you" he whispers in a thick Southern accent and kisses the back of my hand.

"You're welcome." I kiss his cheek. I hesitate only a moment before I head to the other side of the same bed and crawl into the warm oasis beside him. Even though there is another in the room, I figure if he was willing to be intimate with me, he wouldn't mind waking up in the same bed even without the sex. He said that would make for the perfect day, we'll see if that is true.

We don't touch as I drift to sleep, but I can hear his breathing, a deep, steady sound. I can feel the warmth of him radiating next to me. It is a comforting feeling. He is a muscular man as well as gorgeous and he'd shown me nothing but kindness and respect the entire evening. I fall asleep beside him dreaming of a different life, one where this was normal. The Southeast is a place of nightmares for me, but somehow, lying beside Roman, remembering the comfort of his accent and the gentleness of his touch makes me wonder if there are parts of my home that might be worth a second chance.

Chapter 6

Once Upon A Dream

ARIA

I wake from a wild dream of dancing in the streets to find myself in an unfamiliar room. As I look next to me, a beautiful blonde man still slumbers. The events of last night begin to rush back to me. "Roman" I sigh as I watch his chest rise and fall with the breath of deep sleep. He looks so peaceful, I don't want to disturb him. Managing to temper my yearn to reach out and caress my hand across his bare, muscular abs, I instead turn and rise out of bed.

I amble to the window to pull the shade aside just enough to see the empty streets outside past the famous Bellagio fountains. Most people love Vegas at night when it is busy with flashing lights, but my favorite view is first thing in the morning. The quiet takes on a spirit of its own, holding the secrets of the city echoing the experience from the previous night.

I look back at Roman who turns over without waking up and smile. I certainly enjoyed my own adventure. Following a man back to his hotel room was probably the strangest thing I have done yet in Sin City. This wasn't just any man, it was Roman. How can I feel so close to someone I have yet to know for twenty four hours.

The mystery shall continue as I contemplate what to do now. The only thing I can come up in this moment is coffee. I vaguely remember a little alcove on this floor with snack machines and ice as we came in the night before. I hope that it wasn't a dream that it also contained a coffee machine.

I look down at Roman's button up bagging around my small frame. Well, that won't do, even for a short trip down the hallway in a place like this. My small dress lays crumpled in a corner, causing me to shake my head. I glance around the room considering my options.

Roman's suitcase lays opened on the travel stand by the closet with his clothes lazily folded inside. I find a pair of gym shorts and a t-shirt right on top which smells clean enough for my short trip. I put them on and though they also hang a little loose, they will do. I grab the room key, my phone and wallet and with one last look at the slumbering man, tiptoe outside.

I look at my phone to find a message from Leana. I open a picture of her and Alicia holding up mimosas. I guess they got back just fine last night. With the exception of Alicia wearing sunglasses so early in the morning, you cannot even tell the drunken adventures of the previous evening.

I text back, *Glad you see you are both up and about.*

Couldn't miss bottomless mimosas at Hard Rock. They are half price until 9 am. Plus Alicia really wanted a t-shirt.

I smile as another text pops up, *How is the hottie?*

He is good, still sleeping. I'm on the hunt for coffee.

So you did stay, I was hoping you would.

Hoping?

Yes, for someone always on the move, you don't seem to have much fun in the moment.

The comment makes me stop. It has come up several times over the years, this same conversation. She knows why I left and yet I know she has a point. I don't ever just have fun. I coast on survival mode, even after those first months of hardship were over. The realization makes me a little sad, but I also realize that there is no time like the present to make a few changes. I was already braver last night than I was even moving here.

I text her, *Today, I'm going to have some fun.*

Good for you. Cheers!

Cheers! I reply, a familiar farwell.

I round the corner and find the wondrous coffee machine next to a couple of plushy chairs in an alcove. Looking distracted sat none other than Andrew, the one we displaced with my stay. I stop short, "Oh no, you didn't sleep out here did you?"

Andrew looks up at me startled. Then a soft, contented laugh releases from his chest, "Oh no, I was just talking to my family. I wanted to say good morning to my kids before they headed off to school." I notice the cell phone in his hand and nod.

"How are they doing?" I ask.

"Oh, they're good. My wife is spoiling them. They got frozen yogurt for a treat yesterday afternoon after school." He answers with obvious affection.

"That sounds nice."

He chuckles to himself.

"You miss them." I find myself enjoying Andrew talk about his family, it feels happy.

"Terribly." He holds up his cell phone and shows me a picture of his wife with arms wrapped around a small boy holding a baseball trophy. A girl smiles to one side while a younger boy looks up at the trophy his brother holds with wide eyes. It is a charming group. I can see their happiness in the moment.

"Do you go out of town often?" I ask as I walk over to the coffee machine.

"Not much any more. This year I'm only away for this

one trip. I'm training Roman to take my place."

I smile at him, "That's nice. Is he excited about the opportunity to travel?"

Andrew looks up at me and I notice crease forming by his eyes, "Yeah, I think he is."

I nod and then turn to try and figure out how to get coffee out of the machine. When I finally managed to procure a small cup full, I sink into the seat next to Andrew.

We sit for a few minutes contemplating before I break the silence, "It must be nice to have someone love you that much."

He looks at me intently then, "It is, especially when you have to be away. How is our Roman doing this morning?"

I laugh. I can't help it. "He's fine. Sleeping."

"That sounds about right."

"Do you know Roman well?"

"Pretty well. He's been with the company full-time for over a year now. He was an intern before that. He's smart, that's for sure," he pauses a moment and looks at me, "and kind."

I blush as I met his gaze, "Yes, I can sense that."

"Good. I sense that in you, too. That's why I want you to know that he would not bring just any girl back to his bed. He must have seen something special in you."

I am surprised by his genuine statement and I smiled to myself, thinking of the boy I left sleeping. "Thank you. It's not something I do either, stay the night with someone I just met." I pause trying to find the words, "But, I felt something with Roman, something special. It made me want to trust him and that's not something I'm prone to either."

Andrew nods, "Then you are both lucky."

As he moves to get up a wave of guilt washes over me. "Do you need anything out of the room?" I ask.

"Oh no, I grabbed what I needed last night. Believe it or not, I do remember the excitement of being young. I'm going to breakfast with Miguel and Dawson. Roman doesn't have to be back at the Venetian until ten. Why don't you take him out for some breakfast? His treat." He winks at me before he walks down the hallway.

ROMAN

I wake feeling disoriented. For some reason it feels odd that I am alone and more unusual because I am still wearing jeans. I try to remember the events leading up to this moment. I'm in Las Vegas and last night the guys convinced me to go have a night on the town. It was larger than life, the entire night felt like a dream.

There was a girl, Aria. Something about her made me pay attention, it was like she was illuminated from the inside. She was beautiful, not in the supermodel sort of way, but the natural, practical beauty of a kind heart who has been through some rough spots. I looked around the room and realized she wasn't there.

How could I be so stupid to fall asleep when a beautiful girl comes willingly to my bed. From her first smile, she sparked something in me that I didn't even know I could feel. It has been quite a while since I've had those sorts of relations, but I was so caught up in the moment, I forgot to be nervous last night. That was probably the effect of the alcohol, but still. I feel inexplicably comfortable with her.

I shake my head staring hopelessly at the ceiling, she probably already went back home. The thought of not seeing her again covers me in a wave of sadness. I sit up on the side of the bed, still in my jeans and rub my hands over my face, trying to remember what I am supposed to be doing today. My elbow slips from its resting place on my knees when I hear an unexpected noise.

The door swings open revealing Aria in my workout clothes and a steaming cup in her hand. I am too startled to even speak. I look up at her with disbelieving eyes. Not in my wildest dreams did I think she would come back. Yet, here she stands, apparently waiting for me to say something.

"You're still here?" I blurt out astonishedly, half an exclamation and half a question.

"Yep. You can't get rid of me that easily." she responds with a warm smile.

"Nor do I want to." I reached out to her and she came to stand in my arms giving me a kiss on the cheek. "It is the perfect day."

"I was hoping you would say that," she smiles and then offers me her cup, "Would you like some coffee?"

"Sure." I take a sip, and give her an inquiring look, "black?"

"Yep. There weren't any creams or sugars by the vending machine," she says with a shrug. I find myself staring at her, entranced with her voice and the way her hair flows over her shoulder as she talks. She makes a motion in the air, "This may be a fancy hotel, but the vending machines still underwhelm."

I laugh and take a sip of the bitter tang disguised as caffeine. I hand the cup back, "It's not good."

She laughs, "No, it isn't. At least it has caffeine."

I shake my head and then turns serious, "Listen, about last night," I begin, not really knowing how to say what is on my mind.

"What about it?" She asks playfully, "I had a great time."

"Watching me sleep?" I ask.

She reaches out to caress my cheek, "Yep."

I lean back on the bed with an embarrassed groan. She sets the horrible coffee on the nightstand before crawling up beside me. She leans on her elbow offering me a gentle yet playful smile, "There was some nice stuff before that too." She leans down to kiss me, I meet her eagerly, relaxing into her embrace.

"Yes, there was."

After a few moments, she leans up, "We should get food."

"In a minute," I encourage as I reach up to run my hand through her hair. I can't believe this moment is possible, I definitely don't want to miss it. I didn't think I would ever see this girl again, I'm the luckiest man in the world to taste her lips now.

She gives in and embraces the moment, but only for a short time. When she leans back again I let her go and look at her with a content smile, "Okay, food. Let's get some real coffee while we're at it. What are you thinking?"

"I know just the place." She gets up and look down at my clothes, baggy on her. "But first, can we stop by my place?"

"I think my clothes look pretty good on you." I tease. She cuts me a look and then I watch her manner grow serious. In that moment, I realize the significance behind her words. Her offer to invite me into her personal space is a big deal. I want to respect her and her space, so I am going to leave what happens next up to her. This is a moment in our connection that matters. It will be the difference between a one night stand and what exactly? I wonder as I try to answer with a casual, "sure." I guess we'll find out what exactly that something will be.

I watch Aria try her best to press out the wrinkles of her dress, but there is no hope. I can't help myself as I laugh at her fruitless efforts. I reach over to grab the crinkled dress shirt I wore last night and then she obviously slept in. She gives me a questioning look. I shrug and walk over and put my arm around her, "We'll do this together."

She looks up at me and stands on her tiptoes. I lean down, enjoying the sweet taste of her lips. When she leans back, I move to grab a backpack and toss in a fresh change of clothes. I sling it over my shoulder and turn to her laughing at her raised eyebrows. I feel a smile stretch across my face as I extend my hand out to her. She sends warmth through my heart as our palms connect and I try to ignore the butterflies fluttering in my stomach.

ARIA

My small studio apartment stands just over two miles off the strip. The cab ride there takes us only about fifteen minutes. I attempt to make a case to ride the bus, my regular form of transportation, but all Roman has to do is gesture to the ragged state of my dress to convince me otherwise. The trip goes by fast because I am trying to ward off Roman's tickling fingers. I laugh and squirm until tears spring from my eyes. While standing in front of my apartment, I notice the cab driver chuckling at us as he hands Roman a receipt.

As we walk toward my apartment, I playfully ask him, "Will that receipt go on your expense report?"

He stops mid stride and looks at me, "I didn't even think of that. What am I doing?"

The smile that covered his face only moments before disappears making me regret saying anything. I feel sad to see it vanish so quickly, the connection is so new it feels fragile. I watch the moral debate waging war behind his eyes at the realization of possible consequences to his actions. It gives him high marks in my book that he shows concern. It means Andrew was right about his character, meeting a girl and bringing her to his bed is not something he often does.

Still holding his hand, I squeeze it and stop in front of him as we reach the bottom of the stairs that lead up to my apartment. I wait until I have the full attention of his sapphire eyes before I speak. "You were out with your friends and stumbled into a girl you thought was pretty cool. That girl just happens to think you are pretty cool right back. Now your stomach is rumbling because you haven't had any breakfast. I was just teasing, this is not a dilemma that needs to be solved right now."

He perks up a little, "Okay."

"Besides, Andrew said you had to get back for some session or something so we shouldn't wait much longer to eat." I say casually and start up the stairs. I heave a silent sigh of relief when I notice him following me.

"When did you talk to Andrew?" He climbs next to me.

Turning right onto the second floor, we head toward the last unit as I explain, "This morning while I was getting coffee. He was talking to his kids. They seem nice, he showed me pictures."

"Yeah, they're great. Andrew has been my mentor since I started at Benefitfocus just over a year ago. He's a genius. Though he likes the travel, he finds it hard being away from his family so much. I'm trying to learn as much as I can so I can take over the travelling aspects of the business."

"That sounds adventurous."

"I suppose so. I don't mind traveling, though I haven't done much of it. I only have to worry about me, so I'm not leaving anyone back home. It works well all around I guess."

"It sounds fascinating, I love to travel." I say as we walk the last few feet to my apartment. I stop in front of my door and turn to him. "I'm going to warn you, what is behind this door is not glamorous, nor clean. My friends from last night have been here for a few days now. Though that is not an excuse, it is a little more crazy than normal."

"Are they here now?" he asks with his eyebrows raised.

I can't help the sly smile thinking of being alone in my apartment with this beautiful man, "No, they aren't."

He nods and turns toward the door with laughter in his eyes, as a small grin creeps across his face, "I've been warned."

"It's that desperate that I get a new outfit."

"Okay." The laughter he could barely contain overflows into the space between us and it warms my insides. If only he realized how big of a deal it was to let him see my space.

I give him one more warning look, trying not to laugh at myself, and then open the door.

When I say apartment, I don't mean some lavish flat in in the big city. I mean a one room, 580 square foot space that I can barely navigate in. I own no tv, I watch all my Netflix binges on my laptop, which is now perching precariously on a pile of papers on my desk against the right wall. I don't get many visitors, looking at my space this way, from a visitor's perspective, you'd think my novel exploded and all the carnage landed there. I suppose that isn't far from the truth. I never claimed the writing process was a tidy one.

Thankfully most of my clothes are picked up, so at least he won't see my dirty underwear lying around. I suppose I can be thankful that my friends have been here, at least for that. Their luggage is haphazardly cluttered in one of the corners of the living room. My futon is still opened with pillows stacked up from Leana and Alicia sleeping on it.

My bed is the largest piece of furniture in the entire apartment, which you can see through the bedroom door, which is left ajar. It is simple, nothing more than a mattress on a simple frame with a bright purple bottom sheet and a purple, green and brown owl print comforter resting in a ball in the middle of the bed. On top of the pillow rests my e-reader. Honestly I am surprised I managed to force myself to leave home without it last night, it usually goes everywhere with me.

The only bathroom is across from the bed. I have to admit, I love the small walk in closet in the bedroom, though it is slightly embarrassing how little is hanging in it.

The small kitchen just past my desk, holds a sink full of bowls and an empty bottle of wine and glasses sitting on the counter. I've never been especially messy, but not incredibly clean either. It is part of living alone, I suppose.

I am nervous as I watch him take it all in. He says nothing, just looks around nodding to himself. This is my space and I'm comfortable in it, not embarrassed. I also admit that I feel vulnerable because I don't want to chase him away. It is necessary to change into new clothes. I warned him, and he can think what he likes. Being accepted is a hard thing for me to work through. I try not to think about it as I walk back to my bedroom.

My favorite part of the apartment is the large window in my bedroom. I draw back the curtains and fill the room with light causing me to sigh in contentment. The view is not great, but the light is magical. I turn around and pull off my crumpled dress and throw it in the hamper.

Roman chuckles as he plops into my oversized arm chair, the one relatively nice piece of furniture I have in the whole place. "Shouldn't you do that before you pull the curtains open?" he asks, a smile in his voice.

I shrug as I seek a new outfit in my tiny closet. "Probably, but I like the view." I answer.

"I like the view too." He says and I find him looking at me. I smile at his compliment and settle halfheartedly on a simple black skirt and loose periwinkle top. Before I could take off my undergarments to replace them with fresh ones, Roman cleared his throat, "Should I?" He asks, pointing to the living room.

I shrug, "Why?"

"You really have no problem with that do you?"

"With what?"

"Being naked in front of me."

"Why would I? You were taking my clothes off last night."

It was his turn to shrug, though he couldn't hide his smile, "That's true."

"Besides," I said as I slipped on the fresh clothes, "It's natural, why should I be ashamed?"

"You shouldn't be. I certainly don't mind." He says with a sly smile. "It just seems pretty normal for people to be uptight about that sort of thing."

"Oh, I know plenty that are," I laugh. "Are you uptight about that sort of thing?"

Roman smiles a wicked smile and shakes his head, "Never really thought much about it. I don't think so."

"Then I don't really see the problem." As I turn to assess my outfit in the full length mirror in the closet, I catch the questioning look in his eyes thanks to his reflection, "And no, I've never been a stripper if that is the image going through your mind right now. Get your head out of the gutter,"

"My mind is not in the gutter. It's perfectly content right here." his wicked smile continuing to play on his lips. "I really like that shirt," he comments.

I laugh and throw a pillow at him. Only after he caught it laughing did I realize I picked one of the few shirts I wear without a bra.

"You are very beautiful, Aria. I would not be human if my mind were not "in the gutter" at this moment." He emphasises the phrase with his thick southern accent.

I blush and turn back to the mirror focusing my attention to tackling my long brown hair with a brush. I wonder with his charm and sexy, crystal eyes how he doesn't have someone waiting for him back home. He said he didn't, but I find that hard to believe. I suppose I will just have to find out more about this alluring man.

"Besides," Roman continues bringing me out of my thoughts. Though my back is to him, I can feel him stand confirmed by his voice coming closer. "I'm a guy, I think dirty thoughts all the time."

I laugh at that letting my worries fall away for the moment and turning to him, "Well, I'm a girl and so do I. I can't fault you for that."

He smirks, "See, human." I turn to agree with him and witness him take off his shirt. I unconsciously stop brushing my hair for the moment to take him in. He is naturally lean, but the tone in his muscles tells me that he must lift weights too. As he tosses his shirt next to his bag, his eyes catch mine. He bursts into a bright, radiant smile illuminating his sapphire eyes and making my knees unsure of their ability to hold my weight.

"Yeah, I feel pretty comfortable with you. Do you like what you see?" He asks quietly.

I step closer to him and he reaches out to bring me into his arms. "More than you know," I answer as his lips press into mine.

After a few minutes of heavy breathing and lip sucking that lands us on the bed with him on top with his hand tucked under my blouse teasing my nipple, his stomach growls. This causes him to growl. After a playful kiss on the tender spot just under my ear, he raises his head, "First, we need breakfast."

I laugh as I look up into his hungry eyes. I can only imagine what he is actually thinking as I lay under him with a silly smile on my face. I share what I am thinking, "You realize this is the second room to ourselves with minimal clothing on and I still haven't had a taste of you."

I watch many thoughts pass through his eyes: humor, eagerness, fear and through the squint in his eye I can see the torn thoughts of him deciding which of his two heads would win this particular battle. He smiles warmly down at me and I know he decides, "Some things are worth waiting for."

I look up at him and grin, "Yes, they are."

He leans down and kisses me, a gentle, sweet kiss and lifts himself off the bed. He looks back with a devilish smile as he disappears into the bathroom leaving the door open.

I lay on the bed trying to get my head to stop spinning and my breath to return to normal. It is harder than I thought it should be. No one before Roman has left me breathless. What is it about him that has me so intoxicated? I can't begin to guess, but I do know that this is one moment that I don't want to end anytime soon.

He walks out fully clothed, looking refreshed and ready to go, while I hadn't moved an inch. He heads toward the bed and does a little hop, landing right beside me and making me bounce in the air. I laugh enjoying our playful interaction. He turns to me then, "Breakfast?"

"Breakfast." I agree and reach my arms out to him.

He rescues me from the bed. I finish brushing my hair and secure it in a bun and then I'm ready to go.

Chapter 7

Casually Dressed and Deep in Conversation

ROMAN

"We are in one of the most renowned cities for cuisine in the entire world and you take me to a greasy spoon diner?" I ask looking up at the bright yellow entrance to Denny's. Glancing down at Aria, I realize it doesn't matter where we are, but still, Denny's? "I can get this back home you know."

The smile looking back at me is devilish. "Yep, but sometimes, a little familiar is good for you. Besides, you are in my city and this is where the locals go to cure any ailment," she pauses with a little bob of her head, "and possibly gain a few."

I chuckle as we walk into the restaurant. There is so much about this moment that I can't believe. I don't even know where to start. I'm still distracted by the light that fills her eyes as we find a table.

We sit at a table towards the back that looks out the window. As she settles in I feel myself looking out the window at the bustle going on outside and then back to the oasis of our table. I can't help myself, I chuckle again and open the menu, "I can't believe we are eating at Denny's."

"Welcome to America's Diner, good for the east and west coasts." She smiles, "They have excellent omelets."

"Well, I can't argue with you there. I happen to love omelets." I also couldn't argue with her choice. It had quick service even though it was surprisingly busy for a Wednesday morning.

The waitress sets a huge pot of black coffee on our table and hands us each an empty cup. We give her our orders, we both get omelets, and I pour our miracle drink.

It is an interesting feeling to sit with someone. Though I have no idea what to talk about, there is no awkwardness. I feel absolutely relaxed with her and in my own skin. I don't really remember feeling this comfortable even with myself. The thought catches me off guard as I stare at her bright green eyes over the rim of her coffee mug.

She looks up at me concerned, "What?"

Another thought pops into my head, "Am I keeping you from something? Do you have anywhere you need to be? A job? What about your friends?"

She visibly sighs in relief, it makes me wonder what she was thinking. "No. I'm a scriptwriter. The last play I worked on is already in production, my job is done. I haven't been commissioned to work on another one yet. I won't have more work for another month or so."

"What do you do during the lulls?" I ask, curious about her life.

"Sometimes I'll bartend over in Downtown where we met at this little place called *Lights*. I often help backstage at the theater or man the ticket counter. It provides a little extra cash, plus I'm friends with all the performers and stagehands, so it works out socially, too. They perform from Thursday to Sunday, curtains open at 7 pm."

"That sounds fun." I encourage her.

"I enjoy it for the most part. Although, it can be hard without a consistent income. They are offering me another scripting project, but I'm not sure if I'll take it. I've been feeling like something needs to change lately, so I've been thinking of finding a different job, or maybe some freelance options."

I absorb this and find it exciting work. "How are your friends? Did they get back alright last night?"

Aria smiles with a wink in her eye, "They had bottomless mimosas at the Hard Rock Cafe. They are just fine. I talked to Leana this morning."

"Geez, how long did I sleep?" I ask idly, feeling like the whole world has changed in only a few hours.

"Just enough to still be beautiful." I almost spit out my coffee. She looks up at me sheepishly, "Did I just say that out loud?"

I can't believe the ease I feel as I laugh. It is a new feeling. I like it. I put down my mug so I don't spill hot coffee down my shirt. "Shouldn't that be my line?"

She laughs with me, but we are saved by our food arriving on the arm of an older lady who barely let us move our arms before the hot plates appear in front of us.

I can see that her cheeks are still a little red and find it enduring. I want to know more about her I find I love listening to her talk, "Do you like writing scripts?"

She seems to gauge my sincerity for a moment. I'm not really sure what that look means yet, "Yeah, I guess." She replies, "I mean I love writing, but script writing is different, at least the work I'm doing now. It isn't original content, instead, it is always rearranging someone else's ideas into something the actors can rehearse with. The dialogue is the hardest part and also the most important. Sometimes, I don't even know why I stress over it, most of the time the director or cast change little things anyway as they bring it to life on stage. It pays the bills and I see it as research for my novel."

"You're writing a novel?" I find myself leaning

forward, forgetting how hungry I really am.

"I am," She pauses to eat a big bite of her caprese omelet. "It's what fills most of my time and why I'd rather not get another job if I can help it. I love to create new characters and stories and see how far my imagination can take them. Though so far, I don't have anything published yet. I'm not even sure I want my creative expression to have that sort of stress on it. I don't mind picking up odd jobs when I need to. Anyway, my novel is what I would be working on if I weren't here with you. That or sleeping. Probably sleeping. Being here with you is better than sleeping." She smiles at me with that radiant smile and I wonder if she is nervous. I'm still amazed that she is here with me, when did I get to be so lucky. It must be a new development.

I finish a bite of cheddar and bacon omelet. "What is it about?"

"What?"

"Your novel. What is it about?"

"Oh." She looks distracted, or nervous, but I find myself incredibly curious. I watch her take a sip of coffee and contemplate her response. She settles back, mug in hand, apparently deciding to share after all. I get the impression that this, in itself, is an important conversation. I admire that she chooses to let me in.

"It's about a prince who conquers lands for his father until he falls in love with a maid who takes care of a sword wound. Later he discovers, the girl is actually a princess and their love unites the lands."

"Fantasy?"

"Yes. I've been in love with the genre since I was a girl. I've always longed to go to far off places and meet heroic people."

"So you ended up in Las Vegas?" I ask.

"Yes, It's not really far or exotic, but it manages to surprise me from time to time."

"Well, where I'm from, Vegas seems like a distant, exotic place."

She shrugs, and again I find myself wondering what she is thinking. I wait for her to speak.

"It always was for me too. It was exciting when I first got here, I thought I'd finally found somewhere fascinating." She fidgets with her fork, then looks back at me. "It turns out, it's just like everywhere else."

"Is that disappointing?" I ask.

She nods and concentrates on eating. I take a few bites then find myself longing to hear her say more. "I think that's an amazing talent. I can't imagine creating a story. I get surprised by all the most obvious things when I read."

"What kinds of books do you like to read?" Aria asks.

I contemplate for a moment while pushing my eggs around on my plate. "I read mostly news articles on the Internet these days. I like to keep up with new trends in technology and science. When it comes to novels, I tend to lean more toward nonfiction. I like Carl Sagan, Charles Darwin, and Neil deGrasse Tyson."

"Stephen Hawking?"

"Yes, him, too. I also like Stephen King."

"Yeah, he's pretty good. I still don't like clowns after reading *It*. That was just creepy."

"I know what you mean. I don't like storm drains either for the same reason."

She laughs and I notice the subtle chill. I wonder if she likes other kinds of horror, it's never been my thing, but it is interesting to learn what makes her tick.

I fill her coffee mug again and then my own. "I like some fantasy too," I continue. "I've read Robert Jordan and George R.R. Martin. My mom used to read me *Lord of the*

Rings as a bedtime story when I was a kid."

"That sounds lovely. I bet you loved the fight scenes."

"Yes. I did actually. Especially when Gandalf comes over the ridge with his supporting army."

She shivers. "You're giving me goosebumps."

"Yeah, I read those, too."

She laughs, "So did I."

I enjoy how easily the conversation flows. Suddenly I wish I had all day to just sit here and talk with her. "My mom is a librarian. I grew up around books."

"I'm jealous. My mom could care less about reading. Some days I wondered if she even cared if I could read. I had this one copy of Pride and Prejudice, I read it hundreds of times until the cover eventually fell off. Even then I read it until I accidentally spilled soda on it one afternoon. My mom didn't think books were very important," she looks down seeming hesitant again, "we didn't really have the money to buy frivolities, like books apparently. I always wondered how cigarettes didn't count as frivolities, but never found the courage to confront her on the subject."

I could see her growing agitated as she hunkers down in her seat. I wonder if she thinks she's said to much, but I want her to say more. It doesn't sound like she has a very good relationship with her mother, but perhaps that is not something to dwell on now. Hopefully, I will get a chance to learn more later.

"You seem to be well read now." I encourage her.

She looks up and I watch her consider me. I hope she finds the honest interest on my face. She must see something because she continues, "Probably because of my second grade teacher, Ms. Richards, who imposed a love of reading in me. It's something about the words. I love to surround myself with them. I enjoy the puzzle of putting them together to make new ideas. It's probably why I love writing so much now. I used to lie in bed at night longing for a bedtime story. Eventually, I started coming up with my own. I began to write them down and poof, here I am a starving writer living under the bright lights of Vegas."

I watch as she comes alive before my eyes as she talks about writing. "That's not how I see you."

"Oh yeah? You would be in the minority."

I can hear the edge to her tone. It seems there have not been many in her life to lift her up. It makes me yearn to ease some of the doubt she seems to hold so close to her heart.

She seems both hesitant and interested as she asks, "How do you see me?"

I study her for a few moments, taking in the challenge in her eyes and the wavering of her lip before I reply, "I see you as a woman, who against all odds lives her dreams so that others can dream too. You are in the most exciting city, which fuels your inspiration. I bet it's nonstop crazy all the time around here. Lots to write about."

Her lips are no longer doubtful, but hanging open. I think I said something good, but I was just being honest. I wait for her to say something. She continues to stare at me.

"Are you okay?" I ask, concerned that I said too much or the wrong thing.

She shakes her head like she's coming out of a dream. Sitting straight up, she replies, "Yes, I'm fine. It's just no one has ever described my writing that way before. You make it sound like I'm actually doing something worthwhile."

"You absolutely are. I couldn't do it. I appreciate reading stories and the magic they bring. It's very important work that you are doing."

"You've never read my work. It could be horrible." She challenges.

"It wouldn't matter. It brings you joy, that's enough for me."

"Does your job bring you joy?"

I think for a minute. It's been a long time since I've asked myself that question. I think of all the hours of work and study it took me to get to this point. I think of the friendships I've formed over the years and the satisfaction of doing the job right. "Yes, it does. I like to figure out how things work together and I like computers. So yes, my job does bring me joy, most of the time at least. I work with some great people, so that makes the bad days bearable."

"That matters more than you know."

"Yes, it does. I'm very lucky." I agree. Aria pours us each another cup of coffee as we both realize reality is quickly catching up with us. This has been a lot deeper conversation than I would have anticipated during a first date breakfast. I'm intrigued and interested in this woman. There is something about her, a light in her that find myself hopelessly attracted to.

Chapter 8

So Impossible

ARIA

Turns out Roman needed to go do his job, especially since he flew halfway across the world for that specific purpose. With a farewell kiss and promise to meet later in the day, I went to go check in with Leana and Alicia.

Roman's number tucked safely in my phone makes me smile the whole way. I didn't expect this connection, but now I can't imagine missing out of meeting this compelling man.

I feel like I'm floating down Las Vegas Boulevard. No one has ever illustrated my so called writing career quite like Roman did. When he describes my venture, it sounds adventurous and even heroic. Most people tell me I'm wasting my time. Sometimes, I believe them. I'd rather believe Roman.

I keep looking for something else. Perhaps it's time for a change. The problem is, I can't see myself doing anything else. For better or worse, writing is who I am and what I love. I keep writing and figuring out how to make the next month's rent. If I get to behind, Mikey makes sure I get a few hours in at *Lights* to make up the difference. It's worked so far, why does it suddenly not feel like enough?

I never considered writing a novel my dream, but I suppose it is. One that started when I was very young. This man, who I've known for only about twelve hours, found something in me I could never appreciate about myself.

There is a magic when another person holds up the best of you for you to see.

I smile as I walk in the door of Carlos N' Charlie's glad to see the other person in my life that makes it all make sense. I all but fall into the seat. I look to my left and point out to Leana, "Isn't it strange having cocktails with flamingos?"

Carlos N' Charlie's beer garden overlooks the wildlife refuge of The Flamingo Hotel. The novelty is that you can see free range flamingos standing just feet from you behind a fence.

"It adds to the whole Vegas experience." Leana raises her glass to me followed by Alicia who managed to lose the sunglasses.

I suppose there is something spectacular about being able to have a drink in the middle of the day with flamingos. However, today, I had other things on my mind.

Leana must sense that, too. "I guess you had a good night?"

I give her an evil smile, "Yes, I absolutely did."

"Is he as good as he looks?" Alicia leans over toward me with wide eyes. Leana glares at her, but Alicia just sticks out her tongue causing us all to laugh.

I blush a little, "Well, he is confirmed to be kind and generous, and an excellent kisser."

"So you two didn't?" Alicia clarifies.

"No." I reply.

"This just got interesting." Leana speaks up.

"What do you mean?" I ask her.

"Well, if you didn't do it last night, but you are still interested," she pauses and looks to me, I nod encouraging her to finish her thought. "That means you'll see him again."

"We are meeting again tonight," I confirm.

Leana and Alicia both burst out laughing. After a moment, I join in too.

"See." Leana points out. I shrug.

"So, what happened anyway? Could he not get it up?" Alicia asks playfully.

I scowl, "No, nothing like that. All those drinks pressed my bladder to its limits. Even though we were hot and heavy, when nature calls, you have to answer. I came out of the bathroom to find Roman lying exactly where I left him, sound asleep."

"Does he snore?" Alicia asks.

"He didn't last night. Actually, I thought it was kind of sweet. Turns out, he's only human. I find that attractive, especially attached to the rest of the package."

I pause to get the waitress's attention and order my own drink. As she walks away, I continue "To be completely honest, I was tired too. I mean, I would have loved to follow through, but it was kind of nice just sleeping next to each other. It's like a night of innocence in the heart of Sin City," I point out. "Besides, Leana is right. I am seeing him again tonight, so it is a win."

"Are you convincing us or yourself?" Leana asks lightheartedly nudging my shoulder.

"Both?" I shrug the answer becoming a question. "I'm happy at least. He's interesting and genuine. I never saw him coming."

"Pun intended?" Leana asks wagging her eyebrows.

"Haha, very funny." I reply mockingly, but I can't help but laugh so it doesn't have the desired effect.

"The best surprises are...well, surprises." Leana continues, "So, what did he say this morning?"

"He was embarrassed that he'd fallen asleep. He thought I had left. When I came in, he was on the side of the bed holding his head in his hands."

"Was that a good sign?" Leana asks.

"Yes," I reply, "I had gone down the hall to grab a coffee. That's when I saw your text this morning. I ran into his friend Andrew. He seems like a great guy."

"So did his friend give you a hard time about you kicking him out of his room?" Alicia asks.

"No, he didn't." I ponder. "Actually, he seemed grateful in a way. He said he was glad to see Roman so happy."

"Seems like a genuine friend."

"Yeah, and then Roman and I went out for breakfast. I took him to Denny's."

"You took him to Denny's," Alicia asks dumbfounded. "We are in Vegas, we woke up to mimosas at Hard Rock and you took him to Denny's?"

"Yep, he said something local. I happen to love Denny's."

We all laugh. We spent many wayward hours of our high school years within the walls of Denny's in South Carolina. "They do have great omelets," Leana chimes in.

I gesture to her, "See."

"And he still wants to see you again?" Alicia teases. "It must be love."

"I don't know, but it's something I have never felt before and something I want to feel more of."

"Good for you." Leana confirms.

I take a deep breath, thankful that my drink arrives just as my lowdown wraps up. I raise my glass to my friends, "So what else are you up to while you are here?"

The conversation flows easily from restaurants, shows, sun tanning adventures to travel plans. It is a special thing to have friends like these. I've known Leana my entire life, she's the one person I can be completely honest with and always count on during the good and bad times.

I'm glad she and her sister were able to come when

they did. Somehow the fact that they are here at the same time I met Roman makes it all the more meaningful in a way that I can't really explain. To be honest, without them, I would not have met Roman.

I feel bad about not spending much time with them, but Leana would not even let me consider it when I mentioned it to her.

"You have a life here, Aria, I get that. I'm just glad we could come and see you. We're having a great time. You are on a new adventure that I hope you plan to see through." She hugged me fiercely. I am thankful to have such a confident, independent friend.

We've been friends for a long time, much of it apart since I ran away from the South. I miss her, but together or not, it feels like we are always on the same page.

Most importantly, it's nice to know they don't think I'm crazy. At least any more crazy than normal for wanting to see him again. I feel more confident about meeting Roman again tonight after talking with them. If I'm honest with myself, I'm really looking forward to it.

I look at my friends across the table carrying on and laughing obsessively over nothing with a flamingo less than three feet away. It is a good day. I sit back content to enjoy an afternoon with friends and flamingos.

ROMAN

The Venetian is busy today with a wide variety of tech nerds. I feel both worn out and energized by the chaos. It's exhilarating to hear people who speak my tech language. I hardly have time to grab a sip of water and yet I still can't get Aria out of my head. I know I am distracted, but thankfully it doesn't seem to affect my performance.

It is a quarter to five by the time I have a chance to look up. It proves how busy the day is since the conference ended for the day at four. I sit down for the first time in over three hours. Andrew, who is sitting in the hard plastic chair next to me, hands me a bottle of water. I graciously accept his offer and let out a sigh, "That was some crowd."

"It sure was" Andrew agrees. "If all goes well, it will be this busy again tomorrow."

"Something to look forward to." I lift my water bottle to him.

"You're doing great, Roman. The CEO of Intel told me that I was training a natural."

"Seriously?"

"Would I lie to you?"

"Well, you haven't yet." I can't believe this. I lean back in my chair and take another swig of water to calm my mind.

I can do this. I knew I could, but now I've proven it to myself. It's only day three, there is still another day to show my skills and learn more, too. I've worked tirelessly for years to make this a reality.

Why is it at this moment when my dreams are coming true, I think of Aria?

Andrew nudges me with a funny look on his face. "Where did you go just now?"

I smile thinking of how to answer this question. "I was thinking about how much I have worked for all of this."

"Yes, I bet. And" he nudges me.

"And...I was wondering what Aria was doing now."

"You've got it bad."

I shake my head, he has no idea. All the emotions are like a deluge, washing over me. Between my work and these indescribable feelings for a woman I barely know, I feel alive for the first time in about eight years. Opening my senses after all these years is as satisfying as it is frightening.

"I like her." Andrew offers.

I look at him curiously. "You guys talked this morning, didn't you? She mentioned it at breakfast."

"Yes. Did you take her somewhere nice?"

"Ha. Not really, she picked Denny's."

Andrew released a long, deep laugh. "She sounds like one who will keep you on your toes."

I didn't know what to say, so I sip on my water and stare at my shoes. Andrew continues, "She seems kind, smart, adventurous and secure in her own skin."

I listen as my co-worker and friend ticks off all the characteristics I love in her. "I know."

"What are you thinking now?"

"That's hard to say." I pause, "I know exactly what I want and yet I feel confused."

"That makes perfect sense."

"That makes no sense, whatsoever."

"Exactly." I look at him more confused than ever. "So when are you seeing her again?"

"Tonight."

Andrew gives me a knowing smile.

"I want to spend time with her, get to know her better. How am I supposed to do that when we live three thousand miles away from each other." The thought makes me sad. I can't explain the pull that she has on me. I can see her face in my mind, "She has this light in her and I feel like a moth drawn to the flame. It's a silly metaphor. I'm afraid to get burned or worse, hurt her in the process. I don't know what to do."

"True, the risk is there. The best things in life rarely come without risk. Besides, doesn't she get a say in all of this?" Andrew gives me an insightful look. "Why not see her tonight and take tomorrow as it comes."

"Sound advice Obi-wan."

"Smart I am, Padawan. Smitten you are."

I can't help but chuckle at his remarks and his Yoda impression. I realize it is completely true. "I've only ever heard my grandmother use the word smitten."

"Still, it fits."

An idea suddenly forms in my head. Andrew told me the story one time of him taking his wife out once when she could come with him on this trip years ago.

"What is that restaurant you told me you took Sandra too?" I ask eagerly.

"Now you're thinking." Andrew looks like a proud father watching his toddler learn to walk, I suppose it is about time I take a few steps on my own.

Chapter 9

Getting To Know You

ARIA

I stand, gazing into the mirror, holding up two selections of earrings. I want everything to be just right. Finally, I chose the peacock feather earrings. The turquoise of the feather perfectly matches the color of my dress, besides, they are fun and free.

As I slide the earrings on, I think back to my afternoon of writing. It was so nice to be so stimulated. I can't remember the last time I felt this excited about life.

After getting home, I realized two things. One that I missed Roman. It seems absurd to miss someone you've known less than a day. Nonetheless, even though he was only here a short time, the small space seems quiet without him.

Secondly, I felt inspired. I had not had a session of writing go that well in over a year. When I first moved to Las Vegas, everything was new and larger than life. I wrote often in that first year or so. Over time, the desire faded away. I still wanted it, but I had no drive for it. Meeting Roman sparked my mind to create again. That is no small thing.

I don't dare hope that something significant will happen between me and this man, as much as I want it to. We live, literally, in two different worlds, on opposite sides of the country, even. Furthermore, he lives too close to a place I'm not sure I ever want to go back to. I don't know what

I'm thinking of letting this continue, but I want so badly to see him again. I fear it will only end in heartbreak, only fairy tales overcome impossible plot leaps.

As I spent my afternoon writing within the fictional land of castles, princesses and forbidden romance, I wonder when reality and fantasy became so interchangeable? My prince slowly took on the features of Roman and I thought of him even more. In fiction, the characters can overcome even the most impossible odds. In reality, we'll have to wait and see.

After smoothing down my dress, I begin to wonder for the tenth time if the makeup I applied is too little or too much. I gaze at my reflection wondering if I am enough. I shake my head and wonder when I started doubting myself so much. Thinking back on it though, probably a couple years now. Why else am I still here scraping by on odd jobs and scripting someone else's work?

Feeling disgusted with myself, I walk away from the mirror. I reach out to open my window and then slouch into my favorite overstuffed chair to wait for time to meet up with Roman. I stare out at the horizon wondering, what is left for me here?

After only a short time, a knock startles me out of my daydream.

I'm not expecting anyone here. I'm supposed to meet Roman at his hotel in another half an hour. I walk to the door wondering who in the world could be on the other side.

I open the door revealing Roman wearing a charming smile. My knees melt as I take in the large bouquet of flowers in his arms.

"Oh Roman," I ignore the flowers and hug him. He pulls me in with a warm, gentle kiss.

"These are for you." He hands me the bouquet.

"Thank you." I take them and head to the sink to put them in a vase. "They're beautiful." I look up into his eyes and blush at his gaze, "You are spoiling me."

He smiles at my delight. "My girl deserves to be spoiled every once in awhile. Today is your lucky day."

I wonder at his phrase, "my girl." The way he says it isn't possessive, but endearing. I look up into his bright blue eyes and forget all of my hesitations. The look that pierces my heart tells me that he doesn't care which earrings I wear or if I put on makeup.

Damned our locations and time zones, I could get lost in his eyes for days. If he will claim me, I want to be his forever.

I finish fussing with the flowers, setting them brightly displayed on my small countertop. Roman reaches out his hand to me as an invitation. I walk straight into his arms and lean into his kiss.

The warmth of his arms wrapped around me feels familiar, like I've known him a lot longer than just a couple dozen hours. His embrace is steady and satisfying. I am lucky to be in this moment with this man who makes me feel content, my heart flutters.

I pull back, "I was supposed to meet you at your hotel."

"I know, but I wanted to surprise you. Is it a good surprise?" He asks.

"Wonderful surprise." I kiss him again and look back to my flowers, grinning from ear to ear like a lovestruck teenager.

He sits at one of the two barstools with a nervous look on his face. I see it and walk over to stand between his legs pressing my palms into his larger hands.

He doesn't quite look me in the eye as he squeezes my hands, "I was hoping I could take you to dinner."

"Food. Sounds good, a girl has to eat."

"True," He looks me in the eye now and I can see his nervousness, but also the sincerity in his gesture. " I mean like a nice dinner, my treat."

I eye him, "Like a date?"

"Yes, like a date."

"Well, I suppose that would be okay. Maybe I should check in with my other callers."

A confused and questioning look crosses his face.

I laugh regretting my nervous joke, "I'm kidding, I'm sorry. It was supposed to be silly, you look so serious. I told you before, I'm single, no callers, no prospects, not even a recent ex."

"Okay." he breathes deeply.

"Sorry, not funny."

He chuckles and nudges my arm, "Maybe a little funny."

I lean back, "Do you have a girl back home? A caller? A crazy ex lover who still wants you so bad?"

"No." he laughs to himself. "I dated a girl in school for a while, but we wanted different things."

"Like what?"

He chuckles, "She wanted her man to be Italian with black curly hair and teach sailing lessons."

"Ah," I say not really knowing what to say.

He shrugs. "We hardly laughed anyway. If she didn't find mister suave I would have eventually gotten the courage to end it."

"Lucky for me."

He grinned and kissed me, "Lucky for me."

I like that his kisses are becoming familiar and comfortable, but still carry some heat. I think back at how much we laugh together and smile big enough to break our kiss.

"What?" He asks laughing at my expression.

"I was just thinking how much I like that you make me laugh. I never realized how little I laughed before."

"I like that, too. Why did you not laugh before?" He asks his hand taking mine.

"I don't know. I guess I just didn't have much reason to. What about you?" I challenge.

"Not much reason to either, I guess."

"Well then, we'll just have to make up for lost time by laughing together as much as we can."

"I like that idea." he agrees.

Several minutes and kisses later he asks, "So, dinner?"

"Yes," I look down at my dress and then back to him, "Am I dressed appropriately?"

He looks me over and I see the hunger in his eyes, the kind that makes me want to melt into his arms again and never leave this room, "Absolutely."

"Okay, do we need to go now?"

He looks back at my face like awakening from a dream, "Yeah, let's go."

We walk up to the Paris Hotel and Gordon Ramsay Steak. The shock makes me stop short.

"Is something wrong?" Roman pauses and holds my hand a little tighter.

"No, everything is very right, but wow. This is one of the best restaurants on the strip, I mean Gordon Ramsay is world-renowned."

"I know."

I look at him and meet his steady gaze. In that moment, I see his eyes light up, he really wants to do this. The thought overwhelms me. This, us together, means just as much to him as it does to me. I whisper, "Thank you" into his ear and then pause with a light kiss, enjoying the dimple that forms at the corners of his lips.

He kisses my hand and then wraps my arm around his as we head into the restaurant.

At the podium he gives them his name, "A reservation for Roman Wagner, please."

"Of course, Mr. Wagner," the hostess leads, "your table is right this way."

I gave him a sideways glance, and he smiles. I keep his arm all the way back to our table where he holds my chair out for me.

I am blown away by his charm. It's not because he goes through the motions of etiquette but because he wants to treat me, and I suppose himself, to a special night. I feel his eagerness to make our time together special, to show me in his own way that he finds something unique in me.

It makes me search inside a little harder, maybe there is something special in me after all. I've spent most of my life cast aside. Now, I fear I am trying to hold on too hard to the first one who really reaches out to me.

Then again, I cannot deny this connection we share. It is like we are linked somehow and just needed to find each other to realize that.

Of course, I could be living in my head to long and all of this is a dream. Only time will tell. For now though, I'm going to enjoy this moment with a generous man.

After the waiter walks away with our wine bottle order in hand, I notice Roman looking a little chagrined.

"Reservations?" I ask in a questioning tone.

"I was hoping you would say yes. I'm delighted that you did."

I break into a huge smile. He takes my hand across the pristine white tablecloth, an elegant candle burning only inches away. The warmth of his touch relaxes me. I hate that I feel so out of place in this sophisticated setting.

I try not to let my nerves show and focus on being here with a man continues to surprise me. I am excited to get to know him better. His genuineness fascinates me, I've only seen it in a few and I hope it is real.

As I enjoy the warmth of his hand across the table, I realize I learned something new about him. "Your last name is Wagner?" I ask.

"Yes."

"What is your middle name?"

He shakes his head with a little laugh, "Archibald."

"Roman Archibald Wagner. That's a good name, a very dignified name."

"My mom thinks so, she's still proud of it."

"What about you?"

"I like my name. I only got made fun of a little for having such an archaic name."

I chuckled softly, "I like that name. I will put it on my character naming list."

"You would name a character after me?"

"Yeah, maybe. The older names like that work really well in the settings I create."

"Hmm," he contemplates, "that could be fun. Would I get to be heroic somehow?"

"Absolutely." I reply enjoying the caress he teases across my hand. I wonder if his touch will always be this distracting. "It would be fun to meet your mom someday. She sounds fascinating."

His smile encourages me as I list off what I know about her. "A librarian, a woman who purposefully chooses a strong name for her son, and she can't be too bad if she raised you to be such a gentleman."

"Hmm" he ponders again, this time with a devilish smile, "her good graces end when you are late for curfew, believe me."

I'm intrigued by his casualness, he and his mom must be pretty close. "And how often did that happen."

The look he gives tells me enough, "Only once."

I laugh lightly, unable to help but wish my mom would have cared if I came home late or at all.

"I think my mom would like you." Roman continues before my mind can drift too far from this table and this extraordinary moment. "My grandmother, too. Gran is an adventurer just like you."

"Really?"

"Of course. A strong independent woman who fights for her dreams and strikes out at the opportunities life gives her."

I'm beam at his words. I don't know what to say. Suddenly that self-doubt kicks in and I realize that he hardly knows me. I can't possibly live up to the fanciful words he uses to describe me. Still, I look into his eyes and enjoy his kindness and wish that his words could be true.

"You could never meet my mom or grandmother though." He says nonchalantly.

I'm taken aback. I didn't mean to rush things, "Why not? I --"

"Because they would tell you to not mess with me and you'd go backpacking through the alps with Gran and trap yourself in a library with my mom. I would only see you on holidays and when you needed supplies."

I burst out laughing. I had to cover my mouth so as not to further disturb the tables near us in this fancy restaurant. He leans forward and takes both of my hands to kiss my knuckles.

Once I get control of my breathing, he asks, "What is your middle name?"

"Elizabeth, after my grandmother. My last name is

Dalton."

"Aria Elizabeth Dalton." He smiles, "that is a beautiful name."

For the first time in my life I agree with him, coming from his lips it does sound beautiful.

Chapter 10

Story Of My Life

ROMAN

The waiter breaks our trance to take our order. After we choose our courses, I see the fountains of The Bellagio begin their performance out of the corner of my eye. I squeeze Aria's smooth hand and point out the window. We can't hear the music, but the view overlooking the display is breathtaking.

I watch her eyes light up as she gazes at the fountains and lights like it's Christmas morning. She looks back at me, "Are you seeing this? It is so amazing."

"Yes, it is." I answer, but I am looking only at her. The way her hair falls over her face accentuates her strong brow. I've yet to see her look this relaxed, she seems free. Though a different sort than when I met her dancing on the strip. Was that really just yesterday, I wonder? It feels like another lifetime.

I don't think she realizes the open liberation she radiates. I yearn for that illumination, my moth and the flame metaphor rises in my mind again. When I'm near her, I believe I can do anything. The fear and loss that has surrounded me for so many years takes a step back. I can breathe. In this moment all I feel is freedom. I want to hold on to it for as long as I can.

I can dream. I watch her as the majestic water show signals its grand finale. It never gets old, even though I've seen it several times now while staying at the Bellagio.

Experiencing it with Aria, it feels like I'm seeing the world through new eyes. I can only hope she is having a good time with me as well.

I find I don't really know what to say next. The wine the waiter brought when he took our orders sits untouched on the table. As the Bellagio culminates, I decide on a toast. Before I am ready, Aria turns around to look at me with those passionate eyes.

I feel like a deer in the headlights, forgetting even my own name as her beauty stops me.

"How about a toast?" Aria lifts her glass to me.

I lift mine with a smile, "That's a great idea."

"To Vegas, unexpected encounters and following our dreams."

Her words echo my own thoughts. "Here, here, and to dreams coming true." She beams at me as we sip our wine. I am rewarded for my minimal wine research, pleased with the selection. The guttural hum from Aria tells me she also approves.

The brief silence shared over wine is comfortable. Still, it's hard to get to know someone if we don't start talking. "Andrew told me about this place when he came back last year. I always wanted to come, but I never thought I would have a reason to. I realize now it's because I wanted someone special to share it with. Thank you for giving me a reason to come and see it."

Only afterwards did I realize how cliche my statement sounds. And yet, Aria's hand flutters over her heart and I can sense her appreciation. I can't believe no one tells her how beautiful, funny and spirited she is. I want to tell her everyday. She leans in to kiss me and I find myself wanting to do a whole lot more.

In this moment, the connection we share feels bright and real. I reach my hand up to caress her chin as her lips softly massage mine, it seems the only response appropriate for polite company.

As she leans back with a twinkle in her eye, the conversation begins to flow as she asks me about my family. I find myself rambling on about my sister Athena and her recent husband, Seth. "Even though the wedding was only six months ago, they are already trying to get pregnant."

"Do you find that concerning? For them to have children so soon, I mean?" Aria asks with interest.

I think about my baby sister and her remarkable nurturing personality and shake my head in response, "Not at all. My sister has meant to be a mother since she was old enough to hold a baby doll. She is always taking care of people, sometimes when they don't even want the help. It makes perfect sense to have kids and soon. I wish them the best, it could be fun to have a nephew or niece to spoil."

I catch the sad look that crosses her face, but before I can mention it she asks, "Do you like Seth?"

"Yeah, he's great. They met at a homesteading retreat a couple years ago. I'm actually surprised they waited so long to get married. They were hell bent on getting married on their own property. They found a primo spot out in the middle of nowhere, it seems. There is a small house on it now, but they are going to work on building a bigger one in a couple years. They have a ten year plan, complete with multiple children."

"Did you grow up like that? Homesteading and such?"

"No, not really. We had a chicken for a while when I was a kid. We had a fairly big yard and a garden, but I wouldn't call it homesteading. We still lived in the suburbs. I was too busy riding around on my bicycle and pretending sticks were lightsabers to do much with it. My dad was the one who really enjoyed gardening. He and Athena would be outside tending our tiny plot all summer.

"That sounds lovely. I don't know the first thing about gardening." Aria smiles and sips her wine, "What does your dad do?"

"My dad died when I was 17."

I always hate talking about this part. I know it is important and has probably affected me more than anything else in my childhood, but I can't stand the look of pity.

I look to Aria expecting to see what I have in the face of so many others. She gazes back at me, not with pity, but understanding. In that moment, I realize that there is a lot about this woman I don't know. However, I find that I want to tell her more and I am grateful for her reaction.

"He was riding his bike to work, which he always did. It was a day no different than any other, except that a car ran a red light. The impact broke his neck, there was nothing to be done."

"That's awful."

"It was. It's been eight years and I still miss him terribly."

Aria surprises me by leaning across the table to rest her hand on my cheek. I ease into her touch, appreciating the comforting gesture. It is aged pain, but some things never lighten. We have to find a way to live around it. I can sense she understands my suffering. I wonder what ache she carries.

After I moment, I continue, "Honestly, I went a little mad after it happened. Up to that point I was oblivious, most of the time at least, to what other people thought about me. After the funeral, I became all too aware of everyone feeling sorry for me. I didn't know what to do, my dad was invincible in my eyes. Everything I knew came crashing down.

"I started college that fall and attacked it with a sort of

fury. I didn't really make friends or get to know people, I hardly even looked up. I slept, I studied, and I attended class. I never went to parties or bring girls home." he looks at me.

"At least you've improved in a couple areas." She gives me a quiet smile. Yes, something about her sets me free. Even when it comes to my worst nightmare, she brings light and a laugh.

I can't help but laugh. "So really, that's how I got here. I'm one of the youngest tech consultants in the field."

"How old are you?"

"Twenty-six"

"I'm twenty-four."

"When is your birthday?" I ask, eager to change the subject.

"August 1st." she replies, "You?"

"October 8."

"So you're a Libra?" She asks curiously.

"Yep, what does that make you?"

"A Leo."

"Oh no, I'm dating a lion?" I say in mock horror.

"Roar," she teases. "You know about that stuff?"

"Not really," I admit, "but my sister brought home every book about it when she was in middle school."

"Do you remember if the lion and scales are compatible?"

"Not really, do you know?"

"Yes," she pauses intently, "they aren't."

I consider that, "We'll see about that. I think you might be surprised." I wink at her, encouraging her to smile. It delights me at the easy manner in which she does just that. I counter, "Do you know about that stuff?"

She laughs, "I was the girl bringing home every book about it in middle school. Plus my friend's mom is really into the metaphysical and natural medicine and such."

Our food comes on the arms of elegant servers. The plating and portions impress me, I can see Aria's eyes bug out, too. As we begin to eat, Aria states, "I like how you talk about your family. I can tell that you all love each other very much."

I shrug, "Most of the time."

"I wish I had stories like that to tell." She replies quietly.

I look at her then. She has said very little about her family and what she has said makes me wonder if they are very present in her life. I sense she is as ready to share as she will be, so I ask, "What was it like for you growing up?"

She looks at me closely for a few moments. I wonder what she is trying to see. After a minute, she goes back to cutting her fish and says, "It was just me and my mom growing up. And my grandmother before she died. I don't have any siblings. I never knew my dad. Actually, I'm not even sure if he knows I exist. My mom got pregnant one summer during tourist season and the guy gave her false information."

"Dang, that's harsh."

"Yeah, I think it messed my mom up. Mostly my life growing up was lonely. My mom wasn't around a lot, she worked evenings and was out even when she wasn't working. I didn't have many friends, the other kids were all involved in stuff that I couldn't afford to do. I wrote, a lot. I would walk to the park and climb trees and sit in them all day writing poetry. I even got a book of poetry published while I was in high school.

"It wasn't until I was much older that I realized how neglecting my mom was. The sad thing is, I definitely inherited her stubbornness. I hope I'm doing better about not being an ass. For the most part I just avoided her. It got easier as I got older and more independent.

"I did have my best friend Leana though, her family saved me in a lot of ways. We were always together by the time I got to high school. Her mom was more of a mother than my own in those days." she chuckles under her breath. "I still send her a Mother's Day card every year."

Aria looks up at me for the first time since she started talking, "I like that your stories have people in them. I have a few with birds," she laughs.

"Are they happy birds?" I ask absorbing what she said.

"Always."

I couldn't imagine life without my family, especially my mother. I can grasp the pain she carries, at least in part. I want to hug her, but I know from my own grieving that is not always appreciated. I am content to listen.

After a few moments, I ask, "Was it Leana that was with you when we met last night?"

"Yes, and her sister Alicia."

"They looked like true friends."

"She's the closest thing I have to a sister. We are closer than blood. She knows me better than I know myself. She just told me that yesterday actually. "

I smile at her because I can sense the happy thought when it comes to her friend that is more like a sister. I am thankful to have a sister like a friend. Though I realize it is a little sad that I haven't kept up with any friends along the way.

Suddenly, she shakes her head and puts her fork down from pushing food around on her plate, "I'm sorry, I didn't mean to get so heavy."

"We make quite the pair I suppose," I lift my wine glass. She follows suit and though I do not mean to make another toast, it just pops out, "To heartache and pain and still being able to find joy."

"Here, here." Her smile lights up her eyes causing me to suck in my breath, "A beautiful toast."

We clink and sip. As our plates are cleared, we find ourselves laughing again. Our conversation flows freely as we finish the last drops in the bottle and revel in a perfect evening.

Chapter 11

The Heart Won't Be Denied

ARIA

Sitting next to Roman at the table of a fancy restaurant is a dream come true. It's a dream I didn't even know was possible. I enjoy that we can talk about anything and everything. I love hearing him laugh and even appreciate the wrinkle that forms on his forehead when he is thinking really hard about something. It feels like we have known each other for years instead of days and I find that all the hesitations I had earlier today have vanished. I don't want to be a fool to think that we have something special, but I look into his eyes now and know that is true.

As Roman takes care of the check with no reaction at all to the price, he looks up to me and smiles. I feel nervous that he spent that much on dinner. For right now, I'm telling all of my insecurities to quiet down. I'll listen to them again tomorrow. I just want tonight.

During dinner, my mundane existence exploded and came alive. The night holds a sense of magic. I'm not sure if it is the restaurant, the legendary performance of the Bellagio fountains or just being next to him. Maybe it's letting him know about my upbringing without feeling so isolated about it.

I don't want the night to end. I immensely enjoy our time together and I don't want to go home to my quiet apartment alone.

Roman must have been thinking the same. He rises from his chair and takes my hand, asking, "Are you ready for dessert?"

"Are you kidding?" I ask.

"No." He shakes his head with a smile.

I eye him. "Okay. I know a place."

"Oh, you know a place?"

"Yep, it's not far."

"It's not Denny's is it?"

I chuckle as we head out the door, "No, this one is exclusive to Vegas. Almost as renowned as Gordon Ramsey."

"Lead the way."

I wrap my arms around his and head toward Venice. The crisp spring air feels comfortable on my skin as we walk. It will only be a matter of weeks before it is as warm at night as it is during the day now. I enjoy the chill of the evening and the romance that it brings us tonight.

Roman nudges my shoulder, "If you could travel anywhere in the entire world, where would you go?"

"Ah," I sigh. That is a lot deeper question than he realizes. Traveling has always been a dream, but it is hard to go anywhere when you have little funds. I focus on the dream, "Where wouldn't I go is the question. I would love to visit the Louvre in France, ride on a Gondola in Italy, see a bull race in Spain, walk along the Great Wall of China, swim by the great barrier reef in Australia." I look over at him smiling back at me.

"What?" I ask. He shakes his head, but says nothing. "I could go on."

"Is that part of the reason you love Vegas?"

The question confuses me, I look at him with raised eyebrows.

He gestures back at Paris, which we just left and then ahead to Vencia where we are heading, "In this one strip you can go almost anywhere in the world. Paris is back there, New York is up the way a little. You can go back in time to the world of knights and dragons or eat lunch in Caesar's Palace. You can see some of the best shows, premier a sitcom pilot or even journey to the bottom of the sea. The possibilities are endless."

I consider his words as we meander down the sidewalk of this city that constantly bustles with activity. I've never really thought about it much before. When I arrived, I was captivated by the movement and activity. I enjoyed all the different personalities and opinions. I like Vegas because it is a place where you don't have to worry about fitting in because everyone stands out as unique. I'd tried to fit in all my life to no avail. I didn't feel that need here. How could I explain that?

"I never really connected the two before. I suppose it does satisfy my love for travel in many ways. I think I was just looking for the first thing that was the exact opposite of where I grew up. I like Vegas because it is a city that encourages you to be who you are, or perhaps an exaggerated version of who you are in some cases. Besides, it's nice to get lost in a crowd."

"Did you not like where you grew up?" Roman asks curiously.

"I do in some ways. I love the beach. The one thing I really miss about Myrtle Beach is that is right on the ocean. The house I grew up in is just a few blocks from the water. I don't miss all of the emotions that come with the area or my mom. I never really felt like I fit in."

Roman squeezed my hand and then lifted it to his lips. His kiss was tender and understanding. "I too love the ocean."

The abruptness of his comment makes me laugh. He continues, "I love walking on the beach at sunrise. It's something my dad and I used to do."

Now I look at him and see the memories just behind his eyes. Still, he smiles. I think about my dreams of the ocean and can easily see Roman with me there sinking our toes into the sand.

We walk the rest of the short distance to the Venetian in a comfortable silence. I lead him in to Carlo's bakery.

Roman looks up and asks, "Is this the Cake Boss?"

"One and the same."

"Wow, that is very cool." He looks around a few minutes and then gestures further into the Venetian. "What else is here? Our convention is set up on the other end of the resort, but I haven't seen this part yet."

"There's only one way to find out."

We walk through the ornate hallway to where it opens up into an open room with a waterway flowing inside. I look up to see the night's sky painted on the ceiling including shining stars.

"This is amazing. It's like another world." Roman says.

"A fantasy world."

"A dream come true." He says with a gleam in his eye, "Come on."

He leads me over to where a gondola sits ready to embark on the gentle indoor stream. As we reach the entrance, he looks to me. I nod jubilantly. I don't even think as he hands over some money, I am inthralled by my surroundings.

As Roman helps me into the long narrow boat, I understand what it means to swoon. I feel so happy that I may explode. I settle into Roman's side as he wraps his arm around my shoulders. The gondolier bows his head and says, "Buona Sera Signore y Signora, welcome to the

Venetian. Enjoy the ride."

I reply, "Grazie Senior, it is a beautiful night."

"Si, a special night indeed" he bows again and then sets off with a wink.

Roman hugs me close. The feel of his body next to mine vibrates like a gentle hum. I relax into him and enjoy the moment of pure bliss through the waterway until a painted sky.

A soft hum begins in my ear and I turn to Roman realizing he is singing softly. It is a melody that only I can hear. I kiss his jaw, just below his ear. "I like that song."

"My grandmother used to sing it to me and Athena when we were little. She said it was the love song of the doves." He hums a little more of the song in my ear as I melt against him.

I feel him kiss my head and I know what peace feels like.

As we float under the last bridge he lifts his hand to my chin and kisses me. It is a short, gentle kiss. There is an edge to it that tells me he wants this kiss to last a bit longer and to be followed by many more. I lean into him wanting the same.

On our way back to the Bellagio and his hotel room, we stop by Carlo's Bakery and each pick out two delectables. I pay for these gladly and he lets me with a smile.

Though it had been hours since we finished our wine, I feel drunk in love as we navigate the sidewalks weaving through the many people still out among the lights.

Roman promises Andrew will be out of the room and I can't think clearly enough to feel guilt over the generous offer of his friend. I have no hesitations as we make our way through the lobby and up the elevator. The hallways feel endless as the building carnal urges begin to overwhelm my senses. I float through the doorway or maybe Roman lifts me through because I find myself in his arms pressed back against the door.

There is no pausing this time, no time for bathroom breaks or falling asleep. Roman covers my mouth with a generous greed that I have never experienced before. I open my mouth to taste him on my tongue. I revel in the sweet, smoky flavor of him. As his kisses leave my mouth to follow my jawline, I sigh his name. In this moment, under the touch of his enthusiastic hands, I feel alive.

Roman's fingers caress up my side until he finds my zipper. Slowly, too slowly, he pulls it down causing my chest to relax since I didn't wear a bra. He murmurs quietly as he rubs my back with his strong, bare hands. The sensation lifts my chest toward him where he takes full advantage by inserting my rigid nipple between his lips.

I gasp, glad that he is holding me to the wall so I don't fall into a puddle on the floor. His light touch turns more heated as he takes more of me into his mouth. I can feel his desire as I grind into his hips barely able to stand.

He lifts me up taking my lips again. I lock my legs around his hips. After walking a few steps, he sets me gently onto the bed. Before he can lean back, I untuck his shirt and begin to unbuckle his belt. He groans in pleasure as he attacks my ear and jaw, trailing kisses down to my chest.

As Roman teases my neck, I wrestle with his jeans. He helps me get them off and turns to me to pull off the remainder of my dress puddled around my waist. Being this close to him makes me feel on fire, I can't believe I will ever get enough of his kisses or his touch.

I sit up to find his lips and wrap my legs around his

hard member. I explore his mouth while familiarizing myself with the muscles in his back. His hand continues to wander teasing the edges of my panties. He breaks the kiss only long enough to lift me up again to dispose of the thin cloth. I will try to remember which corner he tossed them in later.

As he leans back over me, he gently lays an elbow on each side of my frame. My legs remain wrapped around him. He tilts back and I drink in the eagerness in his eyes as he looks down at me.

He whispers in reverence, "You are so beautiful."

"You are so damn sexy." I reach up until I find his lips and pull him down on top of me.

It feels right, laying here together with him teasing my breast with his fingers and then his lips. I am excited by his touch, and also soothed. At least as long as I could still think.

Roman's kisses lower and lower until the pressure of his lips reach my inner thigh. He continues his motion with his lips as he found my warm center with his hand. Though I ache for it, I still feel like I'm about to combust as he eases a finger in my most intimate territory. I arch my back and remind myself to breathe. He continues his tender kisses and introduce a "come here" motion with his finger that has me writhing in place.

He reaches his hand to massage my hip allowing me to feel the desire in his touch. He adds a second finger to his rhythm as his kisses pepper my stomach.

I can't get enough of his touch, I want more and more of him. To my wonder, he gives himself to me freely. A wave crashes over me and I fall back on the bed.

He patiently rides the whole crest with me and then quickly discards his own underwear and climbs on top of me taking my lips hungrily with his. I incline into him, pushing my body flush against his.

I feel his desire hard against my body and yet he hesitates. "Are you sure?" he breathes in my ear.

I melt in that moment. On edge, ready to take the plunge and yet he stops and makes sure I have a choice. If I ever had a doubt to what kind of man Roman is, this moment erases any hesitation. I know that he wants to be with me, I have no doubt about that, and yet he still puts my needs above his own. Love fills me as I realize I want all of him, his body and his heart. As I look into his intense blue eyes hovering over me I realize I have already made my decision, one of the easiest decisions ever.

I meet his eyes and he looks into my soul, "Yes, I am absolutely sure."

Without hesitation his smile leads him to find my lips, "Me too." Reluctantly he pulls away to reach for a condom. With protection secure, our embrace quickly turns heated again.

As he positions above me I consider the possibility that the anticipation will kill me. When he eases inside of me, I melt to accommodate him. He fills me up and makes me feel whole. As he begins to move inside me he kisses my lips, cheeks, jaw and then behind my ear. I move with him as we connect in the way that only intimacy can bring. I wish it were possible to get even closer to him, but there is no gap left to be filled.

After a huge tidal wave hits me, we both collapsed on the bed exhausted, but fully satisfied.

He leans forward and rests his head on mine, "Now that is the perfect end to the perfect date."

"Yes. A perfect day." I say. He laughs and kisses me.

After we cleanup, I curl up next to him in bed resting in the crook of his arm. We are peaceful, content to lay together. No more words are needed this evening. We have shown each other how we feel and the communion makes us glow.

I begin to doze and hear him humming. I recognize the song from the gondola, and I am comforted by the rhythm. I settle in closer and feel a light kiss on my temple. I lean into his presence as his soft baritone vibrates in his chest.

I fall asleep in pure contentment in the arms of a man I could see myself with for a long time. In fact, I am already running towards that ledge, oblivious of what lies on the other side. In this moment, it doesn't matter that he lives on the other side of the country in a place I fear returning. The only thing I know is that the world is a lot better place wrapped in his arms.

Chapter 12

The Start Of Something Beautiful

ROMAN

I wake to the sound of my alarm, wistful from my dream. I hurry to cease the awful sound then turn to see Aria in the bed next to me. I am thankful, it wasn't a dream after all. I watch her peaceful figure and believe I am in heaven. Our time together last night was the most amazing experience. I had never felt that connected and fiercely united with someone in my entire life. I know I will never be the same.

I remember the look in her eyes as she said she was absolutely sure about me. It gave me confidence that I can't explain. It made our night together truly spectacular.

Aria begins to stir beside me and I can't help myself as I reach out for her. I cannot believe she is lying here next to me. I dream of waking up like this everyday. I can't explain it exactly, but there is something about her that feels like home. It seems odd to travel across the country and feel more at peace in a hotel room in Vegas than I have in my own space for the last several years.

Aria rolls over to face me smiling and reaches out to touch my face. I could die right now a happy man. I cover Aria's hand with mine and lean over to kiss her scrumptious lips, "You are beautiful in the morning."

She laughs exaggeratedly and lays back. I can see her

contemplate her looks as her hand moves toward her hair and then wipes the side of her mouth where a little drool escaped while she slept. None of those things matter to me. She is beautiful on the inside and out. I can feel the truth of it deep in my bones.

Aria must have seen something in my expression because her bright eyes lean my way and sweep me up into a kiss. Yes, I wish I could wake like this every morning. I can't remember the last time I felt such peace.

I settle back on my pillow with the taste of her lips still on mine. Her hand tangles in mine as she shifts to rest on my shoulder. I revel in the ability to hold this exquisite woman in my arms and relent the fact I will have to go to work today.

"I have the convention all morning, but today is the last day. I should be done around three."

She nods pressing into my shoulder. I can tell she realizes, just as I have that our time together here is coming to an end. Aria speaks softly, "They are expecting me at the theater for the show tonight. I have to be there by six. The show starts at seven."

I know she still needs to live her life, Lord knows I've already taken up days of her time when she probably would have been with her friends. "Okay. Do you want to meet for an early dinner?"

She looks up at me with an eagerness in her eyes that sparks my heart. "I would love that. Do you want to see the show? They can manage without me once it's all set up."

"That sounds great." I sigh, gathering her to me. The physical closeness helps reassure me that this isn't a dream. Even if it was, I would be content to never wake up.

A trace of light kisses tickle my neck causing me to look over at Aria wearing a devilish grin. I wrap my arms around her waist and pull her even closer, just to breathe her in. As she continues to flirt with her lips along my skin. I can feel myself harden at her light touch. This woman excites me in a way I forgot was possible. This time together has meant so much, for once in the last eight years since my father's death, I feel truly alive.

"Is it time for a shower?" I whisper into her ear.

She looks back beaming, "Absolutely."

I roll off the bed and reach for her, laughing as her foot gets stuck in the sheets causing her to fall into my arms. Rubbing my hands along her back is a natural response. I pull her close enveloping her lips. My hand finds a sensitive spot just under her back left rib and she breaks our kiss to laugh. Her reaction surprises me, but I love hearing that sound so I go back for more.

She wiggles under my fingers making it very hard to think of anything other than the feel of her skin under mine and the lack of clothes between us.

As Aria gasps for breath, I take her lips with mine for one tenacious moment, "Now it's time for that shower," I declare.

She nods. I lead us to the bathroom, guiding her across the small room.

I start the water and then stand behind Aria, who gazes in the mirror. I'm not sure what she is thinking, but when she meets my eyes in the mirror she smiles. She is the most beautiful woman in the world. Though a familiar stranger, her spirit rages in her eyes and I feel like I've known her a lifetime. Unable to resist any longer, I bow forward to caress kisses along her shoulder moving slowly behind her ear.

A soft moan escapes her mouth urging me on. I turn her to face me pressing a bold kiss on her lips. She arches up for more, but I have other plans.

Moving down her chest, I take her nipple between my

lips and suck gently. Her response is immediate. I have no doubt she can feel my own readiness pressing along her thigh.

The sound of my name distracts me as I pull back. Aria is bowed backwards with her eyes closed and I sense the ecstasy she feels. I bow down to love on her other breast, enjoying every moment with her.

I pull away at the feel of restless arms around my shoulders. The cloudy look of desire in her eyes matches my own euphoria.

Turning slightly in the small space I grab a condom from the box on the counter, then guide her into the shower. With lusty laughs, we enjoy the warmth of the water with passionate kisses. Standing skin to skin, I wrap her in my arms and just enjoy this moment.

The heat of the hotel shower represents a kind of luxury, an occasion seemingly apart from time. I take my time feasting on her body before I move to her warmest center. As I move with her, I can't remember a time that I've felt more alive. Our momentum builds quickly in the heat of the shower as I hold her steady against me. I ride the sensations until I explode, causing my name to ring in a rich alto from her lips.

I gather her to me trying to catch my breath. She kisses my chest with happy giggles and I revel in this powerful connection we share.

After a few moments, Aria gets her feet back under her and I release her with a satisfied kiss. I toss the condom into the toilet and she reaches over and hands me the bottle of tiny shampoo. Just like that, the real world begins to creep back in.

We joke, tease and laugh as we shower and get ready. She surprises me by removing a fresh romper from her large purse. I have to give it to her, she's prepared. We pick up the room a little in case Andrew needed to come in for anything and let the door click behind us as we walk downstairs hand in hand.

We find Andrew in the lobby with Dawson and Miguel. Andrew smiles, nodding to Aria, "Nice to see you still around."

"Yeah," she blushes, "It's good to still be around."

She turns towards me, sharing in my expansive smile, but I say nothing.

"Ready to go?" Andrew asks.

"Yeah," I answer. I am ready, but also reluctant to let Aria go. I know I will see her later in the day, but it feels like the end of our time together is drawing to a close too quickly. I don't want to let her go, I can't stay here in Las Vegas, but I don't know what else to do.

The others walk on giving Aria and I a minute together. I turn to her and take both of her hands in mine kissing them one and then the other, "I'll see you when I'm done?"

"I can't wait."

"You're good to get home?"

I see her eyeing me and hastily backtrack, "I know, I know you are." I don't want her to view me as overbearing, I just want to make sure she's taken care of.

"I'll see you later this afternoon," she voices lightly like we've been giving this parting for years instead of days, "Enjoy your last day at the convention."

"Thanks" I smile and kiss her again, knowing I will never get enough of her affection. I watch her walk away and then turn to catch up with the guys.

ARIA

I glance back as they head off and smile to myself. I'm

sure they're giving him a hard time, but he doesn't seem to care much. Neither do I, not when he looks at me with those clear blue eyes like he can see straight into my soul.

I still feel as if I'm in a dream when my phone starts ringing. "Hello," I answer distracted by my own thoughts.

"So how is that Southern hunk in bed?" Leana practically yells in the phone.

I laugh Best friends always know.

"Pretty damn good." I answer.

Her laughter mimics my own. "You go girl! I want details, but later, right now we are waiting at the airport to board our plane."

"Did you have a good time?" I ask. I felt a little bad for not spending more time with Leana and Alicia while they were here.

From her next words, I knew she understood my remorse and that there were no hard feelings, "Girl, you go and be with that Southern hunk and don't worry about us. We had an amazing time and I'm glad we got to hang out a bit. This won't be the last time I see you, or Las Vegas. You two connected in a way you can't ignore. All of us can see that. Go, see where it goes. I will request that our next visit happen on the East coast. I suspect he'll get you out here sooner rather than later."

"What?" I ask, surprised by her candor.

She ignores my interjection, "I love you girl. Have fun tonight with Southern boy, I know he flies out tomorrow. Thank you for such a great time. I'll see you soon!"

"Thanks Leana. Be safe. I probably won't respond, but I'd love to know when you are both home safe."

"Will do." With a chuckle she hangs up.

I put my phone up and laugh to myself. I don't have a lot of friends, but the ones I have sure know how to cut to the chase. Leana gave me something to think about in that short conversation. What are we going to do when he leaves tomorrow? Roman hasn't even left yet and I already miss him.

I walk through my front door and flop on my chair to look out the window. My mind is in the clouds and I don't want to come back to reality any time soon. My mind drifts to our evening together and then our morning. I am distracted by the memory of his dimples crinkling with his laugh and the feel of his hands along my body.

I need to get work done, but I can't seem to stop thinking about Roman or our short time together. A fresh cup of coffee helps me focus just enough to say I did something productive. I work through an introductory scene in my novel where the two characters first meet. I feel I have a fresh perspective on this at the moment, so I jump on the opportunity to write it out.

Leana's comment about going back east keeps repeating like an echo in my mind. I wonder what is really keeping me here. It is a conundrum because I have a connection with Roman that I can't deny and don't want to. However, that particular area of the world is a minefield in my mind. One that I have taken great lengths to avoid. And yet, would it be so bad to go back?

Charleston and Myrtle Beach are still at least a couple hours away, it's not like my mother and I would be in the same town. It would be nice to sink my toes into the warm sand on the Atlantic coast beaches. It would be even better to be with Roman longer than just a few days.

I didn't really consider the possibility of a permanent move until Leana planted that damn seed in my head. Now,

I can't not think about it. Would he even want me to be with him? Maybe this whole thing is just a good time while away. I don't feel that when I'm with him, but sitting alone in my apartment, it is hard to fathom that quick of an attachment.

I begin to wonder about where he lives, who he hangs out with and who he is when no one is watching. He's seen how I live--in a small mess of a place with eclectic friends and family across the country. I'm curious about him, there are so many questions.

Yet, if he asked, I know I would go. What would I have to lose? I don't really have anything tying me here, certainly not my few convenient friends. I would miss Mikey the most, since he is the one I tend to hang out with the most. My family is actually closer to where he lives. It would be nice to see Leana and Mrs. Grace more often. I don't have a steady job and my primary work seems to be in a lull anyway. Typically, I find work where and when I can. I could even put more focus on my novel.

The real problem is that I don't want to think about these things. What if he wants to end it tonight? What if it is just one final shag before he goes back to real life and I'm expected to do the same? We haven't really talked about a relationship or what comes next. The entire encounter came as a surprise to both of us.

I wonder if this is how my mother felt with the man who would become my birth father. Did she believe he would stay and be more than a vacation fling? She must have. I don't want to make her mistakes. I've been running away from them for so long.

I can't imagine Roman will want me to barge in on his lifestyle. Even if it ends up being a few days with an amazing man laughing and having amazing sex, I think I can live with that. It has been the most incredible time of my life. I don't want it to end, but I am so glad it happened.

The afternoon drags on between reality and fiction, and then sensibility and dreams. It is a distracted stretch of time. I am still going over the same thoughts and uncertainties for the millionth time when I am startled by an enthusiastic knock at the door.

I'm still trying to distinguish between dream and reality as I opened the door to reveal Roman, all smiles, with a backpack slung over his shoulder.

I lean in to kiss him before I back up to let him in the room.

He tosses his backpack next to my bed and then brings his arms around me for a kiss, that starts sweet and promptly grows deeper. "I couldn't get you out of my mind all day."

I bathe in his attention, "That makes two of us."

"You couldn't get you off your mind either? Small world." He laughs holding me close.

"No you, silly. I barely got any work done, but I did manage to get myself stuck on this one scene. It doesn't seem to be fitting together quite right."

He seems to be floating free this afternoon with a light-hearted fun attitude. I want to soak in his goodness and let it wash over me.

Roman frees me and then sits on my plush chair by the window, "That sounds annoying."

Moving to perch on the arm next to him, "It is. I'm trying to form clues to get the prince up to the lady's suite in the tower, but I can't quite get them to add up. I feel like I'm missing something."

"I have the same problem sometimes when I work with code. I've had to research and try things for weeks before the pieces lock into place. It can take five days to find five stubborn lines of code that can be fixed in five minutes."

"Really?" I ask in amazement that he actually understands what I was describing and the frustration that goes along with it.

He nods.

I smile. "How was your last day at the convention?"

Roman pulls me in his lap, "Great. Andrew says I'm a natural at talking in a way that promotes our products to customers without sounding like I'm selling them anything. I looked at him like he had three heads."

"Why is that? It sounds like a great compliment to me."

"It is. I wouldn't say I'm socially inept or anything, but I don't have a lot of practice in crowds like we saw today. Thankfully, I know our products and happen to think they are pretty good, so it works out I suppose."

"That's great though. Are you excited about taking over Andrew's position?"

"Yeah, I think I am. For a long time it was just about checking tasks off a list. I had my head down and did whatever came next. Now, it's starting to feel real. I can do this. I'm seeing all the ways I will enjoy the work."

"What do you like the most?"

"Talking with people. It wasn't really what I originally thought I would be doing within our system, but I do seem to have a knack for it. I enjoy the different personalities, for the most part at least. It is like a puzzle to make sure the customer has the right system set up for their needs. I like that part of it, too."

"You must have a puzzle solving mind."

"I never thought of it that way, I suppose I do." He looks up at me with a smile that lights up his whole face.

"So what do you want to do?" I ask. "We have a couple hours before I need to be at the theater."

He still wears that same carefree smile, but I can tell something heavy is weighing on him because his shoulders are tense in a way I have yet to see. He seems to ignore it, so I do, too. I wonder what is on his mind, maybe he'll tell me later.

Tonight will be our last night together before he leaves to go home. It is the elephant in the room, the one thing neither of us dares bring up. I wonder what will be in store for tomorrow, I suppose a goodbye. The thought makes me sad.

The backpack he casually brought in makes me smile. No matter what tomorrow brings, today will be a good time because we are together. He looks at me like I'm the most beautiful person in the world and answers a question I almost forgot I asked, "I don't care what we do, so long as we do it together."

That is music to my ears. I lean towards him snuggling closer to him while still on his lap. He pulls me in to kiss me, a sweet gentle kiss.

"Are you hungry?" I ask him.

"Yeah, a little. Should we eat before the show starts?"

"It would be a good idea. I know a place we could go. Have you been in the Cosmopolitan yet?"

"You and your places." Roman chuckles to himself, "No, I haven't, but isn't it just right next to my hotel? I thought I saw a big sign."

"Yes, it is and happens to be just across from the theater too."

"Sounds perfect, what are we eating."

"Secret Pizza."

ROMAN

"How secret is this pizza?" I say with a laugh. I'm only

a little worried as Aria leads me through the halls of the Cosmopolitan. We passed the lounge and started through a corridor that seemed to wind back to a lair with vinyl covers along the walls. There were no signs anywhere indicating there was a pizza place even here.

"Not as secret as you would think," we stop as we reach a group of people standing in a line. "It's a local legend, this pizza."

"Wow," I look at the line already formed at four thirty in the afternoon and back towards the Cosmopolitan entry. "This really is secret pizza. I would never know this place existed."

"Thus the secret part. There's almost always a line, but it's worth it. They have the best pizza by the slice."

"I'm looking forward to it." I say and mean it. I watch her smile like she knows a secret and is waiting for the right moment to tell me.

We stand in line and chat about the people around us: a woman two groups up with bright pink hair that matches her oversized purse, the two guys behind us sipping martinis as they wait, a fun juxtaposition to their street clothes of oversized shirts and baggy jeans.

I find Las Vegas fascinating. This is a place where you can be anything and not be judged for it. There is some freedom in that. I can see why Aria wanted to escape here. Still, there are so many questions. Maybe the best way to get answers is to ask.

I gently pull Aria to me, enjoying the way her body fits flush against mine. "What made you come to Las Vegas? Of all the places in the world, why here?"

I appreciate the way her eye furl a little before she answers. I know I am going to get an honest response. "I wanted somewhere I could be free. I feel like I was living life in a shadow never quite sure what was expected of me and never quite brave enough to figure out who I wanted to be. I finally had enough of being scared and set out to the one place I imagined I could figure out who I am. Leana and I used to dream of coming here and being in the shows. I never cared about the gambling or drinking, but there is no other performance stage like Vegas and the nightlife goes all day. The energy here is electric, just like I knew it would be. In the world of performing, this is where the fun and money meet."

"But you don't perform." I stated.

"No, Leana was always the performer, but I still love the show. I love how the characters interact. I love how the lights and sound enhance the story and set the mood. It think it is fascinating and you can feel a good performance with all of your senses. I don't mind being on the stage, but my love is putting the story together. I used to spend hours reading and then I started creating my own characters. I would write out scripts for Leana and I to act out in her backyard. Sometimes her sister or brother would get roped in. Her dog Muffin would star often in our plays."

"What kind of dog was Muffin?" I ask curious, enjoying her happy memories.

"A Beagle. She was the sweetest dog. I think Leana's parents got her so she could help us burn our energy. It worked. We would come in on some afternoons and have milk and cookies and fall asleep at the table."

"Those sound like wonderful memories."

"They were." I watch her reminiscing and can see both light and darkness flashing behind her eyes. She talks of a happy moment, but I am beginning to see that those were surrounded by struggles as well.

All of these good moments were with her friend, I wonder what she was like without Leana around, if she was still able to smile like she is now. It's a good thing she had

Leana, it made me think of my own childhood friend Kyle. We aren't close anymore though, I think he lives in Charlotte, North Carolina, but that's really just a guess.

I'm still lost in thought when it is our turn to order. I look to Aria for advice. She laughs at my expectant look and says with exaggerated arms, "It's all good."

Aria orders a margherita slice and a beer, so I order a meaty slice, a pepperoni slice and a beer. I can't help but have high anticipation for this secret pizza.

I try to pay, but Aria bumps my hip, "This one is on me."

"You sure?" I ask.

"Absolutely." I nod and we find a small table open along the wall. I watch as her hair sways across her face as she puts down her plate. "This place is cool."

I set my own plate down and turn to Aria placing a kiss on her cheek. I can't seem to help myself, I enjoy these moments we have together. I don't want them to end.

"Yes, but wait until you have the pizza. Then you'll know why we wish to keep it a secret."

When our slices emerge hot and ready, I enthusiastically bite into my slice. "Hot, so hot." I exclaim as I gently chew.

Aria laughs at me as a multitude of flavors burst in my mouth. It is a melting mixture of cheese, sauce and toppings. I can't even tell you what kind of style pizza it is, but I do know it is delicious.

"Okay, I get it. This is amazing." I manage between bites.

Chapter 13

Love Will Come To You

ARIA

Roman and I stroll along the Vegas strip since there's still time before I'm needed at the theater. I usually look forward to my time helping the cast prep. It puts a little money in my pocket, but it is also one of my main social events of the week.

Today, I am less enthusiastic about seeing my co-workers and much more interested in spending time with Roman. I thought about calling in, but then hesitated.

I'm still getting to know Roman, but he seems like the real deal. I'm curious how my co-worker friends will react to him, and he to them. Mikey's opinion in particular will mean a lot, since he is the person I'm closest to out here. I can't help but wonder if they will be jealous of each other somehow.

We slowly meander along the wide open sidewalks and people watch. I love how I fit snugly under his arm as we move to our own rhythm. As many times as I've walked these paths, it never felt magical the way it does sharing it with this captivating man. He has an eye for detail that I've never come across before. He comments on color contrast and architecture making the ornate buildings further come alive. I am mesmerized by features I never even noticed before.

"Hey look" Roman points up at the next hotel along the strip, "Did you know there was a place named after you?"

I gaze up to where he points to the Aria Resort, "Yeah, I did know that." I laugh to myself, "Can you imagine how much those rooms are a night? I'd have to be dying and the Make-A-Wish foundation grant me my wildest dream to ever stay there."

"I don't know if I'd go that far," he nudges me with his hip. I can see his brain working, but I've looked at those rooms before, just out of curiosity. Let's just say it's a nice place. He lets it drop though and we head to the bridge to cross over towards the theater.

I like how I relax and take my time next to Roman. I'm usually rushing to get from here to there and don't even look at all the wonder the strip has to offer. I am thankful that I am taking advantage of it now. I suppose I'll have lots of time left to sightsee when Roman goes home.

The thought of him leaving makes me sad. Everything is so much more engaging and alive when he is near. I find I enjoy all the little details he points out and I don't want to miss them. I lean a little closer to him as we navigate the corridors through Planet Hollywood until we get to The V Theater.

We get to the theater and I realize I'm the last one to arrive. It is amazing how fickle time can be when walking with someone so compelling to talk to. I don't regret our pace, but I'll never hear the end of it.

Hoping to put the attention off of me, I enter backstage holding Roman's hand and announcing, "Hi everyone, this is Roman."

I see Roman's face freeze as four pairs of eyes turn toward us. As my co-workers turn, he stays silent offering a windshield wiper wave with his arm. I stand beside him with an enthusiastic smile, witnessing a range of expressions stretch from vacant to unbelieving.

Okay, so perhaps I didn't think this through. This is the first time I've ever brought anyone to the theater, though it isn't exactly uncommon to do. At least I now know Roman doesn't embarrass easily. He wears an amused smile, but otherwise seems content to just let me take the lead.

The cast and crew, all friends, stop and come towards us. Mikey eyes me with a question and I give him a smile with a shrug. He nods and I realize we know each other better than I thought. Turns out we have a silent communication that I didn't even know about.

"Where did you pick this one up?" Brent asks already in his Rumplestiltskin costume.

"The Fremont Experience." I answer.

"They do know how to do it downtown." Teresa agrees as several heads nod.

"What's your name again?" Mikey asks and reaches out to shake his hand.

"Roman," he answers without hesitation giving a firm shake and sporting a casual smile. He's accent rolls thick off his tongue and they catch on to it.

"You're not from around here, Roman." Brent states adding the accent to match how Roman said his name while shaking his hand in turn with the others.

"Where are you from?" Mikey asks before Roman has a chance to answer.

"Charleston, South Carolina." He answers with his accent drawing out the "a" in Carolina and looks at me teasingly.

"So you're from the Southeast, too?" Mikey turns to me, "We must give out some kind of pheromones or something."

I laugh and explain to Roman, "Mikey is from Raleigh,

North Carolina."

"That's good country up there. I applied to NC State, almost lived there myself."

"Then we may have met sooner, I graduated from there a few years ago."

"Small world," Roman comments with a grin.

"It really is," Mikey agrees, "Well, I hate to run but I have to go get everything set u. I'll need to do mic checks soon."

"Good meeting you, Mikey," Roman says.

"You too, man." Mikey responds and looks at me with a wink before he turns to go.

"I have to get Teresa into makeup then help her and Lindsey finish getting ready," I turn to Brent and Trevor, "Can you two please act like civil people, just for a little while?" I plead then give Roman a kiss on the cheek and quietly tell him, "I'll be back in just a few. You okay with these goons for now? This part is girls only."

"Yes," He laughs as he's interrupted by the guys making funny faces, imitating me. "I'll be fine."

I take a deep breath as Teresa and I head back to the wardrobe room to meet up with Lindsey.

"So" Teresa leads me, "Roman, huh?"

"Yeah, we met a couple days ago downtown."

"Wait, a couple days? Is it serious?"

"I don't know. I don't know what it is. I mean, he's leaving to go back to South Carolina tomorrow. Where does that leave us?"

"Well, he's certainly hot enough. I'd go anywhere with him if he is kind on top of it." She looks back before we enter the wardrobe room to reveal Roman laughing with the rest of, dare I call them, men.

"And funny, too." I tell her.

"Damn. And a sense of humor. I'd be done for."

I groan as we enter the room thinking of all the time Roman and I have laughed together, pretty much all of our time together.

"It's about time," Lindsey calls from her dresser. "I was beginning to wonder if you were coming at all. Can you help me?" She gestures to her wig. I realize she barely even looked at us in the doorway so she didn't see the look on Teresa's face. I walk over to help her get her wig in place.

"There's a reason she's late." Teresa calls.

"Oh?" Lindsey perks up in concern.

"His name is Roman."

"Roman" Lindsey repeats with interest.

"Uh huh, and he's a hunk too." Teresa replies, while I focus intently on making sure her all her real hair is hidden under her wig with the magic of bobby pins.

"Wait? He's here?" Lindsey jumps up causing her wig to lean sideways tilting her head at a funny angle.

Teresa nods excitedly and gestures to the door. They both lean out the door, the guys must still be visible because when they leaned out to look far enough they quickly close the door giggling. I slouch on the couch.

"He is quite the hottie." Lindsey agrees.

"Aria's in love with him," Teresa says in a mock whisper.

"What? I never said that." I rise up in horror.

"You didn't have to. Ican see it all over your face. You brought him here, didn't you? You are brave or desperate to introduce him to those goons. You know they will ask him every single question you don't want them to."

"I know. I thought he might like the show. This is the last night we have together before he goes home to Charleston." I explain lamely.

"South Carolina?" Lindsey asks. I nod.

"How did I forget to mention that sexy legs out there

also has an accent?" Teresa quips.

"So, what are you doing here?" Lindsey asks me.

I gesture to her wig which is still leaning sideways.

"Oh come on." Lindsey comes and sits beside me. "You know Teresa could handle it. Hell if I really need help I'll get Trevor, he's better at it than any of us."

I laugh. She is right.

"So why did you bring him here?" Teresa wonders as she pulls up the vanity chair to sit in front of us.

These two are getting serious. I'm in for it now. "He's charming, funny, kind, generous, and handsome." I rattle them off on my fingers.

"Good in bed?" Lindsey interrupts.

"Amazing." There is a collective sigh.

"All I want is a normal day where I can forget that he's leaving and I'll never see him again."

"Oh, I doubt that." Teresa rests her hand on my leg.

"I don't know." I admit.

"What does he say?" Lindsey asks.

"We've conveniently not talked about it." I answer.

"You will." Teresa encourages.

"Well, if he invites you to join him back east, don't hesitate." Lindsey offers.

"What?" I ask, surprised once again by the idea.

"Well, he came knowing he was meeting your coworkers and friends. He could have said no, but he's here. He's out there with tweedle dee and tweedle dum for you, girl. We live in Vegas, he could be anywhere. Yet, he's here with you. He must like you, too. Even love you. Perhaps you just haven't told each other yet."

I look up at her, "It's only been three days."

"Sometimes, you just know. You know?" Lindsey looks deep in my eyes as she talks. She takes a deep breath and continues, "Look, all I'm saying is there isn't really anything here tying you down."

"What about you guys?" I ask.

"Don't use us as an excuse. We will always be your friends. This is too important." Theresa says. It really hits me hard, those are the same words Leana used. Perhaps my friends really do see Roman the way I see him. I trust them, maybe even more than I trust myself.

"Besides, aren't you from the south anyway? I still haven't figured out exactly what brought you to Vegas in the first place. Even if that Southern hunk doesn't work out, this could be just the new start you've been looking for."

She has a point, "I did have a reason for leaving. Going back home would present an interesting dilemma in itself."

"Did you leave a husband back there you don't want Roman to meet?"

I sigh, "No, nothing like that."

"Then you'll figure it out. I still hear your own southern accent when you've had too much to drink, you know. You can take the girl out of the south, but you can't completely take the south out of the girl." Theresa pokes at me.

I laugh because I know she is right.

"Look," Lindsey leans into me. "He's into you, at least a little bit to be here tonight."

That makes me smile. He seemed almost eager to see more about how I lived and the people I knew.

"All we're saying," Theresa adds, "is to go through all the options. Talk to him before you throw in the towel on this one, okay."

"Okay." I look at my friends. "Thanks, guys."

"That's what friends are for." Lindsey hugs me, "Sometimes, we have to tell you to build a bridge and sometimes we have to tell you to go jump off one."

I laugh at her humor. "Now," she continues, "I really do need help with this damn wig."

We laugh and go through our normal routine before the show. Once hair and makeup are complete, we return to the guys so I could help them all go through mic checks.

When we reach backstage, no one is around. We look around at each other confused. With a huge battle cry, all three guys pop out from behind a prop causing all of us to jump.

"Damn you." Teresa hits Brent on the arm. I would be surprised if he even felt it, he was laughing so hard.

Trevor picks Lindsey up and spins her around causing her to laugh, too.

Roman, still laughing comes over and wraps his arms around me. "It was Brent's idea."

"I would have figured it was your idea, except they did the same thing last week." I roll my eyes, though glad to be in his arms again.

He laughs harder. It's hard not to join in, especially when he takes my distraction as an opportunity to tickle me under the ribs where a minute ago his strong hands held in comfort. I wiggle trying to get out of his grip causing another round of hysterics.

The producer, Mr. Julant, enters the stage and clears his throat. "Okay, okay, very funny."

We stop laughing with effort and Trevor introduces Roman, "This is Roman, Aria's boyfriend."

I glance at Roman, he doesn't seemed fazed by the label, a good sign.

Mr. Julant nods hello. I look to Roman who nods back to the producer. He doesn't look at me, but his smile warms my heart, a comfort that I didn't know I yearned for.

"Now, it's time for mic checks." Mr. Julant says and then walks off stage toward the sound booth.

I move forward to help the girls tape their mics so they are hidden in their wardrobe. I notice Brent's mic is still visible so I move to help. He whispers in my ear, "I like him. He's a keeper." I smile and nod, that is high praise coming from Brent. He's a critic, even to the critics.

After mic checks are done and I check that everything is in position backstage, I approach Roman who patiently endured all of the stage prep.

"This is all pretty cool." Roman says in approval.

"Yeah, I suppose. They are all a bunch of dorks, but somehow, they bring it together every night to create a killer performance. That's all they need from me. We can go watch the show now."

"You're all done? You don't stay back here?" Roman asks.

"Yeah. I mean usually I do, but I don't really do anything. I just help them out with wardrobe changes and whatever I can. They can do it all themselves fairly easily. I thought you might like to see the show. It's actually really good."

He nods and I take his hand and walk around the stage to take our seats. I called ahead so they had our tickets set aside.

Once we were seated, Roman leans into me taking my hand in his. "I like your friends. They are funny."

I agree with a laugh, knowing the crass humor of my theater crew, "Yeah, They're a hoot."

"Thank you for letting me meet them"

"You're welcome." I say and immediately begin to wonder what they said. "Wait, they didn't say anything too embarrassing, did they?"

"What?" he asked, "No, they said that you're a lot better writer than the last guy and they are glad when you are around because you are fun to work with."

"Wow." I express, not sure how they could be so nice. "Usually everything just turns into a poop joke."

"Yes, there was that, too," he laughs.

"Well, at least I know we're talking about the same guys."

"I'm serious though." Roman takes my hand and kisses the back of it.

"About what?"

"Thanks for bringing me and introducing me to your friends. Thanks for letting me into your life."

"Oh. You're welcome. You said you wanted to get to know me. This is most of it these days. Writing and these goofballs."

"Sounds like a good life." I see his eyes distance and can tell he's thinking of something far away.

"Yes, but a lonely one." I say quietly. He turns to me and looks me in the eye.

Again, I wonder what he is thinking about. I honestly have no idea. I wonder if I said the wrong thing. It's the first time since we met that I feel really self-conscious about myself, about us. I like him, a lot. I can't deny that. It's a little scary even, to trust a stranger.

Obviously, all of my friends see something genuine since I've been told by three people to follow him back to South Carolina before I even talk it over with him yet. I don't want to intrude on his life. What if, even with a good connection, I'm meant to be a vacation fling? The thought scares me, but I can't get it out of my head. So sue me, I'm afraid of rejection, me and every other person on the planet.

The lights go dim, he squeezes my hand and grins at me as we fade away into another world.

As the lights go on, I stand to my feet with the rest of the audience, tears moistening my eyes from laughing so hard. That handful of divas and goofballs sure can pull off such an entertaining performance. They bring the crowd to their feet night after night and am thankful to get to share the moment with Roman.

He wraps his arms around me as the applause begins to die down and pulls me close. I see that his eyes glisten as well, "That was amazing. My face hurts from laughing so much."

"Occupational hazard," I agree.

We stick around until after the curtains fall to congratulate the cast on an outstanding performance. I walk with the girls to their dressing room to discuss the less glamorous parts of performing like Trevor's breath after eating onions for lunch and how Teresa's mic almost fell off.

"What can I say?" I shrug, "I was a little distracted." Which of course turns the conversation back to Roman, affectionately referred to as the "Southern hunk."

They ask more questions about him some of which just make me laugh. "How does he take his coffee?" I repeat Lindsey's question, "That doesn't really seem that important."

"It doesn't have to be important, but still, it lets you know something about a person." She replies.

"He takes it black, just like me." I answer.

Teresa and Lindsey exchange a look, "What?" I ask.

"It's meant to be." Teresa sighs like a schoolgirl.

Thankfully, removing costumes and makeup happens a lot quicker than putting it on and we were walking back out to meet the guys fairly quickly.

As we come around the corner, we hear laughter echo through the doorway about the same time I see goldfish crackers colliding with the wall. Roman sits next to Mikey with his mouth open wide in an attempt to catch the goldfish out of the air.

I take a goldfish from the bag on the table and drop one in Roman's mouth and then chase it with a kiss. "Hmmm," I hear him sigh quietly.

"Where's mine?" Brent asks leaning toward Roman, puckering his lips.

Lindsey walks over with a handful and dumps them in his mouth. I don't know if he is choking on laughter or the crackers as he coughs.

Mikey comes up next to us and asks, "Man, what are you two still doing here?"

I'll hand it to Roman, he makes quick friends. Though these goofballs are easy to get along with, it's one of the reasons I love hanging out with them so much. Roman smiles big and warm melting my heart and turns to catch my eye. "You ready?"

"Yes," I say. Somehow the moment feels more than just leaving the theater. I am ready to start something new with this person that I have so quickly come to care about. I wonder if it means the same for him?

I give the girls a hug. As I hug Mikey he whispers, "I hope not to see you here tomorrow night," and looks over at Roman slapping hands with Brent, "He's a good one. Make sure he treats you right."

"Absolutely, thanks Mikey." He winks and I grin. I walk over to Roman and take his outstretched hand to leave the theater.

Once we get a couple steps from the closed door a call of hoots and whistles erupts. I turn back incredibly embarrassed, but I try to play it off, "They always do that when I leave."

Roman laughs and stops me, gathering me in a kiss. Right in the middle of the hallway, not five feet from the exit of the theater Roman, grinning ear to ear like an idiot, looks me in the eye, "I love you."

My breath catches as he brings me into a kiss.

He loves me? Well, that changes everything. I give him a piece of myself in that kiss and when we finally part for air I exclaim, "I love you, too."

We are laughing like we are drunk as we walk to the bus stop. While on the bus with my legs resting over his, Roman says, "We'd get home a lot faster if you had a car."

"What's the hurry?" I ask. "I can't do this while driving." I lean into him with another kiss and proceed to make out the whole way home. I don't remember the three blocks from the bus stop to my apartment, only his lips as they divulge mine and his hands as he caressed my cheek, my hips and my breasts. We fall into my apartment drunk on love.

Chapter 14

Dreaming Wide Awake

ARIA

His hands are everywhere and yet I desire more of him. I suck on his ear and kiss the sweet spot along his neckline. Heat pours off of him and absorbs into me. I feel the rise inside me as he cups my breast in the steady palm of his hand. I lean into him, arching my back to further enjoy the firey feeling coursing through my veins at his touch.

He moves his arms so they hold me tight around the waist. I lift my legs and wrap my body around him. He shifts his weight to balance mine and steadies his arms so they support part of my weight. As he finds my lips, his tempo slows from aggressive to savoring this moment of ecstasy.

He holds me close and explores my mouth with his. We're no longer in a hurry. It's time to take it nice and slow. He turns and lays me on the bed gently, covering my body with his.

He explores my body with the detail a sculptor would give to his art. At first his slow pace drives me crazy and I wiggle to get closer to him. He releases a low chuckle next to my ear as he nuzzles my neck with generous intention. I begin to relax into him and encourage his exploratory pace.

This is a night I will remember forever, no matter what happens next.

As we rest together in bed, I lean against his chest. He wraps me snug in his arms as he caresses my back, shoulder to waist. He does it in steady, reassuring movements. I feel myself begin to dose. I don't think it is that late, at least for Vegas, but the glow of sex and the warmth of his touch soothe me to sleep, just like rocking a newborn baby. Just as I brink on the edge of consciousness, I hear Roman whisper, "Can I keep you?"

The quiet question has a sort of ache behind it. Like a crack in the shield that will let a river flow through. The emotion is so genuine that I am not sure whether it is real or a dream.

I do not hesitate, my heart outweighs my head on this one, and there is no turning back. I would do anything for this man I have come to love. "Yes." I whisper back.

"Come to Charleston with me," he asks in the same intense whisper. It is not a demand, but not quite a question. It is a request, a longing that I can't believe he feels too. I breathe in and forget to breathe out again. The dream becomes too good to be true. When I exhale, I breathe out, "Yes."

If I'm dreaming, I might as well dream big.

I feel his arms hold me to him and breathe in my scent as he exhales. It is a comfort to have him so close as he settles into the bed. I snuggle into his calm warmth and for the second time this week dream of South Carolina beaches.

When I wake in the morning, the bed is empty. I reach to acknowledge the crumpled sheets. At least it wasn't entirely a dream. I have no idea where Roman went and can only imagine why he left. I lay on the bed trying my best to recreate the dream of him whisking me away to Charleston to be with him. I can still feel the sand under my feet and the cool ocean breeze on my face from my dream of us sitting by the ocean together.

I sit up at the sound of his voice, "Oh good, you're up." This dream just keeps getting better.

I look at him and grin. He has on dress pants and a belt, but his shirt was unbuttoned, revealing his firm chest. I get distracted and lean toward him running my hands down his chest and bringing him in for a kiss. He gives in to me for a few moments and then takes both my hands in one of his and pulls back.

I don't feel dejected, instead acknowledged, I can tell he has something on his mind. I focus my attention on him as he begins.

"Were you serious last night about coming to Charleston?"

"What?" I ask not being able to follow. I thought that the entire interaction was a dream, though a much desired one.

"Last night when I asked you. You said yes." He smiles then, a light motion that makes his face glow. "I want to make sure. You could have been caught up in the moment, or you could have been asleep. Aria," He looks into my eyes, "I want to be with you everyday. But I have to go home. I can't stay here. You can come with me, if you want. I would really love it if you-" he stops and takes a deep breath, "Will you come to Charleston with me?"

I open my mouth and find myself at a loss for words. I try again, "Yes," I smile meeting his eyes, "How? When? Coffee?"

He laughs and squeezes my hands. "By airplane. Today if you wish. And here." He gets up, takes a cup off the table and brings it over.

"You got me coffee?" I squeak.

"I knew you would want it. Besides, I had a couple

phone calls to make. I needed to make sure it was possible."

"If what was possible?"

"Getting you to South Carolina today. I don't want to miss a day with you if you wish the same. The crux is, I have to go into work Monday morning. Otherwise, my nice little townhouse will be unaffordable. Not to mention Mom and Gran would miss me for Sunday dinner."

"Is it possible?"

"Yes. I had to use a couple favors," he shrugs then grins. "It is very possible."

I take a sip of coffee and encourage him to continue. "How?"

"Miguel will trade his ticket for yours to get you on the flight today. He will stay one more night and then fly home tomorrow."

"Really?"

"Or you could have that ticket and come tomorrow if you'd rather. If you need some time to say goodbye."

"Say goodbye to what? This place won't miss me."

"Don't sell yourself short, you've made good friends here." Roman acknowledges.

I consider his comment, and agree his is right. "Okay, you're right, but I'm not staying another day." I kiss him. "I want to be with you too, everyday, including today. What favor did you have to give?"

He shrugs, "Two tickets to a Carolina Panthers game, a round at the bar and a promise I wouldn't fuck this up. His words."

"I knew he was a good one." I laugh.

"What do you say?"

"Yes. I say yes" I exclaim and hug him tight. Wrapped in his arms, I reward his courage with a kiss.

"There is one thing I want to do for you," he says softly.

"Like you aren't doing enough?" I ask.

"Let me pay for two months of rent here."

"What? Why would you do that?"

"I want you to have somewhere to come back to. You know, just in case this doesn't work out." He dips his head sheepishly. I guess he suspects how that sounds. So do I.

"Are just going to kick me out in two months? Then why even bother?" I challenge quietly.

"No. It's not like that." He takes a deep breath. He gets flustered when he doesn't know how to explain his intentions, I notice. "I hope that you stay forever. I want you to choose me. I don't want you to come and feel trapped. I want to be a choice, not someone you settle for because you agreed to the insane notion of flying across the country after knowing me for only three days all before you've even finished your coffee."

"Do you think this is insane?" I ask using his word.

"Yes, absolutely. But that is also what makes me so sure of it, of us. I don't want to wake up tomorrow and you not be there. I know we are still getting to know each other, but I don't want to wait and miss the chance for something great." He answers, I can see the honesty in his eyes and his words excite me.

I gaze at him and then down at my coffee. I tip the cup and drain it. I set it down on the end table with a hollow echo reverberating from the empty paper cup.

I take his face between my hands. I look into his eyes He doesn't break eye contact with me. I search for any sign of hesitation or trickery. All I see is love, a genuine emotion and a yearning as strong as mine to see where this goes. This connection I feel is real.

"You're serious?" I ask.

"I've never been more so." He answers steadily still holding my gaze.

"Okay. If we are going to choose each other, let me pay for a month and you pay for a month. Then in two months Mikey can come in and sell all my furniture and hopefully make a buck or two."

"That works for me. So, yes?" Roman asks eagerly.

"Yes. I like that we choose each other." I nod.

"Me too. Thank you." He rests his forehead against mine. "I love you, Aria Dalton."

"I love you too, Roman Wagner." I kiss him, a gentle kiss, sealing our promise to each other.

After a few moments basking in the stillness of the moment, he asks, "Can you do it? Can you really just leave today?"

I think about it. My novel would come with me. The guys at the theater would miss me, sure, but the show wouldn't suffer. They were really helping me out with income more than I helped with the show.

My thoughts turn to Lindsey saying, "Don't hesitate if he asks you to come with him," and Mikey saying, "I don't expect to see you tomorrow." Even Leana saying she'd come visit me in Charleston. Three people basically told me I'd be crazy not to make this leap. Even Leana said the same thing before she went home.

In this moment of contemplation, I realize this is exactly what I want. I desire adventure and love, this is a perfect combination. A smile forms on my lips. I look up at Roman and see the anticipation in his eyes. "I need to make a few calls," I mimic his earlier phrase. "But yes, I can go today."

Joy floods his face. He does not jump up and down or make a grand physical gesture like I would, but he leans forward and rests his forehead to mine. The gesture assures me of his love.

Butterflies flutter in my stomach as my heart almost

explodes out of my chest with joy.

As he pulls back, I jump into his arms. He holds me tight and kisses me like he will never let go. I'm holding him to that promise. I wrap my arms around his waist and caress his firm hips playfully. He laughs as he reluctantly drags himself away. "We have to be at the airport by like one o'clock. I want to do" he looks at me and aimlessly gestures, "that more than you want to know. First, you need to pack and so do I."

I nod. I'm feeling that dream state fall back over me. He takes my arms in his hands and stands in front of me until I look at him.

"Why don't you take a shower and I'll go get us another cup of coffee. Then I'll help you pack."

"Okay." I focus on him, it's like he can read my mind. He kisses me again and directs me to the bathroom while he puts his shoes back on to go outside. I hear the door shut behind him while I stare into the mirror.

Who is this girl staring back at me? She is braver than me. I smile, she is in love. Her eyes sparkle with it. I suppose now is as good as any to find out if it is enough. I have nothing to lose and everything to gain.

I'm sitting on the counter in my towel brushing my hair with my favorite bright pink comb trying to figure out who all I need to tell I'm leaving. The list is not long.

I text Mikey and let him know I am planning to leave town and ask if he can use his key to my apartment and check in on it once in a while for the next couple months. *I can do that*, he texted, *Hope it works out with your guy.*

Me too! If it does you can have my couch.

That ragged thing? I may be able to donate it.

That would work, too. Thanks, Mikey.

Of course. After a few minutes, he adds, *Are you going to see that actress friend of yours again?*

Yeah, of course, I am. Do you want me to tell Leana you said hi?

I think I do. She was something else.

She sure is.

I type a quick email to my boss at the theater to let him know I won't be available to write the next screenplay. I wish him luck in future productions and thank him for the opportunities he has given me.

I texted Leana to let her know, too. *I knew it!* she texted back, *Now it's your turn to fly.*

I suppose it is. Wish me luck.

You don't need luck, you've got love. See you on the east coast, girlie! Take care of yourself.

I will. I agree, *BTW, Mikey says hi. Remember my friend you met at the bar.*

Oh really? Well, I wouldn't mind seeing him again if I have the chance.

I think he feels the same. He's going to look after my apartment while I'm gone.

Is he going to take your stuff out of it when you don't come back?

Yes, he said he would do that too.

Well then he is a good friend. Not that you have much.

At least, there isn't much to pack.

True.

I'd better get to it.

Okay, have a good flight. Love you, girlie!

Love you, too.

Roman opens the door and peeks his head in just as I finish my text with Leana. I smile as he enters with a hot cup of coffee in hand. I'm amazed at how comfortable I feel with him, like I've known him for years instead of days.

I take the coffee and kiss his sweet lips. He leans next to me on the counter, "Do you still want to come to Charleston with me?"

"Yes," I answer and kiss him again. I can't imagine I will ever get enough. "Everything is all set, I'm good to go."

"Good. Let's go pack."

I jump off the counter and look under the bathroom counter for my toiletry bag. "Okay, first thing's first." I place the comb in the bag causing him to laugh.

I proceed to use my deodorant and realize it is above the pre-approved weight limit for liquids. I look at Roman, "I'm going to have to get some new supplies after we land."

"Yes, that's fine." he answers with a laugh.

I shrug and put the deodorant back in the cabinet. I grab my birth control, take it and throw it in the bag. I notice him watching me, a pensive look on his face, but he doesn't say anything.

"Wait." I say. "Do you have toothpaste?" I ask him.

He just laughs, "Of course, I have toothpaste."

"Good, then I don't need this." I put the toothpaste back into the draw and keep going through my things.

Once I'm through my toiletries I realize how little I actually need or could even take with me. Most of these things I can get when I get there and not have to worry about carrying it. I need the room for my personal things anyway.

I walk toward my closet with a towel wrapped loosely around me. This is the perfect time to start going through my clothes to take since I have to find something to wear anyway. Something that would be comfortable on an airplane going to South Carolina in May. That would be some leggings and a t-shirt, I imagine.

I turn back around to the bed to glimpse Roman staring at me like he is lost in a dream. It amazes me that he sees something in me worth keeping. Something worth bringing across the country to inconvenience his entire life just to be with me. I can't think of anywhere else I would want to be.

My head keeps telling me that this is all going way too fast but my heart keeps asking, what took you so long?

His eyes lock with mine and I watch his whole face smile. His arms shift open towards me and my response is automatic as if I unconsciously respond to his presence. I race to him, drawn in and protected by the warmth of his presence.

I stand between his legs as he draws me even closer to him. I move my hips so I rest mine squarely on his and lean forward to meet his lips. He deepens my gesture by pulling me in and resting his hands on my hips. Our kiss heats quickly and I forget everything else.

I mean really, who needs clothes? I'd rather not wear them anyway. I'd much rather be doing this, feeling the strong sensual hands of a man who loves me. Believe me, I'm going to cash in his forever claim because the fact of the matter is, I'm in love with him, too.

"What happened to packing?" He asks me.

"It can wait." I say in a deep lusting voice causing him to attack my lips with a new fervor.

He balances my weight with his as he lifts me and moves toward the couch. My legs wrap around him, my head arching back as he carries me. He sits down with my weight pressing into him. I take his lips on mine as I begin to sashay on top of him.

I feel him pressing against me, but he is restricted by the fabric of his pants. Well, that won't do. I climb off of him and bend over to unbutton his pants. He stares at me with an honest desire and yet a slight hesitation. I imagine because of the all important plane ride this afternoon. It melts my heart to feel his sincerity. Still, I know we have time. I find myself feeling strong and desirable because he wants me. It is a powerful emotion.

He arches his back so I can slide his pants over his hips. Once he shakes his foot a little to release the fabric with a chuckle, I disregard them without further thought. I let my towel fall and sit on his lap skin to skin. I take his mouth in mine exploring as his hands caress my back in slow, strong strokes.

I unbutton his shirt and kiss my way down his chest following the path of my hands. He leans back, head resting on the back of the couch with an exhale of pleasure. I continue my way down until I reach his stomach. My hands stroke down his exposed chest while I settle into the position I desire.

I rest my hands on the utmost part of his thighs and take him into my mouth. I hear his sigh of pleasure as I gently encompass his growing hardness. I sense and hear his panting as he creates his own rhythm in the opening of my mouth. I enjoy him as I pick up my pace using my other hand to stimulate myself. He matches my tempo until I can't contain the moans escaping my mouth around his shaft. I finish my wave of orgasm and he brushes my cheek in his hand.

He gives me a look of pure satisfaction, but I see that he is saving himself for me. "Your turn" he breathes, reaching out for me to mount his lap. I yearn for him to be inside me. My entire being tingles with anticipation.

Once I settle my leg over him, I rise up and slowly take him inside of me. I don't stop until I am sitting flush on his legs enjoying the pulse of his erect membrane nestled deep.

I enjoy the stillness, the fullness of the moment, and then I begin to move.

He joins my motion causing me to forget restraint. Heat and friction electrify my blood like lightning. Just when I think the sensation is too much he comes, an explosion that sends me over the edge. I collapse into him and twitch with the aftermath of such a powerful collision. As I lean into him willing my breath to slow, he holds me to him. I enjoy these last moments of wholeness from being connected this way.

When I finally look up, he kisses me full on the mouth, a connection made. This is not just sex, we are making love. It makes me feel tingly all over. I reluctantly release him and head to the bathroom.

I clean up, get dressed and get a drink of water. By the time I walk back to my bed, Roman finished buttoning his pants. He's wearing a big, satisfied smile that makes me laugh. He opens his arms in a welcoming gesture, "How can I help?"

I laugh thinking about how much help he's been for the last half an hour. He is a delicious distraction, but I point to my suitcase still sitting by my door. "I put it on the bed and you pack it in the suitcase."

"Sounds good to me." he agrees and unzips the suitcase on the bed. I open my dresser and start assessing my clothes. I quickly sort through underwear picking out a handful that have holes or don't fit right and set them aside. I gather the rest of them and pile them on the bed. As promised, Roman rolls every one of them and sticks it in the suitcase.

I have four bras and a handful of socks. I grab my house shoes that live under the dresser and add them to the pile. Roman is always waiting for more as I transfer things from the dresser to the bed. I add silk pajamas, two pieces of lingerie, several tank tops and t-shirts. A pair of sweatpants and two sets of workout clothes. I go to my closet and pull out the shirts that I love or are unique. I leave much of the bland filler, I never liked them anyway. I can only fit so much in a suitcase to move across the country, better make sure I get all the important and memorable things first. I came to Las Vegas with less than this even, so I'm not worried too much about it.

My shoes begin the duffel bag. Though I only have four pairs, so they don't take much room. Boots, sandals, sneakers and the flats I am wearing. I add four books, my zipper binder of movies and cds, a handful of picture frames including the one good picture I have of my mom and I when I was eight, my jewelry box containing a gold necklace from my grandmother, a friendship bracelet Leana and I made when we were ten and a ceramic owl Leana painted for me in college because she always called me a night owl.

It seems like too much, but then I look and there is still room left in my suitcase and duffel. I add my computer and notebooks to my messenger bag and zipped it up.

I look around and don't know whether to be proud or sad that I can fit my entire life in three bags. I add my favorite blanket in the duffel bag and zipped it up too. I turned to Roman, "Do you think they would count a pillow as an extra carry on item?" He shrugs. "I guess we'll find out."

I double check everything. I don't know if I'll ever be back. I suppose a couple months back in South Carolina will tell.

Mikey has an extra key if anything happens or if my stay becomes permanent. I can't think about any of that right now. It's time to go.

I follow Roman and look back only long enough to turn

out the light. The funny thing is, I keep waiting to miss it. I don't. I've held no attachment to this place, it was never meant to be home.

I think subconsciously I must have known that because I collected next to nothing while I've lived here. I turn out the lights and lock the door, turning to Roman with a smile.

"Ready?" He asks.

"Ready." I take his hand and walk into the next chapter of my life.

Chapter 15

Cradled in Love

ARIA

We stumble out of the cab and enter the Bellagio hotel lobby laughing, my rolling bag drags behind me and my messenger bag slung over my shoulder. Roman carries his own book bag and my large duffel bag like it weighs nothing.

I playfully hit Roman with my pillow when he teases me about the size of my suitcase. "You try moving in such short notice on an airplane."

"I would for you." He replies in stride.

I stop and kiss him in the middle of the walkway before continuing on to the elevators. To others we probably look drunk, which is not an unusual sight in this city during the middle of the day. I feel drunk but not on alcohol, instead, on life and pure adrenaline.

I'm about to make the biggest leap in my life and that's saying something. I've been zip lining and bungee jumping thanks to my adventurous co-workers. Even moving across the country with nothing more than a backpack and a couple hundred dollars to my name didn't scare me. Taking leaps seems to be part of my life's journey.

I'm not exactly afraid now, more excited. It's amazing how similar those two feelings come across. I'm still not sure if I'm crazy or not to do this, but there's just something about Roman. I see it in his eyes, I hear it in his laugh and I've witnessed his kind heart again and again over the past few days. His generosity has not only been towards me but also to his own friends and even complete strangers.

This decision may be a huge mistake but at least I'll know for sure. It isn't like I'm new to making drastic life decisions in the matter of a day. My decision to come to Las Vegas in the first place happened just as quickly. I am determined to live a life of no regrets. I know I would regret not doing this, no matter how crazy it seems.

I could love this man forever. I want to give us that chance. My apartment is paid for the next two months, that's time and assurance. Roman really has thought of everything and I'm thankful for him. I have no intention of letting him go unless he proves to not be who he says he is or orders me to leave. Those are both worst case scenarios that I hope never come true. I trust this blond haired Southern hunk. It's hard to imagine it so soon but I'm crazy in love with him.

"Roman." We stop and turn at the sound of his name. I almost fall over as I trip on my suitcase. Roman catches my arm to balance me. We look up to see Andrew sitting with Dawson, a pitcher of beer between them.

"Hi guys," Roman says like he just got caught with his hand in the cookie jar.

Andrew laughs, "I was wondering when you would come waltzing in here. You are smiling, does that means Aria will be joining us on the flight home?"

Roman looks to me and I to him. We both turn back to Andrew and nod enthusiastically.

Dawson burst out laughing at our not so innocent expressions.

"Good" Andrew says, trying to contain his own laugh, "Because Miguel hasn't packed a thing." He points to the Blackjack table across the walkway.

"So, you all knew I would come?" I ask.

"We hoped you would," Andrew answers.

"I wouldn't want to be next to Roman on an airplane if you didn't. He gets all mopey when he's sad. Besides, anyone can see there's something special between you two."

"I'm glad you are coming with me." Roman takes my hand and kisses my knuckles, "But I still have to pack."

"Yes, you do. Meet us back here in an hour and we'll ride to the airport together." Andrew suggests.

With a firm nod of agreement and a glace at Roman's watch, we continue through the lobby to the elevators.

We are the only one in our elevator. We spend the few seconds behind closed doors balancing bags and kissing. I almost fall through the door when it opens because I'm paying more attention to Roman's lips than where I am standing. He catches me again with a laugh. We stumble out of the elevator and down the hallway to his room.

Andrew had already packed his stuff, all that was left was Roman's things scattered casually around his bed. Most of them are still in his suitcase. I recognize the gym clothes I wore and his button up right where I left them. Smiling, I collect them and toss them at Roman. He laughs as he catches them and attempts to fold them before placing them in the suitcase. They end up as mostly stuffed balls of clothes, but I can see he isn't really hurting on room.

"You travel light," I point out.

"I don't need much," he answers. "Turns out what I needed was waiting for me here."

I blush as he moves to sit on the bed next to me taking my face in his strong hands. He leans in kissing me, a slow sweet kiss. After a moment of pure bliss he pulls back, "Thank you for coming with me."

"Thank you for asking me to come." I kiss him again.

He gets up and heads into the bathroom.

"So you're sure the guys are okay that I'm coming?" I call out to him.

He pokes his head out to look at me with chagrin. "Yeah, actually, it was sort of their idea."

"Really?"

"Yeah" he looks a little sheepish as he continues. "Dawson made a comment about me spending so much time with you. Andrew noticed the way I smiled at that and asked when you were going to visit Charleston. I knew I didn't want this to be the last time I saw you. I hadn't thought ahead to what that would entail. Miguel asked why you didn't just come now. Andrew shrugged in agreement. I hadn't even considered it, not really. I kept making excuses to myself, you have a life here and friends, we barely know each other, and so on. But I couldn't get you out of my head or the idea of spending more time with you. Eventually, I ran out of time and I went with my instinct. I didn't want to leave you, but I have to leave."

"I like your instincts." I tell him.

He sits next to me on the bed. "I'm glad you're coming with me," he kisses me. It starts out gentle and sweet, but I am interested in a little more.

When he tries to lean back I go with him. His hands move from my face to my waist.

In this moment, I didn't want to think about packing or plane rides or unknown destinations. All I want is to feel the happiness radiating off of this man that has gripped me and found his way to my soul. He kisses his way down my neck. I arch my head back with pleasure. When he gets to my collar bone he whispers into my chest, "I need to finish packing."

I run my fingers through his hair, "You will."

"We don't have much time." he says and looks at me. I

can see the desire in his eyes. I lean into him wanting so much to feel the warmth of his chest against my hands and the feel of him so close to me. He's right though, we are out of time.

I settle for taking his lips in a long, lingering kiss. My tongue caresses his and I smile as he opens to me. He groans lightly, "You're going to be the end of me."

"Honey, this is just the beginning," I respond seductively. He wraps his hands around my waist and pulls me even closer. I breathe him in for a few moments, enjoying his embrace and the warmth of his lips. I take a breath, "But first, I have to pee."

Roman's hearty laugh is infectious as I remember our first night together. With one last kiss, he releases me and I skip to the bathroom.

The moment apart helps me clear my head. I look in the mirror and am surprised by the girl so full of life looking back at me. I like her. I'm glad I met Roman so I can meet her. I can never remember a time I have felt this alive, including the zip lining and bungee jumping. Those were thrilling, but not like this.

Once I'm ready to face the world again, I gather his toiletries off the bathroom counter in my arms. I turn the corner and watch him fold his clothes piece by piece and lay them neatly in his suitcase. I am happy in this moment. It is a good feeling.

"Hey Roman" I call as he stands in front of his bag folding a dress shirt. He turns and I toss him his toothbrush container. He catches it in his right hand like a reflex. He looks at it and then at me. He grins as he tosses it in his bag and then looks at me for the next toss.

It is amazing how simple things bring so much pleasure. I throw the shampoo so that he has to reach for it and the same with the deodorant.

We are laughing until the only thing left is the bag they all go in. I do a little dance and then look at him and crook a finger. He raises his eyebrows at me, a question. I wiggle the bag in front of me and blow him a kiss. He stands up straight with a look of indecision on his face.

With no warning, he races across the room. He doesn't reach for the bag, instead, he grabs my waist and lifts me up. I wrap my legs around him laughing. He spins me around and leans me against a wall for a deep kiss. I settle into him and then begin exploring the sensitive spot I found right behind his ear.

He sets me on top of his suitcase, "Okay, now I'm ready."

I laugh and roll off oton the bed. With a laugh and a kiss, he points to the bag still in my hands. "Here you go," he says as he picks his toiletries and drops them in my lap.

I laugh, "It's a good thing you don't have much, we'd never get there on time."

"You're telling me." He laughs easily, "You are proving to be quite a wonderful distraction."

I grin, accepting his compliment.

Finally, he zips his suitcase and sets his backpack on the floor next to it.

He looks at me with an accomplished look on his face, and then comes to stand in front of me. I split my legs allowing him as close to me as the bed allows. He leans down and takes my face in his hands.

I reach out to him as he kisses me. It feels natural the way I wrap my hand around the back of his legs pressing him to me ever so gently.

He pulls back slowly releasing my lips. I'm awed by what I see in his eyes. A physical desire, yes, but it runs deeper than that. I sense his contentment and pleasure in this moment. I understand his feelings because I want nothing more than to stay right here laughing and playing forever with this person whom I find it so easy to enjoy his company.

I feel confident, capable and light as air. For once in my life, I believe like everything is going to be alright.

It's that look, a moment of true intimacy with our clothes miraculously still on, that assures me I'm making the right decision. Roman is one of the few who I would follow anywhere. I know it as strongly as I know my own heart.

ROMAN

I look over my hotel room one last time before shutting the door on my brief time in Las Vegas. I am confident I have everything. I didn't bring much with me to begin with. It seems I have found something while here though, the very best and brightest of souvenirs. I still can't believe my luck as I take Aria's hand and walk down the hall.

I didn't think I was missing anything in my life. I have friends, family, a good job and a nice place to live. Yet now, I can't imagine my days without Aria in them. It is like she turned on a light in my own life that I didn't know existed. I can't imagine living in the darkness again and I am glad I will not have too. At least not right now.

It was not easy getting the logistics squared away so Aria could join me, but it was worth it. Once Andrew mentioned the idea of her coming home with me, I knew it in my heart I wanted her to. I am thankful she felt the same way.

I breathe in the scent of her as we walk to the elevator juggling our bags. I laugh at her carrying her pillow under her arm and quickly found out that she still had full range of motion despite the messenger bag strapped across her chest.

I feel a lightness when I laugh with her even though I don't recall feeling heavy recently. I reveal in this wonder and can't remember ever laughing this much, even before my dad died. I am thankful for this new life I have found with her.

We find Andrew and Dawson right where we left them, though now their glasses are empty. Andrew smiles when he sees us and makes me wish I looked in the mirror again before I left the room.

I do not think I look as disheveled as I feel but somehow my friend and mentor seems to know what went on in his hotel room while they were down here enjoying a drink and their own last moments of Las Vegas. I am grateful that he says nothing.

Andrew stands with a smile and gestures to the doors that lead to the taxi cabs. I turn to wave to Miguel who moved to the slot machines. I catch his quick glance knowing he will hold me to my promise to be good to this girl.

That is one request I will not have a problem fulfilling. I nod to him and call, "Thanks Miguel, see you next week." He gives little more than an absent minded wave to acknowledge our departure.

I hear Dawson and Andrew laugh behind me and I shake my head. "He doesn't seem too broken up about the change in plans," I comment as we head for the door.

"Did you really think he would? Convincing Miguel to stay an extra day in Las Vegas was probably the easiest part of the whole plan." Dawson responds.

"Yeah, I suppose you are right about that." I agree.

I notice Aria is quiet as I stand next to her waiting for

our turn in the taxi line, "You okay beautiful?"

She smiles back at me with a light shining bright from inside her, "Yes, more than great. Thank you, again."

"I say the same to you." I kiss her lightly on the cheek.

The cab we take is actually a van. It's nice we can all fit in one vehicle with all of our stuff. The driver is nice about helping us get our bags in the back. Within seconds we are ready to go. I hop in first with Aria right behind me. We settle into the backseat as Andrew and Dawson climb into the middle.

For a moment I have a flashback to junior prom - we were escorted in a van by my dad. I have the same butterflies in my stomach today as I did then. I am excited about having Aria in my life at home, I hope she is too. She is so brave. Even as much as I want this, I'm not sure what to expect. I don't know how she will respond to my place or my family. I don't know what she will think of Charleston. Since she's from South Carolina, at least the summer humidity won't surprise her.

As the taxi van starts to move I settle in with the feeling of Aria under my arm a comfort. I remember that night of Junior prom going well, hopefully this day does too.

I hold Aria's hand in mine, still amazed that I can. The weight of it is comforting. She keeps a firm grip on mine during the entire drive.

The day feels like a dream or a story from someone else's life. We are both quiet but comfortable as the landscape flies by on the way to the airport.

I can't believe Aria can just leave everything behind to come with me. She says there isn't much here, but I wonder if she will realize there was more than she thought. Only time will tell.

This is a big change for her. I'm beginning to think of the ways my life will change, too. I have to admit, they are all for the better.

It will be nice to have someone to come home to and share thoughts and opinions with. I look forward to lazy days as well as time adventuring around the city and lying on the beach. Those are both things that I would like to do more of, and would enjoy more fully with someone to share the experiences.

As soon as the taxi stops, it's time to move. I kiss Aria's hand and enjoy her blush as we wait for Dawson and Andrew to get out so we can move the seat forward. We all pile out, gathering our luggage in a rush and head through the sliding doors to start the next leg of the journey.

Airports fascinate me. There are so many people all trying to get somewhere in various states of befuddlement. Getting tickets, going through security and finding our terminal goes by in a blur. There seems to be a hurry up and wait rhythm to it. I will learn it if I am going to travel more.

I sit down placing my bag between my feet. Aria plops next to me, "Wow, that was a whirlwind."

"You are right about that. Are you hungry?" I ask after hearing my own stomach grumble. We didn't really stop for breakfast and we had a workout this morning while getting all of our things together to leave. The thought of Aria naked makes my heart race.

"Yes." She answers through her own daze. "It's definitely time for some food.

I sense she is having trouble focusing on me. I add, "How about some coffee, too?"

She perks up at that, "Yes, please."

I smile and lean down for a quick kiss before heading out to see what I can find to eat. I like that I already feel like I know her well. Even though it's only been a few days, it feels like much longer. It is one reason I am so sure about asking her to come.

I'm lost in my thoughts and don't hear Dawson behind me until he is at my side.

"She's pretty cool," he says getting my attention, "your girl."

"I don't know if I would call her 'my' girl." I respond. I kind of enjoy the phrase though not in an ownership kind of way. I don't think anyone could own Aria. It's more of a nice reminder that she is here with me.

"Well, the girl is leaving everything she knows and flying all the way across the country for your skinny ass."

I laugh at that, leave it to Dawson to put it so eloquently.

"I suppose that is true. I still can't believe she said yes."

"I can," he says knowingly. "I see the way she looks at you. There's something powerful there. You are a lucky man."

"Thanks, I feel lucky right now."

"There's Five Guys," Dawson points out, "Now we can both be lucky. This place is great."

"Sounds good," I chuckle to myself and decide to enjoy the moment. In fact, a melt-in-your-mouth cheeseburger is the energy boost I need right now.

Chapter 16

Gonna Fly Now

ARIA

I sit at our gate grateful for the moment to catch my breath. It has been a whirlwind of a day. In the span of only a few hours everything has changed. I still haven't quite grasped the fact that I am going to live in South Carolina once again. At least this time, it is in a new town with a very different housemate.

It is all happening so fast, and yet, I do not feel any unease. It seems like everything is going according to plan though I don't know whose. I wouldn't have even imagined to wish for something so wonderful as to think a man would want to change his entire life to have me in it.

I feel more steady now that I have had a chance to compose myself. I am thankful that Roman thought to get food. I would have forgotten to eat, a bad habit of mine. If I were alone, I would just sit here and watch the planes land and take off until it was time to board. However, I am not alone anymore.

It it surprisingly nice to have someone around to help look after me and to share the experience. I've been on my own for a long time, even before moving to Las Vegas. It will be an entirely new feeling being with Roman.

"Are you afraid of flying?" Andrew asks, leaning with his elbows on his knees talking over the bags between us in the aisle.

"Oh," I look up at him. "No, I don't think so. I'm

feeling a little overwhelmed, just trying to get my bearings."

Andrew grins and looks at his hands. He must have been deciding on a response because just as I doze back off into my own dream state, he speaks again, "I think you are very brave to come with us."

"Or crazy." I tell him.

He smiles, "Yes, but Roman is a good man and you make him very happy. I am glad you are coming. You are brave because though I know Roman, you do no. It takes no small amount of trust to leave what you know for something so unknown."

Andrew sure has a way with words. I appreciate that he gets to the heart of the matter without all the dramatics. His statement mirrors my own thoughts. Roman has given me every reason to believe he is who he says he is and friends who vouch for him.

"I do trust him." I reply.

"Yes, I know. That's how I know it's true."

"What's true?" I ask.

"The love that you share." Andrew smiles warmly.

I'm left thoughtful by his words. I nod, thinking about what it means. The fact that we trust each other, even though we've only known each other for a few days, shows that what we share is more than just a fleeting impulse. It's something to nurture and grow. But love?

Roman said it once, that he loved me. I even repeated the phrase. Can that be true? Is it that simple? I haven't thought much about what love really is. I never felt it strongly. Is love a shared emotion, a powerful connection, and a promise to see where this will go? We've planted a seed and giving it an opportunity to grow. I don't know what flower will bloom or if it yields any fruit, but I'm excited to find out.

Andrew doesn't say anymore and I am content to zone out as I watch the planes out the windows. I'm in a subtle meditation mode when Roman and Dawson come back with food for us all.

I perk up when Roman sits next to me with a pleasant smell wafting from the bag he carries. I am most excited by the glorious sight of a large cup of coffee in Roman's outstretched hand.

I look at him like I haven't seen sunshine in months and accept his offering with a kiss. I take a cautious sip as the liquid flows through my body warming my insides. Roman laughs and takes a sip of his own.

He settles back and offers me a warm cheeseburger. I take it eagerly. If I wasn't already in love with this man, this moment may have been a deciding factor. My mouth waters as I hungrily bite into my burger, "This is perfect, thank you."

He grins and takes a bite of his own. "Do you like it? I sort of guessed what to get on it."

"It's delicious. I'm so hungry it wouldn't matter much. I can't believe we forgot to eat breakfast."

"I don't know about you but I had other things on my mind," he winks.

I think back to the sex and packing with a smile. Yes, it's been a crazy and amazing morning. "All good things," I reply as I indulge in the mouthwatering burger.

When I put my meal down long enough to take another sip of coffee, I look at Roman, really look. He slouches his shoulders just a little when he takes a bite out of his burger. His hair is starting to encroach on his ears. I wonder if he will cut it or let it grow.

He looks up at me, probably feeling the weight of my stare. I let him catch me staring at him. I smile at the warmth in his eyes. He has the most gorgeous smile, a little humor mixed with the genuineness that I've rarely seen in another. "Want some fries?" he offers me the bag containing a cup filled to overflowing with fries.

"Why yes, thank you." I reach for some feeling a little giddy. We eat and sit in a comfortable silence while listening to the bustle of the airport as people come and go and chatter on the intercom announces this and that. It is little more than organized chaos, but I find comfort in it. I enjoy the crazy because I know it all has a purpose and it's all leading to another door.

That is what life's all about, finding the right door and then stepping through. After I walk through this door, I will exit in another familiar yet unknown land, ready for another life. I feel like I'm living a real life fairy tale. I can only hope mine has a happy ending. Nonetheless, I'm excited about the journey, I have the best traveling partner, he even gets me coffee. I relax and sip it now feeling more energized and more alert than I have in a couple hours.

While we are waiting for the plane to board I ask Roman, Andrew and Dawson about Charleston and their life there. I'd been there a handful of times, but even though it was so close to where I grew up, I never spent much time in the city. It seemed very glamorous and upscale compared to what I was used to. I can't help but wonder if I will fit into the elegance I picture.

"I live in Mt. Pleasant." Roman offers, "it's right across the street from Town Center, a big mall complex."

"Mt. Pleasant?" I ask awestruck.

"Yeah," Dawson adds, "Wait until you try Burtons, it's amazing. They have a great selection of beers."

"What's Burtons?" I inquire with a raised brow.

"It's this bar and grill right across the street from my townhouse. I go fairly often. We meet after work sometimes." Roman answers and takes my hand.

"That's cool." I enjoy sitting next to him and I try not to be nervous about how I am going to fit into his life and his outings with friends.

"There's a lot of history, too," Andrew says. "The Market is a really interesting place to wander through. It used to be a slave market, but now it's just a bunch of vendors selling wares. The sweetgrass baskets are really nice, another local tradition."

"That's really interesting." I smile at him, enjoying hearing about this new place that is so close to where I grew up and yet so unfamiliar.

"If we go down to the battery we can stand on the spot where the first shot of the Civil War took place." Roman adds.

I get more excited as they talk, "I've never seen that kind of history before."

"They also used to hang pirates on those trees." Dawson adds.

Roman leans over to me, "There are a lot of ghost stories in Charleston. It comes from such a long and often violent history."

"I can't believe I grew up so close to all of this and never really knew anything about it."

"Where did you grow up?" Andrew asks.

"In Myrtle Beach."

"Awesome," Dawson exclaims. "That was always the best place to go for spring break."

I laugh, "Now that I know all about."

"Really?" Roman inquires with a nudge.

"Yes," I nudge him back. "People come to party and do all kinds of stupid things. I used to work at a Pacific

Beachwear and people would come in burned. I've heard and seen some crazy stories."

I pause and they all look at me expectantly. "One time I was helping out in the dressing room and a guy opened the door and asked if I could get him a different size. On his sunburned chest were the words 'hug me,' but instead of a 'g' there was a drawing of a penis. I tried so hard not to laugh as I went for the shirt he was asking for."

The guys burst out laughing, "I'm going to have to remember that one," Dawson says.

"Not on me," Roman warm with a smile. Then he turns to me, "We're going to have to watch him like a hawk any time we're at the beach."

"Yeah," I agree, "He's not putting any suntan lotion on me."

"Ah, you guys are no fun." Dawson laughs.

Dawson nudges Andrew, "What about you?"

Andrew playfully swats him away, "I don't think so mister."

Though I am still laughing at Dawson's carefree way of thinking, I realize a very important question has yet to be discussed. I lean into Roman and quietly ask, "Where will I stay?"

He smiles without hesitation, "With me, of course." Then he pauses, "I mean, unless you didn't want to."

"Yes, I would love to stay with you." I reach out and take his hand, "I just didn't want to assume."

"In this case, I don't mind," he smiles and squeezes my hand. I'm not sure if the gesture is meant to assure me or him, but it is comforting to feel the warmth of his hand with the knowledge that he wants me with him.

I notice Andrew grin at our quiet exchange, but he makes no comment. I'm not sure how this didn't come up earlier. Although the words seem strange to ask now when we are waiting to board the plane, I still feel no awkwardness between us. It is important for me to know where I stand. I am quite happy with my choice to be with Roman. It is the beginning of a whole new adventure.

I am still listening to descriptions of Civil War memorials and Waterfront Parks as we board the plane. Though I lived most of my life in South Carolina, I never really explored Charleston much. We were not a family of summer vacations. I've only been twice, once for a junior high volleyball tournament and again on a trip to Folly Beach with Leana's family one summer. I didn't really spend much time in the city either of those times. I am looking forward to getting to know it now.

Dawson switches his seat assignment with mine so Roman and I can sit together. This also gives me the window seat. I am grateful since this is only my second trip on an airplane. Andrew sits on the aisle seat and we all get comfortable. Once the plane begins to taxi, Andrew breaks into a great big smile, "It sure is good to be going home."

Roman looks to his friend and mentor, "It was a good trip though. Thanks for everything."

Andrew looks at me and then back to Roman, "Yeah, it was a great trip." He then settles back in his seat and closes his eyes. I envy him for being able to sleep before the plane even takes off. I'm so excited to even think about closing my eyes.

Roman takes my hand and we gaze out the window at the world below growing smaller and smaller. Standing on the ground, you have to look up at all the buildings and they go up for miles. In the air, the Las Vegas strip has another perspective. It becomes a line of buildings larger than life that form an oasis in the desert.

Roman looks out the window with me, his eyes wide, "I have never seen anything like this place before. It's all so red." I agree with his reference to the mountains entering our view.

The Sierra Nevadas are a small range in comparison with other mountain ranges, but they look huge compared to the flatness of the desert. They are made up of many mesas with flat tops and hold no civilized life.

They are barren like so many things in this city. I pause to enjoy the moment and capture the picture of this place in my head. If all goes well, it will be awhile before I come back here if I ever do. I wave goodbye to the city I've called home for the past five years.

I try to miss it but I feel nothing but gratitude to be leaving. I can't believe it has been five years of hiding. I'm ready to live again, something Roman made me see. I am happy to head toward a somewhat familiar land with a man who has ignited my life in a way the city never could.

As we fly high enough that the clouds cover the view of the land, I sit back and take a deep breath.

Roman kisses my knuckles in the hand he still holds. I find it a comforting gesture. I smile at him, soaking in the moment and the contentment of his eyes on me. He seems to be searching for something, regret or sadness or longing, but all I feel is contentment and joy. After a few moments, he kisses me and then settles back into his seat as well.

After being in the air for just over four hours, I begin to feel a pressure in my head. Roman notices me holding my temples and reaches his arm around me, "You feeling okay?"

"Yeah, I'm fine, I have a headache coming on, I think."

He nods knowingly, "It's probably from the altitude drop. That means we're almost to our first stop."

"Oh, well that's good then." I smile around the pain.

"I have some gum. Would you like a piece?" Roman suggests.

I graciously accept his offer, "Yes, that would be great."

He reaches into his bag and hands me a piece of Double Bubble. "Really?" I ask as I take the gum. "How old are you?"

He smiles a little sheepishly, but responds, "Old enough to blow the best bubbles in my entire family."

"Nice." I honor his boast with enthusiasm, "Thanks for the gum."

"I hope it helps." He says and slides closer allowing me to lean into him. I close my eyes in the comfort of his arms as the plane drifts downward.

The flight seemed easy and even a little fun. There were no screaming kids and I only had to go to the restroom once. I'm sure everyone was thankful for that since I was by the window.

I spent a good bit of the time reading, but was happy when Roman broke out a deck of cards. We played a few rounds of Rummy. Andrew even joined in on a couple hands. I focus on these good memories as the plane finally hits the tarmac with a gentle hop. I popped my ears, thankful that the pressure released.

"It's going to be close to get to the next gate." Andrew announces as he checks his phone.

"How close?" I ask seeing the strain in Roman's brow as well.

"We have forty-seven minutes to get from the B terminal to the D terminal. We should be okay, but we can't lollygag."

"Good to know." Roman responds. Andrew leans over the aisle to let Dawson know as well.

Once the plane lands, it is an act of patience to wait for

our turn to unload. Roman keeps his cool beside me and I try to rest in his calm. We manage to finally get off the plane and follow Andrew as he leads our way through the crowded Charlotte airport.

With about ten minutes to spare, we find our gate and stand around with the small crowd gathering. I can tell the boys are ready to get this last leg of the journey underway. I can't blame them for wanting to get home.

I wonder what my new home will be like. I have no way of knowing if the images racing through my mind are close to the reality I will soon face.

I am thankful when the attendant begins boarding our plane. I want to keep moving so no worry can set in. There's still another short flight to go, so I'm going to try not to think about it too hard.

I stand and stretch, stiff and tired from sitting so long on the last plane and then rushing to get here. It's hard to believe that in just another hour I will be in Charleston ready to begin a new life. I am happy, though a little nervous, to get on this plane and begin my future.

This plane only has two seats on each side. Roman and I sit next to each other while Andrew and Dawson sit in the row across from us. Roman lets me have the window seat again and scoots closer to wrap his arms around me. I settle against him as we takeoff. I barely glance out the window, there is nothing leaving Charlotte that holds my interest more than the man next to me.

"What is your place like?" I ask him quietly.

"It's two bedrooms, which are on the top floor. The kitchen and living area take up the bottom floor. There's even a little patio area out back. It's in a neighborhood called Montclair. There is a pool, tennis courts and clubhouse. It's not too far from where I work on Daniel Island, Downtown, or the beach."

My eyes light up at that and he adds, "Town Center is just across the street with a movie theater and all kinds of food and shopping. The Isle of Palm connector is just on the other side of that, which goes straight to the ocean."

"That sounds nice." I beam.

"Although, this time I'm the one who needs to apologize for the mess because I have no idea what state I left the place in."

I laugh remembering my own mess. "I'm sure it will be fine. Do you live alone?"

"Yep, just me. At least until now," he leans into me to kiss my forehead with a smile. "It's not a big place. I currently use the second bedroom as an office. We can get a second desk for you. It would make a fine place to write for you, if you'd like. The window looks out towards a wooded area. It's pretty quiet."

I snuggle into him thankful for his willingness to make a place for me. "That sounds wonderful, thank you."

"You're welcome," he smiles, " I like that my townhouse is on the end so I never hear anyone through the walls. It also has a fireplace and a pretty nice kitchen, though I don't use it all that much."

"I never used mine either. It didn't seem worth it to cook for one. I would like to learn how to cook at some point though, then I can make dinner for us." Roman squints at me, but before he can say anything I ask, "Does your family live close?"

"Yes, they live in a house a few miles away. It's about a five minute drive. It's the same house I grew up in. My mother takes pity on me and invites me over for dinner at least once a week. We try to do Sunday dinners with Athena and Seth, too."

"Hopefully, she won't mind feeding one more."

He laughs, "I'm sure she won't mind. My mom loves to

feed a crowd." Roman turns to me with a teasing look, "You really want to learn to cook? I mean, do you even own a frying pan? The only thing you brought from the kitchen was that cat clock."

I stop and think of all the things I packed just that morning, "Um, no, I don't actually. I have a pot where I cooked ramen or mac and cheese and a casserole dish, but not a frying pan. I would like to learn though, it would be a fun challenge."

"Okay, well I'm definitely not going to dissuade you. Maybe my mom can give you some pointers."

"Yeah, that could be cool. I suppose I have to meet her first."

"You will. She'll love you, just like I do."

I take a big breath hoping he is right. "What about your sister? Where does she live?"

"Athena lives out towards Goose Creek now. She and Seth bought a house out there with some land. They are really big into gardening. My grandmother lives with my mom. Gran's getting older, but she is a sharp woman. She seems to always know what you are thinking even before you do." He speaks of his grandmother with respect and adoration.

"She sounds like a fascinating woman." I comment.

"Oh, she is," he agrees.

"Will I get to meet her?"

"Absolutely. She will love you, too." He assures me.

"I hope you are right."

He pulls me close. "Trust me."

I smile and lean into him, "I'm so tired."

"It's been a long day."

"Umhum," I agree already nodding off.

"Rest, my love." I hear him whisper in my ear and feel the pressure of his lips against my hair, a comforting gesture. I am nervous and excited about our destination, but it still feels like a world away. In this moment, I am warm and comfortable on the plane in the arms of the man I would give up everything for. Life is perfect. I doze off with the roar of the engine and Roman's deep breathing as white noise.

I wake slowly from my short nap as I feel the plane begin to descend, the pressure hitting my ears once again. It is dark outside the windows and I realize I'm not the only one who fell asleep on this short flight. I rise from Roman's shoulder and take in his peaceful expression as he breathes deeply with sleep. He seems young and vibrant and sculpted like a God. I watch him, content for several minutes.

I look past Roman to see Andrew reading a book. I wave to get his attention.

"Hi there Aria, Did you get some sleep?" He asks with a smile.

I look at Roman as he snores quietly and laugh, "Yes, I did, thank you. What are you reading?"

He holds his book so I can see. "Franz Kafka."

"Metamorphosis" I read off the cover. "That's a great story."

"I agree."

"Have you read it before?"

"Yes, several times actually. I like to think it helps me avoid a descent into madness."

I chuckle, "I can relate. I feel like I'm going through quite the transformation right now."

"You will be great." He assures me.

The pilot comes on the intercom to announce our arrival in Charleston. I gently rock Roman awake as we begin to land.

Chapter 17

Welcome Home

ARIA

As the plane begins to descend, I look out the window with Roman leaning over my shoulder. His hand rests on my knee for balance and comfort. Even though it is dark out, the lights shine bright, illuminating the city. I watch a large bridge come into view and awe at the majesty of this city.

"That's the Ravenel Bridge," Roman points to where I am looking. "It was an engineering phenomenon when it was built. It was the largest cable-stayed bridge in North America and the tallest structure in South Carolina. That's a big deal because there is a strict structure height in downtown, nothing can be built taller than Michael's Cathedral."

"Really?" I ask skeptically. "They couldn't build anything taller than a church?"

"You got it. We are entering the Holy City." Roman replies in an exaggerated voice, though I can hear the humor behind his words. "Though there are about as many bars as there are churches. That's to say there's a lot of both."

I laugh with him, still amazed at how little I know about this city only a couple hours from where I grew up.

"They changed it relatively recently, now they can build an extra 30 feet. That's what Charleston believes to be progress. Then they can house more tech industry." Roman shrugs his shoulders.

I'm not sure what to make of his remark, but I do notice the lack of skyscrapers and lights in the city. It is all very different than the location we left that morning. I feel like I have dropped into a different world. I suppose in many ways, I have.

"It's beautiful though." I comment resting my hand over his still resting on my knee as the plane circles around.

"That it is." Roman agrees. "We'll have to go see it up close very soon."

I nod, enjoying the sights from the sky and the butterflies in my stomach swirling.

Somehow Roman must sense my nerves because he squeezes my knee and plants a light kiss on my cheek. I lean into him gaining strength from his embrace.

Once we land all three boys let out a sigh that I'm not sure they realized they held. They were home. I understand their relief, however, I couldn't quite express it with them.

I found myself silent as we waited for the plane to unload. Roman held my hand, a point of comfort while he joked with Andrew and Dawson. They seemed to be planning an outing of some kind, though I lost what exactly they were saying. I have no plans in this new place where I know nothing about anything. I suddenly feel very small.

I move when it is time. Roman helps me gather my bags as we head off the plane and into the airport following the signs to baggage claim.

Dawson and Andrew part ways with us as we reach the carousel. Andrew was itching to get home to his family. Since they weren't waiting on any luggage, we said our goodbyes. Andrew hugs me and whispers "You'll be great here. Don't worry." Then just like that they were gone.

I stand next to Roman while he rests his arm across my shoulders. I can feel his contentment as we wait for my luggage. We people watch in this moment of comfort.

All the people on our flight begin to crowd around as the carousel begins to move. My luggage shows up about the fourth time around. I gathered it and we balance our bags to find a cab. I watch out the window as we ride along the highway, but there isn't much to see in the darkness. We cross over a couple bridges, but other than that it looks like most cities I suppose, full of restaurants and stores.

Roman points out the Mount Pleasant Towne Centre as the cab turns into an apartment complex. It winds around until it stops in front of a row of townhouses. It is a quaint row of houses with greenery in front.

Roman looks at me with a big smile. "This is it," he says.

I smile back, his excitement contagious, but say nothing. With the help of the driver, we get all of our luggage out and Roman settles the fee. Then he points to the unit on the end and leads the way with me on his heels.

I can tell he's excited to be home, yet this moment has me in a ball of nerves. I can't quite associate it with being my home, too. I'd never even seen a picture of it. I suddenly feel very out of place as the weight of my decision falls on me.

I've really flown halfway across the world to walk up to a strange building I will call home with a man whom I'm still getting to know.

I stand frozen on the sidewalk leading to the door with my back to the row of cars parked in front. I don't even know which one is his. He does have a car right? I am suddenly not sure of anything.

Roman reaches the threshold, unlocks the door and turns on the lights, letting his luggage fall in through the doorway. Then he realizes I am still on the sidewalk. He comes to me and reaches for my luggage and my hand.

"Are you okay?" Roman asks.

I don't know how to answer that, so I stay silent. He eyes are shining bright, beaming with joy. That gives me strength to nod as he nudges me forward.

He stops at the threshold and pulls my hand to his lips for a sweet kiss. I smile up at him, my heart filled with love. Yes, this is crazy but it feels right.

He grabs me under my knees, folding me into his arms and takes a couple steps through the threshold. He stops to hug me close and leans in for a kiss.

"Welcome home, Aria." He speaks quietly, staring so deep into my eyes I swear he can see my soul. Then he lets me down and gestures into the room.

I step into the room and look around. The space is bigger than it seems on the outside, very clean and bright. I notice the stairs in front of me and walk through a little walkway to enter into the living room. A loveseat and reading chair separate the room, looking toward a TV mounted above the fireplace. Next to it stands a floor-to-ceiling bookcase on one side and sliding glass doors on the other.

I continue around to the right and smile at his impressive dining table. It is a dark wood with four chairs around it. The seats are decorated with brightly colored cushions and there is a candle centerpiece in the middle. One side of the table has papers and books piled on it, but with other side is clean. A large canvas depicting the iconic Charleston Rainbow Row at sunset hangs on the wall behind the table.

The kitchen is large with stainless steel appliances. It is a bright space that makes me want to learn to cook. A bay window looking towards the sidewalk opens up the space. I wonder if he eats breakfast at the small two seat table.

I circle back around to the living room, noticing a

small, clean half bath just outside the kitchen. I look to Roman who is watching me. He has brought in all of our luggage and set it next to the accent table behind the couch.

I can see him waiting for a response, seeming slightly nervous. He stands, hands in pockets, leaning on his left foot. He's eyes watch mine as I turn. When his eyes meet mine, he smiles.

Simply by entering into his personal space, I immediately know that the man I met and flew here with is true. Now that I've seen his home, I know beyond a shadow of a doubt that I was meant to come here. I have an overwhelming feeling of being home.

"This is a beautiful place, Roman." I walk up to kiss him.

His smile warms my heart and I enjoy as his arms wrap around my shoulder, making me feel safe and loved. "I'm glad you like it."

I continue to look around, taking stock of his place, my new home. I read the titles of the books on the bookshelf. I flip through his vinyl collection to see what he listens to. I look at the cups in his cupboard and walk around his table to see if he sweeps behind it. He does.

He follows me as I make my way through his small space once again. He doesn't hover, but his is watchful, gauging my reaction to things. He never says a word or makes a reaction of his own. He doesn't try to explain away things or hide anything.

I know this is exactly how he left it a week ago. Just as he was able to do with me the day after we met, I get to see how he lives and who he is. I wonder if he's waiting on me to go running back to the airport to get onto the next flight home.

The nerves haven't completely gone away, but they have been assured by his steady presence. I know that he wants me to be here and for this to work between us. He isn't forcing it, but he doesn't have to. I want to stay and find out what comes next.

I look up at him as I finish my evaluation and smile. He smiles back. Then I realize something interesting tucked next to the bookshelf. He must have noticed the change in my face because he unconsciously steps forward, "What?"

"You have a record player."

"Yes, it plays better music. I would rather listen to it than an mp3 if I have the choice."

"I love you." I grin.

He laughs and steps closer to me. He wraps his arms around me pulling me into a tight embrace. I lean into him and rest my head on his shoulder, "Most people would find that odd."

"We are all odd, you are just my kind of odd."

"I'm glad that you are home. I didn't even know you were missing, but now that you are here, it feels right, like you belong right here with me."

"I agree. This feels like home, you feel like home." I hold his face in the palm of my hand, his beard stubbles making me giggle as they tickle my skin. I pull him close and kiss him.

"I love you, too" he whispers.

"Thanks for bringing me home." I reply. I believe I can truly be happy here with this man. I already am.

I can see the seriousness in his eyes as he looks into mine. I have no response, instead, I lean into his vulnerable honesty and kiss him. I wrap my arms around his neck and step into him. He reaches his right hand up my back and pulls me in close. His left hand snakes up in my hair causing me to moan in spite of myself. He moves then, backing me a couple steps back until I'm leaning up against the wall. As he deepens the kiss, I wrap my leg around him trying to get him closer.

I yearn to feel more of him as I grind on his hip until he lets out a sigh and picks me up. He balances his weight with mine as I wrap both legs around his waist and laugh. He kisses my cleavage and then my lips as he swings us around into the living room. With all wariness of travel forgotten we enjoy each other in a new level of comfort.

"Now it's time to show you the bedroom," Roman whispers with his deep baritone in my ear.

A shiver crawls down my spine and sends warm sensations to my deepest core. "Yes, that sounds like a good idea."

He takes my hand and leads me up the stairs laughing as we climb. He opens the door at the top of the landing entering his bedroom. A large queen bed fills most of the space with end tables on each side. There is a set of weights in one corner of the room, otherwise the floor is clear. I notice a bathroom and another door, which I assume to be the closet across the room. My mind focuses on the dark blue comforter on his bed and the small amount of space we are away from it.

His kisses move from my lips down my collar bone as he gently moves me towards the bed. He continues teasing until he comes to my shirt. In two swift movements, he takes my shirt and my sports bra off releasing my breast from their confinement. I sigh openly as he takes my breast in his mouth and begins to lightly suckle it. I could feel myself squirm as he moves to the opposite breast and continues his caress.

When he takes a breath, he moves me to the bed and continues his kisses down to my stomach. He lifts my pants away, only briefly lifting his lips from my skin. He massages his finger around my opening. I can not lay still. I want more of him and everything his giving so freely.

I feel the pressure of him disappear and I sigh at his absence. I assume he is discarding his own clothes and I yearn to feel him inside me.

However, I am surprised when I feel the warm texture of his tongue begin to play. A sound I didn't know I could make escapes my lips. It was a guttural, pleased noise. For a moment, I forget to breathe as I enjoy the ecstasy of his tongue massaging my most personal area.

The surprise and sensation are too much and I rise to a climax much faster than anticipated. He flitters over a particularly sensitive spot causing me to fly over the edge. I announce my ecstasy with a series of groans and ahs. I can feel the smile on his lips as he continues to lap my juices. I try to remember how to breathe again.

When I raise up to look at him, I am pleased to find him naked. I reach for him with a smile taking his hand to pull him on top of me. I can taste myself on his lips. It reminds me of the rise he just got out of me and I ache for him to be inside me so I could feel all of him.

He quickly puts on the condom he must have had in his pocket. I open my legs as he moves to enter me. Feeling his girth fill me and the weight of him on top of me, satisfies me. This must be heaven.

He began slowly, but I take his lips on mine and express the urgency with which I want him. He picks up his pace and my head rolls back in the waves of sensation. It doesn't matter where we are, I would go to the ends of the earth for this man who makes me laugh and feel alive.

We move together building until I felt like I am going to explode. And then I do, causing him to burst forth within me. I hold him close as he slows and then lays his head on my chest, baring his full weight on top of me.

I yearn for it, the feel of this man exhausted and familiar on top of me. As I kiss his hair, I feel tears spike my eyes. I wrap my arms and legs around him and breathe in the scent of him.

Life doesn't get much better than this, I think to myself as I memorize the feel of him molded to me. He leans up on his elbow and then with wonder in his eyes, he bows down to kiss me. His smile begins at his soul and burst out of him. I mirror his love.

He looks into my eyes and I believe he can see my soul, "I love you Aria Dalton. I'm so glad you are here with me."

I look at him with devotion and kiss his lips briefly. "I love you too Roman Wagner, I wouldn't want to be anywhere else."

He kisses me again and then sighs, taking a deep breath before lifting himself off of me. He holds out his hand helping me up then I skirt into the bathroom to clean up.

I flush the toilet and gathered my clothes. I look up to see him standing in the doorway to the bathroom already dressed, watching me do the same.

"Are you hungry?" He asks when I was dressed.

"Famished." I answer with a smile.

"Digiorno?" he asks.

"I think the delivery man looks great in his underwear." I answered moving closer to give him a kiss. "And without it."

Chapter 18

Everything Changes

ARIA

I slowly became aware of the light behind my eyelids. I was enjoying my dream where I decided to jump on an airplane and fly halfway around the world with a guy I barely knew. It feels like I'm in a fairy tale.

As I blink open my eyelids, I have to remind myself that it is true. I turn to look at the sexy man lying next to me and pinch myself. Ouch! Yep, definitely true.

I take a deep breath to fully be able to enjoy this satisfying moment. So far, I am very glad that I took a leap of faith.

Roman turns, blinking at me, and reaches his arm over to pull me closer. The kisses he brushes along my neck tickle. I giggle as I find his lips and then contently settle onto his chest.

I am surprised at the ease I feel in his embrace. The only other person I have felt no need to guard myself around is Leana. How can someone come into your life out of nowhere and change everything? It's happened to me twice now, both times exactly what I need to get through the next obstacles.

Roman and I say nothing as we lay together matching breaths. He idly caresses my shoulder and then turns to kiss my temple. It is a perfect moment of contentment, pure bliss.

"What are we going to do today?" I ask him lazily. I

would be happy laying right here with him all day; however, there is a great new world that I'm itching to see.

He laughs and looks to me, "Anything you want to do. We could play tourist and check out our little big city here."

"That sounds nice, though I wouldn't be playing. I'm totally going to be a tourist in my new home for a few weeks at least."

He laughs, "Yeah, I suppose that's true. You want to go out and explore?"

"Yeah, though it will involve getting out of bed," I pout.

"True and probably a shower," Roman incites.

"I can help you reach the hard to get places." I tease.

"Oh yeah? I could return the favor." He traces his fingers up my arm causing me to shiver with excitement.

"Well, I do know this one place in particular," I respond, moving closer, grinding against him.

We are tangled and kissing when we hear a loud knock at the door, startling both of us.

He freezes, holding onto me. By the confused look on his face, I can tell he was not expecting visitors on this Saturday morning.

The sound raps again, harder and more urgent than before. Roman sighs and moves from under me. Quickly tugging on some gym shorts, he heads out the bedroom door and down the stairs shirtless.

I sit on the bed for a moment but my curiosity gets the better of me. By the time I hear Roman open the door, I'm in one of his button up shirts heading toward the front door.

"Sis?" I hear Roman say, "What are you doing here? You know, I'm kind of busy."

"Roman," I hear the visitor exclaim. "Where have you been? I've been trying to get a hold of you."

As I walk down the stairs, I see Roman slouching against the door. "I've been here. Well, since last night at least. Again, a little busy." He gestures up the stairs toward me and the bedroom I just emerged from.

I notice the petite lady glance at me and then back to him, "I can see that. You must be Aria."

I look at the lady and notice the shape of her eyes matches Roman's, as well as her high cheekbones. I feel frozen with a deer in the headlights look when Roman smiles and introduces me. "Yes," he responds to his sister. "Athena, meet Aria. Aria, this is my sister Athena."

It is nice to put a face to a name, but this is not exactly the ideal circumstances to meet his sister. I move forward to offer my hand to Athena. "Nice to meet you."

She looks me up and down then returns my handshake, a firm grip. She smiles as she says "It's nice to meet you, too. I'm glad that someone has finally caught Roman's eye."

Her manner makes me hopeful I haven't ruined a possible friendship. After a moment, her interest is replaced with a tired smile. Athena visibly takes a breath and turns back to Roman, "I'm sorry to come barging in on you on Saturday morning, but you are not answering your phone."

"You're not sorry, though I am glad you could meet Aria. My phone was turned off for obvious reasons. Athena, what's wrong?"

"It's Gran. She had a stroke Thursday night. She's still at the hospital. Roman, we need you." Athena says in a rush.

Roman looks at his sister in shock.

I step forward and rest my hand on Roman's arm, but look to Athena. "I'm so sorry. We should go." I say to Roman.

He nods and looks to me. I can see fear and pain in his eyes. I remember him speaking so fondly of his grandmother, telling me how strong she was.

"It's not the worst," Athena breathes and Roman takes a visible breath. "She's awake and as witty as ever. They did tests yesterday and concluded there should be no permanent damage. She's having trouble moving her right side and getting frustrated while talking. She needs you, you were always the one who could make her smile."

He smirks at that, not quite looking at his sister as she speaks. I worry about him, his stance looks defeated and life briefly absent in his eyes.

"She's at East Cooper, Room 306. Will you come?"

He looks at me. I nod slightly, not that he needs my consent yet he seems to be asking for it, "Yes, we'll be there."

Athena turns to me, "It really is nice to meet you. I'm glad you came all this way for my bonehead brother. I look forward to getting to know you."

"Thank you" I respond, not knowing what else to say. With that she leaves, Roman and I staring dumbfoundedly after her.

Something big shifted. It seems the honeymoon phase of this move came to an abrupt end with reality beating down the door. I suppose our tour of the city will have to wait for another day.

I didn't know what to do. I have never met this woman, but it broke my heart that she was sick. I can see it affect Roman greatly. He continues to lean back against the wall staring emptily at the closed door.

"Roman," I murmur to him just above a whisper. He looks over at me like he is in a daze. I can't imagine what is going through his head. And here I am, a stranger, beside him in this most crucial moment. I want to reach out and hug him. So I do.

I am pleased when he wraps his arms around me and pulls me close. He snuggles his nose in my neck and I'm hopeful I can give him comfort. When he leans back, I reach out and rest my hands on his crossed arms. "We should go take that shower, maybe a quick one, and head to the hospital to see your grandmother."

He looks at me for a moment and then his eyebrows furrow ever so slightly. He focuses on me for the first time since his sister left. He shifts his arms to take my hands in his. With a tired smile he nods.

While leading Roman back upstairs to the bathroom, he keeps a firm grip on my hand like a lifeline. I can feel the pain radiating off him and I wish I could help him more. He acts lost, his grandmother must be a very special woman indeed.

I don't know how to deal with this kind of pain. I don't really have many people close to me. I wanted to take his pain away, it was too much for me to take.

I reach out to him and realize he is a world away. His unfocused eyes show a vulnerability that I doubt many people see. I suddenly feel a privilege to be here with him to share in this experience. Being with someone means going through the good and the bad. Maybe, in this instance, he can draw some strength from me as I already do from him. I reach up to caress his face.

"I'm so glad you are here." He says taking my cheek in the palm of his hand. "Thank you for your faith, for coming with me."

"I am here for you, Roman. I promise you." I assure him.

He kisses me hard on the lips. I return the kiss with as much fervor. He backs me gently against the counter and I feel like his soul is pouring into each kiss.

He removes my clothes with a purpose and then I do the same for him. I enjoy every moment of his body, trying to memorize every curve. I hop onto the counter and open my legs for him. I can feel his need, his desire, radiating off of him. I fill him with my own as he moves inside of me. His movements are deep and slow.

In this moment a strong connection is made. I can almost feel the difference in his love making. I can feel his pain, but also something else, a steady love that is unwavering. In this intimate moment, I know I will stand by this man no matter what happens. We will face the world together. I absorb his fear and his desperation all at once as he thrusts into me. I can feel his climax coming and I lean into him so that his explosion becomes my release as well.

As I feel him come over the edge I call out his name.

As our breath slows he wraps his arms around my shoulders and buries his face in my chest. I kiss his hair and hold him.

After a few moments, he takes a deep breath and takes a step back. I sit down on the toilet reveling in the feel of him as he starts the shower. I rise, feeling a little empty again. He kisses my lips gently catching my eye and showing me a love greater than I have ever known. He takes my hand to pull me into the shower with him.

As we wash, I realize that I don't even have shampoo yet. We still need to go to the store. I'll get to smell very masculine when I meet his family.

I can't help but laugh to myself at the insanity of it all. Just last week I was sitting on my couch watching reality TV and eating ice cream out of the container. Now I am worried about the livelihood of a woman I've never even met.

I gaze at Roman, the reason I've come here. I am happy I'm here. I hope his grandmother is going to be okay. Even through his pain, he is a steady foundation to rely on. I can understand why his family wants him there, for the same reasons I do. Only they've known him longer.

I cover his shoulders and back with soap, wrapping my arms around his waist holding him to me for a moment. He holds my arms around him.

There is something incredibly intimate about showering together. We can have all the sex in the world, even the best sex, and it's still moments like this that create intimacy. The little moments together where you fulfill each other in different yet significant ways. When you can be naked and comfortable with each other, you can face the world as one.

In this moment of emotion and uncertainty concerning his grandmother, we bond in a way that is even stronger than what brought me across the country. There is something special about this man and now that I found him, I never want to let him go.

ROMAN

I keep trying to restart my brain, but ever since Athena said Gran was ill, all I can think of is the moment I found out my dad was dead.

I know in my head that this isn't as bad as I fear. Athena said it wasn't. Yet, it is that same emotion I had when I heard about my dad that jumped to the front of my heart. I can't quite get it to calm down. I need to see Gran for myself then maybe I can let this gnawing fear go.

I sit out on the porch soaking in the cool, spring breeze while Aria finishes getting ready. I am so thankful she is here. I can't describe how quickly or intensely I have come to rely on her and that light she emits.

I feel selfish to run out when Aria just got here but also grateful that she is willing, even eager, to come with me. I feel like I am asking a lot of her. Still, her presence is more than I can ask for. With her here with me, I believe I am stronger. She brings that out of me. Our time together has been short, but we have bonded in a way that is deep and significant.

Aria opens the screen next to me and leans against it, "Are you ready?" she asks quietly.

My heart stops once again but this for a whole different reason. Aria stands casually in a knee length skirt and plain white top, but she is breathtaking, an angel in the darkness. I take her hand just inches from my shoulder and kiss it while breathing her in. "I'm ready," I answer as I stand and head toward the front door.

It's not far to the hospital, a couple miles down a rather congested road. The mood in the car is somber. Aria's light still glows as we fight through the traffic offering me hope.

"What is your grandmother like?" Aria asks. I cherish her curiosity and can't help myself when I chuckle as I state, "Gran is the most amazing woman I have ever known."

"That is high praise."

He chuckles. "She always has something witty to say, but in a positive, helpful way. She's traveled all over the world, so she can talk about literally anything. She has a strong opinion, but always listens. She has known love and loss and yet is not bitter. Gran always moves forward and encouraging you to do the same. There is a calm about her and also a fire in her."

"Gran sounds fascinating."

"She is. You remind me of her a lot, actually."

"I will take that as the highest compliment." Aria reaches for my hand which I gladly give to feel her warmth. "I can't wait to meet her."

"I'm looking forward to that." I pause wondering what

state we will find my larger than life grandmother in the hospital. "I hope she is okay."

"She will be. Believe it." Aria says and kisses the back of my hand.

ARIA

Roman seems to know where he is going. I don't want to ask but I wonder if his dad died in this hospital. Roman's sister texted the wing and room number so we didn't even talk to the front desk. We walk in and immediately look for his grandmother's room.

When we reach the room, number 774, I see Magnolia Wagner on the wall next to the door.

"This is her," Roman says as he moves to open the door.

"Wait, she's your dad's mom?"

"Yeah."

"Your mom takes care of her mother-in-law?"

"Yeah, she likes her better than her own mother. There's no one left on my dad's side to take care of her. It works out pretty well for everyone."

"Funny how that happens." I smile.

"I suppose so, I never thought much about it." Roman shrugs.

"Are you ready?" I ask him as I see the cloud cover his eyes.

"No, but then again, I never will be."

I can tell he is worried about Gran being in the hospital. When we open the door, I see his face transform from anxiety into one of confidence and joy.

I witness a beautiful older lady beaming at us as we

enter the room. She doesn't look sick. If anything she seems annoyed to be tied to the bed by IVs.

A lady I assume to be his mother jumps up from her seat beside the bed and runs over to hug Roman. "Welcome home son. I'm glad you made it safe."

"And sound," he finishes for her, returning the hug and kissing her cheek. "It's good to be back." Roman turns to his grandmother, "I was gone one week and you couldn't let them rest, just this once?"

"Now what fun would that be?" she quips. Gran turns to me and smiles, "I'm not the only one making things exciting. You must be Aria."

"Yes, ma'am." I take a step closer, not really sure what to do. Not exactly the best circumstances to meet my boyfriend's family, but it will have to do.

"I'm glad you're here." She smiles at me and reaches out her hand for mine. I take another step forward and take her hand, "Are you completely overwhelmed yet, my dear?"

"Oh no, it is a wonderful place. I'm a Southern girl at heart but I haven't explored this part. I love what I've seen so far." I look back at Roman who is standing with his hands in his pockets and a huge smile on his face.

"Which has been the airport and the hospital so far," he jokes, "at least we got the basics covered."

"Umm humm" his grandmother comments, "wait until you see the old plantation houses then you will see beauty."

I smile and nod as his grandmother releases my hand. Roman steps behind me and rests his hand on my waist and speaks to his grandmother, "It's on the list but it seemed the hospital was a more important destination for the moment."

"Well it is always good to know where it is."

I chuckle to myself. I like her already.

"You gave Mom and Athena quite a scare. How are you

really? How is your arm movement?" Roman seems to know all the right things to ask because his grandmother beams at him.

"Ha, you don't know scary until you've zip lined over the crest of a mountain trusting a bavle to hold your weight and imaging you can fly instead of fall."

I didn't realize my jaw was open until Roman teasingly bumped my hip with his.

"Are you serious?" I ask.

"Absolutely. That was during my trip to Czech Republic." Gran nods.

Roman keeps smiling, "Gran has the best stories. Aria is a writer. I bet the two of you will have a lot to talk about."

I nod in agreement.

"Yes, I love fresh ears and a willing heart for adventure. Let's do that over tea, my dear, not in this dreadful room."

At that Gertrude rolls her eyes, "They are trying to help you Mom."

"I don't need help getting old, it comes naturally to me."

I laugh out loud before I can stop myself. Roman looks at me and I can see laughter in his eyes, too.

At that moment, Athena breezes in with a tall man behind her. She turns to the room and asks, "What are you laughing at?"

Roman's mother is the one to laugh out loud this time. "Your grandmother, of course. We seem to be the only ones worried here."

Athena sighs, "Well, that's normal at least."

Gran smiling says, "You can't get well here. This is a place for sickness and death. I will need time for my arm, but I am doing just fine and ready to go home."

"I know." Gertrude says quietly, "we're working on it."

"Thanks, Trudy," Gran says as she lays back on her pillow. Only in that instance can I see how tired she really is. I wonder how much of a brave face she is putting on her family.

Athena comes over to hug me, "It's good to see you again, Aria. I love your skirt."

"Thanks," I twist my hips to make it shake.

The tall, bearded man steps forward and reaches out his hand "Hi, I'm Seth, Athena's husband. You must be Aria."

"Yes, it's good to meet you." I return his handshake.

I stand back and watch as they all visit together. I see how comfortable they are with each other as they laugh, tease and hug. They seem to hug a lot. Even Leana's family isn't this physically close. At least it makes sense why Roman doesn't mind snuggling. It's all a little new to me since I've never been this close or affectionate with others. I find I don't mind it. There is some security in that togetherness.

I realize I am an outsider in this intimate moment and wonder if I should go. Just as I think that Roman comes over to me. He wraps his arms around my waist and whispers in my ear, "I'm really glad you are here."

"That means a lot," I lean into him grateful for his embrace. "I'm glad to be." In that moment, I realize I am happy. There is love in this room that makes me feel warm. It's something I didn't realize was missing until I found it.

Gertrude speaks up, "Okay, I need to grab some food. Roman and Aria, would you like to join me?" I look to Roman who nods. I have a feeling this may be about more than food. It's time to get the real story.

We follow Gertrude into the hall. As we enter the hallway and the room door closes, Roman's mom reaches out for him. He puts his arm around her shoulders as we walk, a natural stance for them it seems. I follow behind to give them a moment of quiet.

"I'm glad you are here, son. I was really worried about her." Gertrude admits.

"I know. Athena got me worried, too. She seems okay, her sarcasm is as clear as ever. I don't notice any struggle with her speech. It must have cleared up because I could understand her just fine."

Gertrude chuckles, "Yes, I think only death itself could take her sarcasm away."

Roman laughs and I smile at their fondness of this woman. No one in my family is close, it's nice to see some who are.

"What do the doctor's say?" Roman asks.

"They say it was a mild stroke. It seemed to target her right side. She had trouble speaking the first couple days so we gave her a dry erase board to communicate. She spent most of her time drawing various irrelevant and inappropriate pictures on it."

"We'll at least it didn't affect her mind."

"No, which is rare they say. She must be very strong."

"We already knew that." Roman states.

"Yes, I suppose so. She may need a little physical therapy to improve strength in her right arm and leg, but other than that she seems fine now. They are monitoring her vitals and fluids. We got the last test back this morning so hopefully they will release her tonight or tomorrow morning at the latest."

"Let me know and I'll come help you get her home. She is fit, but muscle is still heavy."

"Thank you." We reach the cafe and his mom looks at me for the first time. "Thank you, too, Aria. You must be having a crazy adventure, coming over here and then getting dragged into a hospital and family drama first thing."

I look in her eyes and smile. "I don't mind. I'm glad to be here and to meet your family. I love how close you all are. My family isn't."

She laughs, not exactly what I was expecting. Roman is still smiling, so I don't worry too much.

"You are very brave. You will fit right in. Gran already loves you, I can tell. She has a knack for seeing the fire in people's hearts. You have one, that is undeniable. Roman can see it."

I turn to Roman who shrugs, his face is a shade pinker than before.

Gertrude laughs again, "Alright, let's have a cup of coffee and you can tell me about your trip."

Chapter 19

Speaking My Language

ARIA

I stop short when I shiver and remember the sweater I sat down in Gran's room. Why are hospitals so chilly? It's like they are trying to preserve people through refrigeration. I feel goosebumps climb up my arm and I decide not to brave the cold.

"Hey Roman, I'm going to run back to get my sweater from your grandmother's room."

"Do you want me to get it?" Roman asks.

I notice his mom stop and look back at us. I suddenly feel embarrassed, "Oh no, go catch up with your mom. I'll meet you in the cafe."

"Do you want a coffee?" Roman asks.

"Yes, please."

He gives me a quick kiss and then turns back to enter the cafe with his mom.

I look forward to getting to know his mom, but the few minutes to walk back to his grandmother's room gives me a chance to calm my nerves. Nothing about the hospital itself makes me nervous, but the emotions and open affection of Roman's family are intense.

Roman seems to be able to flow among Gran's sarcasm, his mom's subtle worry and Athena's dramatic flair with grace. I suppose, he has lived with those women and that energy all his life. I am very used to living alone with very little emotional interaction. I must be starved from it because the emotions overwhelm me.

At least everything is going to be alright with his grandmother. That knowledge takes the edge off so I can try to manage my unease with such intense emotions. I am thankful Roman is steady like the eye of a storm. Perhaps his calm is what attracted me to him in the beginning.

I get to the door and quietly push it open.

"Is that you Athena?" I hear Gran ask.

I speak softly. I thought she was sleeping, "Oh, no, it's Aria. I didn't mean to disturb you."

"You're not disturbing me, dear. I'm glad Trudy finally took a break. She is worrying too much over me."

"I noticed she was. Her love for you is evident." I step closer to the bed, "Does she need to worry? Is there something you are not telling us?" I ask more courageously than I feel.

"You are very bold, Aria." I blush as she continues, "I like that. No, I am alright now or will be soon enough. Trudy saw me fall and I think it scared her. Hell, I scared myself if I'm honest but being scared doesn't help anybody. My strength will come back to me. I refuse any alternative."

"You are a very strong lady." I declare.

"So are you, flying across the country to tell an old lady where she stands," she says with a smile. I smile back and silently accept the compliment. "I'm surprised you picked up on her fear. Most would not. She has a tough exterior, that one."

"Yes, I can see that, too. Athena has a flair for the dramatic," I add.

Grandmother chuckles, "You've figured us all out pretty fast."

"I suppose. Roman told me a lot."

"You must also read people pretty well." I shrug at her statement.

"Come over here and sit my dear." She pats the bed next to her, "I would love to hear about you."

I walk around the bed carefully making a wide arc around the IV machine. The stiff mattress crinkles as I sit on the thin beige quilt. "There's not much to tell."

"I don't believe that. We all have a story to tell. What's yours?"

I think for a moment. "I'm a writer who would rather live in my imagination than reality. I love theater and bringing stories to life. When I least expected it, I found someone who broke through my shell and led me by the hand to my greatest desire."

"What was that?" I notice the twinkle in her eye as she waits for my answer.

"To be loved and free to be me."

"You remind me of myself."

"Really?"

"Oh yes. I sense your wandering spirit because I have one as well. I didn't write, but I loved to paint. I backpacked through Europe with little more than a sketchbook, some paints and a sleeping bag."

"You must have some great stories."

"Yes and I love to talk about them. Still, It's hard to describe what happens to me with a paintbrush in my hand. I have to admit though, most of my best stories involve those knuckleheads I call family. I can tell you stories of burnt turkeys, humorous relationships and vacations without asking for directions." Gran's eyes look far away for a moment like she is remembering another time. Then she turns back to me with a curious eye. "You can see people. You've figured out the prevailing attributes of the others. I'm curious, how do you see me?"

I don't hesitate. "You play by no one's rules but your own. Even when you have a stroke, you use sarcasm to strengthen those around you who worry. You are glad Roman is here because he balances out the others so you can breathe. I feel that, too."

"Yes, I believe you can. You are courageous. We shall have to backpack through Europe together someday."

I laugh to myself, "Roman said you would say that."

"He knows me well. I understand what he sees in you. He is happy you are here. I have not seen his eyes light up like that in a long while."

"I feel at home with him. It's something I've never felt before. I'm glad I came with him."

"Even with a batty old woman talking at you?" Gran challenges.

"Especially to meet you." I reply sincerely.

She nods at me and I reach out to take her hand, "I'm glad you are going to be okay. I look forward to many more conversations."

"As do I my dear."

"Can I get you anything? I told Roman and his mom I would meet them in the cafeteria."

"I am good. Thank you. Let them know I'm going to be alright, will you? They will believe you though they don't believe me." She doesn't quite roll her eyes, but I can tell she wants too.

"I will do my best. Rest, I will see you soon." I squeeze her hand before easing off the bed.

She lays back and closes her eyes peacefully. I hope she really is alright. She has a fire in her soul but her body looks frail. I understand why Gertrude worries. It doesn't help that the bed is huge compared to her and the lights are all really white.

As I leave the room, I shut the door silently behind me. I clutch my sweater to me as I head back toward the cafeteria. Although I have only known this woman less than an hour, I feel connected to her. The overwhelmed feeling isn't as strong after talking with Gran.

Meeting Roman and his family has made me see myself a little clearer and helped me see that I can belong. I remember Athena's easy hug, Gertrude's ready acceptance and I sense some of myself in Gran. I look forward to my future with Roman.

I'm still thinking about what Gran said as I reach the cafeteria. She is a wise woman. I see Roman and Gertrude at a table in the middle and walk toward them. His mom, facing my direction, waves to me. Roman turns around and I brighten at his big smile. When I get to the table, Roman gestures to my coffee and a warm bagel with cream cheese.

"Thanks, you're the best." I kiss him as I sit down.

"So how is she?" He asks me.

I stop with the coffee just touching my lips and look up at him innocently, "What do you mean?"

I hear Gertrude chuckle as I watch a smile creep onto Roman's face. "I know my grandmother well enough to know that she wasn't asleep. Whatever you said is between you. Gran has secrets with everyone. I imagine she sees the same fire in you that I see. I just want to know we don't need to worry about her. Mom fears that she is hiding something important about her health because she hates hospitals and medicine. I thought she might tell you."

I finish my sip of coffee as I let a smile of my own glide along my lips. "Actually" I look from Roman to his mom and back again, "I asked her."

"Really?" Gertrude leans toward me in surprise.

I nod and see her turn to a smiling Roman.

"I told you they were made from the same cloth." he laughs.

Gertrude turns back to me. "I can see this. Well, what did she say?"

I shrug. "She says it was a bad fall. She doesn't blame you for being afraid, it scared her too. Though she would never tell you."

She looks down, "I know that."

"She also says she refuses to live in fear. That is no way to live. She's determined to recover from this. I can also understand why she wants to get out of here, this place feels sick. Honestly, it makes sense to me why she zip lined down a mountain. I would do the same if it could help me overcome my fears."

"She did that two weeks after my husband died. I never understood. I always thought it careless and a bit selfish." Gertrude admits.

"Well, it may be but that's not how she saw it. I would have done it to prove to myself that I am still alive. I've been ziplining. It's a rush of adrenaline that can restart your entire system. It would be like a flood of light to overcome the darkness. Then again, I just moved from Las Vegas to Charleston because my gut told me I would regret not taking the leap."

Roman took my hand.

I feel reassured, but shrug. "I think she just wants to feel strong. Maybe we are both crazy. "

"Well, she's definitely crazy but most of the time it's a compliment." Gertrude resigns. "It makes sense in a Gran kind of way. She's always been very bold."

"Thank you." Roman brought my hand to his lips.

"For what?" I ask.

"The missing piece. We've always wondered what drives her. I know she has extreme impulses and a strong will. It's nice to understand what motivates her a little more," Roman explains.

"Well, it is only my perception of her after just meeting her but it makes sense to me. Give her a couple weeks to gain strength in her arm and I bet she'll do something else elaborate. Just wait."

"I'm sure she will." Gertrude sits back in her seat with a sigh. "Let's keep an eye on her. I trust her," she looks at Roman, then me and shrugs. "I just worry."

Roman lays a hand on his mom's arm, "That's a mom's job to worry. She'll be alright. We'll keep an eye on her."

I nod in agreement, "We'll keep two." Gertrude closes her eyes and takes a deep breath.

"Thank you." she looks up at us still holding hands on the table and smiles, "So tell me all about Vegas."

I look to Roman and he to me then we laugh together. His mom scoffs, "Oh you know what I mean."

Roman squeezes my hand and turns to his mom, "It was my second night there. Some of the guys we met at the convention suggested going up to Fremont for the night. It's apparently the "old Vegas" before the current strip was built." He pauses and looks at me, making sure the details were factual.

I nod and he continues, "We go up there and it's amazing. All the old time neon lights illuminate the buildings. There is a dome covering the main street that's lit up. We stopped at this one stage with a cover band playing 80's music. They were pretty good so we stopped and enjoyed our drinks.

"There was this group of three girls in front of us dancing. I remember being awed by their energy. They were so free. They moved like a flame, lucid and free."

Roman looks at me and smiles before continuing. "Andrew told me that I needed some of that in my life."

"Really?" I ask. "He said that?"

"Yeah. I didn't think to ask at the time whether he meant the feeling of freedom or the girl. After a few drinks, I didn't need much nudging to go talk to the girl that stood out to me in the group. Dawson was my wingman so it helped that her friends were there."

" Leana and Alicia said he was hilarious. My friends from home were visiting me for a couple of days," I explain. "Roman caught my eye before he ever came over."

"I didn't know that. I'm glad I found the courage to talk to you."

"Me too." I squeeze his hand.

Roman smiles at me before editing the story a little, "We got lunch out the next day and things just sort of clicked."

I nod.

Gertrude gave us a suspicious glance and a sarcastic "um hum." After a moment, she smiles broadly, "Well, I'm glad you are here. This one could use some looking after."

"Thanks, Mom."

"Anytime. Well, I need to get back to Gran. Why don't you two go on. I'll call you if there is any change or if she goes home today."

"Okay." Roman answers. "I would like to see if she's sleeping so we can tell her goodbye."

We stop by Gran's room and she surprises us all by actually being asleep. We slip out of the hospital and head to the car. I feel a little guilty leaving and mention it to Roman.

"She would want you to be outside," he assures me. "She'll want you to have seen as much as possible so you can discuss it over tea."

I laugh, but I know he isn't kidding. It makes me feel good like part of the family that his grandmother seems to like me. "Okay then," I ask. "Where to?"

"Should we go find you some shampoo and supplies? We need some groceries, too."

"That's probably a good idea. Let's do it."

The grocery store is busy, probably because it's the weekend. Even though it's a mundane task, it's the first time shopping together. It feels exciting to find out what he likes. We get some fresh fruits, including raspberries and blueberries, which are my favorite. We get a handful of frozen pizzas and quick meal. I share with Roman again how I would like to start learning to cook. "It will be fun to use that big kitchen."

"I'd be glad for it to get some use but don't feel pressured."

"I don't. I want to."

"My mom has all kinds of recipes and so does the Internet. Figure out what ingredients you need and we'll pick them up."

I laugh appreciating his encouragement, "Frozen pizzas are good for now but I'll get there."

"I trust you will," Roman smiles at me.

His whole face lights up with the sun's rays beaming down on him through the skylight. He could be a prince or a God like his name suggests. I am overjoyed by this simple moment. I kiss him on the cheek as we walk down the frozen food aisle. I feel like I'm glowing from the inside out.

Roman calls his mom when we get home and reports

that Gran has been sleeping most of the day thanks to the painkillers they gave her. We conclude not to return tonight so she can rest. We decide to return in the morning when they release her to help her home.

Once we get the groceries put up, I collapse on the couch. It's been an emotional and exhausting day. Roman and I have bonded even more through doing ordinary things like grocery shopping and laundry. It is nice to feel like we're settling in together.

I look at the clock and realize how late it is. I did some quick math in my head and realize what time it is in Vegas. It's only been two days since I left and it already feels like a different lifetime.

I keep waiting to miss that life or to feel uncomfortable here, but I don't. This feels right. I look over at Roman sitting next to me on the couch with his head leaned back, his eyes closed and smiling. This feels like home.

Chapter 20

Everything Is Going To Be Fine

ARIA

An alarm wakes me though I don't remember setting one. Something moves beside me, and I open my eyes to figure out where I am. The room looks familiar like a dream.

I look over to find bright blue eyes scanning my face. I smile causing the corner of his mouth to raise as well. I reach up to caress his face, "Now this is the kind of dream I could wake into every single day."

He leans down taking my lips in his. I taste the heat of his breath and it lets me know that he's real. And that I probably need to go use a toothbrush.

"You are a dream come true."

It's so corny. I laugh.

"What?" he leans back, but he starts laughing too.

"Did you read that in a greeting card?" I ask.

"Yes, if you must know. I thought it was very romantic."

I lift myself until my lips meet his again. I pull away smiling.

"Oh it is romantic but overly cliché."

"Touché," he relents and starts tickling me under my ribs. I laugh and squirm ending up with him on top of me and our lips swollen from kissing.

Roman looks into my face with serious eyes, "I love you, Aria. I want you to know that. I know we haven't known each other long but I look into your eyes and I see my future. I see laughter and happiness. I see courage and power. I see your beautiful soul radiating with passionate. I want to wake up next to you, take chances with you and face hardships with you by my side. I want you to know how glad I am you are here with me. It makes my whole world a little brighter."

I look up at him, awed by his impromptu speech. "You didn't get that off a greeting card."

He chuckles. "No, I came up with it all on my own."

"I love you, too, Roman. There's nowhere else in the world I would rather be." I smile up at him and watch his eyes widen with love. "Now I suppose we need to get ready to get your grandmother."

"Yes," he pauses, "you don't need to feel like you have to come if you don't want to."

I question him with my eyes and answer with my heart. "I would like to come and be there for her if you would like me to join your family."

"Absolutely. I would love for you to be there, thank you."

I nod as he kisses me before rising with my hand in his.

We are comfortable together in the morning. We don't talk much, each in our own world of thoughts, but we kiss and touch as we shower and get ready to go.

I can see him through the mirror watching me put on makeup. "What?" I ask.

He startles like he didn't realize I could see him. "Sorry," he says, "I got caught up in your beauty. It's amazing how you highlight your natural tones with your makeup."

He ducks out of the bathroom and I pause to consider

the moment. He has a mother and a sister, he is practically surrounded by females. I wonder if he's ever stopped and noticed them before.

As I finish my lipstick, I realize that he really didn't know I could see him watching me. I stumbled onto an honest moment, one where I could witness the tenderness in his eyes and how he truly sees me. I know in that moment that the love we feel is real and I am so thankful for it.

I meet him in the living room as he ties his shoes. He looks up at me, "Sorry, I didn't mean to be awkward, I just --"

I stop him with a kiss, "I like the way you see me."

We don't talk much on the ride to the hospital. I'm still learning to read him. He seems nervous about something. I want to assume it has to do with his grandmother, but I can't tell. I don't know how to ask so I keep my thoughts to myself.

Tomorrow he goes back to work. We haven't talked about what I'm going to do here. He hasn't suggested I get a job, but I can't sit still all day I would go crazy. I need a purpose.

I wonder if I should look for a job. I've lived off contract work most of my life. I'm sure I can find something, maybe another contract or go back to bartending. Those thoughts make me feel a little sad. I would love to finish and publish my book. I imagine Roman would support that, even though it doesn't exactly bring in big bucks. It feels odd not having an income for myself.

Spending time writing would be a good purpose. That

thought makes me very happy. Perhaps the time has finally come to focus on my work and not anyone else's. It is my dream to be able to write full time. It is also terrifying to put so much time into something that could never amount to anything. Maybe it's time to go for it. Is it too early to take another leap of faith?

I guess it's up to me where I go next. I've gotten this far. It's still hard to believe I moved back across the country. Believing in myself and my passion seems harder. It's strange how the big jumps seem easy compared to the everyday choices that define us. What will Roman think after he realizes I'm just a boring person that he has to live with every day?

Lost in my thoughts, I didn't realize we arrived at the hospital.

Roman turns to me, "We'll park here and go check on things. Mom said they should be ready to leave at about 9 am, that's half an hour from now."

I nod as we get out of the car. I slam the door behind me locking all my doubts inside. I take his hand as we walk noticing the nervousness in the corner of his eyes again.

"She's going to be okay." I assure him hoping I am right. He looks at me, his eyes open a little more. I hit the nail on the head. He was worried about her.

"I know." He answers with a sigh and hangs his head. "I just worry. Maybe I get it from my mom. Gran just doesn't have the best track record for telling things straight. It's like she wants this larger-than-life life and refuses to acknowledge anything bad. I'm afraid she's going to push herself to get better and hurt herself more. I have to go to work and so does mom. I don't want her to be home alone, but I don't know what the solution is."

I watch his face as he talks and can feel the frustration come off of him.

We walk a few steps and then I look up at him. Could it be that easy? I may have found my purpose after all.

"I could stay with her during the day while everyone is at work." I suggest immediately loving the idea.

He looks at me and a light goes on in his eyes, "You would do that?"

"Of course. I mean if it's okay with her, your mom, and you."

"That would be perfect. If you are sure. I mean you have the whole city to explore and your writing."

We stop at the entrance to the hospital. I step forward and kiss his cheek, "The city isn't going anywhere and I will still write. I would love to do this. We seem to get along well enough. I'm available and I want to."

Roman smiles, "Thank you. I think she will like spending time with you. You two have a lot in common."

"So I've heard."

He stops with a startled expression on his face.

"What?" I ask concerned.

"Wait a minute. I'm not sure that is a good idea. You two might decide to go jump out of an airplane or something."

I laugh and so does Roman.

"Well, not today at least." I assure him.

"Okay," Roman says, in a lighter mood than he was previously, "Let's go check on them and see how the discharge paperwork is coming along."

I nod as we walk in and straight up to Gran's room.

ROMAN

The walk up to Gran's room is long. I can't figure out

why I am so concerned. It helps that Aria stands right next to me holding onto my hand. She seems to understand exactly what is going on with me. I'm glad she does because I can't seem to understand it myself.

After Dad died, I lost it for a while. My mom was a wreck and so was Athena. It took me a long time to understand how calm Gran could be about the entire situation. It was her son, her flesh and blood that she lost and yet, she was calm and graceful. Only now am I beginning to see that is how she carried her own pain. It also didn't occur to me back then that she has already come across profound pain like this. Someone needed to keep it together.

Being back in this hospital and worrying about another person is getting to me. I can tell Mom is barely keeping it together with her own worry. Athena kind of flutters in and out. Somehow I'm left to be the one everyone counts on. It is a lonely feeling because they expect me to be strong. I'm not feeling very strong today. Gran is usually the strong one. I take much of my strength from her, something I didn't realize until she became the one we all worried about.

I don't know what I would do if anything really happened to Gran, she is the glue that holds our family together, not me. I'm afraid that she is going to leave us all. Then I will be truly alone. I still fear she is not telling us everything.

What Aria said yesterday really made me feel better though. It was a bad moment, but we have to move on. It also helps to understand more of why Gran acted the way she did when Dad died. I always wondered a little if I was missing something. It seems that it is just how she deals with life, the good and bad. I see that same spirit in Aria.

I am so thankful I met Aria. It seems like coincidental

circumstances, but maybe we can be what each other needs. She makes me feel more confident, just by being with her. Her strength is similar to Gran's, which I've always admired. No wonder I am so drawn to her.

She smiles tentatively at me. I can tell she worries about Gran as well and probably also about me. It amazes me that she can care so much, so deeply so quickly.

I'm glad that she may be able to stay with Gran. That will really help all of us out and reduce some of the stress. I know those two will get along just fine. I squeeze her hand as I consider this. I'm reassured by her illuminating smile.

I can't explain why I feel so strongly for this girl I just met, but it feels like I've known her my entire life. It's all surreal. Even though we've only known each other a short time, I can't imagine going through this without her.

She didn't want the easy out. She didn't demand time to herself. She wanted to be with me and help my family. Not just today, but for the foreseeable future. I can't explain to her what that means. It is a powerful thing.

As we turn into Gran's hospital room, I can see she is already dressed and ready to go. I can't blame her for disliking hospitals. I hate them, too. This is where people come to die, just like she said. I, for one, will be very glad to put this scenery behind me. I can tell by the look on her face that Gran is too.

Gran sits up in the bed donning her favorite red blouse and a determined look on her face. I don't see my mom in the room. I hope she is figuring out the release paperwork.

Once Gran sees Aria and I walk in the room, she beamed up at us. I am amazed at the difference in her expression. I know she is glad to see us, but there is something that Aria brings to her that I don't quite understand. They are like sisters of another time.

Aria heads over to her side and immediately plants a

kiss on Gran's cheek. The act surprises me but I don't know why. These two seems to have some sort of telepathic connection I am not privy to.

Gran takes Aria's hand and holds it to her cheek, "You know just what an old lady needs."

Aria laughs and pats her leg with her other hand, "What you need is a wheelchair so you can escape this refrigerator box."

Gran laughs, a magical sound, "Yes, that also works. The quicker the better." Both of them look to me like they are expecting something. I stare back distracted by my thoughts. Then I realize what they intend, "I'll go get that wheelchair."

I walk to Gran and kiss her other cheek before turning around to begin my quest for the escape vehicle. What have I gotten myself into?

ARIA

The chair beside the bed look extremely uncomfortable so I scoot onto the bed next to Gran. "How did you sleep last night?"

"Oh, just fine once I got a second blanket. You are right, it is cold here. My blood is not as thick as it once was."

"Maybe, but you couldn't prove it to me. You may be cold, but you are handling this whole thing like a pro. I will let you know that Roman and his mom are still worried."

"Oh I know, but that can't be helped. They would worry anyway. I couldn't convince Trudy to go home last night. There's nothing she can do here that the nurses can't."

"She can know you are safe."

"I suppose." Gran shifts on the bed like she's telling a secret, "but there was this young boy on the night shift that was totally making eyes with me."

"Oh yeah? Was he muscular, lean and look like Chris Hemsworth as Thor?"

Her laughter made me feel better, "Not exactly, but it made for some nice dreams of the good old days."

"You'll have to tell me about those days sometimes. I'm looking forward to your stories."

"Well, stick around, I have a few of them."

"I'm planning on it, trust me. I want to hear them all. Maybe even be part of a few new ones."

"I know a certain grandson of mine who will be very happy to hear that."

"I tell him every chance I get."

We both turn at the sound of voices in the doorway. Roman guides a wheelchair next to the bed followed by Gertrude and a doctor. The small room begins to feel claustrophobic. I don't know who reaches for whom first, but Gran's hand is in mine. I feel her tension like she's waiting for bad news.

The doctor talks first, "Alright Mrs. Wagner, you are cleared to go. Please, take it easy for a few weeks. Be sure to take your medications with meals."

"I can finally go?" she asks in reply.

"Yes, you may go. I wouldn't be able to keep you another day without tying you to the bed. I'd rather not deal with the fall out of that decision."

"Good man," she says.

"Thank you, doctor," Gertrude interjects giving Gran a look. "You've been very helpful and patient."

"My pleasure. No offense Mrs. Wagner, but I hope not to see you anytime soon. Stay well and don't give these guys too much trouble. They really do mean the best for you."

Gran smiles, "I know they do. Thank you, doctor."

With that, the doctor leaves and it is time to go. The entire room sighs in relief as soon as the door shut.

"Finally." Gran exclaims, "Let's get out of here."

Roman positions the wheelchair next to the bed and helps Gran into it.

As we walk down the hall, Gertrude says, "Roman mentioned that you offered to stay with Gran during the day. That would be wonderful. You sure you don't mind?"

"Not at all. I'm glad that I can help. I enjoy spending time with her."

"It seems she thinks the same of you. You have certainly won her over. She doesn't always take kindly to new people, but she really likes you. That is a huge compliment."

"Thanks." I reply not knowing what to say. I am humbled and honored by this declaration.

Chapter 21

Happiness Does Not Wait

ROMAN

I help Gran into Mom's van. I appreciate the ability to focus on this task so I can quiet the restlessness in my mind. Once Gran is settled in, I turn to my mom.

"Thank you, Son."

"You're welcome," I respond and give her a big hug. "See you at the house."

"Sounds good." She smiles and I release a breath I didn't realize I was holding.

Aria and I head back to my car. I feel reassured by the sensation of her hand in mine. I open her door and she turns to me with a sparkling smile.

"She's going to be okay, Roman. You know that, right?" Aria reaches out and places her hand on my chest right over my heart.

I place both of my hands over hers and breath in her warmth, letting it radiate through me like a furnace. "I know that. Thank you for making me believe it."

"She is strong and stubborn."

"Apparently, features I like in women." I tease.

Her quick kiss is a comfort. "Because you are strong, too."

"Sometimes I wonder." I say honestly. I don't always feel as strong as I pretend to be. I haven't felt strong the last couple of days. Yet with Aria, my strength feels rejuvenated somehow.

"You are stronger than you think."

"And smarter than I think."

"You know Winnie the Pooh, too?"

"Librarian mother."

"Dream man."

The warm pulse of her neck excites me as I taste her lips, so sweet. She is the dream.

I enjoy her longer than I should in the parking lot of the hospital, but not nearly long enough. She settles into the passenger seat and I run around the car.

As we head to my mother's house, I sit in the joyous silence. I didn't expect Aria to have such an abrupt introduction to my family. Though the circumstances were not ideal, I'm glad they could meet her so soon. She has a grace about her that is undeniable. Not many strangers could come into my family and flow in so easily. Gran would be the first one to put her in her place, but even she seemed to find strength from Aria. I could sense it the night we met, but now I am sure Aria has sort of magic about her. We have experienced so much together in less than a week. Aria is assuredly a special lady. I'm thankful she has seen something worthwhile in me as well.

Once we pull in the driveway behind Mom's van, Aria gets out before I can even turn the car off to help. I see Gran is just getting out of the passenger's side door with Mom offering her a hand. By the time I get out of the car, Aria has Gran's bag over her shoulder letting her lean on her arm while Mom opens the front door. I guess they don't need me after all. I follow them into the house shaking my head.

Gran settles into her favorite chair by the window and the old cat comes over to nestle her feet. "I'm okay now, sweet kitty," Gran coos as she leans over just enough to pet her arched tail.

Aria sits on the floor next to the chair and pets the cat, "What's her name?"

"Petals," Gran answers. "She was a rescue when Roman was still in high school. She's old now, just like me."

"She's lively." Aria says over Petal's purring.

Gran chuckles, "That she is."

I smile at their interaction and head to the kitchen. I find Mom leaning on the counter with her arms extended and her head bowed between them.

"Are you okay, Mom?" I ask.

She looks startled like she wasn't expecting anyone to find her there. "Oh, yes Son. I'm fine. Just a lot on my mind."

"I can understand that. I've been feeling the same way."

She smiles gently with a nod. "Aria sure seems like a sprightly woman."

I grin, only my mother would come up with a word like sprightly. "She is. I'm finding out more and more about her everyday."

"Are you concerned that it is all happened so quickly?" She asks in her motherly way.

I lean back against the counter and cross my arms, considering her question. "Not really. I wonder if I should be but it feels so right. I can't explain it exactly. We just clicked. Right from that very first moment I felt like I found something I didn't realize I had lost."

I notice the smile creep along her lips, "Then you are very lucky. Gran seems to like her."

"Yes, she does. Another reason I'm not worried. That would have been a hard one. It sort of worked out that we didn't have time to think about it. Aria insisted that we come quickly, which I appreciated because once I heard the news I needed to see Gran."

"You are a good man, Roman. I am proud to be your mother. Gran told me not to bother you."

"So you sent Athena after me instead?" I peer at her.

The chagrin look makes me laugh. "Maybe a little," she admits. "Athena suggested it. I just agreed."

"Eagerly."

"Perhaps."

I step forward to kiss my mother on the cheek, a familiar gesture for us. "It all worked out. Gran is going to be just fine. Apparently, she has a guardian angel watching out for her."

"Aria seemed delighted to stay with Gran when we go back to work tomorrow."

"I agree. I think they will enjoy each other's company. It couldn't be any more perfect timing."

"I thought the same," she agrees. "We'll have to make sure Gran is okay with it, too."

"We will." I listen to Gran and Aria chatting away in the living room, "I don't think it will be an issue though."

"They do seem to get along very well."

I nod, "They are so much alike. I've never met anyone like Gran before, never thought to look."

"May be why no one ever stuck before."

"Yeah, maybe," I consider.

"Well, it's Sunday night and Athena and Seth will be here for dinner. I was planning on pork tenderloin, mashed potatoes and green bean casserole."

"Mom, you don't have to cook all of that if you don't want to. You know no one is going to fuss over it tonight."

"I know, but it will settle my nerves," she explains.

"She's okay. You have to believe that." I assure Mom the same way Aria assured me.

"I do. I need the routine of cooking Sunday dinner to make it feel real."

"It is real Mom," I smile. "I'm going to go make sure they don't need anything. Do you need help?"

"No, not yet. Thank you."

"You're welcome." I smile turning to leave.

Mom catches my eye then, "No, really, thank you. You have a strength that I sometimes take for granted. Everything felt better once you were there. I really appreciate you, Roman."

I see the tears leak out in the corner of my mom's eyes. I embrace her before they can roll down her cheeks. "I love you."

"I love you, too."

I hold her for several minutes. She has been steady all of my life, it feels good to be strong for her.

"Okay, I need a cutting board and some onions. Then I can really cry." Mom pulls away.

I laugh, "Food preparation will make it all better."

"It always does."

I leave Mom to her cutlery and head into the living room to find Aria with Petals in her lap, a true rarity. It's nice to hear Gran laughing.

"I see you've made a new friend." I sit down next to Aria.

"I have. I think Petals likes me."

"Yes, she does. That is an honor. She is very picky."

"That's what Gran said." Aria replies.

"Well you've won us both over." Gran smiles.

"Does that mean I can come back?" Aria asks.

"I sure hope you do." Gran nods.

"What if I come over tomorrow while Roman and Gertrude are at work? You can tell me more about your time in Prague, that sounds fascinating."

"I would love to. Do you like tea?"

"Yes, Ma'am."

"Then we will get along just fine." Gran answers with a yawn.

"Want to lay down and get some rest, Gran?" I ask as I get up.

"Want to, not at all, but I suppose I should. I hear your mother is cooking a big dinner tonight. I need to be rested so I don't fall asleep in the gravy."

We laugh as I help Gran up. I chauffeur her down the hallway to her room. She leans into me, "You found an exceptional gift in that girl, cherish her."

"Always." I breath. I couldn't agree more as I look back at Aria meandering into the kitchen.

ARIA

I enjoy talking with Gran, she is so full of life and wisdom. I understand why her family loves her so much. I love her and I just met her. This family is so easy to love. I understand Roman better through their relationships with him. I like learning what makes him work. I feel like I know him even better now.

I can't help but consider the striking contrast to how I was raised. I envy the openness and interest they have in each other. I wish I could have experienced that growing up. I'm glad that I have found it know. I'm thankful for how open they are toward me as well.

I walk into the kitchen searching for Roman's mom. The room already smells good as Gretchen stands behind the counter with a knife in hand.

"Do you need any help?" I ask her as I move toward a stool at the countertop.

Gertrude looks at me with a smile, "I can always use a couple extra hands in the kitchen. Do you like to cook?"

"Um, no, not really," I shrug. "But I never really learned how. Only if mac and cheese out of the box counts."

I try not to take her tentative smirk as a negative sign, "It's a start. Have you ever snapped green beans?"

I shake my head.

"It's easy." She sets down her knife and pulls out a colander of green beans freshly washed from the sink. After setting them on the counter, she opens a cabinet and adds another bowl to the setup. I stand watching her glide gracefully around the kitchen.

"All you do is snap of the ends like this and then break it into small one inch sections." She shows me as she explains.

"Okay." I hesitantly pick up a bean and try to break off the end. When it snaps, I grin. It was as easy as it looked.

"There you go. You're getting the hard part of the ends off, you don't want to eat that, not on this style of bean. The size doesn't have to be perfect, just bite size."

I finish the first bean and pick up another one. Once I have four small sections in my hand I show her, "Like this?"

"That's perfect. Then you just put them in this bowl and we'll wash them again, just to make sure they are nice and clean."

As I pick up the next one I feel a little more comfortable with the process. I hear them clank into the bowl and feel a sense of satisfaction. I can understand why people like cooking. There is a sense of meditation in this process.

"How are you going to cook these?" I ask as I snap.

"These are going into a green bean casserole."

"That sounds good. My friend's mom used to make those for potluck dinners at our school."

"It is a southern favorite. Where are you from?" Gertrude asks interested.

"Myrtle Beach."

"Oh nice. That's not far from here."

"No, it's really close actually." A little too close, I think.

"Are you going to visit your family soon?" She asks innocently.

"No," I say too quickly causing Gertrude to look up. I smile and try not to sound as bitter as I feel. "I don't really talk to my mom very much."

"Oh." She says as a moment of silence fills the air. "Those green beans are coming along really well."

"Thanks," I focus on this moment and try to forget why I lack cooking skills.

"The secret to a good green bean casserole," Gertrude interjects, "is to blanch the beans first. You get them boiling hot and then put them on ice to cool them down really fast. The cold water stops the cooking process so you get a juicy inside without the mushy outside."

"That's really cool. I didn't know that."

"One of the many little tidbits I've picked up over the years. The only time I could talk to my mom was in the kitchen. She was intent on being the picture perfect wife and mother. She was locked into the stereotypical 50s lifestyle. I never saw her without makeup on or her hair perfect."

I enjoy listening to Gertrude talk with she idly chops vegetables. "She was a hard lady, nothing was ever good enough for her standards. You wouldn't think about coming home with your school clothes dirty. Her pride was in her cooking. It was also the only place I saw her smile. She was very technical, so I learned very young the proper way to chop vegetables. They were good skills to learn, but I did it just so I could watch her dance."

"That sounds nice."

"Yeah, I suppose. My relationship with my mother wasn't always so great. I didn't cook for a long time after I left home because I didn't want to be like her. I wanted a relationship full of love, not of duty. Cooking was considered a duty in my mind for a long time. After I met Liam and had the kids, I realized the kitchen was a place of peace for me. It was a space I could think and feel free to be me. I had the culinary background thanks to my mom, but it wasn't until I did it my way that I learned to love it. Now it is how I manage stress. I also happen to love feeding people. Sunday is my favorite day because I can cook and gather around a table with people I love."

"That sounds really nice."

"I'm glad you are joining us today, Aria."

"Thank you. I'm glad to be here." I smile.

"I haven't seen my son's face light up like it does when he looks at you since he was a kid."

"He's a pretty special guy."

"Yes he is. You seem like a pretty special girl. I'm glad you found each other."

"Me, too." I look down at the bowl full of snapped beans. "The beans are ready."

"Perfect. Would you like to learn how to blanch them?"

"I would love to."

ROMAN

I decide to get out of the house and work out my lingering stress over yard work. Even though I mowed the grass just before I left on my trip, it already needs to be mowed. The bushes around the side of the house could use a good trimming, too. With Gran resting and Aria in the kitchen with Mom, this is just the distraction I need.

I'm thankful that I had an extra set of workout clothes in my trunk because the sweat is pouring down my back. There's still another month until summer begins, but the sun is already pouring down over the lowcountry.

I'm sweating like a pig in line for the butcher while finishing up the bushes when I see Athena and Seth pull into the driveway.

Athena gets out the passenger side and waves, "Hi big brother, you look like a drowned poodle."

"Thanks, Sis. Nice to see you, too." I see her laugh and head toward the front door.

Seth walks over to me, "Hey man, how are you?"

I put down the trimmers to give him a fist pound. "Not bad. Yourself?"

"Can't complain. The bushes are looking good."

I chuckle, "Yeah, just trying to stay busy, you know."

"I hear you. How's Gran doing?"

"She's good. As far as I know still asleep."

"Well, that's good. Rest is probably the best thing for her."

"Yeah, I agree."

I get distracted as Aria comes around the corner in a red polka dot apron with a glass of sweet tea in her hand.

"Hi Seth," she greets as she approaches us.

"Hi Aria, good to see you." She gives him a quick hug. I'm amazed at how she has already melded into my family. Seth looks toward the door, "Well, I'll go on inside and say hi to your mom."

I wave him off and then swoop Aria into a kiss. I can feel her laugh on my lips. "I like this apron, it looks good on you."

"Thanks," I release her and she does a little swirl. "I'm helping your mom cook dinner."

"Should I be scared?"

"I don't think so. Your mom is teaching me. I can blanch green beans now."

"That sounds exciting. Maybe we won't have to live off frozen pizza and mac and cheese after all."

"I hope not. I'm enjoying learning. I've never really had anyone teach me before. Your mom says she has an old family recipe book she'll let me use."

"My mom has tons of old recipe books. I'm glad you're enjoying cooking."

"I brought you a glass of tea." She hands me a glass which I upend and drink half of on the spot.

"This is delicious, thanks."

"Athena said you were drowning out here, but I think you look hot."

"Oh yeah?" I ask and kiss her again. I enjoy her hum of pleasure. As I lean back, I look up at the bushes. "I just have this last one left and then I'll be in."

"Okay. Your mom says it will be about forty five minutes until dinner is ready.

"Perfect, I'll finish up, grab a quick shower then check in on Gran."

"Sounds good. She'll either be asleep or watching African animal documentaries," she says with a laugh.

"Now that sounds like Gran." With one last kiss, I watch Aria walk back towards the house. How did I get so lucky?

Once I clean up, I head to Gran's room. I knock on the doorsill as I enter. She shakes her head awake and turns in my direction. The smile she gives me, as always, warms my heart.

Just as Aria suggested, an African safari documentary plays on the television. I move to sit next to Gran in the armchair next to her bed.

She smiles at me, "You sure know how to pick them."

I laugh knowing she meant Aria. "I think in this case, she picked me."

"Perhaps. The best ones pick each other. Still," she pauses a moment with that look of consideration in her eyes, "She has been in and out of here all day making sure I am comfortable and entertained."

"She did all that and helped Mom in the kitchen." I credit her.

"She is a savvy girl."

"That she is. I think it's cool Mom is teaching her how to cook. She says she wants to learn."

"I think you'd be surprised at what she would do for you. Leaving you out of the picture, after talking with her more, I wonder if she ever had anyone to show her how to cook or to care."

"Well, that is true. From what she told me, I bet she hasn't had either." We sit in silence for a minute before I ask, "So how are you doing?"

"I am doing just fine, don't you worry. I am tired, which I don't like. I can't even stay awake to watch this very attractive fellow grind rice."

"Oh yes, now that is a thriller that will keep you going."

I smile at the laugh Gran makes. It is an airy sound and I can't help but wonder if that was always how she sounded. It makes me want to notice things that I didn't before, life is too precious to let it pass me by.

A soft knock distracts me as I turn to the doorway. Aria stands in the open door like a goddess. I can't help but smile at her gentle, radiant energy.

"Dinner is ready." She says softly.

"Okay." I answer then look at Gran. "You want some help up?"

I notice Gran in a moment of peace looking from me to Aria. I wish I knew what she was thinking. There's a look in her eyes like she is remembering a time long ago. Then she nods and I stand to help her.

After she has her walker, we slowly make our way to the kitchen. I can't help but gaze at Aria head to toe as she leads the way. I am glad for dinner, but I can't wait until it is time to sweep her up and take her home to show her how much I love her for everything she's done.

I am overwhelmed by her beauty, inside and out, and that bright light that shines from her.

ARIA

The Wagner table is very large and welcoming. I appreciate all the little touches Gertrude adds to the decor like cloth napkins and accented playmats. The plates are already set as we all come to the table with a feast ready to serve. I thank Roman as he passes me the rolls and get very excited when I add the green bean casserole to my plate. I am thankful I could contribute to the meal. It was a perfect first lesson in cooking.

I enjoy the chatter of the family that knows each other well. Athena and Seth give an update on some renovations they are doing to their house on about seven acres of land outside of town.

"It is a cute house," Athena told me, "but it needs a lot of work. We just got it earlier this year so much of our focus has been outside during the spring to get some fruit trees planted and the gardens tilled up."

"Now that the heat is coming in, we are moving inside so we can avoid the brutal humidity as much as possible. The bathroom is one of the most needed renovations so we are starting with it." Seth adds.

"The kitchen is also outdated but everything works for now. That is going to be a big project." Athena describes.

"That all sounds amazing. You are doing this all by yourself?" I ask.

"Yes, for the most part. We have a friend that is a contractor, so he is helping us with some of the structural work and to make sure we meet all the codes." Seth looks at Athena and smiles as he continues, "the demo is the most fun. Then we can put it back together however we like."

"I think that part is the most fun," Athena winks at me causing the entire table to laugh.

"What do you do?" Seth asks me.

"I'm a writer." I respond, "I was a screenwriter in Vegas. My last project was an adaption of old fairy tales and folk stories with a humorous twist for the stage."

"I was lucky enough to see the production," Roman interjects. "It was very well done, absolutely hilarious."

"Thanks," I look to Roman. "I had a lot of fun with that one. Not all of them have been so entertaining to create. Now I'm working on a fantasy novel."

"Oh that sounds interesting," Gertrude chimes in.

"Yeah, I'm really excited about being able to work on my own story. I started it a long time ago but it has been sitting and collecting dust for quite a while now. It's time to dust it off and make it come alive again."

"I would love to read it when you are finished," Gertrude states.

"Me, too," Gran says. I look around to see Athena, Seth and Roman nod as well.

"Thanks," I say delighted by their support, "I can't wait to share it."

The conversation continues to flow easily. I feel at home at this table. I appreciate how Roman's family folds me in.

"How are you getting around?" Seth asks. "Did you have to leave your car in Vegas?"

"I didn't have a car," I answer.

"You didn't have a car?" Athena gasps, "How did you get anywhere?"

I pat my legs, "With these. And the public transportation around Vegas is pretty good. I never had a need to roam outside of the city, so what I had was enough for me."

"Not everywhere is as hard to get around as this city," Gran remarks. "I miss the public transportation of New York and Paris. The traffic here is a nightmare, unfortunately a car is pretty much the only way to get around."

"I hadn't really thought of that," Roman admits. "We can get you a car so you can get around while I'm at work if you want."

"Did you keep your driver's license active?" Seth asks.

"Yeah, I did. It seemed like a good idea."

"Sweet. Then we can definitely get you a car." Seth says surely.

"Really?" I ask.

"Oh yeah, your cousin works at that car repair shop out in Goose Creek." Roman comments.

"He sure does. It might not be new, but it will run great." Seth nods.

"That's enough for me." I comment. It's amazing how well things are working out. Solutions are showing up before I even realize there is a problem.

I greatly enjoy Sunday dinner with Roman's family. There is so much love and laughter in this group of people who really seem to love and care for each other. I am glad to be a part of that. I catch Roman's eye while we clean the table and it makes me melt right in the middle of the dining room. He shows me so much love and affection in a simple look. I feel like the luckiest girl in the world. I'm thankful everything worked out with Gran and that we are able to share such a peaceful dinner together.

Chapter 22

Never Too Late

ROMAN

Saying goodbye is always a process coming out of the Wagner home. Mom and Gran needed one more hug from us and to sneak in another helping of desserts. As Gran slipped me the small tupperware she winks and whispers, "These are great for snacking on in bed."

"Gran," I groan, unable to conceal my laughter.

Dinner was great. Aria has come a long way in one afternoon from not even owning a frying pan to making a delicious green bean casserole. I know my mom helped her but that was a special contribution in the eyes of my family and me. I realize there is still a lot about this girl that I don't know. It makes me want to learn more.

Finally, I follow Aria out of the foyer and head toward the car. I increase my pace so I reach the passenger door before her and hold it open. I reach for the leftover tubs in her hands and add it to mine. I sit them on the back seat of my small two-seater sports car and then pull the seat back up ready for her.

Before she can slide into the seat, I catch her eye and wrap my arms around her. Looking into the chocolate brown eyes of this dynamic and beautiful girl, I sigh unable to believe we are here together.

She giggles, probably at the dumbstruck look on my face, and then steps closer and takes my lips with her own. I believe the best kisses are the ones shared by laughter. I can't help myself with her, I think as I savor her kisses. We both know Mom and Gran are peeking from the window, but neither one of us seems to care. I know I don't.

"Well, that went well." I nudge Aria. "I think it was the best family dinner in quite a long while."

"Wow. Well, I had a good time." She gives me a peak on the lips. "Was the green bean casserole okay? Your mom helped me with every step, but I just knew I was going to mess it up somehow."

"It was delicious. You did great." I nuzzle her neck, enjoying the smell of her.

She wiggles in my arms. "That's good, at least I can make one dish."

"I'm sure there's more where that came from. My mother is an excellent teacher. So is Gran for that matter, but she is more interested in the creative arts than cooking."

"Well, I hope to learn much from both."

"You and Gran seem to get along particularly well. You guys act like you've known each other for years instead of days."

She laughs and leans back, "Well, that sounds familiar. I love your family. They are very easy to get along with and they make me feel like I belong here. It is a very nice feeling, one that I've not had often."

"Really?" I ask, absorbing what she says. I want her to feel like she belongs. I want her to belong here with me forever.

"Yes. I wish I had someone like Gran around when I was younger. I wonder if I would have been able to cultivate a little more confidence earlier in life."

"Well, Gran has that to spare. You said you spent time with your Grandmother when you were young. What was she like?"

Aria hesitates causing me to backtrack, "How about

let's head on home now. Maybe then Mom and Gran will get back to their own business." I chuckle lightly as I gesture to the two blinds slightly pulled from inside the house. Aria glances and adds her chuckle to mine.

I hold Aria glad that she is in my arms, "I didn't mean to spoil our fun."

"Oh, you didn't spoil anything. Nothing can taint a great day, especially since you're here with me." She leans in and I hug her close. "But yes, let's go home. I'll tell you on the way."

"Only if you want."

"I don't mind." With one last kiss, she eases into the passenger seat. I close the door and head to my side. I wonder what growing up was like for Aria. Very different from my life, that's for sure. Tragedy was forced on me later in life but I've always had people love me on all sides. I've known the depth of that love and probably took it for granted.

The more she talks, the more I realize how few people were around her. Not many showed her love at all. She must have been very lonely. It makes my heart hurt for her and even more thankful that I found her.

I back out of the driveway and head towards home. I want to reach for her hand but it is very difficult to drive a manual transmission through traffic without both hands. I settle with rubbing her knee a moment and offering a reassuring smile. Her returning smile is weak.

She seems in a far off place where I wish I could join her. All I can do is let her talk. She seems ready to share and I'm ready to listen. I look forward to understanding her better.

"This is hard for me," she begins, "but only because it makes me sad to tell it. It isn't really my story but it is my family history. My grandmother was a catch, beautiful and young. She and my grandfather met in high school and were married right after graduation. Not an uncommon thing in those times. Nor was the draft notice. My grandfather was going to war.

"My grandfather was lucky to be able to stay and see his daughter born. When my grandmother kissed him goodbye, she didn't know that he would never come home. Killed in Action was the declaration. My mom was about eight months old at the time. At least they were a family for a short time.

"After the delivery of a folded flag, I don't know that my grandmother was ever truly happy again. She became depressed and bitter. It's the only way I ever knew her.

"My mother was a handful and very high maintenance. From what I could understand, their relationship was strained since she was a child. My mom wanted a larger than life existence and my grandmother focused on only the most mundane tasks to get her through the day. In the end, my mom turned bitter just like the unhappy widow that raised her.

"I can't help but wonder if my mom's bitter came from being afraid of love. She never committed to anyone, not even me. She was always looking for something but was never able to find it.

"I was conceived after a one night stand during tourist season. My mom threatened me to never search for my dad. I knew better than to anger her. She was a bitch on a good day and a devil with a few drinks.

"She lived the same life my grandmother did, an unhappy one without love. She didn't even accept the love of the daughter she decided to keep. I never knew why my mom didn't give me up for adoption. It sounds horrible, but sometimes I wonder if we would have both been happier.

"We lived with my grandmother until she died when I

was eleven. That's when I began to feel so lonely. My grandmother was not exactly fun to be around, but she was there for me when my mom wasn't. That's about the time Leana and I started hanging out so much.

"By the time I was in high school, I was like a ticking bomb. I knew I wanted to leave but I didn't know where to go. Eventually one of my mom's abusive boyfriends, Doug, became the trigger. After he came after me, I didn't care where I went. I was ready to go.

"I knew I had to break free of the cycle. I refused to live the life of my mother or my grandmother. I wanted to give myself the chance to have happiness and love in my life. I'd seen enough of Leana's family to know there was another way. I didn't know how I would find it, but I knew I had to escape. That's when I went to Vegas."

I park the car and turn to her, able to listen to the last part while looking into her eyes. They seem to sparkle from the moisture in her eyes. My heart broke for her and the pain of abandonment she had to endure. It was a lifelong bondage that I can't imagine even as she lays it out for me to see. I reach over to rub the wetness from her eyes and hold her face in my hands.

It feels good to touch her, but she still isn't looking at me. "Aria," I whisper.

She looks up her eyes shining into my own. I am shocked to see fear staring back at me. Could she possibly think telling me the hardships of her life would somehow send me away? This is all part of who she is today, the bright, quickly girl I fell in love with. If she could only sense how much I want to make up for all of the lack of love she's had in her life. I want to show her how incredibly beautiful, smart and intoxicating she is. I could not leave this woman if I tried, not after finally finding her.

I hold her eyes with mine hoping to convey this to her.

She relaxes under my hands as I speak. "You have found love now and I am not letting go. You will no longer feel without love and affection. I can promise you that."

She leans into me with fresh tears, this time happy ones. "I can't believe I found you. I can't believe this is true."

"It's true, my love. It's more real than anything else that's happened to me. I love you, Aria. Always know that."

"I love you, too." I don't know who leans in first, but our kiss is passionate. It symbolizes a declaration of the love we share sealing this promise to each other and ourselves. We've only known each other for a week, but it feels like I've known and loved her all my life. I've been waiting for her to wake me out of my stupor and she needed to feel my love to thaw from her freeze. The circumstances are crazy but our love is real.

We clumsily get out of the car, almost forgetting the leftovers. I juggle the boxes while Aria teases my neck. I unlock the door, missing the key hole twice before I get it in. Once we tumble inside I turn to her, "Gran said these cookies were good in bed. Want to find out."

"Absolutely." She says kissing me deeply. "First bed then we shall eat cookies."

I can't argue with that.

We tease and kiss going towards the kitchen. I manage to balance the boxes on top of the eggs, not caring about the order of the fridge. I follow Aria and the trail of her clothes to the bedroom where she lies naked on the bed. I toss the cookies down on the nightstand and scoop her into my arms.

I kiss her lips, face and neck slowly making my way to her breasts. I feast on this delicious buffet she lays out for me. I am urged on by her sigh as I let go of one breast only long enough to devour the second.

I feel her hands in my hair and it sends sparks of electricity through my body making me aware of the bulge against my pants. The tightness makes me focus more on her delicate skin as I trace kisses down her stomach. I like the feel of her muscles moving under my hands and my lips. I want to see her enjoy even more, to know my love for her is real.

I continue moving down until I reach her moist tender spot. My hands gently widen her legs and make room for my mouth to feast once again. I slow down for a moment to appreciate the long, deep moan that escapes from my love's mouth as I teasingly lick along her tender core. She arches up, a signal for more. I run my tongue down her center and grin as she continues to squirm.

I build her up with slow, long movements in an effort to express my love and desire for her. She begins to push into me, "More," she breathes. I feel like my manhood is going to explode from my pants as I add a finger then two below my tongue and increase the pace. She pumps her hips into the beat of my thrusts until she releases a most erotic moan and falls back on the bed.

I continue to caress her with slow, lazy strokes as she catches her breath. I enjoy watching her chest rise and fall, thanking my stars I found her.

She looks up at me with a huge smile on her face. She reaches for my mouth, kissing my lips. I wonder what she tastes like to herself. I enjoy her sweet yet spicy flavor and gladly share it with her. I lift up to undo my shirt and she stops me with her hands.

"I got this," she breathes huskily and begins to unbutton my dress shirt. She follows her hands with kisses. I appreciate the torture but I must get my jeans undone before I explode in them from sheer anticipation.

I move to release the pressure on my pants and she

shifts with me. Leaving my shirt opened, she moves to my jeans. I can see the gleam in her eye as she releases my quivering member.

After quickly releasing me of the remainder of my clothes, she takes me into her mouth. As if the warm pleasure wasn't enough, the moan she releases as I slide in her mouth has me close to the edge. I tense up and breath, "Aria."

She looks at me. I imagine my face has a strange contortion of pain and pleasure. She hums, like a purr, and mounts my lap. I enjoy the shape of her breasts as she saddles to a comfortable position. It is her eyes I truly get lost in.

We lock eyes sharing a promise for a lifetime of love. As she settles with me deep inside her, I am the most content and aroused man in the world.

I feel my eyes roll back in my head as she finds a rhythm. After she sets the pace, I reach around cupping her bottom in both my hands so I can match her thrusts. I have never felt more love or desire in my life.

As we crash together, I catch her eyes once again. There is a sparkle there that wasn't there before. Something powerful is happening between us. I couldn't be happier.

"I love you." I whisper hesitant to break the silence and yet unable to contain sharing my heart with this spectacular woman.

"I love you, too." She whispers back, eyes just as intense. In that moment a pact is made, something even more powerful that the leap of faith it took to get her here. Now, we face the world together and it looks bright.

Chapter 23

Way To Normal

ARIA

I have not slept that well in forever. Yesterday was an emotional day but it ended on a note of power and love. I didn't realize how much I needed to tell my story and share my loneliness. He didn't pity me or reject me as I feared he might. I should have known better. I feel like I know him so well.

He embraced me and once again declared his love for me. I can't help but believe him. I can see the genuineness in his eyes. His words came straight from his heart.

He showed me his sincerity in his lovemaking creating an undeniable bond between us. Who knew a complete stranger found across the country was the link I was missing. He unknowingly brought me home again and showed me what it meant to be loved.

All I can do now is be grateful I found him and cultivate our love in anyway I can. For now, the amazing sex helps. I enjoy a quiet moment watching the man I love sleep peacefully beside me with tousled hair and an arm wrapped around my waist. Blissful, that is the only word to describe this moment.

Today I will go be with his grandmother, again. I am looking forward to spending time over there. I enjoy Gran's company, her spirit and her wisdom. I am thankful we get along so well. His family is wonderful and make me feel wanted.

Roman's family seems so close. I am almost jealous of their connection but I am glad I found it. I hope they allow me to become family, too. I didn't realize when I fell for Roman that his family would be such a pleasure. I got lucky.

I am so wrapped up in my thoughts that I don't even notice Roman move until I feel a kiss on my neck. "Good morning, beautiful," he says sleepily accentuating his southern drawl.

I love that voice, the baritone vibrations go straight to my loins. "Good morning, yourself, handsome." I quip back, kissing him. I know he is still sleepy, but we have time. I leave heated kisses trailing along his neck and down his stomach until I reach my destination. "I think it's time to finish what I wanted to start last night." He looks up with a lazy "hmm" until I pull him into my mouth. Then I hear his intake of breath and smile as I wake him properly.

Roman drops me off at his mom's house with a big smile which I mirror. After a kiss full of promise for more soon, I walk to the front door. I knock so they know I'm here then use the house key Gertrude gave me yesterday.

Gertrude comes around the corner to greet me. "Aria, I'm so glad you are here." She pulls me in the kitchen. "I've already started some tea. You're welcome to have coffee if you'd rather. There's some pancakes and sausage still on the stove if you are hungry." As if on command my stomach growled revealing my lack of breakfast.

I chuckle nervously, a little overwhelmed with the welcome. "This is amazing," I note. "You did all of this and it's only --" I look up at the clock on the stove, "8 o'clock in the morning?"

"Yes," she looks around and the kitchen. "I know. Roman says I carry on a little much but it helps settle my nerves. I worry too much for my own good sometimes."

"Thank you for everything. I can handle this. You have nothing to worry about. Gran is in the next best care after your own."

I watch Gertrude relaxes before my eyes. She takes a deep breath and looks at me. "She is, isn't she."

"Absolutely." I comfort her.

"Roman really did find a gem in you."

I blush not quite sure how to reply to that. I feel more like a stone that hasn't been polished yet, still rough around the edges. I can't deny how much her son means to me. Maybe she can sense that somehow.

"Okay," Gertrude interrupts my thoughts as she rests her hands on my shoulders. "Thank you, Aria. I want you to know how much I appreciate you being here. Both for coming here to care for Gran and for making my son so happy."

"I'm happy to be here. Thank you for making me feel so at home."

She envelopes me in a hug, "You do belong here. I can feel it in my bones." After a moment she steps back. "Okay, I'd better go before I am late."

From the other room we hear, "Get on out of here, Trudy. The party won't start until you leave."

I see the amusement in her eyes but she looks at me with a thoughtfully. "I suppose she's had quite enough of my company for now. She's all yours."

With a wink and a "bye" called out to the other room, Gertrude leaves. I take a moment to breathe in the quiet and show gratitude for all that I have.

As I feel a sense of peace come over me, the tea kettle signals with a blaring whistle. From the living room, I hear clapping hands and the exclamation, "Finally, there's tea." I laugh to myself and put together a tray of what I'm learning to be Gran's favorite fixings and some tea for myself.

ROMAN

Waking up with Aria in my bed is still new. I feel like I am dreaming each morning. Getting ready for work is a little harder when I am preoccupied with a beautiful brunette. We managed to get out the door in enough time for me to drop Aria off with Gran.

I pull up in the familiar driveway and pause. "You gonna be okay today?" I ask, feeling a little nervous at leaving her alone with my family for the day.

"Of course I will. I'm in good hands."

I chuckle, "That's what I'm worried about."

"We'll be fine. I'll try not to get Gran into too much trouble."

"Will you tell her hi and I love her. I've got to get going if I'm going to be on time. I don't want to be late for my first day back from the convention."

"I know. I'll tell her." She kisses me and then adds, "Say hi to Andrew for me."

"I will. I'm sure he'll be very interested in how you are enjoying Charleston."

"I love it."

"I love you."

She climbs out of the car and heads toward the door. I smile when her turn around on the doorstep and wave. I watch as she disappears inside the house and head on to work.

Meeting Aria has changed me in so many small ways. I feel warmer and lighter but it has also made me a little off centered. I don't know what to expect. It is an odd feeling having so much emotion.

It is different with her though, I don't feel drained like I usually do with groups and socializing. She is someone I could come home to forever. I hope I can. Right now, I'm enjoying the moment and spending time together.

I'm a little anxious to get back into routine. It feels like months since I've been into the office. So much has happened and changed since I left Charleston a week ago. It will be stabilizing to get the debriefing from the convention and have a steady, familiar day.

I walk into the office and see everyone hard at work. The familiarity is comforting and I yearn to get back to routine and try to settle my mind.

My bag feels heavier than normal as I approach my small cube of space. Looking at it now, I can see how empty it is. I've never been much for clutter but I get the sudden awareness that I've been feeling more empty than I realized.

The only personal things I have are a small black notebook that I use to take notes during meetings and a picture of my mom, Gran, Athena and I from last summer pinned on the wall. I shake my head.

Maybe I'm reading more into it than there is. It is hard not to see the contrast between how I feel today and how I felt when I left work a week ago. Aria has made all the difference.

As I walk over to Andrew's office, I decide that I will bring some color into this world, too. So much for wanting to get back to normal. I suppose it is time for a new normal.

I have a lightness to my step as I peak my head into Andrew's office.

"Good morning, boss," I call. He looks up and waves me in. I sit in one of the chairs facing his desk and wait while he finishes what he is working on.

After a couple moments he looks up with a smile, "Nice

to see you, Roman. How was your weekend?"

I can't contain the sigh that escapes, "It was good, but I found out Saturday morning my Gran was in the hospital."

"Oh, no. Is she okay?" Andrew asks concerned.

"Yes, she seems to be. It's hard to know with Gran. She had a bad fall due to a mild stroke. She is bouncing back well. She was very thankful to be out of the hospital yesterday."

"I imagine. She doesn't like to be told where to be or what to do. You sir, are surrounded by strong, independent women."

"That could not be more true."

"How is Aria adjusting to Charleston?"

Now my smile explodes across my face, all of the weariness from the stress melts away when I think of Aria. "She's doing great. I still can't believe that she came. I'm so glad though. It makes everything a little easier with her here. Gran and Aria get along great. It's amazing how much they have in common. Aria is going to stay with her while Mom and I work."

"That's really great to hear. It doesn't surprise me that she and your Gran get along well. Those two are made of the same cloth."

"I said the same thing. So now that's all settled, I'm actually a little grateful to be back at work. It's nice for something to feel steady when everything else is changing."

"I could see that. We'll I am glad you are here."

"Did Miguel ever get home?"

"He did, but late last night. He took the day off to recover. We'll have the official meeting tomorrow so that we can all be there to review."

"Okay, is it on the calendar already?"

"Yes, I put it on this morning. I have one more thing to

discuss with you."

I don't know why, but that always makes my stomach sink just a little, even when my boss is as great as Andrew is. "Okay," I encourage trying not to let my nervousness show.

"You have been working really hard here and you did really well at the convention cultivating interest and exhibiting the ease of our integration. You have proven yourself to me and impressed the higher ups as well. You've been wanting the traveling ops. Do you still want that?"

I think about that. When I pushed for the travel, I hadn't met Aria and Gran was well. Now things have changed. I realize I do still want to travel. I've always wanted to, but never really had a reason.

I wonder what Aria will think about it. Maybe she can come with me. Andrew's wife used to travel with him before the kids were born.

"I do," I answer simply.

"Your job title will still be Solutions Engineer and it comes with a slight pay raise." I look at him dumbfounded as he hands me a slip of paper. I take it and look at the numbers. It is a small increase but it feels like a big deal.

I have worked so hard. I've kept my head down and forgot to live. There is so much changing at once with Aria coming, our new concern for Gran and now more responsibilities at work. It feels like a lot, but really, this is what I've been waiting for. Things are coming together for the better.

Glancing up at Andrew, I see his proud smile. "You've worked really hard for this, Roman. You deserve every bit of it. I know you are the right person for this job."

"Thanks, Andrew. Thanks a lot," I beam.

"We'll have a one-on-one tomorrow after our debriefing

and start going over a few more details. Most of it you have already begun working on, so it won't be much of a transition. The next convention will be in a few months and you'll be the lead. We'll make sure you are prepared for it. I know you will do great."

I stand and shake Andrew's hand, "Thank you."

I walk out of his office and feel like I'm floating on a cloud. This entire week has felt like a dream. One which I never want to wake from.

Chapter 24

Come Talk To Me

ARIA

I can't get over how nice their house is. It isn't huge but there seems to be plenty of room. It is clean and is full of comforts. These are stark contrasts from my childhood home. I lived with my mother and grandmother in an old house that was falling apart. It was always cold during the winter and hot in the summer because there was little insulation and we never fixed the air conditioning unit. All of our furniture was ancient and tearing. We never got new things. I barely even got new clothes when I outgrew what I wore.

The only saving grace was that it was really close to the beach and to Leana. I am told it was once beautiful before my grandfather died in the war. I wish I could fix it up now. I can't imagine my mother would let me touch it. I don't know if she stays there or still even has it. There's a lot I don't know since I left. Leana said one time that it looked abandoned. I suppose that is a fitting end to an unloved house.

It was a house but never a home. It felt even emptier after my grandmother died. That's one reason I spent so much time with Leana. The Davis's had a modest house but it was clean and well stocked with food and love. I could never get enough of being there. I ended up with my set of chores at one point because Leana's mom teasingly told me if I was going to eat over there so much I would have to work for my supper.

I never minded. The less I was at home the more I didn't want to be. By the time I graduated, I never went home. My mom had to pick up her own messes then, which she didn't most of the time.

The day goes by easily with Gran. We talk or read, she'll knit, or at least hold knitting in her hands as she falls asleep in the chair. I write during the afternoon when the day is quiet and she drifts off to sleep in her recliner. I enjoy the peace of the day as we move from one topic to another. Roman and his family seem to run on entirely different energy.

I try to recall last week at this time of day. I would have probably been eating chips straight out of the bag while bing watching the declared best television drama. Instead, we played backgammon during tea time while listening to Mozart. I'd never played backgammon before. It was a fun experience.

Gran's words were, "If you like backgammon, just wait until I teach you cribbage or better yet, parcheesi." I am amazed by her level of excitement for the smallest things. I mentioned it once and she shrugged it off, "You only live once. Might as well make it count." I like that.

I find comfort talking with Gran. She preaches living in the moment. I realize I want to do exactly that. Gran exudes great wisdom and has absolutely no filter. I love hearing what she has to say about everything.

It was after lunch as we sat on the back porch under the fan when I asked her about the war. I'm not sure what brought it up exactly. Perhaps, telling Roman about my family last night. I never realized how powerful that confession was. I couldn't quite get it out of my mind how much the war changed my family. It made me wonder if it had the same effect on others. I imagine Gran handled the war with finesse and grace. I want to know more so I decide there is only one way to find out.

"Gran, how did WWII affect your life?"

I watch Gran's face as she contemplates my question. She didn't remark about how out of left field the topic came from. Instead, like everything else, she took her time and answered with honest wisdom.

"The war changed everyone. The entire country, the world and everyone who lived and breathed in it were different. Nothing was the same on the other side of that damned war. I was no different. It changed me right along with everything else.

"I married my Nicholas just out of high school. That was not an uncommon thing to do in those days, but still, we were head over heels in love. We almost waited until we were married to consecrate our union. Getting the draft notice was about as inevitable as our positive pregnancy test. Both happened within the first month of our marriage.

"That soon?" I gasp.

"Yes, it did feel too soon. We wanted to be together and were happy to start a family. We were young and in love. We thought that would carry us through."

"Did it?" I ask.

She contemplates for a moment. "Well, yes, I suppose it did. Nicholas did two different tours. On the second one, he got bit in the ass with grenade shrapnel sending him home with a purple heart. His recovery was hard. He had scars on his rear and the back of his legs for life. I am thankful he got to come home and see our Oliver grow up, a blessing that we did not realize the value of until much later."

"Who was Oliver?" I ask before I realize this may be a painful story for her.

"That would have been Roman's uncle. He died of pneumonia when he was eight."

My inhale of breath shocks even me. "I'm so sorry."

"I know dear. So am I. It was tragic, his death. He had asthma but we didn't realize how bad it was. When the pneumonia took over his lungs, there was nothing we could do. They tried everything they could but we lost him. It hit Roman's dad pretty hard. Oliver and Tim were very close. We made it through together, doing our best to move on, but missing him always."

"I haven't heard of him," I admit.

"Yes, no one likes to talk about death. It is very sad. I don't like to often but that is how the people we love live on in our memories. I feel the same about my Nicholas and Tim, too. It doesn't get easier but you learn to make room for them to live in your heart."

I feel heartbroken. I never even met these people and I miss them. Roman has hinted at the depression that hit after losing his dad. I wonder if it is harder to love and lose them or to never feel loved at all. I don't know that answer, but it makes my struggles feel so miniscule.

This woman has lost so many loved ones who were young and in the prime of life. Still she remains so upbeat and enthusiastic. I can't help but ask, "How do you stay so positive after all that heartbreak? My grandmother didn't, neither could my mom and she never really had heartbreak. They were always so bitter."

"Everybody handles life's tragedies and circumstances differently. I was a mess after Oliver died. I deemed myself unfit to be a mother. Without Nicholas and Tim, I don't know that I would have been able to piece myself back together. Somehow I grew stronger in the process. Losing Nicolas was hard. He was my best friend and I felt really lonely afterwards. He had pancreatic cancer, an aggressive cancer. He was in so much pain. I knew I needed to let him have peace but it was still hard. Tim was another tragedy. Losing another child, even though he was grown, was almost unbearable. I'm sure Roman or Gertrude have told you I went to the Amazon and stayed for a week."

"They did. Roman mentioned that he didn't really understand it. You went zip lining?"

She laughs, "Yes, I did. I was overwhelmed. He was my baby, a mama's boy. We were really close and I still miss him. I needed to get away and experience a reason to keep living. I was feeling as dead as my family. I needed to remember what it means to live."

"That sounds pretty reasonable to me. All I know is I don't want to end up like my grandmother or my mom. It is one of my biggest fears in life. I don't want to be bitter. I want to make the most of this moment and then the next and find a reason to keep love in my heart in the process."

"So don't be bitter." She says with a shrug. "You are what you choose to be. Even happiness is a choice. Simply by deciding you don't want to hold onto bitterness, you won't. Is that why you went to Las Vegas?"

I ponder that for a moment. "I suppose it was. I ran away. It seemed like the only option at the time. I didn't even stop to think about it, I just left."

"You are already staying away from bitterness by making the most of each moment and opening your heart to love. Aria, you have a fire in you. I can see it. I know Roman can see it, too. It is bright and powerful. Nothing can come between you and your dreams except you."

"What do you dream of?" I ask spontaneously.

"To paint," she responds just as quickly. "I did a lot of it when I was young. Especially while Nicholas was away. It calmed my nerves and focused my energy. Much the same way cooking does for Gertrude.

"As I added details I could see a painting come to life. For a brief moment, the world would make sense. It was a place where I was in my own world even in a crowd."

"Why did you stop?" I ask, curious.

"That's the kind of question I usually ask," she nods at me.

"I'm a quick learner," I tease.

"Now that you mention it, I don't really know my dear. I guess as I got older and busy with other things. I kept painting sometimes but not like I did before. Come to think about it, I never even set up a spot in this house. My stamina isn't what it used to be. I'm not sure how steady my hand is now. I don't know if my paints are any good anymore, but I believe there are some blank canvases, brushes and other supplies in one of the closets we use for storage." She sits quiet for a few moments before turning to me, "Do you have something like that? Like what painting is for me?"

"Writing," I blurt out. I was already thinking about it and how it was the same. "The act of writing calms me, helps my brain slow down and process information. Books, poetry and writing have been what keeps me going. It gives me hope and some much needed therapy at times, too." I say laughing.

"Oh yes, I understand that one. Is that what I saw you doing earlier when I woke up from my little cat nap?"

I smile and nod, "Yes, Ma'am."

She smiles and continues, "Painting was part of my healing after Oliver's death and then Nicholas's. My painting was angry after Tim died. I felt as if the world had betrayed me once again. It made me a little afraid of myself, thus the trip to the Amazon. I haven't painted since."

"Would you paint again?" I wonder.

She seems lost in thought for several minutes, but then looks up with a mischievous smirk, "I think perhaps I would. It is past time to put paint to canvas again. I wonder if we can find my old supplies?"

"Let's find out." I exclaim ready for an adventure.

We sit down with a cup of tea and review what painting supplies we found. We searched through several old closets and even in the attic. Their house was even bigger than I realized. I asked Gran if this was the house Roman grew up in.

She responded, "Oh yeah, he and Athena used to get into all kinds of mischief. Hide and seek was their favorite game. There are so many nooks and crannies to disappear in. It is a secret of these old houses.

"I remember one time Roman was hiding and Athena looked for a good fifteen minutes. She couldn't find him so she gave up and started playing with her dolls. Roman got so mad when he finally came out. If I remember correctly, he hid for almost an hour waiting for her to find him. After that, he kidnapped her dolls and held a ransom for her to do one of his chores for leaving him hanging like that. They were always at each other but they loved each other, too. They were good kids and they still are if you ask me."

"I think so, too," I respond. "It's nice to think of Roman as a boy. I don't really have a lot of stories to tell from my childhood. I spent all of my time in a book or writing in my journal."

"Well, there's nothing wrong with that, my dear. Besides, you are still making memories. We never stop creating who we want to be just because we get older."

I think on that. It seems a profound statement. I am

thankful I get a chance to create memories with Roman and his family. Hopefully, one day we will have kids. That thought surprises me the most. I've never thought about having kids before. Never really wanted them. Not that I don't like kids but because my childhood was so messed up. I can't think of imposing my insecurities on a tiny human. I imagine with Roman it would be different. I know that he would make a great dad one day.

Finally, Gran said we found all the art supplies that we were going to find. She seemed most surprised that she had her best set of brushes and palettes right there in her closet. "Trudy must have put them there." Gran says thoughtfully.

In the end we found two full sets of brushes in great condition, a varied collection of palettes in different shapes and sizes with different hues forever stuck onto the boards, some paints that had gone bad, three different easels: one standing and two meant for tables, and several stretched canvases of varying shapes and sizes.

"That's pretty good," I comment.

"Yes," Gran says, "It seems most of it is her. We will need new paints."

"We can do that. Do we need anything else?"

"Not to get started. I think we are good." She looks around at the things we pulled out onto the table with a reminiscent look in her eyes.

"Are you okay?" I can't help but ask.

She looks up at me like through a fog, "Oh yes my dear. I'm great. This is going to be interesting."

"I'm glad we can do it together," I share.

She nods and then looks at me with new interest, "What about your writing, my dear? How is it going these days?"

I'm a little taken aback by her interest. Few have ever really cared about my writing or what it means to me. Leana will ask sometimes and now Roman does quite often. It's nice to find people who care about my work. It makes me feel like they care about me too, a strange sensation for me. It makes me care about my work more, too, like I can actually finish this story and publish it instead of just dreaming about it.

I have to refocus before I can answer Gran's question, "It's been going well. My narrative writing is starting to flow well. I'm still working on my very first novel so I don't really know what I'm doing half the time. I'm figuring it out a little bit at a time. It is my dream to become a published author, but it's scary, too. So it's here and there I suppose."

Gran gave me a knowing look, "You can tell that grandson of mine to take care of himself once in a while if you need too."

I laugh almost spitting tea across the room. I really appreciate this woman's humor. I hope I'm still this candid when I am her age. She seems to have no qualms with imagining Roman and I doing the dirty. Then I remember, "Well, you were right about those cookies being better in bed." I wink at her. It is nice to hear her laugh with such abandonment.

"He's not my problem," I continue. "I'm enjoying him just fine. It's from before I met him. I got really stuck there for a while. I've written more since I met Roman than I had in months. Everything is happening so fast. I'm enjoying the moment. Some positive changes have begun this week. I need to get back in the story and devote some serious effort to the project. It's been a while since it has been able to be my priority."

"What's it about?" She asks curiously, pouring more tea.

"Oh yes," I comment as I offer my cup for more as well, "The question every writer loves to hate to hear." The more often I talk about the story and what it is about the more solid the characters become in my head. They are like old friends that I haven't talked to in a while. I tell Gran of the princess in her castle and her daring rescue.

"Does the guy swoop in and save the damsel in distress?" Gran interrupts me at one point.

I chuckle, "Gran, don't you know me at all? The princess is the hero in this story. She saves the prince and herself all at the same time. Well, I suppose they save each other but still. Sadly, though I don't have an ending yet. I know the direction the story is going but happily ever after is boring and not real. I want something more for them. I haven't figured it out yet. "

"You will dear, just give it time. I like the story. Have you ever tried painting a scene?"

"What do you mean?" I ask.

"A sculptor friend of mine would paint what her piece on canvas first so she could find the shape easier in the clay. You could paint what you want a character or location to look like, maybe even an entire scene of the story like a panel so you can craft the words you need."

"I love that idea." I proclaim. "I've never thought to try it. You are very wise, Gran."

She chuckles at that, "I've seen a lot of things in my life and I try to pay attention. If you can't take in some useful information along the way, what is the use of the journey in the first place? Besides, some would say wise and others would say smart ass. I'm a little of both I suppose. Either way, people usually don't want to hear either."

"That's true, most don't like hearing the truth. I'll take anything you can offer. I could use a little wisdom and smart ass to help me along."

That got a roar of laughter out of her, "Where have you been all my life dear? I haven't laughed this much since I was a youngster thinking the world owed me something. If Roman doesn't keep you around, I might just have to steal you away for myself."

I smile, basking in the feeling of wanting. "I believe I am just where I belong. It took me a while to find it. Ironically, I had to go all the way across the country to end up not far from where I began. I've never had a real place to belong, it is a good feeling to have found it with Roman and you, too."

"I'd give it three months, tops." She grins.

"For what?" I ask.

"Roman to propose."

"Really? You think so?"

"He probably would today if he thought it wouldn't freak you out. I can see the love he has for you. It shines out of his entire face. It doesn't matter that you haven't known each other for a long time. Once you know you know. The time doesn't make it any less real." She considers a moment, "Yes, I'd give it until the holiday at the latest, and he will propose. Don't let it take you off guard, it's just how he works. He comes from a long line of romantics."

I let this sink in. In my heart I know she is right. I suppose I was thinking about our future kids already, a very uncharacteristic thought for me. Is Roman really so accepting of me and all of my flaws? I come with a lot of emotional baggage, too. Marriage would be a logical step but am I ready? It's a scary thought.

Chapter 25

Paint A New World

ARIA

The comfortable noise of Burton's washes over me as I sit across the table from my favorite person. It's been a good day all around. I am thankful that Roman's work is going as well as my own ventures. I mention my quest with Gran to find her painting supplies and how she is considering painting again.

"Really, she wants to paint?" Roman asks. "She hasn't painted since my dad died."

"I know." He looks up at me. "She told me. She said she was really angry then and it scared her. I think painting may help her get through the days and give her purpose. She won't say as much but I know she is in pain sometimes. I think this will help distract her and give her something else to focus on. We'll do it together."

He considers, "I suppose that makes sense. She never explained why she stopped. She's painted off and on my whole life and longer I imagine. I sensed that something changed about it but understand why. There are so many things about Gran that are perplexing." He looks over at me with considering eyes, "You seem to understand her."

"Yes, I suppose I do. We see the world through a similar lens if that makes sense. Like painting, for example, I get how it became too much. I didn't write much when I left home for the same reason. The thing that gave me comfort became the manifestation for all of my hurt and pain. It took time to process. I was lucky I had Leana reminding me of my strength, especially when it came to my writing. Eventually, I could circle back around and let it help me heal." I pause remembering that hard time in my life. I look back at Roman's furled eyebrow and know he is trying to understand. "I'm excited that she wants to go back to painting now. She is so strong."

"Yes. She is." Roman agrees. "I don't always understand her methods but she has proven to always come back firing on all cylinders."

"I'll drink to that." I say as I raise my glass of wine. Roman smiles as he lifts his to mine. "She loves painting. I can see it in her eyes. We talked about passions and what helps us through those hard times. At least she isn't ziplining in the Amazons this time."

He laughs. "Yes, that is true. For now at least. This will be enjoyable for both of you. Do you think any of those bad feelings will come up for her again? Did they for you?"

I pause to think about that honestly, "I don't think so. Those kinds of feelings tend to come up when we least expect them. I think it will be a rewarding experience. If not, we'll chalk it up to a bad idea and move on to the next bad idea. Maybe eventually one of them will surprise us."

"You amaze me."

"How?"

"You aren't afraid to try something even if it may go wrong. You still try."

I shrug, "Calculated risks are a part of life. The question isn't whether it will fail but what if it works. What if it changes everything? I won't risk never knowing the answer. It's easier to try."

He looks at me considering. I leave myself open for a moment under the weight of his gaze. After a few moments I add, "And I'm stubborn. So that helps."

My bluntness makes him laugh, breaking the seriousness of the moment. He looks at me meeting my eyes like he is peering into my soul. Finally, he nods, "Okay, so painting. Do you need more things?"

"Yes. Mainly fresh paints. Everything else she has is in pristine condition."

"That also sounds like Gran. Do you paint?"

"Not really, but there's no time like the present to give it a shot. Gran explained some of the more unique tools she uses. I'm excited to try."

"Thank you for spending so much time with Gran. It means the world to me. You are good for each other."

"Yes, I think we are."

When I get to Gran's house the next day, I lug two big bags through the front door using the key Roman's Mom gave me last week.

"Is that you Aria?" I hear from the parlor.

"Yeah, it's me."

"What did you bring, a herd of elephants to squeeze through the door?"

"Maybe. I brought a surprise." I call back.

I hear her laugh, "I love surprises."

I leave the paint supplies Roman and I bought last night in the den and greet Gran.

"I hope you like peanuts as much as the elephants do." I tease as I kiss her on both cheeks, our customary greeting.

"Oh my stars." She puts down a pair of knitting needles and leans back with a smile.

"I have a couple things to set up. Finish your tea and we'll see if it is a good surprise."

She looks at me with a little twinkle in her eyes. I

challenge her with a surprise that she may or may not like. She nods approvingly, accepting my challenge.

"Trudy left some muffins if you want one," Gran points.

"Thanks," I take one as I leave the room.

"Thank you." I hear Gran say softly.

I turn in the doorway to look at her sip her tea. "You don't even know if you like it yet."

"No, I may hate it. Don't worry, I'll let you know." She winks. That piece of truth makes me chuckle. "Thank you for going out of your way for an old lady."

"What old lady? I don't see any. I'm glad to do it for you." Gran smiles at me.

"Now, engage suspense build up. I'm going to set it up." I flee the room in a dramatic fashion leaving laughter in my wake.

I gather the paint supplies we found yesterday and add the fresh paint and new canvases that Roman and I bought. I have a vision of this dormant passion healing her and bringing her balance and her soul joy. I'm looking forward to that feeling myself. I hope it works. The supplies will not go to waste in any case. With all the paint supplies in a pile I'm excited to realize we could create our own little studio. I was hoping it would work out that way. I set to work placing everything so it's easy to get to and we each have our own space to create next to each other.

"Gran," I call as I walk into the kitchen. "Would you like some more tea?"

"Tea? Darling, I'm ready for this surprise."

I laugh. Gran is much like myself, always ready to get right to the point. "Okay, come on in. It's ready."

"Finally." I hear her get up, "I've never had so much trouble focusing on my knitting before. I lost count three different times. I even had to redo an entire row after my needle slipped."

Gran walks slowly around the corner leaning on her cane. She gasps as she sees my makeshift art studio. I set up two easels with canvases at the ready on a table in the den overlooking the windows into the backyard. The paints are all lined up with palates ready for mixing and brushes laid out by size.

I watch the expressions pass over Gran's face. Surprise, hesitation, pain, questioning, interest, and finally her lips spread into a big smile. It takes her several minutes before she can speak. I give her the time, I would have wanted it.

She looks up at me with a glisten to her eyes. "This is a beautiful surprise."

"I'm glad you like it. Roman wasn't so sure."

She chuckles to herself, "That boy, always worrying about what other people will think."

I laugh coming to realize that statement is all too true. "I couldn't wait to get started so we got what we needed right away. I want you to have the experience of painting again and I would like to give it a try. Maybe even try to paint that scene like you were talking about. We can take this journey together and ride the waves with our brushes in hand."

"I would love nothing more, my dear."

I move forward to take her elbow as she made her way to the table. She has most of her mobility back after being in the hospital. It felt good holding onto her, connected somehow to this wild woman who opened up my world.

It makes me realize that my leap began with Roman but it is very quickly becoming so much more. This family feels like a lifeline, a connection that I've never really had before. I want to spend time with Roman's family, not something I would even ask from my own. It is amazing how one chance encounter and an act of faith can change everything.

Gran, seemingly as lost in thought as myself, reaches out for a paintbrush. She studies it for a minute. I can't help but notice the moisture in her eyes. I can only imagine what she is remembering in this moment. I will have to ask her sometime but for now the moment is hers.

I begin gathering colors, "Gran, what color palette would you like to use today?"

"I'm thinking some dark reds, deep purples, yellow and light blue." I set the colors she asks for on her palate with the basic white and black next to her easel.

"You know what else sounds just perfect right now?" Gran asks with a devilish grin.

"What's that?"

"A glass of chilled wine, something sweet."

"A perfect request." I go to the wine cooler and pick a bottle of sweet Riesling and pour two glasses. I hand Gran her glass and then sit down with my own raising it out to her. "To painting, creativity and family."

"To life and love," she adds. We clink our glasses and sip the delicious sweet wine. It's a perfect start to an afternoon of creating art.

Gran reaches out for me, taking my hand in hers. "Thank you, Aria. You have breezed into this family like a breath of fresh air. You are not afraid to try things and don't mind pushing people a little when they need it most. Roman has never been happier. I have felt lighter and stronger since you started taking care of me."

"I don't take care of you. You do that yourself," I reply. "I take care of the laundry and the tea."

She laughs, "Yes, but you take care of me, too. Roman is very lucky to have you, a beautiful, smart, strong, independent, creative woman in his life, and so am I."

I am overcome by her proclamation. I don't know how

to respond. I squeeze her hand then wrap her into a hug. "Thank you," I manage but somehow it doesn't feel like enough.

"Thank you, Darling. Now," she pulls back with a smile, "let's paint."

Painting with Gran increased my inspiration and my drive to write. I went home and got comfy in the second bedroom Roman turned into an office. I open up my laptop and start typing.

Roman startles me when gets home. I hear him come up the stairs and peek his head into the office. "Hey honey, what are you doing home so early?" I ask him, barely looking up from my computer screen.

"Early, Aria, it's after six. I thought I was getting home late."

"Oh, it's really that late?" I'd been working for over two hours. I shake my head letting the thought rattle around a little.

Roman walks over and kisses my forehead, "It's great to see you writing."

I finish the sentence I am on and respond. "I painted with Gran today and now the words are sort of falling out of me."

I turn to Roman and kiss him enthusiastically on the lips leaning my body flush with his. He responds instantly, wrapping his arms around me and pulling me closer to him. I love the feeling of his warm, strong body, I will never get tired of this.

"So I take it the painting idea went well." He asks.

"Even better than I imagined. She seemed really lost in thought a lot but she was smiling. I figure it was a success."

"Do I get to see what you painted?"

"Yes. I left it there to dry. You can see it when we go over there for dinner tomorrow night."

"I can't wait. How is your writing coming?"

"Wonderfully, I'm getting so close to finishing the first draft. I still have to figure out how to end the story. I can't decide whether to put in feelers for a sequel or tie everything up and let it stand on its own."

"Do you think the characters have more to tell?"

"I think so. I'll know in another 10,000 words or so. I have this instinct that it will come to me when the time is right. I'm trying not to focus on the future so much. I want to enjoy right now because life is pretty awesome these days."

"Is that so?"

"Absolutely." I start kissing his neck and move up to behind his ear. I feel him shiver and let it wash through me. He turns and wraps his arms around my back and deepens our kiss. As we lean into each other and laugh and kiss, I think that life doesn't get much better than this. There is no other place I would rather be right now. Roman picks me up and I support my weight on his hips as he carries me into the bedroom.

"Wait, what about dinner?" I ask laughing as he kisses my neck hungrily.

"Later, I have more interesting things on my mind right now than food."

"Hmm," I murmur into his ear and give in completely to his embrace and seductive kisses.

Chapter 26

Bad News

ARIA

I feel the sweat beam beneath my Riverdogs baseball cap as I nudge my way through the crowded grocery store. I'm trying to remember what is on the list I forgot on the kitchen counter before I head to the checkout.

I'm not sure why I am so distracted today. Maybe it's the heat or the unusual amount of people at the store on a weekday. I mean really, don't people work? I look around at the young women with baby strollers and the older ladies in sunhats and realize, probably not. I mean, I'm here, so I shouldn't judge others.

I seek out peaches to make a peach cobbler. Gertrude gave me the recipe after Roman said it was his summer favorite. I'm not sure how it will come out but I've enjoyed trying to make new things.

Thinking of Roman, I find myself distracted again. I hope he is home in time to eat it. After a couple blissful weeks together, work began to take more and more of his time. He has been so busy in the office the past week that he comes home and practically falls asleep while he eats a late dinner at the kitchen counter.

I decide I have everything I can remember on my list and head towards the checkout. While waiting in line, I realize I am worried at how stressed Roman has been. Gran has assured me it is a phase that has happened before and will happen again. I hold on to her promise that it will pass.

I appreciate how close we are. I've started writing down her stories and we often paint together. She is showing me how to mix colors and work with shapes and textures. I'm learning a lot.

Athena laughed about it when I mentioned his distance to her after family dinner last Sunday and said, "He's moodier than a thirteen year old girl. Haven't you realized that by now?"

That made me laugh but I've yet to see him so distracted or stressed. It is more complex than I thought getting used to someone else's schedule. I know he needs to work but being alone is harder now that I've experienced what it's like to have someone come home at night. It's only been a month but this does feel like home.

Roman says it is the project that they are working on and life will go back to normal after they close their sale on Friday. He apologized for being so distracted but I do understand. Still, I don't know what to do with myself during this change.

Three days feels like an eternity away. I suppose I can be thankful for the extra time to work on my novel. I also see Gran almost every weekday which is always a joy. His family has accepted me as one of their own.

I enjoy seeing Gertrude on Wednesdays since she gets off work early and gets home before I leave. I love their closeness. We all get together on Sunday afternoons to spend time together and eat dinner. I could never imagine that with my family.

As my thoughts keep cycling, I am glad to finally be out of the stuffy store. As I walk to my car, compliments of Seth's cousin Mack, I think about how much I miss having some friends to hang out with. I enjoy sitting around talking about nothing over a glass of wine or a beer. Even though I never felt Las Vegas was home, I did have that with Mikey or the theater crew. Roman and I often do but not lately since work has him running ragged.

I suppose I need to find some of those friends here. Even though it feels like home, there are still times when I feel lonely. What I really need is my lifelong best friend. Just as I think of Leana, my cell phone rings. I toss the last of the groceries in the trunk as I answer.

"Speak of the Devil and she calls." I hop in the car and start the air conditioner.

"You're saying good things I hope."

"Actually, I'm not saying anything. I was just thinking about you," I confess. "I miss you."

"Oh sweetie, I miss you, too. I wish this call was social but I'm afraid I have some bad news."

"What happened? Are you okay?" I inquire.

"I'm fine. Aria, it's your mom."

I almost dropped the phone in my lap. I lean my head on the steering wheel feeling my head begin to ache.

"Aria, are you there?" Leana asks.

"I'm here. What about my mom?"

"She's in the hospital. Some guy beat the living shit out of her and dumped her in an alley."

"That sounds like my mom." I reply thinking of her long list of bad choices in men.

"I know, Aria." Leana says sounding sympathetic. "The hospital wanted to call you but I asked if I could give you a heads up first."

"Why did they contact you?" I wonder.

"Well, technically they contacted my parent's house."

"Really?" I ask surprised.

"Yeah, it was the only number she had as an emergency contact in her phone. Mom forwarded the message to me. I guess she doesn't really have many people around her."

"No, she never did. Including me." I resign.

"Aria." Leana says in comfort. She knows exactly how it was because she was there with me every step of the way.

"Not your fault. How bad is she?" I say to relieve myself of the growing gloom that arises when I think of my mother.

"Pretty bad. She has a broken arm and nose, massive bruising along her face and chest, and a concussion." Leana lists off.

"All in all, that doesn't sound so bad. Why the panic? She'll heal and go back to the next asshole of a guy that gets his kicks from beating her up. You know this won't change her."

"I know, but Aria, there's more." Leana says with a sigh.

"There always is." I wonder what it could be this time.

"She has Syphilis."

"Syphilis?" I ask. "The STD? Can't that be cured with a dose of antibiotics? Good as new?"

"Well it could if they caught it early on. Unfortunately, they said this is at the tertiary stage. It's been latent for some time and now it's starting to shut down her body. There's enough damage they fear her days are numbered."

"Damn." I pause to absorb this. "Figures, my mother always wanted to be considered special."

"She wants you to come home." Leana says quietly.

"She wants me to come home? How many meds do they have her on? She's never wanted me."

"Well, quite a few actually but that's not the point."

"How is that fair? I'm finally making a life for myself. She gets herself fucked up and wants me to come take care of her? Where was she when I needed taking care of? It was your mom that took me to the emergency room when I broke my wrist roller blading, helped me fight fevers, and sat with me the week I had chicken pox. If your mom ever gets sick, I'll be there in a flash. My mother never even knew where I was or if I was safe. She never cared. Why would I go see her now?" I all but yell into the phone. I can not stop my blood pressure rising. I know it is all an irrational response and I don't care.

"She's dying, Aria. If you don't see her now, you may never see her again." Leana whispers.

"It couldn't have happened to a better person." I spit out.

"Aria." Leana says sternly.

"I mean it." I reply feeling seventeen and mad at the world all over again.

After a pregnant pause, Leana continues. "Look, I get it. I know you mother was an absentee parent. I was there, remember? Still, she is your mom. I knew this was going to be a hard conversation and I don't really expect you to come. I wanted you to know what was going on and save whatever nurse happened to call you from a bad day." She pauses. I stay quiet enjoying my brooding. "Think about it, okay? I don't want you to realize one day that you should have seen her to say goodbye. Maybe you could even make peace."

I sigh heavily. I realize once again how good of a friend Leana really is. She is better than I deserve. "Thanks, Leana. I know you are just looking out for me. I just," I pause looking for words, "I can't. I have to let this sink in. Can I call you back tomorrow and we can talk some more?"

"Yeah, that's fine. Hey, whatever you decide, know that I have your back girlie, always."

"Thanks. I really appreciate that."

"Alright, bye now. Go kiss that Southern hunk of yours."

I smile thinking of Roman working late. "I will. Thanks

for letting me know. It is better to hear it from you. You saved that poor nurse from having a bad day."

"That's what I was hoping. Don't kill the messenger, okay." Leana reminded me. "I love you, girl."

"Love you, too."

I hang up and feel tears well up behind my eyes. The last thing I want to do is cry for my mother. I sit with the car running and my head resting on the steering wheel. A knock at my window startles me. I roll the window down to reveal an older lady with a large blue hat matching her suitcase sized handbag.

She asks quietly, "Are you okay dear?"

I try to smile, "Yes, I just got some bad news."

She nods knowingly, "I'm sorry. Can I call someone for you?"

"No. Thank you." I reply sweetly. Most of the time I enjoy Southern hospitality but right now I want to be alone.

The lady nods politely and leave me alone. I put the car in gear and head home before any other well doers try to help.

Even with the air conditioner on full blast, I can feel the oppressing heat from the sun blazing through the windshield. It looks like a beautiful day, but it feels endless. All I can think is I wonder if this is punishment for moving back east and being happy?

Once I'm home, I put the groceries up and begin to make pork tenderloin like Gertrude taught me. It is supposed to be a surprise for Roman. I put on the apron his mom got me and play some relaxing music.

The last few times I've cooked new recipes like this I have danced around the kitchen filled with love. Today I feel like a robot working through an assembly line. The food has no flavor and there's no joy in my actions.

As I clamor around the kitchen following his mother's directions, I hear my phone buzz with a message.

Good evening, beautiful. I'm leaving now to head home. Sorry it's a little late. I'm so thankful we are almost done with this thing. It should be ready earlier than expected.

I smile, at least I try to. I appreciate that he lets me know these things. What he does matters and he's been sweet, though tired, during the entire ordeal. I understand what it's like to be overworked and feel drained by a deadline.

Only today do I wonder if that's really what he is doing. Then I chastise myself for that thought. That is my mother in my head not me. It is my choice to trust him and I do. I wouldn't have moved across the country if I thought he was a man like that.

I reply. *Sounds great! See you soon.*

If he is just leaving that gives me at least twenty minutes to finish up. The pork and potatoes will be almost done. It is all going according to plan. Robot me finds this satisfying. Now if I could just make my doubts go numb like my mind.

I pour two glasses of wine in time for Roman to breeze through the doorway.

"Sorry, I'm late getting home. It's been crazy at the office lately," he says as he has for the past week. He comes straight to me for a kiss before he even puts down his bags. I can feel his desire to be home and it warms me for a moment.

"I'm glad you're home," I reply as he settles in. With him home, everything feels okay. I hand him a glass of wine which he gladly accepts with another kiss.

"Do I smell something coming from the kitchen?" he asks eyes perking up.

"Perhaps."

"It smells good. Are you sure you cooked it?"

I smack him lightly in the stomach, "Yes, I cooked it."

"I can't wait," he says. "I'm going to go get washed up and I'll help you finish up."

"Thanks, Love," with another kiss he leaves the room and I let my smile fall. While he was in the room I felt love and joy. As soon as he left all the emotion and confusion came back. As if I didn't dislike my mother enough, now she is apparently dying and I can't even enjoy a night with my overworked boyfriend without feeling lousy.

I know I need to tell him what I learned today. I doubt he will take long to realize something is on my mind. I'm not exactly great at hiding such things. I don't know how to breach the subject of my mom. She so frustrating to talk about. I don't even know what I think about the whole situation yet. The bitterness is creeping in, a curse upon me like my mom and grandmother. It scares me. Suddenly, I'm not far enough away from my mother. The need to run hits me like an itch I can't scratch.

My mind has quietly become a dark place today. First feeling lonely and now angry. I'm thankful when Roman comes back into the room. I feel him before I see him as my back is to the door placing dishes on the table. Roman's arms wrap around me hugging me close from behind and I feel safe. He is a light piercing my darkness. I hold onto him enjoying his radiant warmth. I am thankful he is here with me.

"I can't believe you cooked, again. You're really getting good. We might not have to live on frozen pizza after all."

"If we're lucky and as long as your mom keeps teaching me these new delicious recipes."

"She has a bunch of them. I don't mind being a guinea pig for food."

"That's a good thing because I'm still learning." I kiss him as he reaches to help me plate the pork. "She walked me through everything so I could make it special for us."

"Special? Uh oh. Did I forget something important?"

I laugh at the look on his face. "No." I reassure him. "You've been working so hard. I am feeling like I'm finally getting into a routine here and finding my place in it all. I wanted to make a special night for us to celebrate our first month together."

"It's been the best month ever."

"I agree." I smile.

"I'm sorry I've had to work so much. It's only like this a couple times of year. We launch our programs once in the fall and once in the spring, generally."

"Roman, I understand. You have a commitment to your work. You don't need to apologize for that."

"I don't want you to think--"

I cut him off by putting my finger to his lips, "I don't think anything. You work hard and I'm proud of you."

"How did I get so lucky to find you?"

He feels lucky? How can it be lucky to find someone with so much baggage and a mother that can't even take care of herself? I'm the lucky one to find someone who works so hard and is so generous and loving.

I suddenly feel like I don't deserve to be here in his house or in his arms. I have too much bitterness in me. I don't know what to do about that or about my mom. How do I explain any of this to him? I don't even understand myself.

Roman must have noticed my hesitation because he leans back with a crook in his eyebrow. "What is going on in that beautiful brain of yours?"

I look at him and then look away. He reaches for my chin to lock eyes with me. "What's wrong?"

I take a deep breath and tell him the truth, "Leana called me today with bad news."

"What happened?" He asks concerned.

"It's my mother. She got beaten within an inch of her life and is in the hospital. While there they also found out she has a late stage of syphilis."

"What? Aria, I'm so sorry."

"I'm not. She probably deserved it." I notice the confused look from Roman but chose to ignore it. "I was just thinking you might not be so lucky after all. I mean look what I come from."

"Aria, where you came from only has the impact on you that you let it. You are not your mom. What does a late stage of syphilis mean? Isn't that an STD?"

"Yeah, it is. There's another name for the stage but I don't remember it. Apparently, she's had it for a long time but never had it treated. Now it's starting to affect her organs."

"That sounds serious."

"It is. The diagnosis isn't good."

"Wow, that's a lot. Are you going to go see her?"

"What?" I exclaim, "No. Why should I?"

"I hear your mom is not a pleasant person but don't you want to see her?" He takes a deep breath, "What if she dies?"

I think of my response to Leana and want to repeat those words but something holds me back. Roman doesn't understand my mom like Leana and I do. I try to explain. "She didn't want me. She practically forced me to leave town and not be a part of her life anymore. All of a sudden she wants me to come home? It's not fair."

"No, it's not. But Aria, she's your mom. Don't you

want to try to make peace? At least to say goodbye."

"Not really." I try to smile. "I'm not sure if that is even possible."

Roman studies my face. I can see him making the decision to fight or to make peace, "Aria, if you want to go see your mom, do it. In my mind family trumps everything else. Don't worry about the cost or time away. I want you to know that."

"Okay, but I don't really think I --"

He cuts me off, not harshly, peacefully, "Think about it. Please? You don't get a second chance after death. It's final."

I look up at him and can see that he doesn't really understand my decision. Still, it is mine to make. I can also see that he is thinking of his dad and that he never got the chance to say goodbye. What does this have to be so hard?

I wish I could have met his dad. Why couldn't my mom be the one hit by a car? Then again, my mom would never be riding a bike. That's only one of many differences between the two. Still, it would have been a lot easier all around. The benefit of visiting a corpse is that they can't yell at you about how you ruined their life.

Even my thoughts are making me feel guilty. This is a vicious cycle I can't win.

Roman has no doubt in his mind that his father loved him. Whereas I have no doubt in my mind that my mother didn't. My mom ruins everything. I finally had something good going here. I was happy. Now I watch as it all crumbles around me.

I already feel myself pulling away waiting for it all to crash down. It's inevitable that Roman will ask me to leave. I thought it could be different this time. I don't see how Roman could love me after he realizes where I come from. The overwhelming need to run fills me. My feet itch with it.

"Let's eat this amazing smelling meal and enjoy the evening." Roman lifts his hand to my cheek. I didn't realize my cheeks were wet until he wipes tears away. "Take some time to process. We can talk about it more tomorrow."

"Okay. Thank you, Roman"

"I love you, Aria. I'm here for you." He says. I can feel that he means it. How did I get so lucky? Even though he doesn't agree with my defiance, he is still here with me. He's not yelling or demanding his way. He is better than I deserve.

I need his love and strength too much to run away. Yet, I am pulled by the urge to leave and protect him. For now we sit and eat pork and potatoes. We'll deal with the rest tomorrow. I look up at him and once again am so thankful I found him.

"I love you, too."

Chapter 27

What If I Was Nothing

ARIA

I toss and turn all night. I can't get my mother off of my mind. I don't want to go back but there is something inside gnawing at me. Not even a bottle of wine or Roman's loving words could make it go away.

I wake in the middle of the night leaving my warm bed where Roman still sleeps soundly. Though it is dark, I walk downstairs and into the kitchen by memory. The quiet of the night unsettles me. A street light illuminates the window allowing me to see the small access road. I sit in the bay window witnessing the nocturnal wildlife. The bugs hum as they congregate by the light. An owl perches in a nearby tree watchful and waiting.

That's what I feel like now, watching and waiting, but for what? I don't want to see my mom. I have no desire to go back to my hometown. Why am I so restless? What am I waiting for?

Roman seems so sure that I should go. Even Leana encourages me to come. What do they think will happen? Nothing new, that I can tell you. My mother will be mean and spiteful like she always is. Does it matter that she's dying?

Perhaps it does.

Part of me feels relieved that this may be the end for her. Does that make me a horrible human being? Guilt settles on my harsh reaction. It reminds me too much of my mother. I don't want to be like her. I want to be honest and loving. I am trying so hard but it doesn't feel like enough. I can feel her bitterness inside me and it makes me so mad.

I look back at the owl, still watching and waiting in the cover of night. If only I had some of his wisdom. I don't know what to do or why I feel so torn with emotion. The itch to run away crawls along my skin. I've done it before. It didn't solve anything but it felt good for a while.

The problem is that I feel good here with Roman. I want to be here with him and be good for him. I can't run away now because he is too important. My quarrel is not with him. It's with my mother in a town too close to ignore. Running from this place wouldn't help at all. It doesn't even make sense.

So I stay. I watch the owl watching. I fixate on him memorizing his feathers and the way his eyes shift without his head ever moving. I'm amazed how long he stays in one place. As I sit quietly near the window sill, I notice my breath deepening almost like a trance. I listen to the wind lightly caressing the leaves and enjoy the warm evening.

This place offers peace in a way I've never experienced before. I love the openness and slow comfort the people here have here. It's much different from the tourist mania at Myrtle Beach or Las Vegas. I never realized how similar my childhood home and my escape location are to each other. They are both busy, loud and cater to people who don't live there.

I lost the close proximity to my mother when I fled across the country but I wonder if that tie to her ever ceased. The move also made me sacrifice the ocean which is the one constant that always made me feel good.

I'm thankful to this new haven, a place that is peaceful and full of love. Roman and his family have been so gracious and accepting. They have opened their arms to me in a way that I could never have dreamed.

I've never really felt like I belonged anywhere not even my own childhood home. Perhaps that is why I was so ready to come here and am now so hesitant to leave it. This understanding of home is new. This is a place I feel safe and loved, an unfamiliar yet desired place.

I keep trying to figure out what good it will do to go see my mother. I come up empty. It will be peaceful when she dies. Yet I can't ignore this pang of guilt reminding me that I am not strong enough to face her. She makes me feel weak, worthless and incompetent. If she is dying those projections get worse not better.

I look back into the house from my seat at the window. The kitchen is clean with both of our mugs ready to be filled with coffee when the sun calls for a new day. I put out picture frames with us, friends and family as well as some art and pillows to add my own personality to the place. The few things I brought with me are predominantly placed to give me the reassurance that this is my place, too. I have one more month where I could go back to Las Vegas but I know that I won't. Now, I have a home. Roman peeled back his own space to allow me a place to live and call my own. That in itself tells me how much he loves and respects me.

Somewhere deep inside I know I should go see my mom. I haven't been home in so long. Leana will be there to support me. Mom is stuck in a hospital so she can't follow me to tirade me about her poor life choices. Just thinking of listening to my mother's intense negative attitude makes me depressed.

I can't go back. My life is here now. I don't want to get swept away again. Roman's words, "family trumps everything" comes back into my head. I'm so torn. I sit by the window ledge contemplating life as the sun peaks over the horizon. I didn't hear Roman get up.

"Aria, are you okay?" He asks with squinted eyes as he comes into the kitchen.

He wears a pair of shorts without a shirt leaving his chest bare. I smile at him with bare feet and bed messed hair. I stand and wrap my arms around his broad shoulders, "I'm okay. I have a lot on my mind."

"Do you want to talk about it?" He asks rubbing my arms.

I see the genuine concern in his eyes and I wish there was something that he could do or say that would take this pain away. There isn't much to do. I must bear it.

I let him console me. I take all of him as he offers himself to me while we shower. I feel the love and passion he has and I absorb all of it. As we ready for the day, filling coffee mugs, gathers bags and kissing goodbye, I know that this day will bring some sort of revelation. I can feel the winds begin to whirl in my heart. I wish I could prepare for it.

As I drive over to visit Gran, I call Leana. I need a friend. Someone who has known me forever and understands the situation I'm in. I need the hard love from someone who has experienced the "love" from my mother first hand. I want someone to tell me I don't have to do this. I want to be selfish and happy.

"Hi girl. How are you doing?" Leana answers the phone.

"Not so great. I couldn't sleep last night," I reply.

"I'm sorry." I appreciate Leana's compassion.

"Is there any change?"

"Well, I changed the color of my kitchen wall from blue

to purple last week. I'm still getting used to it."

I laugh, despite myself. Leana always knows how to diffuse my focus. "I bet that would take some getting used to. It seems exciting and very you."

"Oh it is. I like it a lot."

"About the other thing?"

"No change. She's still going in and out of consciousness. She's still a bitch. The doctor says there is only so much they can do until the narcotics completely leave her system.

"I visited her yesterday and she asked if I'd called you. I told her yes and she said 'She's not coming, huh?' I said no, probably not. She said, 'That selfish twat. Who does she think she is moving across the country.'"

"Wait, she doesn't know I moved back?"

"I didn't tell her."

I consider this, "Believe me if I could have gotten any further I would have. I kind of want to run away again."

"I don't blame you but don't do it. You have too much going for you. There are people who love you that are a lot better than your mother. Me for instance and that hunky southern man of yours. Where's your head?"

"There with you, where I know I should be." I answer hesitantly.

"But."

"But, my heart is here. Leana, what if I can't handle it?"

"I'll be here. You know Roman has your back. You are not going into the lion's den, Aria. You are just coming home."

"Feels like the same thing."

"Yeah, I can see that. Look, you know I have your back. I'll be here to check on your mother."

"Thanks, Leana. Do you really think this might be it for her?"

"She looks pretty bad. I think her body would physically heal if it weren't for the tertiary syphilis diagnosis. The doctors fear that will cause her heart to fail. I don't think she has the will to live. Not like you do. You are not your mother, Aria. Remember that. Coming home to see her doesn't mean you will turn into her. You are stronger than that and you have people who love you."

I take a deep breath. I knew this would be a heavy conversation. I don't think I will ever be ready for it. Being in the middle of it is even harder than I thought it would be.

I turn into Gran's driveway and pause. I feel stuck between two worlds. After a few moments of silence Leana asks, "You okay over there?"

"Yeah, I suppose. Hey Leana, I need to let you go. Keep me updated, okay."

"I will. I'm in your court, always remember that." Leana emphasizes, "I love you, girl."

"Thanks, I love you, too."

I take a few more moments before I get out of the car. Gran and I are supposed to paint today. I always look forward to that time with her. Now, more than ever, I can't wait to get lost in my art.

When I reach Gran's house, I knock on the door twice before using my own key to open the door.

Gran calls from the den, "Why do you still knock, my dear? I know you are coming and I look forward to your arrival."

I laugh as I come in and lay down my things. "To let you know I'm here in case you are in the living room in nothing but your underwear."

"Oh, well when you put it that way it makes perfect

sense. I should really try that sometime."

"I like doing yoga in my underwear, so you might get a peak if you didn't knock on my door first."

"All the better reason to walkright on in." Gran retorts with a wink.

I laugh, amazed at the ease in which we communicate and tease each other. I've never had this sort of relationship outside of Leana. Gran is the mentor I wish I had growing up. I'm glad that I have her now.

"Do you still want to paint today?" I ask her as I kiss her on each cheek. It feels natural, a family tradition that I picked up much quicker and easier than I expected I would find comfortable.

"Absolutely, I found a picture I took of a bird on my last trip I wanted to use as a focus point."

"That sounds perfect."

"It feels right at least. What are you going to paint."

"I don't know yet. We will see."

Gran made tea while I set up the paint supplies on the kitchen table overlooking the window to the yard outside. I love this setup. I'm so glad Gran and I can paint together. It makes me feel alive to be in this place and feel love from those around me. The family support brings me to life and makes this place feel like home in a way nowhere else ever has.

We work in silence for a while while classical music plays in the background. I sip the last of my tea as I view Gran's woodpecker. "That is a gorgeous picture, Gran. It's coming out really great in your painting. I love your colors. It's great contrast."

"Thanks, my dear. I noticed your colors are dark today."

I look at my picture and see the deep reds and purples. My outlines are heavy and dark. It is a picture of the sunrise through a storm.

"I suppose it is," I respond. The scene matches how I feel. It doesn't surprise me that Gran picks up on that. I like my work. I predict that Gran's comment is going to bring up what I have been avoiding all morning.

"What's going on?" Gran asks as she turns back to her own painting though still focused on me.

I sigh. What is it with everybody picking up on my moods so easily. "Leana called me yesterday to tell me my mom got beaten within an inch of her life and has been diagnosed with a late stage of syphilis."

"Wow. That must have been a hard phone call for Leana."

"Yeah, it was." I commend Gran on knowing just what to say. "She wanted to save the day of an innocent nurse. She's a great friend. She went and saw my mother for me. She says she doesn't look so good but mean as ever."

I can feel my face relax as I release the effort of trying to keep up a smile. I don't know why I felt the need to try to make the day feel normal in the first place. Of course, Gran would be able to tell. She quietly gets up and walks over to her teapot. After refilling our cups, she opens a cabinet and pulls out a bottle of Jameson whiskey.

"Gran," I exclaim. "You have whiskey for your tea?"

She laughs easily, "I'm old, dear, but I'm not dead. I still like a little kick in my tea once in a while. I say if life is giving you a kick, it's okay to have some motivation to fight back."

I shake my head amazed by this lady who still has such spirit after such a long life full of her own trials. She makes me want to be stronger. She raises the bottle with a little shake asking for permission. I nod, "Thanks, Gran."

I watch as she pours a generous helping into each cup and hands one to me. She sits next to me giving me her full attention. "Now for the big question if you're comfortable sharing. What exactly happened between you and your mother?"

Gran goes right for the kill shot same as I would. I answer her honestly, "My mother was selfish all of her life. I was an accident that seemed to get her attention at first. As I grew I became baggage that she had to figure out what to do with. I spent most of my younger years under my grandmother's care. She died when I was eleven and then I felt completely alone.

"Thankfully, I could at least take care of myself by then. My mother was never around and when she was she was usually drunk. She would often forget I was even there. I felt like an unwanted vacation souvenir that wouldn't go away.

"I knew my mom didn't want me but it hurt less when I didn't see her. I tried to become invisible. I spent all the extra time at school I could and stayed with Leana a lot. Still, I couldn't completely avoid her.

"One night during my senior year, I was at home reading a book at the kitchen counter eating a snack. I didn't expect my mother home that night because she usually worked a shift. I wasn't prepared for her to come home in a drunken rage with her good-for-nothing boyfriend. She came in screaming that this was her house and I needed to leave. The guy came in behind her reeking of alcohol and slapped me.

"I didn't know what to do. I ran out with my book still in hand and Doritos scattered across the counter. I never saw my mom again after that. I watched my mom get worse and worse over the years. It was the last straw for me. It was only two weeks until graduation but I couldn't stay in that house anymore."

"Where did you go?"

"To Leana's house. Her mom popped us popcorn so we

could stay up late watching movies. I believe we ate a pint of ice cream each that night."

"That's a traumatic experience for a young lady. No to mention a very bad role model."

"I don't think my mom and role model belong in the same sentence. Maybe not even on the same page.

"Leana helped me get my stuff out of the house while my mom was out and I never looked back. Leana's been the one person in the world who has always had my back. She was there for me when the one person in the world who should have loved me kicked me to the curb. I was devastated. I knew no one wanted me and that I was alone. Leana is the only one who stood by me through everything. She is the one person in this world who knows all of me."

"What about Roman?"

I look at Gran who had a curiosity in her eyes that made me pause. I can feel her understanding of what I am going through. "Don't worry," she smiles, "I'm your friend right now not his grandmother."

I continue. "I love Roman. He is the reason I am gaining confidence. I am honest with him but there are some experiences that I wish I didn't have. I don't want my past to taint what we have now. I'm not proud of who I was then. I was mean, mad and lonely.

"I ran to Las Vegas, the place where lonely people go, and hid behind characters as a screenwriter. All I wanted to do was hide and be left alone. I was trying to survive. I'm not sure I ever learned how to live.

"It was Roman's radiant smile and steady presence that woke me up. He promised me something more. He gave me someone to care about that would also care about me. Those first few days with him were such a whirlwind. I'd never felt emotions that strongly before, not positive ones at least. Leana was there, too. There was something about her fast approval combined with the passion I felt from him that connected us so quickly.

"When he asked me to come here with him, I knew I had to. I could feel that this was my chance for a new start. I didn't want to let that chance get away after finally finding it. I wanted those feelings with Roman to last and it has. It has been such a wonderful experience for me. I should thank you, too. You were a big part of that."

"You have made quite an impression on me, too." Gran pats my hand with hers. "Roman and Gertrude are so much more relaxed with you here. You helped me when I needed. More importantly, you are a calming presence for them. They tend to get really worked up over the silliest of things."

I laugh understanding her all too well on that one.

"Thank you for letting me in. It helps me know you better." I nod and she continues. "Do you let Roman in like that? You say you don't want to share your past, but my dear, that is how we connect with people. We can be truly in the present when those closest to us know what it took for us to get here and love us anyway."

I think about what she said. It sort of makes sense. At the same time, I am nervous about letting someone so close to me. It's hard to show those vulnerabilities you've spent your entire life trying to cover up. "That's scary," I confess.

"Yes it is," she agrees. "So now, what are you going to do about your mother?"

My body stills but my heart rate increases. "I don't know. I still don't want to go."

"But you feel like you should?" Gran urges.

"I can't shake it," I say shaking my head. "It's constantly on my mind."

"Then I believe you have your answer." Gran suggests

"I know but she doesn't deserve it. She was never there

for me. In fact, she is the sole reason I left. I got as far away from her as I could at the time. I'm not sure that was far enough. Maybe a trip to the moon next." I remember to breathe again at the end of my rant.

Gran grins at my overdramitisation. I start to laugh, unable to help myself.

Gran says, "My dear, your mother is not worth all the anguish."

"So you agree with me?"

"Yes, but that doesn't matter. Don't you want to go tell her exactly how you feel? To share what you wish she would have been capable of fulfilling as a mother."

"What do you mean?" I ask wondering where this is going.

"You have been spending your days with an old lady you barely even knew at first. You would do anything for me if it brought me even the tiniest bit of joy. I can sense that about you." Gran states.

"What does that have to do with my mom?" I ask confused.

"Everything. Don't you want to bring a little bit of joy to someone you've known all your life?"

"She won't appreciate it. Somehow it will all become my fault. It always does." I argue.

"I know." Gran agrees. This is getting really annoying.

"But?" I start for her.

"Is it?" She asks.

"No." I answer definitely.

"Of course it isn't. Does it matter?"

"No. Of course it doesn't. What does that mean?" I try to make her words make sense.

"It means that she won't appreciate it. She can't. But if you don't go and try then you will not forgive yourself. That, my dear, is far worse. Don't poison yourself for her sake. You once said that you didn't want to become bitter like her. Don't let her win now. Be better. Let her know you love her because you do." Gran states passionately.

I step back in defeat. Those words hit home. I hate her but I love her. She's my mom, even after all these years of indifference. It does matter.

"Win, not for her, but for yourself." Gran urges me.

"Gran?" I study her, "I can see the haunt in your eyes. Who?"

"My sister. She died unexpectedly while we are arguing. She had just a couple of days and I didn't come. I could have, but I wouldn't leave. I like to tell myself I didn't realize how bad she was." She shrugs. "The truth is I wish I had gone. She died and I never said goodbye. I can never say "I'm sorry" or "I love you." I can never fully get rid of the poison of that sting."

"I have to go." I resign.

"It will cause pain. I'm sorry for that. Life is full of pain but also of hope that there will be something better. Somewhere along the way you realize it's worth it. Not for them but for you. Go. Bear it. Then you can move past it. It is the only way."

Gran is so wise.

"I love you." The words just fall out of my mouth as I reach over to hug this woman who has grown to mean the world to me. She is like a mother, not my mother or grandmother, but like a mother should be. I appreciate her hard truths and her steadfast encouragement.

I think of Roman in this moment and know that I will not be able to face him. He has given me love and family. He has saved me in so many ways. Maybe I can save him from this pain.

"Aria, my dear, I love you, too. I wish I could bear it for you," she confesses.

"This pain is meant for me. Roman's right, family trumps everything. I have to believe it."

She nods. In that moment, I know we are in many ways the same. Her soul sees mine in a way that I can barely fathom. I will heed her advice and learn from her mistakes. I don't know how I will survive this trip but I know I have to.

Chapter 28

Walking Far From Home

ARIA

I know Roman isn't home. I pack a small bag. It is nothing. I want nothing to follow me to this barren place I head. I am nothing. I leave a note. It is pathetic really. "You're right," I write onto a pink sticky notepad, "family trumps everything. I love you. I'll be back in a few days." I leave it on the kitchen counter and turn toward the door feeling more sad than I have in years.

The last time I ran away I had anger fueling me. This time, I only have a begrudging duty to face what I have been running from for so many years. I suppose this time I'm not running away as much as towards. I wish it made me feel better or stronger somehow. Instead, I feel like a piece of glass ready to break at the slightest blow.

I can't face Roman, not this humble man who has warmed my heart and shown me what love means. I want to see him and tell him that I'm doing what he wants me to. I want to kiss him and lie in his bed. I want to forget the world and ignore the pain. But I can't. If I don't go now, I will not leave. I can't see his smile when I go. I wouldn't be able to tear myself away to face the bitterness that awaits me. I can't see his joy and bare the pain it brings me to leave him. Through cloudy eyes, I realize pain is where I have to go.

As I begin my journey, the wall slowly goes up. All the laughter and joy I've felt slowly sinks away from me. By the time I reach the forested back roads that lead to my childhood home, I am a shell. I am even more hollow than when Roman found me. Now, I know his warmth and joy. It has completely filled me. At least, it did. Now all I feel is lacking. I feel nothing.

I am nothing.

That is what my mother taught me.

As I drive into Myrtle Beach, the first thing I notice is that traffic only gets worse with time. Tourist season is in full bloom and there are lots of extra people in the city. There are always lots of people. One of the benefits of being local is knowing how to get around them. Well, as much as possible at least. Myrtle Beach is one of the biggest destination spots in South Carolina. I learned very early on how to get lost in a crowd.

It is amazing how much and how little changes all at the same time. I head towards Leana's apartment. I called her after I got on the road to let her know I was coming. I know I picked the best of best friends when her response was, "I'm proud of you. I'll have a bottle of wine ready when you get here." That made me smile. For once small moment I am glad for this trip because I get to see Leana. She always knows exactly what I need. If only I could leave my mother out of it.

I pull into Leana's apartment complex and park in front of her unit. I see her sitting on the porch reading a book with two wine glasses on the table and a bottle breathing in between them.

I get out the car and hear, "And you said you would

never come home again."

I dip my head, "It's a start anyway. I wouldn't be here if it weren't for a sweet old lady who is too smart for her own good."

"Well, I congratulate her."

"Of course you would." I shake my head as I walk toward the porch and my best friend.

"Yep. I think you deserve this now." She pours the wine and offers me the glass as I walk up to her. I ignore the glass and hug her. I needed her in that moment a lot more than the wine.

"I miss you girl," she says while we are embrace.

"I miss you, too." I agree and reach out for the wine she offers. "It's only been a little over a month and yet it feels like another lifetime."

"It's amazing how fast the world can change. I think we have to move right along with it." Leana clinks her glass to mine before we both take a big swig.

"That's easier said than done." I admit causing her to nod.

We sit quietly sipping on our wine for a few minutes and then curiosity gets the better of me. "So how is she anyway?"

Leana smiles big. I knew she was waiting for me to ask. "The same. I went by this morning and she cursed me out saying that I ran you away from her. I let her rant and eventually the nurse got tired of hearing her foul mouth and gave her some drugs to keep her quiet."

"I'm sure she's loving that. She gets to mouth off and then gets the happy pills. If the syphilis doesn't kill her, a drug overdose should do the trick."

"Or your sarcasm."

I glare at her, "My mother always brings out the best in me. Can't you tell."

"Oh honey, this is just another loud and annoying call for attention."

"It might be the final one." I let out a frustrated sigh taking a big gulp of wine. I try to relax a little in the company of my friend. "I'm sorry. I've been a mess ever since you told me the other day. I want to run far away and never look back."

"You've already tried that."

"True. It didn't really work out the way I thought it would. That is in part why I am here."

"I wish I could take this from you."

"Ha," I laugh, "I wish I could let you."

"I know how she gets under your skin. I understand but you are better than her. You have so much going for you right now. What does Roman say about you coming up here? Is he as proud of you as I am?"

I hesitate, "I didn't tell him I was coming."

"What?" she exclaims. "You just left?"

"I left a note."

"A note? What do you mean you left a note? I thought you loved this guy? Wouldn't he have your back?"

"Yes. He told me to come but I was being stubborn. His grandmother gave me a hell of an inspirational speech and then I just left. I couldn't face him. I wouldn't be able to leave if I saw him so I just got in the car and drove."

"You are a piece of work. You know that?" Leana asks looking me over.

"Yep. I know I am not good enough for him. I'm about to face why head on."

"You don't really believe that do you?" she asks concerned.

"Nothing has ever been good enough. One person doesn't just change that."

"Your mom really did a number on you."

"You know that better than most."

"Well, hopefully, I can help you more than most. You need it. Aria, you have to let me in. You have to give me a chance to help you. You have to give Roman that same chance. You can't keep pushing us away."

"I will try." I look at her and reach for her hand. She was always the one there for me when no one else was. I think of those same words that Roman said to me yesterday. It seems they must have a point because they are both saying the same thing. Maybe it is time I listen. "Thank you."

"Always. You should call Roman," she states matter of factly. I think about this amazing man who has already changed my life so much. I have such mixed emotions with my mom I don't even know what to say to him. Still, I look at my friend and know she is right, "I will."

"Good. Tonight we drink wine. Tomorrow we'll face your mother together."

"Sounds like a plan." Leana and I finish the bottle and debate about opening a second. However, Leana declares that this would be a special bottle for after we visited my mother tomorrow. I agreed that wouldn't be a bad idea. She picks her best bottle and sets it aside with a note of our future victory.

I still don't feel settled. My anxiety keeps switching between guilt of leaving Roman without saying anything and the overall frustration my mother causes me. Lucky for me, it is hard to feel too down in Leana's company. She always makes me laugh.

ROMAN

I know Aria is gone before I even get home. When I

pull into my parking spot and her car is missing, it is confirmed. It's only been a month but I am learning a great deal about this woman I have fallen for. The biggest thing is that she doesn't like conflict. If the choice comes down to fight or flight, it isn't even a choice. She will flee.

Also, Gran called earlier to warn me that she may have been too helpful with Aria's situation concerning her mother. I walk into the house which feels empty without a bubbly brunette having something witty to say about nothing.

I notice the note on the kitchen counter. A wave of emotions flow through me: pride, sadness, understanding and loneliness. Why won't she let me in? Why does she run when there are so many who want to help her?

I put down the note and open the fridge for a beer. I look over at her quirky cat clock hung on the wall and my heart hurts. All I can hope is that she comes back. I pray this situation with her mother doesn't cause her to run away from me. I want to believe that our love is stronger than this, but I don't know. We've only known each other for a very short time. Her mother has created a very vulnerable abandonment issue for her.

I don't want to go after her only to have her push me further away. However, I fear that when she goes and fights her battle, she will forget how good we are together and never come home. The thought makes me sad. I want it to sound silly, but fears have a funny way of not happening the way you expect.

It doesn't help that I'm running on empty these days. I feel my tendency to shut down pull so hard on me. It always does when there is a lot going on. I'm trying really hard not to do that now. It helps now that I realize I'm doing it.

I know this is hard for her, but ultimately, I am a selfish

man and I don't want her to go. The last few weeks with her here have been the best of my life. I want to help her through this. I wish I knew how.

I imagine Aria feels my stress with this big account looming. I can't get around having to work a little extra right now. I keep trying to encourage her and remind myself that is a temporary thing. Thankfully, we are closing a little early. It will be done first thing in the morning. I only have to make it until then. With Aria gone without a word and this sale impending, I feel more stressed than normal. I take a swig of beer and sit down on the patio. Hopefully, some fresh air will help clear my head and soothe my heart.

My mind turns to Aria. I miss her. I miss her energy, her smile and the way she makes everything better. I hope she is okay. I want to talk to her and make sure she is alright. I'm not sure if I should call or wait her out. They always say that if you love someone, you have to let them go. They just don't mention how hard that is to do.

I don't know how long I sat there staring out at the horizon when the phone rings. I have to resist jumping for it when I hear the sound startling me out of my daydream. I relax a little and smile big when I recognize Aria's number.

"Hello, beautiful" I answer.

"I'm sorry," she bursts out sounding close to tears.

"Aria, honey, are you okay?"

"Yes, no, I don't know. I'm sorry I left without telling you goodbye. I should have been stronger. I just panicked. I knew if I saw you I wouldn't be able to go and your grandmother just lit a fire under my ass and I had to leave." She rambles so fast I almost can't keep up.

"Aria, I told you to go. You need to see your mother. I do wish I could have said goodbye first. I could have given you a proper send off."

"You are too good to me."

"I don't think that is possible. I think you do need to be better to yourself."

"I miss you. I miss your strength."

"It's only here because you hold it up for me to see. Have you seen her yet?"

"No. Leana is taking me over in the morning."

"You can do it. You can face her," I insist. "You are stronger than you think."

"I don't deserve you." She says quietly and my heart breaks. If only she could understand how bright her inner light burns for any willing to look.

"That's not true. You are kind, creative, beautiful and the life that I want. Aria, I love you. Don't you ever forget that."

"I love you, too, Roman. Thank you for believing in me."

"Always," I tell her, meaning every word. I don't know what else to say.

"How was your day?" she asks.

I smile, she really is the most wonderful woman in the world. "Another rough one," I start and ramble on about work. It is a nice break in the tension from her being away. I hope the conversation gets her mind off her mother even for a few minutes.

When we get off the phone I feel more relaxed but still a little concerned about how this is going to play out. I miss her terribly. I want to be there with her to comfort her after she sees her mother. I bet I can make it. I wonder if she would want me there. I feel worried and confused. I wish I could wrap my arms around her now. Maybe then, it would all make sense.

Chapter 29

We Will Become Silhouettes

ARIA

The day starts bleak and it's not just my disposition. A storm brews over the ocean with dark, threatening clouds. It's going to be a little more than our normal Southern summer showers. The sky looks angry. I understand exactly how the sky feels as prepare to see my mother this morning.

As Leana drives up to the hospital all I can think is, I've seen enough of these for a while. Hospitals make me nervous. I can't help but think about death here and I haven't even known someone who died in a hospital. I think back to how Roman handled our trip to see Gran in the same hospital his dad died in. I am once again overcome with his strong spirit. Even though I didn't even know Gran yet, the hospital made me nervous for her.

This hospital makes me more nervous for myself. I try so hard to hold onto Roman's steadfast belief in me and will myself not to have a panic attack as I sit in the front seat waiting for Leana to park.

She looks over at me now. I can see the concern on her face. I notice my hands clenched into fists beside me and loosen them realizing only now that my nails are making deep marks on my skin.

"Are you sure this is a good idea?" I ask Leana, hating

how shaky my voice sounds.

"Well, it's an idea. It's time you face her, Aria. I've known you for a long time. Your mother only holds power over you because you let her. You give her too much power. It's time to take some of it back. This is a good first step."

She's right. I know she's right and yet the fear of an eleven year old girl unsure of how she is going to get to school in the morning overtakes me.

I take a deep breath and open the car door. Leana waits for me as I set my resolve to face the person who gave me life without any tools to actually live it. I feel resentment and anger creep in as I rise. Right on cue, the thunder booms signaling the storm is close. I am thankful for this. I use nature's power to propel me forward.

Leana takes my hand and squeezes it. I add her strength to my small kindling and slowly start to believe I am capable of this interaction. Still, it is only Leana's hand in mine that keeps me moving towards the building.

The influence of my friend has been a secure harbor for me over the years. It meant a lot that she would check in on my mother. I mean, I would do the same for her. The difference is that her mom, unlike mine, actually likes me. It would be a joy to care for her, not a burden. I think not for the first time in the last twenty-four hours, let alone twenty years, that I have one heck of a best friend. Even as she pulls me, unwillingly, to meet my maker.

The hospital is cold and sterile, void of any personality. We walk past the receptionist and the local coffee shop right to the elevators. Leana has a firm grip on my hand. I hope it's to give me courage, but possibly also to make sure I don't bolt for the doors. I can feel the tension in every part of my body as we watch the doors close on the huge elevator.

We walk down a pristine white hallway filled with

mobile machines, nurses always moving and a big row of doors. The room we stop at is only recognizable as my mother's by the label to the left of the door with her name on it. Leana gives me a look then squeezes my arm and opens the door.

The room is nondescript and smells like antiseptic mimicking the rest of the hospital. There are no flowers on the tables or anything personal in the room at all even though, according to Leana, she has been there for three days. The woman on the bed is swallowed by the nightgown they have placed her in. Her face is drawn. Her eyes are closed with sleep and her mouth is shaped into a sneer.

My mother was once a pretty lady. She may not have won the Miss America pageant but more because she was too busy getting high in the bathroom than parading around on stage. Still, this woman before me is shrivelled and almost void of life. It surprises me to realize I feel sorry for her. All this time I've hated her because she goes out of her way to strike at me anyway she can. I wonder now if she was really taking hits at herself.

I lean into Leana afraid to speak. I don't want to wake her. In fact, I'm ready to go. I turn to head back towards the door, but Leana holds me in place and walks towards my mother. "Ughhh, why'd you do that?" I whisper to Leana as I notice my mom beginning to move.

"For your own good." She whispers back.

My mother opens her eyes groggily. "I brought someone for you to see." Leana says in a kind voice, revealing me by her side. I realize I am trapped. I smirk and offer a half wave in her direction like a scared child.

"Hi Mom." I say thinking how simple I sound.

"What are you doing here?" My mother taunts at me.

"Well, a little pixie told me you weren't doing so well

and wanted me to come see you."

"Why? You can't help me. All you did was take take take," she scorns in a sing song voice, "then you left me with nothing. Besides, I'm fine."

I have no words. I stare at this sunken woman who is supposed to be my mother. I look over at Leana her eyes wide. "If this is your definition of fine," I spit, "I can't imagine what bad is."

"Look in the mirror. I change my mind. I'm am doing bad but only because you are here."

"What is your problem?" I practically scream at her. I suddenly feel six years old again throwing a temper tantrum to get my mother to notice me. "Why do you hate me so much? It took a lot for me to come here today. Why do you have to always push people away?"

I stop and realize my words. The echoes of Leana and Roman both asking me not to push them away haunts me. I really have become my mother. Well, I'm not taking her abuse any longer.

"I don't have to push. They leave anyway. Besides, there's no one worth having around." She says bitterly then presses the button on the bed that calls the nurse.

"You are one miserable piece of shit. You know that? I am embarrassed to call you my mother."

"So don't. Leave. I don't want you here. You're the one that's shit. I'm embarrassed to have given birth to you. I wish I hadn't."

I step back as if I've been slapped. I don't know what hurt worse, the words or the laxidasical way she says them.

Leana steps forward, "Okay, I think that is quite enough from both of you."

I get my breath back and decide I've had enough. "No, Mom." I say quietly, but firmly as a new resolve comes over me. I step forward and stick out an accusatory finger,

"I am not shit. It took me a long time to realize that, no thanks to you. If you are fine with abusive boyfriends and drug problems, then be fine here all alone with your nurse wiping your ass. I am sick and tired of being dejected and torn down. You are not worth it."

I want to say more, but the nurse had come in during my rant and was staring at me with astonished eyes. She looks to my mom and then Leana like she doesn't know what to do. In a way she just entered into a war zone. I was the one speaking but it seems she is unsure who to blame for the disruption.

Leana swoops in for the rescue. "Attend to her," she says to the nurse, "we were just leaving."

"Probably for the best," the nurse sighs. From her reaction, I have a feeling she knows my mother's ire all too well. Looking towards Leana she adds, "The doctor wanted to talk with you if you have time to wait. He'll be finished with his morning rounds in about half an hour."

"Thank you." She looks to me and I nod. "We'll be in the waiting room at the end of the hall."

I am still seething as we walk down the hallway. I feel more like I'm stomping. I hate that my mother brings out the worst in me. I want to say things to hurt her like she does to me. In fact, I think it is worse now than when I lived with her. The separation only gave me the perspective that it isn't meant to be this way. It's hard to be mature when she draws from such a negative place. I would feel low about the whole encounter but at this point I'm still too damn mad. It's been the same routine for most of my life, but this was a whole new level of mean. It makes me want to be rude right back. I can't seem to think about anything else. I can't even consider it may be the drugs affecting her. She's been on and off drugs for longer than I understood what they were.

As we enter the small waiting room, Leana sits down with a heavy sigh. "Well that went well."

"About as expected, I suppose." I say with more ire than I mean to. I can't contain my energy so I pace around the small waiting room. Leana lets me be. There really isn't anything she can say. She, like I, have heard some version of this all before.

A strange thought occurs to me. There is something missing in this room. I turn to Leana, "Where's the fish tank?"

She looks at me like I have three heads. "What?"

Maybe I have finally snapped, "The fish tank. Aren't there supposed to be a fish tanks in waiting rooms? It's calming and something to focus on. I know I could use the distraction."

Leana bursts out laughing.

Now it's my turn to stare blankly, my hands still in the air from my exaggerated gestures. "What?" I ask innocently as my arms fall back down.

"After all that, you're worried about the lack of a fish tank?"

"Yes." Then I look back at the wall, "No." I sit down next to her defeated. The mad is finally dissipating leaving me tired. "I don't know. I'm so mad. It's always the same. I don't know how trying to care for myself when she wouldn't has become an attack on her. I don't understand and I don't know what to do about it. I never have."

"Oh honey, I don't either." Leana reaches out and covers my hands with hers on top of my knee. "She wasn't like that before. Don't get me wrong, she was spiteful and mean but not venomous. That was new."

"I guess I bring out the best in her, too." I lean into my friend more lost than I've felt in a while.

It's not long before the doctor steps in and gets our

attention. I let Leana take the lead. I'm too drained to even think.

"Thanks for waiting," the doctor comes over and shakes Leana's hand.

Leana introduces me, "This is Marilyn's daughter, Aria."

I shake his hand, too. "Good to meet you. I'm doctor Michael Yaris. I've been watching over your mother since she got here a few days ago."

"What's the word, Doc?" Leana asks, quickly getting to the heart of the matter.

"After considerable observation of Ms. Dalton from myself and my staff, I have decided to suggest we bring in a psychotherapist."

"What brought you to that conclusion?" Leana asks as I stand dumbfounded.

"Several things actually. Ms. Dalton does not seem to have a solid grip on reality."

Finally, something I could get behind. "She never has. What is a psychotherapist going to do about it?"

"A diagnosis can go a long way. With treatments she could have increased function and better cognisant reasoning."

"Doc, I've known her for a long time. I don't know if that is possible." I admit.

Leana steps in, "Could be the reason she's always been so distant and -" she pauses for a polite way to voice her thoughts.

I interject, "distrusting, irresponsible, uncaring, demeaning," I stop as both Leana and Doctor Yaris stare at me.

"Yes." Doctor Yaris says simply. Then elaborates, "By being analysed we can determine what is going on with your mother. Perhaps even why she is acting in this manner.

We will take care with the process, especially since she was admitted for an abusive attack."

"Why wouldn't something like this have been diagnosed before?" Leana asks.

"How long have these symptoms been going on?" the doctor asks us.

Leana looks at me. "All my life." I answer.

Doctor Yaris nods. "I can't really answer that. If your mother has not sought out help or been in the hospital under care before, it is possible that no one has ever considered it. The symptoms could be worse due to the recent trauma. Honestly, your mother probably doesn't realize she has a problem. With her particular case, I would expect the latter."

I look at Leana and she back at me. Best friend intuition says that this is not a new development.

"Would it still be helpful even though her physical diagnosis is bleak?" Leana asks.

Dr. Yaris grins, probably from her word choice, "Yes, it could help us with treatments of her physical body, too. It may be the key to the puzzle."

"I never considered there might be a key to my mother." I say mostly to myself.

"What is the next step?" Leana asks.

"We bring in the physiotherapist and see what the diagnosis is. Then we will go from there."

"Do we need to be here?" I ask.

"It's not necessary. Honestly, in this case, after hearing the reports from the nurses, I would advise against it. It would be prudent to get her perspective. It seems your mother did not respond kindly to your visit."

"Yes well, she seems to be personally offended by not only my presence but also my existence."

"That is unfortunate. However, it also adds to my

suspicion that there is more going on here."

I nod. I'm ready to get out of here and take a deep breath.

Before the doctor leaves he adds, "I would recommend a therapist for you as well."

I try not to react but I know a little came through, "Thank you doctor, but not yet. Let's see where this goes first. After that perhaps I'll reconsider."

"Okay. I will set things up and have some information for you in the next day or so."

"Thank you, doctor." Leana adds.

We shake hands again and then sit back down as he leaves. Curiosity finally overpowers my anger and hurt. I look at Leana. "So, she might actually be sick? Like out of her mind?"

"It seems that is a high probability. It sure would begin to explain a few things."

"Perhaps," I retort, "But it doesn't excuse them."

"No, it doesn't." After a pause, she slaps my knee and stands. "It's time for lunch. I know a great sushi bar."

"I'm there." I reply, then look around, "Anywhere but here."

The sushi was good but overpriced. Something you get used to in a tourist town. I grew up with the problem and dealt with it in Vegas, too. Even Charleston is a tourist stronghold. Are there so many places in the world that make selling to others a way of life or do I just pick the few that live that way to reside in? Maybe I'm drawn to the lifestyle because I feel the need to present myself in the same way a tourist town would.

As I swallow my last Philadelphia roll, I sigh at the

state my mind is in. Nowhere good, I can tell you that. I am worn out, frustrated by the situation and I miss Roman. It is still strange for me to feel so attached to him. I've never felt like that before with anyone. He has shown me again and again that he is different than the rest. I hope he can forgive me for leaving without saying goodbye and my attitude surrounding my mother.

I've never wanted to make myself better. He makes me want to try. That leaves me with some hope. I need anything I can get when it comes to dealing with my mother.

I glance up at Leana as she finishes her rolls. She is off in her own thoughts as well. We spent much of our lunch in silence trying to absorb the new information.

When Leana looks up from her empty plate, I say, "I can't seem to take it all in. Too many emotions are warring at once. I don't know what to feel about this. I just feel numb."

"That doesn't seem too surprising. It is a difficult situation."

"I'm hurt. I'm mad. I'm confused. Yet, there is also this kind of relief at the same time. My mind keeps coming back to this one thing. At least it is her that is messed up and it's not about me at all. That's messed up on it's own, though. I mean, she's my mother. I want her to get her shit together already. I mean how has she gone this long without being diagnosed with a mental illness?"

"That I don't know. She doesn't even really understand that she is sick now." Leana pauses and then looks up at me with serious eyes, "I never thought it was you. Remember, I've seen her neglect and berating. I asked my mom later why she never called child services."

"Really? I never thought about it."

"She said it was because she thought she could help you

more by being next door and having me as a friend than taking a chance in the foster system. She never saw any physical abuse so in her mind she just sort of adopted you as her own."

"Wow. I will have to thank her. She always felt like a second mother to me. In a lot of ways more of a mother." I think about how kind Mrs. Grace has always been to me. "No, there wasn't ever anything physical, at least not from her. By the time that boyfriend came around I already had one foot out the door waiting to sprint. Your mom definitely helped me. I survived despite the odds. It helped having you around."

"Yes it did. Now we are here, two fabulous ladies." Leana raises her sweet tea glass in the air, "Cheers!"

"Cheers." I return the gesture with my own.

"You can thank my mom tonight. She has invited us to dinner."

"Oh, that would be nice. How is she anyway?"

"Good. Bored now that we are all out of the house. She's taken up quilting."

"Ha," I exclaim. "I can totally see that. I bet she's good at it, too. She's always been so crafty."

"Yes, she is. She even goes to a club. Apparently, it's a bunch of older women who sit around drinking wine and gossiping around a quilt in progress."

"Doesn't sound so bad actually." I surprise myself by saying.

Leana laughs, "No, it doesn't. That will be us one day."

"To old friends. We can become senile together." I toast.

"Something to look forward to."

The conversation lightens. We laugh and carry on like we always have. I still don't know what to make of the new revelations about my mother. I put it out of my mind for now.

I feel better, probably the best since Leana first called with the news. I'm glad I'll be able to see Leana's mom for dinner. Mrs. Grace has always been a rock for me, helping me and providing stability where no other existed.

Chapter 30

Wherever You Will Go

ROMAN

The day has been a long one. It felt strange waking up this morning without Aria next to me. It's amazing how fast habits are made. I miss her. It's probably a good thing work was so busy today. I couldn't get her off my mind even with the distraction. I couldn't imagine going through the day without something else to occupy at least some of my mind.

I have this feeling that I need to go to her. That she needs me. I can't tell if it is my desire to be near her or if she's actually in trouble. I'm not a hundred percent sure she would call if she were in trouble.

I believe she trusts me but I'm not sure if she feels able to depend on me yet. I wish she would. I figure she probably wouldn't call me. She's known Leana most of her life and even she seems held at arm's length.

I've noticed when faced with hardships, Aria tends to run. I'm not sure she would run to me. I hope that changes in our time together. She is so stubborn and has a hard time relying on her childhood friend let alone her lover that she barely knows.

I completely zone out in the last meeting, a debrief from closing the sale this morning. Thankfully, all the hard work paid off and everything went without a hitch. Once I finally get out of the meeting, I leave the office for the day. I'm not helping anyone there. I am ready to focus on more important matters.

I call Aria and catch her as she's finishing lunch with Leana. I'm glad she has her friend. I can't imagine who she would be without Leana's positive energy to keep her afloat through all of this. She seems to be in a positive mood when she answers. I breathe a little easier when I hear her voice. it feels like I've been holding my breath all day. I didn't realize it until I finally let it out.

"Hello, handsome," she answers.

"How are you, beautiful?" I ask.

"Okay now. Leana and I just finished eating some average sushi at extravagant prices."

"That sounds good." I encourage.

"It was a good pick me up after this morning. So is hearing your voice."

I smile and miss her even more. "So you saw your mother?"

"Yes." She pauses.

"How'd it go?" I inquire.

"Not pretty, but we did learn something new."

"What's that?"

"My mother may have a mental illness. That could be why she's always been so...frustrating."

"That's never come up before?" I ask.

"No, never. The doctor said that unless someone saw the signs it wouldn't necessarily get noticed. Especially if she didn't recognize or acknowledge that something was off."

"What do you think?" I ask digesting the new information.

"I think it explains some things. I'm not sure how I feel about it."

"That's big."

"Yeah," she sighs. I can hear her exhaustion in that one

exhale.

She doesn't offer any more. I decide to share my desire to see her. "What would you think if I came up there and help you through this?"

"Oh, Roman," she proclaims, then pauses. I wait for her to continue not wanting to push. "I don't know what you could do. I'm not doing anything but bugging Leana and worrying."

"If Leana doesn't mind, I could sleep on the couch and worry with you. Look, I don't want to come off as pushy or that you can't handle yourself. I know you can. I miss you Aria. I want to be with you and share this with you."

"I miss you, too." she sighs. I can hear the longing in her voice that parallels my own. "What about work?"

"I can take the rest of this week off. Andrew knows you are out of town attending to your mother. He already cleared it. We closed this morning and everything is going smoothly. If something happens, Andrew knows how to get ahold of me. I can handle it remotely."

"You have this all figured out." She laughs making me feel lighter.

"All you have to do is say yes."

"You drive a hard bargain, Mr. Wagner."

"Yes, I do. Please let me in."

"When can you be here?"

"How long is the drive?"

"About two hours."

"Give me two and a half hours. Would Leana mind if I crash there with you?" I ask to cover all bases.

There is silence on the other end and then I hear giggling, "No, she wouldn't mind. In fact she asked what took you so long."

I grin at that. Yes, Leana is a good friend. "I have no idea."

"We've been invited to Leana's mom's house for dinner. Would you like to join us? It'll be like meeting my family. The one that really took care of me."

"I would love to." I reply enjoying the idea.

"Then it's a date. I'll send you Leana's address. Drive safe and I'll see you soon."

"I love you." I tell her because I want her to know it is true.

"I love you, too."

With that I hang up feeling over the moon. I was truly afraid that she would say no and again not let me in. My heart is overflowing as I grab a few changes of clothes, my toothbrush and my laptop. I throw it all in a bag and head out.

I get the address from her and pull up the map. Within twenty minutes, I'm in the car and on my way.

ARIA

I feel a lot better knowing Roman is on his way, stronger somehow. At the same time, I feel weak that I need him so much. I've spent all of my life not relying on anyone for anything. Then again I've also spent that time lost and alone.

Spending time with Leana lets me know that that isn't entirely true either. I relied on her and her family a lot more than I realized at the time.

I haven't lived an elaborate life, but it has been mine.

At the same time, Roman has never tried to control anything I do or who I am. He seems to like me just as I am even the not so proud parts. He also encourages me in my writing and creativity. Even his family seems to have my back. So I know he is true. I feel it in my soul.

Not twenty minutes after I hang up with him, Roman texts to say he's on his way. I can't deny the leap my heart makes at hearing that. He will be here soon.

I look over to Leana as we head back to her place, "Are you sure it's okay Roman is going to come stay?"

She rolls her eyes as she turns on her road, "I'm still amazed that you just left without telling him. I figured he would have come up with you."

"I'm sure he would have. He seemed excited to come be with me."

Leana looks over at me and I can see the question in her eye before she asks, "What do you think about that?"

"It makes me happy. I feel stronger when he's around, more capable somehow. I wonder if I should need that."

"Everybody needs that." Leana interjects. "You came all the way across the country to be with him. Maybe this is his way of letting you know he would take a leap for you."

"Maybe. I never know what to do when it comes to my mother. I don't want him getting in the crossfire. I'm still nervous about that."

"He would be the first one in the line of fire," Leana tells me. "That boy would do anything for you. Those stars I saw in his eyes the night you met are still there. Now they are sparkling. I think he can handle some heat. Besides, he's done wonders for your self-esteem."

I take my turn rolling my eyes. I have to admit she is right. I have found my inner strength since I met Roman. It's like he held a mirror where I could see myself through the filter of love instead of contempt. It is a powerful perspective.

I have a funny thought, "Is it strange that he's going to meet your mom before he meets mine?"

"In this case, not at all. You are family, Aria. Even if it

isn't blood."

"Thank you for that."

"Always," Leana pats my leg in reassurance as she pulls into the parking lot of her apartment building.

I am excited to see Mrs. Grace. I feel bad for not keeping in better touch with her while I was away. She sent a few cards over the years. I did not always reply when she reached out. I hope she isn't disappointed in me.

So many emotions pull at me in this city. Coming home is hard like navigating a minefield. I never know what will set me off.

I am looking forward to Roman coming here. Maybe then I will feel complete and able to handle all the confusion a little easier.

Leana and I sit on the front porch, drink sweet tea and chat while we wait for Roman to get here. We'll head over to Leana's childhood home soon after he arrives.

"What do you think about the doctor saying your mom may have a mental illness, now that it's sunk in a little? It a big deal." Leana asks softly.

I sigh and sit back, suddenly wishing I had something stronger than sweet tea. "I think it makes a lot of sense. She's never been stable or responsible. It makes me mad that it hasn't come up before now."

"I can't blame you there. I guess we'll have to wait and see what the doctor says. Mental illness is a pretty broad spectrum. I don't know what can be done about it now. She's not exactly young and she's been diagnosed with this advanced form of syphilis, too. Even if she was physically well, she already seems to have lost her grip on reality."

"Yeah, I don't know what to think about all of it right now or what to do. We still don't have enough information

anyway. It does feel a little too late. Roman reminds me
that she's still my mother, but he hasn't met her. You saw
her today." I lift my arms exasperated. "Roman lost his dad
in high school. A dad who loved him whose life ended
tragically and way too soon. I don't know if I can forgive
my mom, even knowing that she's suffered. How much was
she in control anyway? She had no business raising a kid."

"I don't know what to tell you. I have a pretty normal
family." She shrugs, "It still isn't easy sometimes. You had
nothing compared to a normal upbringing and yet here you
are shining bright. You are a strong lady. Please know I'm
here for you. However I can be." Roman pulls up, "And so
is he. Don't shut us out, okay."

I've been hearing that a lot lately. Maybe it's time I
finally start listening. "Okay," I lift my hand to complete
the pinky swear she offers.

A huge smile breaks out when I see Roman. I look over
at Leana and say honestly, "I will try."

"That's all I can ask." I hear Leana say as I jump up to
run towards Roman. He's barely out of his car before he
catches me in his arms. I wrap my legs around him and
hold him close.

"Hello, handsome." I whisper in his ear as he hugs me
tight.

"My beautiful, strong girl." He whispers back in my
ear. He kisses neck, my cheek and then my lips.

"I'm so glad you are here." I say delighted.

"Me, too. Thanks for letting me come."

We look up at the loud throat clearing from the porch.
"Hi Leana," Roman calls up to her.

"Hi again." She waves. "Glad you could make it."

Roman looks back to me as he answers. "Me, too."

He kisses me again then lets me down and grabs his bag
out of the backseat. He leans his arm around my shoulder

as we go up the steps. Just like that, everything feels right with the world. At least for this moment.

ROMAN

I feel at home in this place I've never been because of the two people fluttering about the room. I relax and enjoy some sweet tea while I wait for them to get ready to see Leana's family. I'm looking forward to meeting them. It seems important somehow. It represents a connection to Aria's past. No matter how hard she tries to hide her childhood, it is important for me to see.

This trip seems to be all about memories. The drive up was fairly easy. It brought back visions from the spring break we came up to Myrtle Beach my ninth grade year. Along the drive through the back roads, I was suddenly fourteen again in the backseat fighting with Athena over who gets to choose the music.

Thinking back on it now, I don't know why we always fought. My parents had a system so we'd all get choice. There were a lot of things I realize now that I had no idea about then.

Even now, it seems random that we came up to Myrtle Beach that one year. There are several really great beaches in the Charleston area so we never felt the need to leave for a beach vacation.

However, that one year Dad won free tickets to the Carolina Opry at a work raffle. Instead of selling them, my parents decided to take us all on a trip north along the coast to see what the fuss was all about. Maybe just to say we had been.

We stayed in a hotel on the beach. Athena and I played

outside all day in the sand and surf. We went to that show at the Carolina Opry. I don't remember much about it.

Those are times when I look back and remember my dad the most. They were great years before he was swept away. It took me a long time to remember the good times without feeling mad or betrayed.

On that stretch of road, going towards the person that has shown me once again how to love, these memories feel happy again. I made peace with myself and my past on those back roads. It makes me thankful to be here now even more than before.

Once I found Leana's apartment and saw Aria on the porch, I felt like I was home. It is a strange feeling to be so connected to someone.

I am still afraid that I will lose her, especially when she ran here without even telling me. I also understand how hard it was for her to come. In a way I feel like I pushed her here.

I don't want to pressure her or think I know better. I want to support her like she does me every time she smiles with her warm open heart and looks at me with her soul shining through her eyes. I am thankful to have my arm around Aria once again.

Since I'm still in my work clothes I am ready to go. I'm thankful for the moment to rest. The girls give me a quick tour Leana's one bedroom apartment and I put my duffel bag next to Aria's backpack.

Now I sit back and sip my tea watching Aria fuss over what to wear.

"Aria, it doesn't matter what you wear," Leana says, "It's my family. They would love you in a potato sack."

"I know," Aria groans, "I just want to make a good impression. I feel bad about how little I kept up with them while I was gone. They mean so much to me and I couldn't even be bothered to send a note. Who does that?"

"You haven't seen them since you left after high school?" I ask.

"No." Aria looks at me like she is about to cry.

"Oh, honey," I lean toward her and take her hand.

Leana interrupts. "Aria, you are family. How many times do I have to tell you that. My parents love you. They can't wait to see you. It's time to leave anyway, you'll feel better once you see them. I promise. They have already forgiven you. Now you have to forgive yourself."

I see Leana's pep talk hit home. "Okay," Aria straightens up. I squeeze her hand before she heads back into the bedroom.

I look to Leana, "How's she doing? Really?"

"Overwhelmed I think. I didn't realize she had this guilt about my parents. They just wanted to see her since she was here." Leana smiles at me, "Aria is a whirlwind of emotions. She is wholeheartedly in the moment which is great most of the time."

"I am beginning to learn that. I don't mind. I almost forgot what it was like to have emotions."

"You guys are perfect for each other."

"I wish I knew how to help her." I reach out to the only other person who might have a clue.

Leana looks at me with a face that imagine mirrors my own, of reluctant hope, "I wish I knew. I'm trying to be there for her while we figure out what is going on with her mom. It doesn't look good and Marilyn's as hostile as ever. Aria gets some of it honestly. You'll find out soon enough. In the meantime, I'm trying to make sure she doesn't run away from it all. She likes to do that."

I nod, understanding completely. Aria is so strong, but sometimes she forgets to believe in herself. "Well, I'm here to help however I can."

"She's lucky to have you."

"I'm lucky we found each other. She was so brave to trust me. I want to prove to her that it was the right choice."

Only a couple of moments of silence pass before Aria appears in the doorway. "I'm ready," she states.

"Let's move out." Leana leads the way out the door.

Chapter 31

What We Cannot Speak Of Must Be

ROMAN

The small brick house reminds me of my own childhood. The look I see cross between Leana and Aria is one of relief and happiness. Aria told me that she always felt more at home at Leana's house than her own. I'm not even to the front door yet and I feel welcome. This was a place of comfort and refuge for Aria. I love it already. I'm curious to learn more about who she was before she ran off to Vegas.

I get out and move to open Aria's door in front of me. She turns to me and looks up with a childlike smile. I am glad to see her relaxed in a way I haven't seen her before. It seems like the stress she held at Leana's apartment has melted away just by being here. I take her hand to help her out of the car, "This place is nice."

Aria nods. It is Leana who answers, "This is where we grew up." She has no hesitation using the plural pronoun.

A lady with brown curly hair wearing a kitchen apron opens the door as we come up the stairs. She gives Leana and then Aria a big hug. I hear her comment in a mama bear tone, "Welcome home, it's been too long. You look all grown up now."

"Thanks," Aria responds. I try to hang back and let them have their private moment.

Leana's mom steps back as she takes me in, "You must be Roman. I've heard a lot about you from my girls."

"Good things I hope, Mrs. Davis." I offer my hand. She ignores it and steps in for a hug, which I readily return. This is a woman who has a motherly disposition. One you can always talk to. Aria was very lucky to find such a loving person in her life and Leana to have her as a mother.

"Why yes," she says, "all good things. You are more handsome than they let on. You can call me Mrs. Grace. All the others do." I blush and back out of the spotlight. She continues "Well, I'm very glad to meet you and see both of you girls together again. Come on in."

She waves us in opening the door wider. I know another hospitable Southern lady, who taught me the place of a man. I reach for the door and hold it open for her and my companions before following them inside.

"Thank you." Mrs. Grace smiles at me as she passes.

I watch them move naturally to the right into a bright square kitchen with an oversized middle island. Aria leans back into me as I move to stand behind her, "This was our favorite spot in the house when we were young. We would come home after school, do homework and have snacks around this counter. It was the heartbeat of this house."

"Still is," Grace explains, "except now there is much less homework and much more wine." We all laugh. I find laughter comes easily here. No wonder Aria always felt so safe and loved in this space.

Mrs. Grace must cook up some magic in this kitchen. I smell lasagna wafting like my mom makes. My mouth starts watering and I realize I forgot to grab lunch.

Aria asks, "You're making lasagna?" She must be thinking with her stomach like me.

"Of course I made your favorite. I did invite you didn't I?"

Aria laughs, "You always know how to make me feel special."

"You are special, Sweetie. Don't you forget that." Mrs. Grace gives her a warm smile and then turns to me. "I hope you are hungry, Roman. I'm glad you are here, but I didn't get a chance to ask if you have any dietary restrictions."

"Oh no, Ma'am, thanks though. The lasagna smells amazing. Thanks for letting me come at the last minute."

"Of course. Leana knows there is always plenty to go around for surprise guests. Please, make yourself at home."

I'm finding that won't be hard to do as I slide onto a bar stool next to Aria.

A tall man with a dark, full beard comes in causing me to sit a little straighter. I instinctively believe this is the man in Aria's life that I need the okay from and I'm determined to get it. He comes over with a big smile and wraps Aria up in a hug. "Good to see you, young lady. It has been too long since you've come to visit."

"Yes, it seems it has." She answers leaning into his hug.

He looks over at me and offers his hand, "Who might this fine young man be?"

I take his hand in a firm grip, "Roman Wagner, sir. Leana and Aria have graciously extended the invitation for dinner to me. I'm glad to come and meet you."

"Well said, Roman," he nods with approval. "I'm John. It's nice to meet you. I hear you have stolen the heart of our young Miss Aria here."

"She has stolen mine, sir."

"I think you have found a keeper," he winks at Aria.

I relax as he turns to Leana, "Why can't you find a respectable boy like this one?" he asks.

"They seem to all be taken." Leana responds with a flip of her wrist as she leans up to kiss her father on the cheek.

"All in do time, I suppose."

Mrs. Grace moves to the oven pulling out the lasagna and garlic bread saying, "Dinner is almost ready. Honey, would you uncork the Merlot so it can breathe while we fix the table and let this rest for a few minutes."

"Of course, dear." He replies with a kiss on her cheek.

There is so much love in this house. I am thankful I could come and meet these wonderful people that have been there for Aria. I can see in a lot of ways these are the people who encouraged her own inner strength.

I watch as Leana goes to a cabinet and hands plates to then cups Aria. I move to help but they seem to have fallen into an old routine to set the table. I sit back with a smile as these two friends laugh and cut up in their sanctuary of sorts.

Aria seems to have a carefreeness here that looks beautiful on her. I've seen glimpses of it when we sit together in the evenings or playing Rummikub with Gran. Here, it is like she has taken a deep breath. I am glad she came back to visit. This is an experience I hope she remembers during the harder times of her stay. I wonder if she even realizes how comfortable this place is to her.

I have heard hard things about Aria's mother. I can hardly imagine a person being so cruel. I know she hurts Aria on an emotional level. I've learned that is often much harder to overcome. I don't know what to say or do when it comes to her mother. I hope Aria knows that I would do anything, be anything, for her.

My thoughts are heavy as we sit down at the Davis's large oak dining room table. I can tell this is one of the keystones of the house by the subtle wears in the wood and the simple, happy place setting. Eating at the table was always a cherished time for my family growing up, especially to my mom. I imagine Leana's family shares that tradition. They all seem happy as they come to sit together.

Mr. Davis pours wine all around then sits to my right at the end of the table. Aria sits to my left. I take a moment to clear my thoughts and be in this moment.

"Go ahead and toast now Leana. I know you want to." Mrs. Grace lifts her wine glass to her daughter.

"You know me well, Mother." Leana beams and lifts her glass as I catch a wink from Grace to John across the length of the table. "It feels special to have Aria back at this table," she looks to her friend, "You have always been family to me. I raise this glass to my friend, who is like a sister, and to this wonderful man she stumbled into that brought her back home. Thank you Roman for being such a handsome reason for me to be jealous of my friend." I blush as the table laughs. "Thank you Mom and Dad for being there for us both throughout the years. I know we weren't always easy." I catch Grace and John give each other a knowing glance. "To family," Leana concludes, "and to being together."

"To family and being together," everyone at the table repeats as we raise our glasses. This moment feels like an initiation of sorts. I am thankful to be part of this custom. Leana seems to always have the words to say. It is her gift. According to Aria, she has many.

"Well said, Leana," Grace applauds as she sets down her glass. "Now let's eat. Aria can you please pass the bread?"

We dig in. There is plenty to go around and more to spare. The food is delicious and the company delightful.

I share about my work and Aria updates them with her progress on her novel.

Aria and I tell the story of how we met. Leana even joins in. It is fun to hear about that night from their perspective.

Grace and John also think Aria was brave for coming to

stay with me. For them, it also meant Aria came home or close enough to it at least. I can see their immense love for her by the way they greet her with open arms.

However, we could not avoid the reason that Aria was here in Myrtle Beach for the entire evening. After the plates were empty and the wine refilled, the conversation turned to Aria's mother.

"So what is the current status on your mother?" Grace asks Aria bluntly.

I can feel Aria tense up beside me with her wine halfway to her lips. I'm sure she knew as well as me that the question was coming but still was unprepared. I gently rest my hand on her leg as she takes a deep sip of wine.

Sitting down the glass, she looks up. "Well, I'm sure Leana has told you that she ended up beaten and in the hospital. Also that she was diagnosed with a bad stage of syphilis." Grace and John both nod encouraging her to continue. "Somehow, none of those things surprise me about my mother. Perhaps even an inevitability of sorts. The interesting part is that now they suspect she has some sort of mental illness."

"Oh," Grace lets out.

"Exactly," Aria continues. "I'm still coming to grips with that. It makes a lot of sense but I don't know what to do with it. I mean, could she even get better now? I don't know that she would want to even if she could."

There is a heaviness in the air after her last words. I see that her hand is shaking and turn slightly to take it in both of mine. I turn to Leana expecting her to say something, but she is unusually quiet.

"Do they have any idea what sort of mental illness?" Grace asks. "The diagnosis could make a difference in how you come to terms with it and possibly treat it."

"I don't know," Aria responds. "The doctor said she has

lost grip with reality. That could be a number of things. I wonder if it might just be all the pain killers she's on and how they mix with the narcotics that were apparently in her system. She doesn't respond well to the staff. She was about ready to jump off the bed to attack me. "

"Hmph." John grunts.

Leana opens her mouth then closes it again. The entire table looks over to her waiting for her to speak.

"Go on," Grace gestures.

Leana looks at Aria and then back at her mom. "You taught me that when I don't have anything nice to say, I should not say anything at all."

"When have you ever listened to that particular piece of advice? You always say what you think." Grace chuckles.

"That fair." Leana turns to Aria who squeezes my hand. "Look, I've been doing some research and your mom could have anything from bipolar disorder to schizophrenia and several things in between. We've known she was messed up since we were kids. We didn't know what to do about it then either. I don't know that she's ever going to be the mom you want her to be. Especially now that her organs are literally shutting down. Even her own body doesn't like her anymore." Aria snorts at that and after a moment Leana continues, "It makes me so mad that she got herself all messed up. I wish she could get better. I'm afraid that's not going to happen."

Leana gets up and comes over to hug Aria. She lets go of me to wrap her arms around her friend. When they let go, I realize they both have tears in their eyes.

"I wish I would have done something sooner." Grace whispers. I look over to see her also tearing up.

"Oh, Mrs. Grace," Aria gets up and wraps her arms around her role model. Leana follows and embraces them both. "It wasn't this bad back then. Besides, I wouldn't have wanted to go into the foster system. I would have rather stayed here."

"That's sweet of you," Grace says. "I suppose I tried to hide the worst of it from myself. I hate to see your mother so despicable. I'm sorry that you have to live through it."

"You once told me that the trials we live through makes us stronger." Aria quotes.

"I did say that, didn't I?" Grace smiles

"Yes, Mom. You took care of us the best you knew how. You loved us even when we tried your patience. You gave Aria a place to feel safe and allowed me to be there for my best friend. You built us up to be triumphant no matter what was thrown our way," Leana assures.

"I love you girls. You two grew up so lovely."

"Thanks." Aria and Leana say in unison and each kiss Grace on opposite cheeks.

It's not until my nose itches that I realize tears are emerging from my eyes, too. Even John is not immune to the emotional show.

A peace floods the room. Aria surprises me by coming up behind me and kissing my cheek. "Whatever happens with my mother, I will be okay because I have all of you. I don't know that she will get better this time. I'm not a little kid anymore. Leana's right, it's time I finally face her."

ARIA

Being in this house again with Mrs. Grace and Mr. John, makes me realize how much this felt like home. They have always been so important to me.

I remember my mother's cold empty house when I think of this town. That is not all my childhood was. These were the moments that really mattered. I can't dismiss the hard parts of my childhood but I can appreciate the good things I had.

There is so much love here it almost makes up for having none at my own home. I can't deny all the good, warm memories here. They wrap me up like a warm blanket and let me know that it will all somehow be alright.

I've been so focused on all of the bad times and the reason I ran away that I forgot all of the love waiting for me to come home. I don't know if they ever knew how much of a haven their house was for me or how encouraging it was to see that they really did love each other.

In this seeming vortex of time I can't help but think how much and yet how little has changed. They are still pillars to lean on like they always were.

Mrs. Grace was right about being all grown up now. It means there are some hard decisions to make. It is nice to feel welcomed at the family table in the meantime.

As I stand next to Leana at the sink helping her rinse off dishes, I get a call from an unknown, local number. I answer to hear an older woman's voice, "Hello there, are you Aria Dalton?"

"Yes, ma'am."

"My name is Beverly. I'm from Grand Strand Regional Medical Center. I'm calling about your mother, Marilyn Dalton. I apologize that it is so late. We received the results of your mother's physiatric evaluation and Doctor Yaris asked me to contact you immediately."

"Is everything okay?" I ask leaning into the phone.

"Well, yes and no. There is no urgent concern. Your mother's condition has not changed. They did expedite the process so the medical staff could try to help her more adequately. She is being defiant and seems to be causing some disruptions."

"That sounds like my mother," I sigh.

"Doctor Yaris has asked if you would be able to meet with him tomorrow morning to discuss the results."

"Yes, I can do that." I nod as she gives me the details and then look up to an expecting audience as I hang up the call.

"The test results came back, so I," I correct myself, "we can go in the morning to talk to the doctor."

Roman reaches out and takes my hand, "Then that's what we'll do." I squeeze his hand and look over to Leana, who nods.

We say goodbye to Grace and John. I thank them again for the delicious dinner and their gracious support.

The ride back to Leana's apartment is in the comfortable silence of friendship. The dinner went well. I'm glad they didn't hold those years I was gone against me. It's also nice to know how absolutely they approve of Roman.

I wonder what my mom will say about him. I can't imagine it will be anything positive even with how great of a guy he is. I suppose we'll find out tomorrow. I'm suddenly dreading the sunrise.

When we park, Roman is once again at my door. Knowing his mother, she would be proud to see him being the very definition of a southern gentleman. I accept his kindness and kiss his cheek as I step from the car.

I still think he is too good for me but I can not let him go. Instead, I lean into him as we climb up the stairs.

"You have a great family, Leana," Roman comments as we enter the apartment and begin to settle on the couch.

"Yes, I suppose they are okay. Most of them anyway. My parents are cool. It's amazing how they had such different kids from the same upbringing."

"I'll have to meet your siblings someday."

"You already met Alicia, briefly." I comment.

"Oh, yeah," Roman remembers. "I suppose I did."

"If you stick around, which I hope you do, you'll meet Caleb too. They aren't strangers." She chuckles, "you might get more than some drunken conversations when you meet them outside Vegas."

"They are the family I know," I surprise myself by saying. Perhaps I am more tired than I realize. I snuggle into Roman's side. "I'm glad you got to meet them. They seem to like you."

"I felt very welcomed, so that's a good sign."

"Oh yes," Leana interjects. "They love you. Thanks for giving me such a high bar to reach, Aria."

"You're welcome," I nudge my friend, "I hope you do find someone awesome who treats you right. It would be a nice change from the string of nitwits you bring home."

"Who says I bring any of them home?"

I stick my tongue out at her making her laugh.

"Yeah, I know." She turns to Roman, "Are you sure you don't have any brothers?"

"Nope." He laughs, "only a sister and she's already spoken for."

"Dang it. Maybe that's what I need then, a nice lady to warm my bed."

"You know I will, just say the word." I tease.

Roman looks from me to Leana, "Okay, I'll stand by and protect you."

"Sounds good." Leana yawns. "I'm exhausted. Why don't you guys take my bed tonight."

"We can't do that," Roman says, "I'm already intruding enough. I'm not going to kick you out of your own bed."

I stay quiet. I slept in the bed with Leana last night. I don't have a case in this argument. I wait to see who will win.

Leana won. I'm glad as I snuggle up to Roman in her bed.

"I can't believe she tricked me." He shakes his head making the pillow rustle.

"She is a sly one."

"Like a fox."

"Her favorite animal."

"That figures."

"Thanks for coming here to be with me."

"Thanks for letting me come. Do I get to come to the hospital with you in the morning?"

"Yes, please."

"Good." He kisses my forehead and settles me close.

"It was the hardest thing to leave without you. I didn't realize how much I would miss you."

"Why did you leave without me? Why did you feel like you had to?"

I sigh and take a moment to answer. As I feel the warmth of him next to me, protecting me, I tell him the truth. "My mother brings out the worst in me. She always has. Nothing is ever good enough. She likes to rub that in and every piece of negativity she can muster with it. She blames me for most of the things wrong in her life even before I was old enough to understand them.

"Now that I do I resent her for not being responsible enough for her own actions. I didn't want you to see her attacks on me or how I can't seem to help retaliating. I'm not proud of it but I can't seem to get past it either.

"I'm afraid you will decide you made a mistake about being with me. I keep waiting for you to realize I'm not good enough for you."

"That will never happen, my love." Roman says softly and kisses my forehead.

I breathe that in for a moment and hope that it is true. "I fear I'm too much like her. I don't know that I could go back to my life like it was in Vegas now. I don't want to try."

He rolls toward me, "I've been sufficiently warned about your mother by various sources. Nothing she says is going to sway my feelings for you. I also don't believe you are anything like her. Your soul shines so brilliantly. It is my beacon of light." He caresses my face as he continues, "I hope you never go back to Vegas. At least not alone. You have brightened my days too much for me to ever want to live in darkness again."

I press my head into his shoulder and find strength in his arm around my waist. He speaks softly into my ear, "I want to share my life with you. That means good times and hard times. You were there for my grandmother who you haven't even met yet. I want to be here for you. Let's face our struggles together. It's not how will you get through this, Aria, but how we will get through this. I'm going to be by your side the entire time."

"I'm so thankful to have you."

"That goes both ways. I love you. Aria. We can handle anything when we face it together."

"I love you, too."

Chapter 32

One Day You Will Teach Me To Let Go Of My Fears

ARIA

The taste of salt water fills my mouth. I am out in the ocean at my favorite beach. It is a beautiful summer day. The shore is filled with people. I hear joy and laughter all around me. I can't focus on that because my nose is breathing in water. Wait, that's not supposed to happen.

I realize I am caught in a riptide. Another wave crashes into me pulling me further under. I lift my head and think I see Roman and Leana on the beach throwing a foam football. I try to get their attention. Before I can even get my hand in the air to wave, the riptide pulls me under again. I am being beaten by the sea.

While my head is underwater, I hear a cackling that sounds like the wicked sea witch in "The Little Mermaid." I always said she had the same laugh as my mother. I am drowning. I know I am as I swallow an entire mouthful of the ocean. All I hear is my mother laughing at me.

"Aria," Roman exclaims. "Wake up!"

I come to with a start and immediately start hyperventilating. Roman rubs my back trying to soothe me. I try to breathe, but I can still taste the salt water in my mouth burning my throat.

The door bursts open. "I hope this is not your form of kicks." Leana comes in karate stance ready. "Who's strangling who here?"

My gasps increase, but now with laughter mixing with my fear.

Roman turns to Leana very seriously, "She had a nightmare."

"I can see that." Leana comes over to the other side of me and pounds her fist on my back. "You're being too nice. Can't you see she is drowning."

"Huh?" Roman questions.

I start coughing like I would if I were expelling water from my mouth. Thanks to Leana I am also already feeling better. Of course, she remembers.

I reach out to both Roman and Leana on either side of me. "Thanks," I whisper.

"Are you okay?" Roman asks and holds tight to my hand.

"I am now." I appreciate Roman's patience. I don't think I would be so calm. I can tell he is not entirely calm, but he isn't screaming like I would so he gets major points.

"You're going to be okay. We're here." Leana rubs my back.

After a few deep breaths, I try to explain. "I was in the water at the beach. The riptide got ahold of me. I was drowning. All I could hear was my mother's raspy cackle."

"Oh, honey. I figured it was that again." Leana leans back and takes my hand as I rest on Roman's shoulder.

"It's an old nightmare of hers," Leana explains to Roman. "She used to have this dream a lot when we were younger, especially right before she left."

"I haven't had it in a really long time though. I forgot how powerful it was."

Roman pulls me close, "We're not going to let you

drown."

"Never." Leana agrees.

"I believe that." I say almost inaudibly as sleep and the weight of the dream pull at me.

I was able to doze back off for a little bit but it wasn't good sleep. Leana got up at some point and went back into the living room. Roman slept with his arms protectively around my waist.

My last conscious thought was that dreaming of drowning in riptides can't be a good omen.

No one is up for much conversation in the morning. We all get our coffee and sit in comfortable silence. Long before I am ready, it is time to go face the monster. I mean, my mom and her diagnosis. Same thing.

The hospital is cold and smells of disinfectants. It seems to me the cold is an attempt to keep back the death as long as it can. It's only delaying the inevitable.

I sit in Dr. Yaris' office between Roman and Leana feeling safe yet still scared. I can't shake my nightmare. I swear I can still taste salt water in my throat.

Dr. Yaris comes in with a daunting handful of files. I am thankful for Roman's hand in mine. He keeps saying that we're in this together. I need to trust him.

"Well, it seems Mrs. Dalton's fan club grows." Dr. Yaris chuckles.

Leana murmurs, "I wouldn't call us fans. More like obligated spectators."

"I'm glad you are here," he acknowledges.

Roman offers his hand. "I'm Roman Wager, Aria's boyfriend. It's good to meet you, Doctor. I'm here to help however I can."

"It's good to meet you." Dr. Yaris smiles then sits behind his desk. "The psychiatric test results show that your mother is exhibiting signs of schizophrenia and PTSD."

I appreciate that he went straight to the punchline, but I am confused. "I anticipated the schizophrenia, but PTSD? Isn't that what you get after a tragic event like a war or something?"

"Yes, but it can come from smaller traumas, too. When the brain is faced with a deeply distressing or disturbing experience, it ignites the fight or flight reaction. In some cases, the mind will freeze or completely shut down.

"Personal trauma means something different to each individual. In your mother's case it could as easily have come from something she experienced while in an altered state of reality. PTSD can build up over time from seemingly small events. Even something as simple as a heartbreak could initiate it."

"My mother had a number of those." I comment.

"So it seems. According to her assigned psychiatrist, each one of those was worse than the last. They built on each other in a unique way. Those traumas also include you, Aria."

"Me?" I gasp "She drove me away."

"From getting to know Mrs. Dalton, I don't doubt you. You have to remember this is your mother's perspective."

"Hmmmp." I sit back hard.

Roman sits up and asks, "What about the schizophrenia? Could that have a greater play here?"

"It does, absolutely. It means that part of her brain compartmentalizes while another is working. She could have pushed you away in one breath. Then be traumatized in the next never realizing it was her own hand to drive you away. All she sees is you leaving."

"That's a lot to take in." Leana says softly.

"Yes, indeed." Doctor Yaris agrees.

"So what do we do now?" Roman asks

"That is up to you," Dr. Yaris answers. "Some options include medications or sedation therapy. We also have to take into account the tertiary syphilis that is already wreaking havoc on her system."

"At what stage is that in exactly?" I ask.

"Unfortunately, a very late stage. It is affecting her circulatory system the most right now. She is barely getting enough blood throughout her body making her heart work overtime. This condition has also been known to target the brain which may be intensifying her schizophrenia. She may have been experiencing the influx for a while without even realizing it."

"So this goes beyond the physical trauma she had coming in here?" Leana asks.

"Yes, those were all fresh surface wounds. This goes much deeper and has been going on for a while."

"What happens now?" I ask.

"The physical wounds will heal with time. We can give her medication to combat some schizophrenia symptoms. If your mother would accept it, psychiatric help could be of great use. With the degenerative nature of the late syphilis, the best option is to keep her comfortable. There's not much we can do to reverse it at this point."

"So she's going to die?" I jump forward in my chair.

Dr. Yaris lifts his hand, "Not necessarily. We will continue to monitor how her body is healing from the physical injuries and how significant the heart and brain damage are. In the meantime, we will continue to give her painkillers to keep her comfortable and calm."

"That sounds best." Leana agrees.

"Since she is currently unable to make decisions, the

choice to give her medication to subdue the schizophrenia effects is up to you."

"Do you think it will help?" I ask meekly.

I can see his sigh in his body language, though he does a very professional job of not making it audible, "It's hard to tell. There is a lot going on in her body right now. It can't hurt to try."

I look to Roman and then to Leana, they both shrug. I look to the doctor and say, "Sure. Give it a try."

I feel heavy as we leave the doctor's office. We thank him for his time and expertise. I don't intend to see my mother. I want to have time to consider all that I have learned this morning and what it can possibly mean.

Still, there is no way to leave without walking by her door which happened to be open. I didn't even acknowledge the room until I heard my name, "Aria, you little twat."

I freeze stone cold in the middle of the hallway. My heart turns to ice. Leana must have felt my tension. She turns toward my mother and spits out, "What do you want, Marilyn?"

"I want you to tell me why in the hell she got some psychoanalyst on my tail asking all these questions."

Leana answers for me. We both know it is impossible to ignore her. "The doctor suggested it and we gave the go ahead." Roman holds a tight grip on my hand. I wonder if he is doing it for me or himself. Either way I am thankful. I imagine he can feel my anxiety.

"How dare you. You don't know anything about me. Neither does that cunt of a daughter I have. Now they think I'm crazy."

"No." Leana responds sounding like she is talking to a toddler who was told she couldn't have candy. "They want to know where your irrational behavior is coming from."

"I can tell you that. That little devil I gave birth to. She did this to me. If I'm crazy, they better take her out first."

"That's enough, Mom." I practically scream at her. "Why do you talk to me like that? I want to help you."

"Help me? How can you do that? First you ruin my life and then you leave me. You run away with your tail between your legs and don't even look back."

Before I can gear up to continue my rant, she sees Roman. In an instant, her demeanor changes. She bats her eyes at my boyfriend and speaks in an entirely different voice, "Well, who is this handsome fellow?"

"Roman Wagner, ma'am," Roman steps forward without letting go of my hand. "It's nice to meet you, Mrs. Dalton. I'm-"

She cuts him off, "What are you doing later? I just have to get my purse and I can take you anywhere you want to go, sugar."

Roman stands there dumbfounded.

"Mom, this is my boyfriend," I introduce.

"Your boyfriend? Ha, that's a good one. He's too good for you and way too handsome. You leave him to me."

I can see red form at the edges of my vision. I have no words and no sympathy for the thing sitting in that bed who doesn't even want to be my mother.

A rush overcomes me. I can't contain it any longer. I turn away from everyone and run through the halls towards the exit.

I hear Roman call after me. Leana, too. The sound is distant like in a dream. The smell of salt water overwhelms my senses. I feel the burning in my throat like I'm drowning even on solid ground.

This is why I didn't want Roman to come. He witnessed all of the horrible things she said. I can't shake the awful way she makes me feel. No wonder I have no self-confidence. Still, I ran away just like she said I would.

Instead of this new realization slowing me down, it propels me forward. Harder. Faster. Further away from the pain. I am worthless. Whatever is below that it shares my name.

ROMAN

"You know what Marilyn, you are crazy. That girl you hurt is wonderful. You pushed her away, again." Leana all but yells at Aria's mother. She surprises me by grabbing my hand on her way out the doorway pulling me into the hallway. I believe she intended to slam the door, but it closed slowly on resisters behind us.

"The nerve of that woman." Leana grumbles angrily letting go of my hand and leaning back against the wall with her arms crossed.

"So that's the infamous mother, huh?" I ask.

"Oh yes. You have seen her in her bright and shining glory."

I can't help myself, I laugh. "Well, you guys weren't exaggerating. I see why Aria was always with you growing up. Has it always been this bad?"

"No, it seems to have gotten worse over time. It was never good. Aria mostly avoided her. Marilyn worked a lot anyway. She did something with her time away from the house. I don't want to think about it too much. I hate how much and openly she hurts Aria. It's not fair to her." Leana drops her head, "I'm the one who made her come."

"Don't blame yourself. It is her mother. She's going to

have to face her sooner or later." I comfort.

"She would choose later or never. I can't blame her."

I look towards the room, "Neither can I." I look up and down the hallway trying to see a trace of where Aria might be. "Where did she go?"

"I hope downstairs. If we were still teenagers, I would say probably to the pier. That's where she always ran to when we were kids. It's a little further from here than it was from our houses though." She smiles reluctantly, "We're not as young as we used to be."

"She just ran?"

"Yeah, she ran all the time. She said it helped her think. She used to run track in high school. Even lettered in it though she would never get a jacket. She used to run all over town."

"You ready to go find her?" I ask hesitating before moving towards the elevator.

"No, I need a minute," Leana sighs. She looks up and down the hallway like it has the answers, "Somewhere quiet."

"I think I saw a waiting room at the end of this hallway."

"Okay, that sounds good."

We walk to the waiting room and sit in a couple of uncomfortable chairs. I hear Leana audibly take a deep breath. I watch her focus and begin to understand how tough she is. Aria must have relied on her quite a bit throughout the years. Their relationship fascinates me.

I believe that Leana being with Aria when she met me had a lot to do with her decision to come back east. In this quiet moment I realize I have a lot to thank Leana for. "Thank you for being here for Aria all these years. You are a good friend."

Leana looks at me. I can see her warring within herself

whether to be serious and sarcastic. Under all of it, I can see her exhaustion. "Thanks. Being friends with Aria is great. She is so fun and positive. She is always ready for an adventure. She has this fire in her that makes everything more interesting."

"I know exactly what you are talking about. I saw a light in her eyes that first night we met. I knew I would live my entire life and never meet anyone else like that."

"You are right about that." She looks back out into the hallway. "Her mother has done a number on her. She lacks confidence to stand up for herself. Marilyn is cruel and has been a role model in how not to be. Do you see now why Aria wanted you to stay away? I'm still amazed she let you come, though also thankful, you must really have a hold on her."

"I love her. That's all I have." I shrug. "I know Aria wanted to shield me from her mom. I got some perspective today. It helps to meet her mom and see what she's been dealing with all of these years. I can understand her a little better. It's a lot to overcome."

"You can say that again. She didn't get the love and nurturing that we got growing up. She's on her own. At least that's how she sees it."

"Until now. I want her to feel loved and safe."

"I know you do. That's why I like you so much. You are good for her."

"I try but she has to let me. I will not force anything on her."

"You and me both. She still pushes me away even after all these years. Honestly, I was surprised she came. For her to even try to face her mother is a new development. I probably have you to thank for that."

"I can't take credit," I chuckle. "I tried, but it was Gran who somehow persuaded her to come here."

"I must meet this Gran. She has superpowers."

"It's very possible."

"I think it's good that Aria is here. She needs to face her mother. However, she will see this encounter as a huge set back and be embarrassed that you saw her mother say those things."

"I am sensing this. I have to figure out how to let her know that I'm here for her no matter what."

"Just be here. No matter what. That's more than most have ever done for her."

I nod, "Ready to find her?"

"Yeah."

I pull out my phone and send Aria a text, *Remember we're in this together. Where are you? I want to kiss your beautiful lips!*

ARIA

I sit in the courtyard outside the hospital not sure if the two people I love most in the world even want to see me again. I can't imagine they are happy with me after how my mother acted and the hurtful things she said.

I don't know what to do when faced with my mother's ruthless words. Part of me wants to turn and start yelling back at her. I've tried that and it didn't make anything better. It does the opposite actually. I feel worse and my mother has more fuel to fire back.

This time was different than before. With my hand in Roman's, I couldn't speak the malicious words in my mind. Instead, I ran again executing my familiar escape plan.

I hate this horrible feeling. Mostly because I fear I am the cause of it. Even though they are my mother's words, I brought this out of her. I'm to blame.

It is because of me that Roman and Leana are subjected to her harassment. I wonder, not for the first time, if I should run away for good and save them the trouble.

I think of the pier and all the times I ran to it from my house. The wood on that pier knew me about as well as Leana did. She came to find me there on many occasions. She always knew where to find me and what to say. I don't know what I would have done without her.

My phone buzzes. It's Roman. He is a much newer source of support. He proves his love everyday. It means a lot that he is the one to reach out to me. I read Roman's message and smile. Maybe he will pardon my actions. I am not worthy of their love. They would be so much better off without my broken spirit weighing them down. Yet, I can't help myself. I finally found stability in Roman and Leana has been my anchor for so many years. I don't know what I would do without either of them today.

I wipe the tears out of my eyes. It's not helping anything to sit here feeling sorry for myself. My companions are sacrificing their time and offering me love and support. Perhaps it's time to stop running and lean on them the way they want me too. They are so freely giving me encouragement. I need to learn how to receive their help. Why is it so hard to do?

I text Roman back, *I'm in a little courtyard just pass the main entrance. There are signs on the main floor.*

I try to stop the tears as I wait for them to find me. I'm in front of the parking garage ready for a quick departure from this awful place. I wish I could go to the pier but that would mean more running. It is quite a way from here on foot still it calls to me. The pier is my place of solace to both escape and find strength. I try to remember the comfort it brings but I am coming up empty. All I can think of is the madness of my mother and the incoming pitying faces of my friends.

I see Roman first. He looks around the corner to my quiet perch. I watch his face soften as he comes over to me. He stops in front of me taking my face in his strong hands and kisses my forehead. He kneels in front of me, "Are you okay?"

I have to sniff back my tears I thought I had under control. "Am I okay? She said all of those...vulgar things." I try to find the right word and shiver. "I should be asking if you are okay. I'm surprised you even want to talk to me right now."

The look Roman gives me makes me tremble. His eyes pierce into my soul with determined authority. "Now Aria, I've been getting to know you pretty well over the last month. I have never heard you speak with such skepticism. You are not your mother. Nothing she says can make you feel less unless you let it. You are powerful and courageous. I look forward to seeing that bright light shining from inside you every single day. Do you not know how much I love you?"

"I love you, too." I weep with joy mixing right in there with my sorrow. Though confused, I am reassured by this wonderful man that has swooped into my life making me feel alive and stronger than I ever have. I expected his pity. What I received was relentless support. Maybe it is time to start trusting it and rely on him not push him away.

"Good," he kisses my wet lips. "Now that's settled. Remember I'm here to face this with you. I can't do that if you don't let me in. Now, how are you?" He sits down next to me and wraps me in his arms.

"Not so good." I lean into this shoulder. "She is so cruel. She goes from one mood to another without even blinking. I get sideswiped by it all. All I want to do is to attack her, make her hurt, too. That doesn't help. I end up hurting myself." Roman listens to my broken rambling while rubbing my shoulder. "Then when she started hitting on you like she wasn't shriveling up in a hospital bed, I started seeing red. I wanted to yell at her. That reaction is what makes me like her. I felt your hand and knew that I couldn't. I had no other response so I ran. I couldn't be in that place surrounded by her malice. All I do is run. I don't know how to do anything else. I want the misery to end so I get as far away from it as I can and try to ignore her. Ignore it all."

"How's that working?"

"Not very well," I snort.

Roman wipes my face with his knuckles. "You are here. You are facing your mother. Leana said that she was surprised you came or let me come. But you have. Don't you see, you are so much stronger than your mom. You also have a couple of things that she doesn't."

"What's that?" I look up at him.

"Me," he kisses the tip of my nose making me smile, "and Leana."

I look over to her standing at the end of the courtyard giving us space. She walks closer at the sound of her name until she is sitting on the other side of me patting my leg, "Are you done running for today?"

I can't stop the chuckle that escapes my lips. Of course Leana would make light of it. We've been through this many times before. "Yes. I don't think I can handle anymore today."

"Pinky swear?" Leana holds out her hand, pinky extended.

"On my honor." I respond with words scripted long ago and connect my pinky finger with hers. We commit to the ultimate promise between childhood friends.

"Good. Now can we go home. I want a shower to get all

the Marilyn negativity off of me."

"That sounds good." I sit for a moment embracing Leana's hand in mine. I embrace Roman's caressing hand on my shoulder. "Thank you guys. I couldn't do this without you. You make me stronger."

"That's the plan." Leana comments.

"You don't have to be alone. We are here for you." Roman assures.

"I'm beginning to believe that. I don't know why it's taken me so long." I reply.

"It doesn't matter how long it takes. So long as you do." Leana grants me instantaneous forgiveness.

"I'm here as long as you want me," Roman says.

"Forever?" I ask.

"And always." He finishes.

"I'll be here even longer than that." Leana says getting up. "I'll haunt your dreams if I can't get that shower." We all laugh and head to the parking lot.

I feel different leaving the hospital today. I am stronger. I had Roman and Leana before but now I understand how to rely on them in a way that I didn't before. I can see how I've been what's holding me back this whole time. They are giving me their love and support. I have to accept it.

Love is a powerful thing. It's better late than never to believe in it.

Chapter 33

Remember Everything

ARIA

We get back to Leana's apartment and burst through the door like we've been gone on a week's long holiday. If only it were even a little bit enjoyable.

Leana orders pizza then hops in the shower. I hear the water running and her singing show tunes. I go into the kitchen for some water with a smile.

When I turned around, I notice Roman studying me. I'm still surprised he didn't go screaming back to his car once he realized the crazy I came from. I hate not knowing what he is thinking, especially since he's now seen my worst.

I walk over to him stopping in front of him. I don't look into his eyes or touch him. "I'm sorry," I start but pause as I try to figure out how to apologize. "I'm sorry I ran away at the hospital and that I left you in Charleston without saying goodbye or explaining.

"This place brings out the absolute worst in me. I didn't want you to see me here. I didn't want you to get caught up in the path of the tornado that is my mother. I don't want you to see me like this, weak and angry. I hate it. I hate myself like this. I hate this place and what it does to me," I finally got enough courage to look up, "and the ones I love."

I don't know what I expect from Roman, but the smirk and kind eyes was not it. "I want to see all of you, my love.

The good and the bad. You are the only person that can send me away no matter what you mother says or does." He brushes a piece of hair from my forehead and rests his hand on my cheek.

I reach for his hand and kiss his palm, "I don't deserve your kindness. I've been horrible to you lately."

"I believe that is what love means. We forgive, support and stand together through better and worse."

"Why did you want to come after me?" I ask.

"Because I knew you needed me. Even if you wouldn't let yourself believe it. I want to be here for you when you are struggling. You don't have to face things alone anymore. We are stronger when we face things together. Besides, an old, wise bird encouraged me to come save you from yourself."

"Gran?"

"Who else?"

"She's the one that got me to go."

"I know. I think you are brave."

"I don't feel brave. I feel broken."

"You are not broken. You are hurting. The only way away from the pain is through it. Let me walk with you."

"Thank you. I love you."

"I love you, too." He leans towards me closing his beautiful blue eyes at the last minute. All I can see is his love. All I can feel is his warmth as he pulls me close deepening the kiss. Oh, how I missed him.

How deep into the rabbit hole I have fallen in only a couple days. I feel like I've been lost forever. I am thankful for my handsome prince to come and pull me out of the water and back onto dry land.

We are snug on the couch when Leana practically slams the bedroom door, announcing her entrance into the living room. "Pizza will be here in about five minutes. Do you want a beer?"

"Yes." Roman and I both answer simultaneously, making me laugh.

"How did I manage to find such amazing people to share my life with?" I say to myself.

"You knew when to leap." Roman whispers in my ear.

I nod. "I suppose you are right."

He kisses my forehead as Leana comes over with our drinks and falls into the recliner next to where we sit on the couch. "That feels a lot better."

"I agree." I take my first sip of beer and enjoy the coolness going down my throat. It is refreshing. So is the company. I feel like I've run a marathon, though thankfully, I'm not doing it alone anymore.

A knock at the door sends Leana flying towards it. She must be hungry. I should be but I'm still a little unsettled by the whirlwind of emotions these past couple of days.

I stand up, too. "I'm going to wash up." Roman smiles up at me and kisses my hand before I head to the bathroom.

Once alone I inhale deeply, letting it all rush out of me. I wash my face and look in the mirror. I don't even recognize myself. The person I was and the person I am now overlaps into twisted shadows. My mother is one burden I wish I did not have to bear. At least I have pizza and friends to share the stress.

When I return to the living room my stomach rumbles. Maybe I'm more hungry than I think.

Leana lounges in the recliner with a slice of pizza already in her hand. It amazes me how nothing ever seems to get to her. She is the ultimate go-with-the-flow kind of girl. I wonder how she does it. So many little things bother me. To her it is all part of the ride of life.

I get my slice and settle back in next to Roman who grins through his bite.

"So," Leana begins with a brush introduction, "Roman tells me that you haven't told him the whole story. Are you still shutting him out of your life?"

I turn to Roman and then back to Leana, "No, I - " I start.

"It's okay. I told him I know what it feels like to be on the Aria freeze. You always comes around eventually."

I sigh, looking cross at Leana who just smiles wide and takes a big bite of her pizza.

I turn to the man I love, "I want to let you in Roman. I am trying. Anytime anyone gets close, I corrupt it destroying the connection. Nothing has survived my mother. I barely did."

"That's true." Leana commentates.

I roll my eyes this time. I chuckle knowing what Leana is doing. "Thanks, Leana."

"No problem," she looks to Roman. "Absolute bluntness is the only way to get her to open up when she gets like this. Mild annoyance goes a long way when it comes to communicating about her mother."

I see Roman trying to absorb it all while trying not to laugh at our antics. After a minute he gets serious. "What happened?" He asks.

It is a simple question. If only it were so simple.

I look to Leana who gestures with her slice of pizza to tell him.

"By the time I was seventeen, I hardly ever even saw my mother anymore. She was fired from her job at the salon the year before and became even more elusive than she was before. She would leave forty bucks on our kitchen table every Friday like she'd been doing for years for groceries and such. I honestly don't even know where that money came from. I don't want to think about it." I cringe and see Leana shiver as well.

"She came home drunk one night with her good-for-nothing boyfriend who slapped me. Then my mother kicked me out of the house. I was done then. I was living in this void where it didn't seem like trying was worth it anymore. That nothing was."

"That living wasn't worth it, you mean." Leana adds.

"Yeah."

I watch as Roman realizes what I meant. His eyes grow wide and he looks from me to Leana who nods.

I quietly continue, "Leana found me on the pier in the middle of a thunderstorm."

"She scared me to death that day." Leana adds.

"You didn't say anything." I point at her then turn to Roman. "She walked up and punched me causing me to fall back over the railing. I had a black eye for a week."

"At least you were alive long enough for it to get better."

"Fair point."

"That was my thinking. You were too damn important to me to let you take that leap."

I nod, "After that, I stayed with Leana for the last two weeks of school and then flew to Vegas three hours after my last class. I didn't even go to graduation."

"I wanted to kick her ass for that, too."

"This is the first time I've been home since then."

"Damn. Why didn't you tell me this before?" Roman asks.

"I didn't think it mattered." I shrug knowing it wasn't enough. "I didn't want to think about it. It's not who I am anymore. At least it wasn't until I came back to town. I felt so trapped by my mother back then. Now I just feel lost."

"Do I need to punch you again?" Leana asks punching her fist into her palm.

"Please don't." I chuckle.

"Just checking. No more jump attempts okay. That's a dumb way to die and your mom is a stupid reason."

"Yes, on both accounts."

Roman turns to me laying his hand on my knee. "Aria, I knew you and your mom didn't get along. If I would have known how deep it ran, I would have understood better why you didn't want to come home. I pushed you so hard. I'm sorry, love."

"You were right. I wasn't letting you in. You deserved better than that. I wanted it to all go away. If only avoidance actually worked. I handled it all wrong."

"I'm right here for you. Please know that." Roman says.

"You've proven it. I can't thank you enough." I squeeze his hand on my leg. "You were right about another thing, too."

"What's that?" he asks.

"I did need to face my mother. I needed to see her through adult eyes. She is a flawed person, apparently with a mental disorder. It's about time I stop taking her actions so personally."

"Here, here." Leana toasts with her beer.

I take a big sip of my own and a much needed breath. "What am I supposed to do now?" I ask.

"Eat pizza," Leana exclaims. "Aren't you starving? You've barely touched your slice."

"A little," I admit trying to let the comfort food settle me.

"Does knowing about your mom's mental illness change how you see her?" Roman asks.

"Honestly, it does. I see that not all of what she does is by choice which helps some. I always felt like I was never good enough. Now I'm realizing that it wasn't really me at all. It never was."

"If she's had these illnesses all along, it does make

some things more clear in hindsight." Leana adds.

"Yeah, especially when she would act like two different people. She did that today. I never really paid much attention to it before. She's done that for a long time."

"That is what schizophrenia is right? It means she has a hard time deciphering reality." Roman observes.

"It's strange that it was never noticed before. I didn't see it and I was around her more than anyone. I never thought to look for it. Even through all of the upheaval, I didn't consider that there might be something wrong with her. I was too concerned that there was something wrong with me." I admit.

"It seems to be resting squarely on her head. Looking back on it now, it almost seems like she was jealous of you. She never liked being tied to any place or person. Maybe she envied your freedom. It could be she lashes out at you because you remind her of all the things she wished she could be." Leana suggests.

"I could see that. I was just a kid. I didn't ask to be born that was her choice."

"Was it her choice?" Roman asks.

"I always thought it was," I answer, "but my grandmother would have disowned her if she got an abortion. I suppose in a way she was stuck. She relied on her mother for a lot."

"What about the PTSD? When did that happen?" Leana asks.

"There's no telling. I mean, she didn't exactly get lots of love and support from my grandmother either." I turn to Roman, "My grandmother was always depressed and never really showed her emotions. She took care of me a lot when I was young, before she died. I was expected to do for myself as much as I was able. She would read to me sometimes but those were the only tender memories I have with her. Otherwise, she kept everyone at arms length."

"Sounds like it was a generational tendency." Roman offers.

"Yes, it does. I was on my way to being next." I bow my head in disgust.

"Not anymore. You have broken the cycle. Deciding to leave and live your own life was the start. Turning to face your mother means that you will rise above the curse of depression and mental illness." Leana exclaims.

"I hope you are right." I declare.

"Believe it and it will be." Roman says.

I nod and take a few moments to contemplate. I know what I have to do and I don't like it. "I have to face her. I have to tell her that I love her but I can't live her pattern. I want more for myself. I choose love and people who love me for me. I wish I could help her but I don't know how. Even the doctors seem perplexed by her. It doesn't seem like having me around is helping her. It might even be hurting her. Roman is right. I need to face her for myself so I can get past it."

"That is a very brave decision." Roman says.

"I don't want to." I admit. "I need to. I can't let her keep bringing me down. I have to face her so I can move on without this shadow in my past."

"We'll be there with you." Leana reassures.

"I hoped you would. Can we go tomorrow? I want to get this over with while I still have the courage."

"That's a good idea. We'll go back tomorrow." Leana agrees.

Roman takes my hand, "I'm proud of you."

"Right now I'm scared. Hopefully you will still be proud after I see her tomorrow."

"I will be. We'll face it together."

I lean into him as Leana turns on the television. "Okay,

enough with the heavy. Have you guys seen Stranger Things? Season two is amazing."

"Yeah, that's a great show. Can we start from the beginning?" I ask ready for a distraction.

"Absolutely."

I hope that I will be strong enough to face my mother. I'm not sure I'm ready. I doubt I will ever be. Roman and Leana are right. If I want to get past this, I have to face her. I'm tired of running. I sit back and relax as 80's style theme music plays. Tomorrow I will face my demons. Tonight, I'm going to enjoy good company and watch someone else face theirs.

Chapter 34

I Believe in Your Victory

ARIA

The doors to the hospital feel like the gates to hell. It seems every time I've walked through them something bad happens. I hold Roman's hand to give me strength. At least this time I am ready for battle.

As we walk by the nurses' station, one of the nurses I recognize calls out, "Aria Dalton?"

I turn to greet her. It must be early in her shift because she still has a smile on her face. "Yes?"

"I'm glad you are here. I was about to call you."

"Is something wrong?" I ask.

"Dr. Yaris wanted to speak with you again and give you some updates. If you want to wait in Mrs. Dalton's room, he's doing his rounds now."

"Would it be okay if I wait for him in the waiting room? I would rather hear what the doctor says before I see my mother."

"That's fine." She says understandingly. "I'll let Dr. Yaris know you're here."

"Thanks." I reply. We head to the waiting room.

"I wonder what it'll be this time?" Leana asks as we find seats.

"I don't know." I reply wearily. "I don't even know what to hope for anymore."

I want to face my mother so I can get this over with before I lose my nerve.

Roman sits down next to me with his arm around my shoulder. "Gran always says that knowledge is power. It may be good to know what we are facing before we enter the room."

"That's a good point," I agree. It's important to know all the information about the situation before I confront her. For all I know my mother could have drastically changed for better or for worse during the night.

"More waiting," Leana sighs.

Thankfully, we didn't have to wait very long. Within fifteen minutes, Dr. Yaris walks around the corner of the waiting room to greet us. "I'm glad you stopped by."

"How is she Doc?" I ask.

"All the narcotics have cleared out of her system so per your request, we gave her medicine to begin countering the schizophrenia effects. It seems to be going well. She is much more responsive and less combative to the nurses."

"That's good. I wonder if she will be any less combative towards me?" I wonder.

"I'm curious about that as well. I guess we'll find out." Dr. Yaris smiles.

I nod.

"There is one more thing," Dr. Yaris adds. "Her heart is continuing to work harder and harder. I fear she is susceptible to heart failure. We have her on fluids and gave her an extra pint of blood to increase circulation. It seems to be helping but it is still too early to tell. Now it is a matter of her body overcoming the damage it's been through and her will to live."

I feel Roman squeeze me in reassurance as I hear this news. This might be the end of the line for my mother. I can't decide whether to be sad or relieved at the thought.

What kind of person does that make me?

"Thanks for the update Dr. Yaris. Do you think she will recover from this?" Leana asks.

"It's hard to say," he replies grimly. "She is making some incremental improvements so there is hope. We will continue to monitor her."

"Okay," I respond. "I need to go see her now."

Dr. Yaris nods and shakes all of our hands before he leaves.

"Are you ready?" Leana asks rubbing my arm as we all stand.

"No, but I'll never be ready for this. Let's go." I say more confidently than I feel.

We walk down the hallway to her closed door. I stop in front of it readying myself for her attack. I turn to Roman and Leana, "Stay close okay? I can't run again. I have to face her."

"We face this together." Roman says and tightens his grip on my hand.

"You can do this." Leana reassures.

With their encouragement, I open the door. My mother looks like a kid lying in the bed. She is cradled in the fetal position, small and frail. Seeing her like this, I don't know how I've given her so much power of me for so long. She seems to be asleep. As we enter she rustles awake.

"Oh, it's you." she mutters. "I thought it was one of those nice nurses to give me some more meds."

"Hi, Mom." I say hesitantly, "How are you feeling?"

"Like I got hit by a bus." I realize this is the first time she has actually talked to me. Up until now, she'd only been yelling. I don't know how to continue. I start with taking a step forward and resting my hands on the bottom side of her hospital bed.

"I want to tell you something." I begin with uncertainty.

"Oh yeah?" She snarks, "that you're sorry for pushing me away all these years?"

I squeeze my eyes shut and say what I came to say. "I love you, Mom."

She stops and looks at me. "I can't remember the last time I heard you say that."

"I was eleven and Grandmother had just died."

"That was a long time ago."

"It feels like a lifetime. Do you love me?" I ask instantly regretting the question.

"Yes. You were everything I wanted to be."

"Which is what exactly?" I ask.

"Free." Her words make sense to me in a way. In another they make me sad.

"Do you regret having me?"

She looks up at the ceiling for a moment her eyes vacant like in a memory. "No, I don't regret having you. I miss the life I would have had if I hadn't gotten pregnant." She smirks, "You were a lot more work than I realized. I was tied to you. I wanted to go have fun not stay home with a fussy baby."

"Why didn't you give me up for adoption?"

"My mother thought it a sin to have you out of wedlock but a greater sin not to have you at all. Giving you up was never an option. She helped take care of you and never complained."

I hung my head. I knew she was right. My grandmother was not one to complain. She simply did what needed to be done.

"Why did you always run away from me?" she asks quietly.

I wasn't expecting this question. Honestly, I wasn't expecting any of this conversation. At first I want to point my finger at her. I bite my tongue. I no longer need to run or blame anyone else. It's time to be honest and get to the source of our trouble. That means I need to face my choices, too.

"It didn't feel like running away to me. Home was not a very good place. Especially after grandmother died. I never knew if you were coming home or who you would bring. Some of your boyfriends were not very nice to me.

"You were drunk all the time or on drugs. I was trying to keep my head down and pay attention in school. To me, it felt like surviving." I feel the tears begin but I keep going. "You kicked me out of my own house, Mom. How was I supposed to feel about that? I didn't know love or support. I knew fear and uncertainty.

"I wanted to be normal and loved. I wanted to play with you and learn from you. You were never around. Even when you were home, you wanted to be left alone.

"I ran away because that was the only thing I knew how to do. I didn't think about fighting back. I didn't even consider there was something more going on with you. I always thought I was broken and unloveable. I wanted to disappear."

I spoke the last of my words in a whisper. I felt spent but there was more I needed to say. "You made a lot of choices mom. I don't know what your motive was. It wasn't because of or in spite of me. You made them for yourself.

"I can't keep being drug down and hidden away by your choices. I will no longer suffer for your mistakes. I have to live my own life and make my own choices. I don't want to run away anymore. Leana has loved me for as long as I can remember, despite my flaws. Now I have found someone else who loves me. I want to love them back, wholly, without being afraid I'm not worthy of their love in return."

My mother is quiet for a long time. She seems off in a daydream. I start to get frustrated and it must have shown because Roman put his hand on my back and Leana put up a finger signalling me give her a minute. So I wait. All the while feeling vulnerable and defenseless.

"I don't remember that," my mother finally says looking at me with a sad look. "Kicking you out of the house, I mean. I don't remember doing that. I liked it when you were around. You had such a bright presence."

I want to be mad. That was a defining moment for me and she doesn't even remember it. Then I think of the diagnosis the doctor gave us before we came in. She's been mentally ill for a long time, not understanding what reality she was in. She finally has some medication for her mental limitation but there is little help for her physical recovery. Just when she may have some redeeming qualities, she will probably die.

There is no reason for me to be mad now. It's not going to do much good for her or for me. I feel the pressure of Roman's hand on my back. I am thankful that I could finally let him and Leana in. It is already making a huge difference. Their presence in the room help me find the strength to forgive my mother.

I tell her honestly, "That day changed everything for me. It was then I decided I would leave. I never wanted to look back."

"Why did you? I wouldn't have."

"Because I found someone worth changing for." I look to Roman who gently rubs my back with a smile.

"I wish I could have found that." Mom says then gets that far off look again. "I'm sorry I wasn't a good mother to you. I never really stopped to think about it much. I think this is about the longest I've ever been sober. Have I ever told you I hate hospitals?"

I watch her shift uncomfortably and reply. "I kind of do, too."

"Will you keep the house?" She asks.

"The house?"

"I put it in your name back when you were still in high school. That was before you ran off."

"I never knew that."

"You do now. Will you keep it?"

"I would like to. Grandmother loved that house."

"Yes, she did. I never understood it. The house was old and creaky. I always thought there were ghosts in it."

"I always pretended there were. It gave me someone to talk to."

"Hmph." Mom grunts. I try to figure out what she is thinking. I'm also trying to process the fact that apparently I have a house.

"You're grandmother would like that you keep the house. I haven't stayed there for a while though, so I don't know what kind of condition it is in."

I don't know what to say. This conversation went in a direction I didn't expect. At least we aren't yelling. That is the first time that's been accomplished in about ten years.

I notice my mother start to nod off. It seems like her body is losing its life force right before my eyes. Without yelling, there is nothing left of her. I wish I could have known her like this more.

It seems the medications have done wonders overnight. Without her own inner demons, or me, to fight with, I wonder how much fight she will have.

The doctor said it was up to her will to live and how her body fights off the injuries. Looking at her now, I get the feeling that this is her way of saying goodbye.

She said she was sorry. That was much more than I expected to get from her. I wonder if I will get to see her again. I suddenly feel this overwhelming sensation that I won't.

I step closer to her frail body, "I love you, Mom."

She looks at me and smiles, "I love you, too, my little songbird."

I lean down and kiss her cheek. I haven't heard her call me that since I was about six. It's paired in my mind with rainbow sherbet ice cream and a walk down the pier. I look at her now and feel sad.

I didn't think I would miss my mother. She had never been much of a mother to me. I miss the opportunities we lost to have any sort of functioning relationship. At least we have this moment. Roman was right. Coming to see her was something I needed to do.

My mother drifts off to sleep. I look at my companions through wet eyes nodding that I'm ready to go. They turn toward the door and we leave my mother in peace.

Once the door closes, Roman wraps his arm around my waist. "I'm proud of you, Aria."

I look up at him glad he's leading the way, "That was more than I ever thought possible."

As we enter the elevator, Leana mentions, "I haven't heard your mother speak coherently in years."

I laugh causing a wet snort to escape my nose, "I was thinking the same thing."

"She was like a different woman than she was yesterday," Roman observes.

"She was more like the glimpses of times when she was actually being my mom. I haven't heard her call me songbird since I was a little kid. It reminds me of the few times we used to walk down the boardwalk, a rare good memory."

"That's a happy thought," Roman agrees.

I smile and share my sentiment. "I have this strong

feeling that I'm not going to see her again. Somehow that moment will be the peace that she needs to be done."

Roman squeezes me tight as we walk out of the hospital to the car. Neither of them say anything. I wouldn't know what to say either. I feel it is true.

"Do you think we could go by my old house? I mean my house." I correct in disbelief. "I can't believe I have a house."

"Yeah, we can do that. I didn't know she wasn't staying there. Someone must be cutting her lawn. I go by it every once in a while when I visit my parents."

"I'd like to see it." Roman says.

"Thanks for pushing me to see her, Roman. I really needed it."

"You're welcome, love. I'm glad everything worked out."

"Me, too."

"Me, three." Leana exclaims as we reach the car.

Roman opens my door and looks me in the eyes, "Are you okay?"

I meet his gaze, "Yes, I believe I am." He nods and kisses me sweetly. We pile into the car and head out to my house. I still can't believe that Mom put the house in my name. What a bizarre day.

Chapter 35

Home By The Sea

ARIA

I smell the ocean and feel at home. That concept is so confusing to me right now. Home has always meant trouble and uncertainty. I never got a good grasp of what it could mean. I think of home now being more about the people. Leana and her family were my home growing up. Vegas never felt like home because I kept myself so set apart. Then I found my home in Roman. The townhouse we live in is nice but even him being here with me now feels like home.

The house I grew up in is beautiful. I always thought so. Admittedly it is quite rundown. I didn't see it so much a home growing up as a place to store my things.

My grandmother inherited it from her father to raise her family in. She could not have suspected my grandfather would die in the war. She raised my mom there and loved the house as she loved my grandfather. It was built in the 1920s a few blocks from the waterfront. This area, being mostly residential, did not get built up as much as other parts of town when tourism exploded in Myrtle Beach.

I love that the house is so close to the ocean. I can see the majestic waters now as we drive down the lane. Leana turns into the driveway. I hear Roman voice from the backseat, "Woah. This is where you grew up? It's exceptional."

I look at it now with the grass long but not overgrown. I

will have to find out who has been cutting it and thank them. I am sure my mother never paid them. The trim is worn and the paint fading but the house stands like a majestic ghost.

"Yeah," I sigh. "This is it." The memories flood back as I begin to walk toward the front door.

There is a blood stain on the third stair. I point it out, "I remember sitting on the front porch steps with a bloody knee after falling off my bike. My grandmother gave me an ice pack and a glass of sweet tea. She said 'You can't get through life without falling down once in a while, but you just have to keep going.'"

"I remember running up to the widow's walk so we could see the ocean." Leana adds.

"It's magical up there. You'll have to see, Roman."

He smiles at me, "I'm looking forward to it."

The front door is locked. I run around to the back and find the hide-a-key still under a gnome almost buried in the grass. I open the back door and let Leana and Roman in the front door.

I look around. My mom hasn't been here in a long while. There is a thick coat of dust over everything. The hardwood floors look to be in good shape. They need to be polished and they'll be good as new. Most of the furniture will have to go judging by the mouse droppings and holes in the cloth.

We walk into the kitchen, which is brightly lit by large east facing windows. The appliances are old. It'll be hit or miss whether they run or not. There doesn't seem to be any electricity because the fridge isn't on. Thankfully, there is nothing in it. I watch Leana and Roman do their own inspections. The space feels sacred after such a long time of disuse.

I am lost in my own thoughts and surprisingly sweet

memories. "My grandmother used to make biscuits in this kitchen every Sunday morning."

"Your grandmother made some good biscuits."

"Oh yes, they were buttermilk from scratch."

"That sounds delicious," Roman grins. "I'll play guinea pig if you ever want to try out the recipe."

"I just might." I grin. I like the idea of mixing some of my family recipes in with those his mother gave me. I'm sure my Grandmother has a recipe book around here somewhere.

We continue through the rooms. Though stagnant, there isn't any noticeable damage from its vacancy. I'm thankful no kids or passersby ransacked the place.

The bedrooms look eerie like someone left one day and never came back. I suppose that is not far from what happened. There were still clothes in the closet and the bedspread made. Knowing what I do now, I wonder what state of mind she was in when she abandoned this place. I can't imagine it was a good one.

My old room is exactly how I left it. My childhood bedspread covers the mattress. A picture of my mother, grandmother and me sits my nightstand next to my bed. I walk over and pick it up. I didn't realize I made a sound. Roman comes over to peak over my shoulder.

"Is that you?" He asks.

"Yeah, this was my eighth birthday. We went out to dinner that night. It was one of the few times we all went out and did something together."

I look across the room at my bookshelf, still full of books. I reach it and grab Matilda off the shelf. "This is the book I got that year. My grandmother always got me a book for my birthday. I can't tell you how many times I've read this. I always wanted to do pranks to my mother like Matilda."

I barely remember the old cedar chest at the foot of the bed. I go to open it and cough at the dust flying. There is a crochet quilt that my grandmother made for me as a baby, more books and my journals. I take one out and open it, "Wow, these are my old notebooks. You can find all of my thoughts, hopes and fears in these pages."

"You used to have a notebook with you everywhere you went." Leana laughs.

"Yeah, I did." I chuckle, "I still do, there's one in my bag right now. I can't believe my mom just left all of this. I never really thought about what happened to my old stuff. I wouldn't have been surprised if she burned it." I look around again, "This is exactly how I remember my room when I left. It's like a time warp."

I look out my window facing the ocean. Coming back here makes me realize there were good times, too. I've been focusing on all of the bad things for a long time. I overlooked the little things that make this place special to me.

I turn back around to Leana and Roman sitting on the bed, "I can't believe this is mine now. I didn't think it would matter but I am really glad." I stop and think, "Roman, will we be able to keep both of our houses? I wouldn't expect to live here. I know our life is in Charleston. Could we make this a vacation home or something."

Roman gets up and wraps his arms around me lifting me in a spin. "Of course, Aria. We can make it whatever we want it to be. Maybe a writing retreat for you?"

"Oh, I like that idea." I kiss him, thankful for his willingness. "Now you have to see the widow's walk. It's the best part."

The creaky, spiral stairs will need some attention, but they hold our weight for now. As we round the top, I push through the frail door to expose the salty sea breeze. We file out onto the widow's walk and lean against the white wooden railing. I breath in the ocean air. For this moment, all feels right with the world.

"This is really something else." Roman announces.

"Yes, it really is. I used to come up here with my grandmother and watch the sea. I don't know what was going on inside her head. Looking back, I wonder if she thought about my grandfather up here. She never remarried or fell in love again. She didn't even keep many friends. She was alone for all of those years. With that perspective, this could be seen as a somber place. For me it was magic. I imagined all kinds of stories up here. With the sea on the horizon and a constant breeze, I could be anyone and anything could happen." I explain.

"We used to come up here and pretend we were wives waiting for our men to come back from the sea or pirate wives waiting for our pirate husbands to come home with treasure." Leana describes.

I laugh at the memories. I feel alive.

"I'm glad that you have this. This place does feel like magic. Anything can happen." Roman smiles and hugs his arm around my waist. I'm glad that I can share this with him and remember some happy time amidst all the anguish.

Gurgle, gurgle. A strange sound came from Leana's stomach. She looks at her belly and then at us, "Sorry to ruin the perfect moment, but I'm hungry. What would you two say about grabbing some lunch?"

I laugh, thinking it is still a perfect moment. "That's a great idea."

We go back through the house and lock it up. I make a mental reminder to get copies of the key and perhaps even new locks for the doors.

As we head back to Leana's car, an older man stops his

red Ford 150 along the road in front of the house. He rolls down his window with a stern look on his face. "Hey, you there," he calls out to us.

Roman starts to walk over but I run ahead of him, "Mr. Carter, is that you?"

"Well, yes," he looks confused for a moment before he recognizes me. "Aria? It can't be? She is just a youngin'. You are all grown up."

I laugh, "You're older than you think, Mr. Carter. What are you doing here?"

"I come by once in a while to make sure the place stays somewhat maintained. I know that is what your grandmother would want. I don't know where your mother ran off too. I haven't seen her around for quite some time now."

Roman walks up behind me catching Mr. Carter's attention. "Mr. Carter, meet my boyfriend Roman," I introduce.

"Roman Wagner, sir. Good to meet you." Roman offers his hand through the window and receives a firm shake.

"Same to you, son. Are you taking good care of Miss Aria? She can be quite the handful." Mr. Carter asks.

"Yes, sir. She sure does make life fun." Roman answers with a wink.

Mr. Carter laughs, "Is that Leana trying to hide over there?"

"Yes, sir" I answer.

"It sure is good seeing all of you here. It has been too long."

"I agree with you. I didn't ever think I would come back but it's good to be home." I reply. I turn to Roman, "Mr. Carter is the landscaper that used to take care of the house. He's does work all over town. He and my grandmother would spend hours in the garden tending to plants and roses."

"The roses were her favorite. I was so sad when your mother let them die off. It was like your grandmother died all over again." Mr. Carter expresses.

That made me feel sad. I remember them blooming every year. My grandmother would tend to them like a child. After she died, I stopped paying attention. I suppose I let them die, too. I would like to plant more. I believe we can bring this place back to life and give it the happiness it deserves.

I turn to Mr. Carter with the not so great news. "My mom is in the hospital. She hasn't been for all the time she's been gone but she is now. She's not doing so good. The doctor is concerned about heart failure."

"Hmm," he murmurs. Then adds, "You're mother never really took very good care of herself. I'm sorry to hear about her being ill. I wouldn't wish that on anyone, especially you."

"Thank you, sir. It's been hard. I was finally able to talk to her. That's something I haven't been able to do in many years."

"A light beaming down through the clouds." Mr. Carter says with reverence.

"My grandmother used to say that." I remember.

"Yes, she did. She was a complicated woman. She loved you, I hope you know that."

"My grandmother or my mother."

"Both, I suppose."

I nod, it is nice to hear. Then I think, "Can I offer you something for taking care of the house all this time?"

"No dear, I did it because I respect your family. It was the bare minimum anyway."

"Thank you, Mr. Carter," I reply, then add, "Could you go back to doing more than the bare minimum? I can pay you for your services from here on out. My mother left this house to me. We live in Charleston currently. I intend to keep it but we won't be here to do regular maintenance."

"Now, that I can do." Mr. Carter agrees.

"Perfect. Let me give you my number. You can let me know what works for your schedule. I do have one request though."

"What's that my dear?"

"Could you plant some new roses. I would like to remember my grandmother when I am here."

"It would be my honor," He beams. "Now I must be on my way. You be good now, you hear?"

"I will. Thank you, Mr. Carter. It is good to see you again."

I look to Roman as the truck rumbles down the street, "Now that was a pleasant surprise."

Roman nods, "It answers the question to how the place is so well maintained while your mom was gone."

"Yes. What are the odds he happens to come by while we are here?" I wonder.

"It seems like things are starting to come together." Roman declares.

"Yes, it does. What a good feeling."

Chapter 36

Six Days At The Bottom Of The Ocean

ARIA

"I win," Leana squeals.

I toss my cards on the table, "that's the third time in a row. Rummy is not my game."

"We could play poker," Leana raises her eyebrows.

"You are on a roll. I'm not going anywhere near your poker face," Roman declares.

"Aww, you guys are no fun. Where's your sense of adventure?" Leana asks.

"It drowned in the butter along with my crab legs." I proclaim.

"It was so good though." Roman declares as he sits back on the couch. "I hope you don't have anything planned for dinner. I'm still full from that all-you-can-eat buffet."

"I ate it all and then some," I relax into the couch next to him.

Leana laughs and collects the cards. "I'm going to pour another glass. You guys want more wine?"

"Yes," we both call out.

Leana gets up and I lean over and curl up on Roman's shoulder. He wraps his arms around me with a content sigh. "This is nice," he states.

I listen to his breathing for a few moments, "It's

perfect."

I am lying peacefully content thinking of the sea breeze when my phone rings. I freeze with a sense of dread in my stomach. Somehow I know this is not a good call.

I reach over to the coffee table and retrieve me phone. The caller id says Grand Strand Medical Center, definitely not good. I look to Roman causing him to sit up straight. I notice Leana come back into the room with a wine bottle in her hand also at attention.

"Hello?" My voice is weak when I answer.

"Hello, is this Aria Dalton?"

"Yes, ma'am."

"I am calling on behalf of Dr. Yaris about your mother, Marilyn Dalton. Would you be able to come by the hospital tonight?"

"What happened to my mom?" I ask in what I think to be a calm voice.

"I would rather you talk to Doctor Yaris in person."

I pause a moment looking toward Roman and Leana for support, "Can you tell me what is going on, please?"

"I am sorry to tell you this Mrs. Dalton, especially over the phone. Your mother died this afternoon of heart failure."

I am speechless.

"Mrs. Dalton? I am so sorry for you loss." The nurse comforts.

"Heart failure? Just like the doctor said."

"Yes ma'am. The staff did everything they could. Her system couldn't take it. Her condition worsened rapidly. Then she was gone."

"I see. Thank you. We'll come in shortly to discuss arrangements." I say and hang up.

Roman and Leana are by my side by the time I look up, "Arrangements?" Leana says.

"Aria?" Roman questions as he puts his hand on my shoulder.

"It happened like Dr. Yaris said." I lean into Roman's arm and catch Leana's eyes, "She's dead. It was heart failure."

"Oh Aria." Roman says and envelopes me in a hug. I feel Leana join in the embrace. I am numb. Yet I knew it was coming. I take solace in their love. I hold on to both of them figuring out how I felt about it all.

ROMAN

The ride to the hospital is quiet. When Aria got the call, I could tell she was not surprised but still affected by it. I am glad that she was able to come to a peace with her mother before the end. I pushed her for it. I am thankful it worked out. It will take time for her to process all of this. I'm glad she is opening up for me to stand beside her.

I don't have words to console her but I can be here for her. That is often more important anyway. I appreciated her presence when Gran was sick. Thankfully though, Gran got better. Aria healed her as much as anyone could. I truly believe that. Aria has a light shining from within her, even her mother noted it. It is hard to see it dim during this trial. I pray it is only temporary.

I have witnessed the complicated nature of Aria's family. It's a lot to figure out. Now there is a finality to it. Hopefully, it will help her come to terms with her mother and herself. I'm not sure Aria knows what to think about it all. It's hard to know where to begin. I am trying to trace the story so I can continue to understand her better and help her heal.

I can see Aria's profile as she watches out the window

while Leana drives toward the hospital. She looks sullen. She hasn't said a whole lot. I wonder what is going on in her head. I reach forward and place my hand on her shoulder. I want to offer her comfort. This is the only way I know how. I have such a powerful connection with her. I want to share my strength for this next part.

Aria takes my hand and presses it to her cheek. I can feel her warmth and it makes me smile even in the somber environment. She kisses my hand and holds onto it. I feel stronger knowing we are connected. I hope she can feel it too.

I know she wasn't close with her mom but this part is always hard. I remember being with my mom when she received Dad's death certificate. The circumstances in this scenario are about as different as they can get. Still, the weight of that paper is significant.

There is a finality in death that is undeniable. It closes a door. Ends a chapter. Moving forward has to be different because there is something missing.

I don't know how Aria will need to process this change. I will be with her the entire journey. I squeeze her hand to somehow pass along this internal monologue. We face things together. She is finally believing that. I plan to stick by it.

Leana pulls into the hospital and I feel Aria tense. I don't let go of her. Once the car stops Leana looks over, "It's time."

Aria nods. She releases my hand and moves to open the door. I jump out and hold it open for her. She smiles up at me, a melancholy look. She leans into my chest wrapping her arms around me. I pull her close and kiss her hair. "We face this together," I whisper. It is becoming our mantra. A strong beginning to a lifetime together.

"Thank you," she looks up at me. "I'm so glad you are

here. I can't believe I kept pushing you away."

"You wanted to protect yourself. I get that. But I want to protect you, too. We are stronger together. We always will be."

"Yes, you have proven that already. I'm glad I got to have a real conversation with her first. You were right, I did need the closure. At least I could tell her I loved her."

"I'm glad you did." I kiss her gently on the lips then pull back to close the car door. We move toward Leana arm in arm. She waits by the front of the car watching us with a soft smile.

Aria pulls away from me to enfold her in a hug. I hear her whisper, "Thanks for always being there for me. No matter how many times I've tried to push you away you've always stood by me. I'm so glad you are here now."

"Me, too." Leana replies. "Remember, you are stronger than you think."

Aria pulls back nodding. She takes a visible breath.

"You ready?" Leana aks.

She looks from her friend back to me. Reaching for my hand she answers, "I can do this. With you two by my side I believe I can do anything."

"You've got that right." I say quietly as we begin our trek into the hospital now seeming even more cold and dreary than before.

Leana leads the way with Aria and I following hand in hand. Our pace is slow but purposeful. Leana checks in with the nurses station who directs us to Dr. Yaris's office. We sit and wait for him to come by. We don't talk. The weight in the room is unwieldy.

Sitting in the stiff, high back chair is enough to put

anyone on edge. I hold Aria's hand still as I watch her leg bounces anxiously. I catch Leana's look over Aria's head, she notices it, too. I don't know how to make her feel better. So we wait.

Though it feels like an eternity, it's probably only about ten minutes before Dr. Yaris breezes through the door. I imagine Dr. Yaris is a busy man. I am thankful he has been able to be so available for us regarding Aria's mom.

Dr. Yaris comes right in front of Aria giving her all of his attention. "The nurse told me she let you know the situation on the phone. Aria, I am very sorry for your loss. We did everything we could to hold onto her." He pauses and looks off for a moment. "I've been a doctor for many years. I've seen a lot of things. It seemed like your mother was ready to let go."

I watch Aria nod, "That sort of makes sense."

After their conversation earlier in the day, it does make sense that she may have felt like she did all she could do. Her body was already failing and her mind seemed barely pieced together with that one precious moment of clarity. It would be hard to live knowing that what you see and think are not based in reality.

"I understand that you and your mother didn't get along very well," the doctor begins but is interrupted by both Aria and Leana's chortle. I smile in spite of myself. It was not a secret to anyone that was the case.

Even the doctor grins, "But you seemed to have had a nice talk right there are the end. She died peacefully during her sleep. She did not struggle or suffer. It was like her heart just stopped."

Dr. Yaris leans up and gets a folder off of his desk. "The official cause of death is heart failure. Though I imagine it was a combination of things in the end. Here is her death certificate. The administration team will get you the rest of the paperwork and any reference numbers you need to make arrangements. Once you know where you want her, they can take care of transport and everything else."

Aria nods and hesitantly takes the paperwork from the doctor.

"Again, I am very sorry for your loss."

"Thank you, doctor. Thanks for all of your care and patience when it came to my mother."

"Not a problem, ma'am," Dr. Yaris pauses with a shake of his head. "She sure did keep things interesting around here."

We all chuckle. That is an understatement for all of us.

"You take care of yourself now, okay." Dr. Yaris says.

"I will," Aria responds. We all shake his hand. He breezes out of the office in the same manner he did coming in. He's probably off to the next crisis leaving us all feeling a little out of it.

There it is. That weighted piece of paper sitting in Aria's hands. She looks at it like it has all the answers. It is just a piece of paper but it is the beginning of a big change.

ARIA

The talk with the administration team was a blur. They were kind and efficient, but I don't remember many details. Thankfully, Roman and Leana were there to make sure all of the specifics are covered. The entire interaction was like looking through a fog. I knew it was all very important. I just couldn't seem to care.

We decide on the funeral home closest to Leana's apartment to make it easier on ourselves and made an appointment. By the time we left, I am dazed and drained. I still had no idea how I feel about any of it. The commitments are made for now.

We get home late. I can make out the stars as we sit down with a glass of wine on the patio. The warm summer evening feels happy, a contrast to my current bewildered mood. I know Roman and Leana are talking but I'm not paying them any attention.

"Aria," Leana gets my attention.

"Hmm?" I look at her questioningly.

"Hey, girl. Where are you at?" Leana asks.

I think for a moment. Where am I at? I look at her and answer honestly, "I don't know."

Roman reaches over to take my hand, "How do you feel?"

I look from him to Leana and then down, "Relieved." I look back up to them, "Does that make me a horrible person?"

"No." Leana says.

Roman agrees, "In this instance I would say it makes you human, love."

"You've been through a lot with your mom. I mean a lot," Leana emphasises. "That her end comes after the first real conversation in over ten years seems like a reason to feel relieved."

I nod feeling better. The guilt was starting to gnaw at me. "I don't know if she could have gotten better or even would've tried. I've been running away for so many years. It feels good to have it over. It makes me feel guilty, but I'm thankful I don't have to fight anymore. I'm ready to rest."

"And now you can. Your mother can, too," Roman says. "Everyone I've met has agreed that she didn't take care of herself or anyone else. It's like she's finally been able to accept you. Now you can let it go. Maybe it's time for you to let her go, too."

"That sounds nice. I hated her for years. It's strange to think of her as a mom that loved me but didn't know how to show it. She had so many demons in her head making it hard to know what was reality. I don't know that I can ever love her the way that you guys love your moms, but at least I can forgive her and try to understand. That's more than I had a couple weeks ago."

"It's way more." Leana agrees.

"It's helped me overcome my fear of letting people in, at least beginning to. I've never felt safe in relying on others. Even those closest to me. I now realize it's because I was never able to rely on my mom." I look off into the distance trying to make my thoughts make sense. "It's a comfort to realize there was something wrong with her not with me. I've been afraid I would poison any relationship so I ran away the same way I did from her. Turns out the one I was poisoning was myself."

"Not anymore." Roman kisses my hand and looks into my eyes. "You can rely on me, always."

"It's a powerful thing." I acknowledge. "I'm going to call it a night. Maybe some sleep will help me process it all."

"Okay, love. I'll be in a little bit."

"Sounds good," I hug him with a goodnight kiss.

"Night, girl," Leana says as she hugs me as well.

"Night. See you guys in the morning."

I take my wine glass into the kitchen and replace it with a bottle of water. It tastes refreshing after such an exhausting day. I've ran 5k races and not felt as tired and I do today.

The bathroom is too bright. I can feel my eyes droop. I run on autopilot as I brush my teeth and wash my face. I'm about ready to turn to go to the bedroom when I catch my eyes in the mirror. There is a vitality in them there wasn't before. Even through the fatigue I sense an intensity in me that I'd never noticed.

My emotions have been muted through this process. I don't know what to think about my mother's death. By facing her and seeing the situation through, I have gained confidence in myself. There is a certainty in my heart that I am on the right path. I can trust the people in my life because it is my choice and theirs to be there. There is a power in that which I am only beginning to understand.

I take a deep breath and exhale my doubt. Everything is going to be okay. We will face it together.

Chapter 37

Bird Set Free

ROMAN

The humid air is the same here as it is in Charleston. Being close to the ocean under the southern sun is home to me. Being here with a friend and a woman that I love and connect with so strongly makes me certain there isn't anywhere else I would want to be.

I hear the bedroom door shut. I hope Aria can get some rest, it has been an overwhelming day. It is amazing the topsy turvy roller coaster life can be. I try to think of my evenings before I met Aria. I can't even remember what I did. It's hard to imagine her not being in my life, I never want to. It has only been a month since we met, yet I can't see a world where she is not in it.

In some ways that scares me. I loved my Dad fiercely, but I lost him. Love isn't enough to save someone. It is enough to make life worth living. The light behind Aria's eyes is starting to come back. I noticed it when she said that she was relieved.

I'm still trying to puzzle together Aria's story in my head. The past I've heard about and the mother I saw in the hospital.

Leana has been curiously quiet. I glance at her across the table with her nose in her uplifted wine glass. She catches my eyes, "What do you make of all of this?" I ask.

The smile that spreads across Leana's face is almost evil. "Could you imagine living your whole life in a cage?

We do it to birds. They can fly anywhere, yet we put them in a prison so we can look at them."

"I'm curious as to where this is going," I encourage her as I sip my Cabernet.

"Now imagine the owners of that cage dies and the birds are set free. Do you think the birds are going to be sad that their maker dies or happy that they can fly?"

"They would die because they wouldn't be able to fend off predators." I tease her.

She scowls at me and counters with, "The bird has a courteous friend and a compassionate mate to help her."

"Courteous, huh?" I say causing Leana to reach over and whack me. "Okay, okay, I get it. It's hard to be too upset when the situation ends with being set free."

"Yes," Leana exclaims. "When Aria went to Las Vegas she didn't see her mom, but she was still in the cage. Wherever she went it moved with her."

"Then she moved back after she met me." I add.

"I believe you helped her forge a key. She could get out once in a while. She always seemed to find her way back into the confinement of her mother's influence."

"Facing her mother made her see the cage that surrounded her." I ponder.

"This time she was strong enough to push away from the cage entirely." Leana continues.

"Then the maker of the cage died setting her free for good."

"I like you, Roman. You speak our language."

I chuckle, "I'm learning as I go."

"You are a quick learner, my Padawan."

"Thank you, Obi Wan." I bow to her and we both laugh. I lift my glass for another sip, "I like you, too, Leana. I am glad that Aria has you in her life. I can see why you guys stayed such good friends through it all."

"Yeah, how's that?" She asks with a tilt of her head.

"You have your own language." I explain.

"That is true." She lifts her glass to mine.

"I bet there is more." I inquire.

She looks at me for a moment. I'm not even sure what I am asking. I am curious what makes them work. They support each other so fiercely, yet they only share a few commonalities.

"Aria is interesting," Leana confides. "She has this spark about her that is undeniable. She had a shitty home life, but she was always kind and never got in trouble. I used to see her sitting in the back corner of the library after school with her nose in a book. I asked her one day why she was there instead of home. Her answer was, 'It's peaceful here.'

"It took me a while but I eventually understood what she meant. She started coming to the drama club with me after school. She didn't really care about the production. She would help with the staging and run lines with me. We got really close and started hanging out all the time.

"Life for me was boring. My family loved me, I know that, but they didn't really need me. We spent time together. I would go to school then go home. Nothing exciting ever happened. I didn't zone out into books like Aria did. I like to reenact other people's stories. When I found Aria, I figured I found the writer of tales I would produce.

"Aria used to write plays and all kinds of things when we were young. You've heard us talking about that before. That's what we did all the time. We lived in a different world together. She would write and I would set everything up to act out the scenes. I suppose it all created a powerful connection that stuck even as we grew up and lived our own lives. We have a stable foundation. I was one of the few people who knew about what was really going on with her mother. She didn't like talking about it. I don't even think my mom knows all the stories. We were always together. She is like my sister. We are closer than blood."

"That's extraordinary. So powerful. I hope we have a story like that one day." I remark.

"You already do." Leana tilts her glass toward me. "You may not have been around long, Roman. But I've seen you two together. It's not something you see very often. Aria doesn't let people in, like at all. It was different with you right from the start."

"I can feel that." I agree then ask curiously. "Why do you only date assholes?"

"How do you know?" Leana counters.

"Aria is worried about you. She says you need a new type."

"I know. She's right. I don't know where they are at. I keep trying. A guy seems nice at first but they all end up the same. I need to get out of my routine and do something new."

"What would you do?" I ask.

"Get back to singing." She answers easily.

"You sing?"

"Yes. I enjoy it. I used to be a lead in our high school musicals. The songs were my favorite part."

"I've never heard you sing." I realize.

"That's because we haven't been on a road trip together. Nothing beats belting out to Christina Aguilera with car acoustics."

The image makes me laugh. I can imagine her and Aria singing together. "I bet that is quite the spectacle."

"I wanted to write my own songs. I just never knew what to say. That's always been Aria's department. I like doing covers and singing show tunes. My mom even got me a piano so I could compose and make my own arrangements."

"You play piano, too." I ask.

"I sure do," she nods.

"That's something we have in common."

"Ah, something new about you. Classical or contemporary?"

"Classical. My mom made me take lessons when I was young. I fought her for so long. It turns out I really love it. It's like a puzzle to turn the notes on the page into music. I've never composed anything. I read sheet music."

"I would like to hear you play sometime."

"You will have to come meet my mom sometime. That's where the piano is."

"I have a keyboard. I haven't pulled it out to play in a while." She pauses lost in thought. After a minute, then looks up at me. "Maybe I will have to come visit. Gran lives there, too, right? Aria has told me all about her. I think she may be my spirit guide."

"She has a knack for it. Just like you do." I say and don't miss the twinkle in her eye. "What kind of music do you play?"

"Contemporary. I like to take the fast songs and slow them down. Take the slow songs and speed them up. It's fun to play with rhythm. I like giving people the unexpected."

"You have a good sense of what people need. I remember that first night when I met all of you. You practically told Aria to stay with me. I didn't think anything of it at the time. I remember being thankful. Now that I know you better, I bet you sensed the connection between Aria and me."

"Perhaps. I have a gut instinct on things. I don't question it. I'm glad she went with you. I think it's done wonders for both of you. I didn't know you needed her, too."

"I did. Though, I didn't realize it at the time." I agree. "What about you? What do you need Leana?"

"It's a lot easier for me to see it for you than it is for myself."

"Maybe it's time to start looking inward." I suggest

I can see her thinking. The weight of the day is beginning to weigh on her, too. "I'm going to call it a night."

"Yeah, me too." She gets up and starts clearing the table.

"Hey, Leana," I begin.

"Hmm?"

"I'm glad I can call you friend."

"Same here," she sets the glass and bottle back down and reaches to give me a hug. "I'm glad Aria found you," she pulls away. "I'm glad you found each other."

"It was definitely one place I didn't think to look."

"Funny how that happens," she ponders.

I follow Leana inside and set my glass in the kitchen before heading to the bedroom. I turn back to Leana, "You're sure you don't mind me sleeping in your bed? You could sleep next to her tonight if you want. I know she won't care."

"Thanks Roman, but I think she needs you tonight." Leana smirks and goes into the bathroom.

I'm not going to argue with her. She really does seem to know what people need. I open the bedroom door silently to find Aria lying in bed with her eyes open.

"Hey beautiful, what are you still doing up?"

She smiles over at me and shrugs, "I can't sleep. Too much on my mind, I guess."

"They isn't all sad is it?" I move to lay down next to her on top of the covers.

"No, I had a realization. It made me feel good. I'm still trying to figure out what it means."

"What's that?" I ask.

"I'm free." She smiles at me.

"Like a bird freed from a cage."

"Yeah," she says surprised. "How did you know?"

"A little bird told me." I lean over to kiss her cheek.

"Leana?"

"Of course."

"Yeah, that seems like something she would say. A bird is what I imagined, too."

"You two speak the same language."

"Yeah, I suppose we do."

"What is the bird going to do?" I whisper.

"Whatever I want. Right now, I want to kiss you."

"I would like that very much." I agree leaning down meet her lips. The moment we connect I feel whole. I know that no matter what happens today, tomorrow or in the future, as long as face it together, nothing is impossible.

After a few moments, her mouth is not enough. I leave traces along her jawline and find a sweet spot under her ear. I enjoy her squirming under my lips. I smile into her neck and adjust myself to continue my line of kisses even lower.

Melody flows in from the living room. We pause and look at each other. I hear a piano playing a slow refrain of Zedd's "Stay." It is hauntingly beautiful.

"Is that Leana?" Aria asks.

"I suppose so. She was talking about playing earlier. Do you think we're being too loud?" I ask with my arm wrapped firmly around her shoulders keeping her close to me.

"No." She says with a smile. "I'm glad she's playing again. That means something is about to change for her."

"How do you know?"

"We speak the same language, remember?" She laughs nodding, "Something good always happens when she starts to play. She loves it and it makes her stronger. She sometimes forgets how important it is. She always comes back to it. Good for her."

"It seems this has been a week of breakthroughs." I notice.

"A new chapter beginning."

"As long as I get to kiss you through the next one, too."

"Through the whole book."

"I only get one?" I tickle her making her laugh.

"You get the entire library."

"As long as you're there with me."

"Always." She breathes.

I consume her mouth attaching my spirit with hers. My hands glide up the length of her body and pull her tank top off. Her silky skin makes me ache to be closer to her. She sighs into my mouth. I take the opportunity to move my kiss down to her stomach. I reach up to caress her breast and feel her rise to my wandering hands. Her breathy exhale excites me. I remind myself to go slow. She comes alive under my hands and I yearn for more.

I lean down and trace my tongue over her nipple. She arches back giving me more access. I take her breast in my mouth and gently suck on her smooth flesh.

I feel her hands flexing on the bed next to me as she angles closer. My fingers reach into her pajama pants for her moist center. I brush her, causing her to release a gasp.

The melody in the living room builds as Aria does. I stroke her orgasm with my finger and tongue. She builds into a crescendo and crashes over into release.

After a few moments, she looks over at me. "You are an amazing man."

I bow forward to kiss her lips, "You are an amazing

woman."

"I want you," she reaches up under my shirt to place her hand on my chest.

"You have no idea." I say as I pull my pants off along with hers. I crawl on top of her and gaze into her eyes enjoying this moment. "You are so beautiful. I love your body and your soul."

"Kiss me," she breathes.

"Always," I answer and devour her lips.

Making love has always been amazing between us. Every time has been special and immensely pleasurable. Being with her in this moment is beyond anything I have ever experienced. It was transformational.

She let me in entirely. We connected both physically and emotionally. I could feel her pain, her joy and share her freedom. Maybe those were all my own emotions. My heart opened and our union deepened, two became one. We will face all things together because we are one. We are two separate people sharing our lives, our hearts and our love.

My release is powerful. As I fill her, I enjoy the feeling of her wrapped around me. We are a solid merger fusing our life force together in the most intimate, primal way. I look into her eyes and see the stars looking back at me.

She smiles and reaches up to lay her hand on my face, "I love you, Roman."

"I love you, too, Aria. More than there are stars in the sky." I kiss both her cheeks, her forehead and her mouth before I surrender her to clean up.

Afterwards, the weight of her head on my chest feels light as a feather. I cradle her to me as I slowly drift to sleep feeling invigorated and revitalized.

Chapter 38

Closer To Fine

ARIA

Light streams through the window piercing my dream. I was a bird flying across the vast landscape below me. I could go anywhere but I kept coming back to this window. There was a piano inside it with a cushion to perch on. The piano's tune felt like a calling, a beacon home.

Waking up feels surreal. The world goes on without my mother to throw anymore kinks in the works. The best part is, I can forgive her of all of it. The years of abandonment, rejection and carelessness wash away like dirt from a strong rain. The storm left fresh air in its wake. That will be my mother's legacy.

Roman is still asleep beside me so I get out of bed quietly. I notice Leana asleep on the couch as well. It's still as I make my way into the kitchen. My stomach growls as I make my coffee. I decide to cook some breakfast. Only after I have bacon sizzling and bread popping up from the toaster does Leana stir.

She calls out from the living room. "Do I smell bacon?"

I poke my head around the corner, "You sure do."

"It smells good. Is it a special occasion?" she asks.

"Yes." I reply, "I'm hungry. We will need our energy today. And I wanted to make breakfast."

She gets up with a blanket wrapped around her and sits on a stool. I pour coffee for her. I notice her inquisitive eye but she doesn't say anything.

With her first sip of coffee I watch her melt on her perch. Satisfied, I turn back around to finish breakfast.

A few minutes later I hear the water running in the bathroom. Soon Roman walks into the kitchen in sleep pants without a shirt on. "Good morning, handsome." I greet him with a kiss, enjoying the feel of my hand resting on his bare chest.

"Good morning," he returns the kiss. "Do I smell bacon?"

"Yes you do. It's almost done."

"Is it a special occasion?" Roman rubs sleep from his eyes.

I turn around, spatula in hand, and look at him. I point from him to Leana and back again. "You two," I laugh as Roman sits down next to Leana with the same drowsy eyes. "No, I'm hungry and I felt like cooking breakfast."

I see them look at each other and then back to me. "What?" I ask. "I cook."

Roman laughs, "Yes, you are turning into quite the chef." He walks over and wraps his arms around me as I flip the bacon and stir the eggs. He kisses the back of my neck causing me to giggle before moving to fix his own mug of coffee.

I put the food onto plates. "All done." I announce.

We eat contently. The mood is light and peaceful, a stark contrast to the schedule for the day. I am glad for these moments. I feel stronger this morning than I have in a long time.

Whatever comes today, I can face it. Especially with the two most important people in my world by my side. It makes me happy they get along so well. They fight with their forks as lightsabers while putting their plates up. It warms my heart.

I try not to think about what will happen next while I

get ready to head out. I have no idea what to expect at the funeral home. I try my best best to not stress over it too much.

Just like when I go to the dentist, I have to trust that these people know what they are doing. They can help and lead me through all of the details.

We approach a plain brick building with a large covered awning at the entrance. "This place looks dead." I say offhandedly.

Leana laughs, "Really?"

"Huh?" I look at her confused.

"That was a horrible pun," she chuckles.

"What?" I ask and then realize what I said. "Oh," I laugh when I realize it. "I must be nervous. I'm making puns and I don't even know it."

"It's going to be fine," she reassures.

I nod. I don't really have a choice so best to get on with it. I find Roman's hand as we walk through the door. A middle aged man greets us, "Hello there. Are you Aria?" He asks.

"Yes," I step forward to shake his hand.

"My name is Ralph. I'm the funeral director. I'll be helping you make arrangements."

"It's nice to meet you. This is Roman and Leana." He shakes their hands as well.

"If you'll follow me, we'll start in my office." He leads the way down the side of the building where a series of doors stand. He chooses one and opens it ushering us in.

The place is chilly causing me to shiver. I sit in a lightly cushioned chair across from Ralph. "I'm so sorry for your loss," he begins. "Were you and your mother close?"

"No," I know he is only trying to be polite. I'm not very good at small talk, especially when it concerns my mother. "It's complicated."

I shift uncomfortably in my chair and he gets the hint, "Well, the first question is cremation or burial."

"Hmmm," I think out loud. "I don't know what she would have wanted. We didn't exactly talk about these things."

"What do you want?" Leana asks.

I smirk in spite of myself. All I can think is 'She's a witch, burn her!' Too many late night Monty Python marathons are not very helpful in this moment. Though the inspiration sticks, "Cremation seems right."

"Okay, would you like to have a viewing? You can do this before or after she is cremated." Ralph asks in a professional manner.

It seems strange making these kinds of decisions. They all seem very grown up and final. I didn't want to see her in life. I don't know what to do with her. I am ready to move on. I try to be respectful while I push through these details. "No, I don't think that's necessary."

"What about the service?" Ralph asks, "Would you like an open casket or to display the ashes in an urn?"

"I don't think anyone would come to a service. Do we have to have one?"

The funeral director looks cautious, "Not necessarily, but most find it resolving to have a service to help them make peace and move on."

I'm ready for that part to hurry up and get here.

"I think it would be good to have a service," Leana offers. "People will want to come say their respects."

I open my mouth then close it again. It seems like the right thing to do. I still don't think anyone will come. I'm not sure I would have. Definitely not before we talked yesterday. Wow, she was alive yesterday and today she is not. My head starts to spin.

"How soon can a service be put together?" Roman asks.

"The average wait is three days to allow for notification and preparations to be made. There is a twenty-four hour hold after we receive the body. Since you do not want a viewing service, we can begin the cremation tomorrow. You can hold the service as early as tomorrow evening. I recommend an extra day to allow time for notification. We have both evenings available here unless you would rather hold the service at a different location."

Everyone looks to me, "Here is fine."

"Which day would you like to book?"

I look to Roman and Leana for this one, "You guys are the ones with jobs to get back to. What do you think?"

"I think we should wait the extra day." Leana suggest. "Let's give everyone a chance to come."

She seems determined about this. I look to Roman and he nods. "Okay. The day after tomorrow it is."

"Alright, we will get that all set up. We received the paperwork we needed from the hospital and the body is already here."

"Can I see her?" I surprise myself by asking.

Ralph looks at me curiously, "Yes, of course. Then I can show you some options for urns."

Ralph leads us down a somber hallway then down some stairs. I read morgue on the wall as we enter through the double doors. Ralph shows us where my mom is and then leaves us in peace.

She seems to have shrunk even more since I saw her in the hospital. It doesn't feel real. I keep waiting for her to wake up and start yelling at me. Not this time, though. The quiet in the room is unsettling. The only thing I hear is our breathing sounding very heavy among the dead.

I don't know the right answers. I'm just trying to get through this stage so I can finally feel free. "I believe I was right to say cremation." I say quietly. "She looks like she needs to be set free. The same way I want to fly from my cage."

"I think you're right." Leana agrees.

We chose an urn, a black cylinder with three birds etched in silver. One for mom, one for my grandmother and one for me. I don't know if I will keep it or spread her ashes. We finalize the dates and details about stationary and obituaries. There is a that needs to happen when someone dies. I couldn't imagine going through all of this if I were truly upset over the death. I'm overwhelmed enough as it is. I am glad when we are finally able to leave the stifling building.

On the way to the car Leana speaks up, "I'm dying to know what you were chuckling about while we were talking with the funeral guy?"

I laugh again, a sweet release after that stuffy place. "He asked about burial or cremation and all I could think of was the quote, 'She's a witch, burn her!'"

"Ha, that sounds about right," she laughs. "I knew you had something going on in your head."

"Guilty."

"All I could think was about how he could speak without his mouth moving. It was kind of creepy." Leana confesses.

"I'll have to notice next time. I was glad when he finally ran out of questions." I sigh as we reach the car. "I still don't think anyone will come to a service. I can't think of many who will miss her. I'm not sure I will."

"Harsh but true," Leana agrees. "They aren't coming to see her. They are coming to support you. Ask anyone. They know that your mother wasn't often there for you. Ask them also if they would have helped if they only knew what to do. They will come to encourage you. They will come because you matter to more people than you think."

"I doubt that." I react. "I can't really oppose it either."

"I would come," she shrugs.

"You are already here."

"I wouldn't be anywhere else."

I'm glad to be back at Leana's where I can change into fuzzy pajamas and relax. I decide I deserve the comfort even if it is still afternoon. Before I can relax too much, I feel an urge to call Gran. I know Roman has talked to her and his mom to keep them up to date but I need to talk to her.

I sit alone on the porch snacking on gummy bears as I dial her number. She picks up on the third ring, "Why hello dear. How are you holding up?"

"Hi Gran. I'm alright. I miss you. I could sure use a painting session right now."

"I imagine you can. Well get to it shortly."

"Has Roman told you what's going on? I'm sorry, I haven't been in good head space to call you before now."

"That's perfectly fine my dear." I can hear her smile through the phone. "Yes, he has said the worst has happened."

"I don't know about the worst, but she is dead." I pause. "Wow, that's still strange to say."

"I wish I could tell you it gets easier. At least you got a chance to see her."

"Yes, you were right about all of it. I needed to come and face her. It helped me find my own strength. I also think it helped her let go in the end. I didn't realize there was so much going wrong with her. Not only at the end but for probably most of her life. She never even knew it."

"We do not always recognize the demons we face. It sounds like she had a few of them."

"Yeah, she did. I'm glad Roman was here too. Thank you for telling him to come."

"He would have come anyway. He wanted to be there for you. It sounds like you have let him in."

"I have. I feel like the Grinch. My heart has grown three sizes through all of this. I've been able to rely on him and Leana more than I ever have let myself before. It feels like a big change. It's an important transformation for me."

"That is wonderful to hear. I can't wait to meet Leana. She sounds like a fascinating friend."

"She is. She wants to meet you, too. I'll have to get her down to Charleston soon."

"Please do. I'm glad to hear you are hanging in there and making breakthroughs while you are at it."

"Yes, it has not been easy but it's all working out."

"Keep me updated. I will talk to you soon darling."

"Thanks, Gran. I will."

Gran always makes me feel good. I silently kick myself for being so out of it and not calling her. I'm glad Roman was able to. Before I can get up to see what is going on inside my phone rings. I look down at the caller ID, "Mikey," I practically yell into the phone as I answer it.

"Hey girl, how are you?" It's nice to hear Mikey's relaxed baritone. He's the only one I really miss from Vegas. With so much going on, I haven't had much time to think about it.

"Not doing so great at the moment actually," I admit.

"What are you up to?"

"What's going on?" he asks.

"My mom, you know, the greatest living bitch on the planet." I continue at his acknowledgment. "Well, now she is the greatest dead bitch on the planet."

"Damn. Short story long?" He encourages my explanation.

"About a week ago," I pause. "Wow, it hasn't even been a week yet." I say absently. "I get a call from Leana. She's the one that was at Lights with me that night when I met Roman."

"Oh yeah, I remember her. She was a spirited one."

"That's definitely her. She called to tell me my mother was in the hospital. I didn't want to go home to Myrtle Beach to see her, but I got talked into it. Turns out she really wasn't doing so hot. I finally went. It all seemed really bad for a minute. She was yelling at me and making me feel even worse."

"Oh man, that sucks."

"Yeah, but then I learned that she may not physically recover. She was also diagnosed with schizophrenia so her mental health was possibly worse. It took her a few days to detox. They gave her some medicine to try and combat the crazy in her head."

"Did it help?"

"I guess so because then the most unimaginable thing happened. I had a conversation with her. A real grown-up conversation. I still can't believe that happened."

"That sounds nice."

"It was. She said she loved me but she didn't know what to do with me. We had a moment of peace. She died yesterday afternoon of heart failure." It feels good to get it all out there. When I put it all in one explanation it feels more manageable than it all happening a little bit at a time.

Maybe I can use this to continue trying to process it all.

"Woah, that's a crazy story. Have you already had the service?"

"Well, technically it's a memorial because we are having her cremated. But no, not yet. It's the day after tomorrow."

"That's a lot going on. How are you doing?"

I turn inward for a minute and answer honestly, "I'm doing okay. It's a little sad and a little relief all mixed in. In truth, I'm still processing all of it. So much has happened in such a short time it almost doesn't feel real."

"I can understand that. Take your time." He pauses. I can tell in his voice that he has something else to say. After a couple beats, he continues, "When my Dad died, I didn't know if I liked him or not. I'm still not entirely sure. Over time the memory becomes less intense. I think my mom is happier without him so it's hard to say."

"Your Dad was a piece of work."

"So was your Mom. Something we had in common," he laughs. I contemplate the past tense and realize that is only partly true. Our parents may be gone, but their influence remains.

"Aria?" Mikey asks quietly after a few moments of silence, "Would you want me to come out there to be with you for the funeral?"

"Really? Would you?" I ask excited about the idea.

"Yeah. You were there with me when my father died. I know you have Roman and probably your friend, too. It's a hard time even when we don't like the ones who died. Besides, I haven't been out to see my mom in almost two years."

"Oh Mikey, that would be amazing. You'd be able to get the time off work and everything?"

"I'm not worried about that. I've been thinking it might

be time for a change of my own. I'm just not sure what that is yet. Ever since you've been gone, it's different. I get up, go to work and come home. It's not much of a life."

"I know the feeling. That was me hard core before I left."

"Yeah, I figured. I'm not sure that it's enough anymore."

"I hear you there. Are you thinking of moving back to the east coast?"

"Maybe. I don't know. Why can't life make sense?"

I laugh a lot harder than I mean to. "That would be nice. I suppose it wouldn't be as much fun, though."

"Right," I can hear him roll his eyes through the phone. "Now you're going to think I'm crazy."

"You're preaching to the choir. I'm already crazy. What's up?"

"You know how you are always telling me to listen to my dreams because they have power behind them?"

"Yeah, I completely believe that."

"I had a dream last night of a bird being set free over the ocean. There was a sign in my dream, a billboard that said 'Welcome to Myrtle Beach.' Isn't that where you are?"

"Yeah, it is. Are you serious? That is beyond coincidental."

"How so?"

"Myself and Leana both independently had the thought of a bird being set free from a cage last night after we learned my mom passed away. We are at the ocean. We were over at the water yesterday. That's not even including the Myrtle Beach part. Was there anything else in your dream?"

"I'm trying to remember. It's actually why I called you. I can't seem to get it out of my head and you always know what these things mean."

"Well, thanks. I'll take that compliment."

He laughs at that, "There wasn't anything else in particular. I woke up with this urge to go somewhere like something or someone was calling me. There was a melody in my head, a song from the radio. It didn't sound the same, it was slower."

"Do you remember the song?"

"Umm...The same band who sings "Clarity," but it was their other song."

"'Stay?" I ask.

"That sounds right," then he hums a few bars.

"Yep, that's 'Stay.'" It is the same song Leana was playing last night. Chill bumps race down my arms. Something is happening here and it is powerful. Dreams have great meaning to me. I always pay attention to the feelings I get from them. Mikey may be coming to support me through my mom's funeral but I can't help but wonder if Leana is what he'll find. They connected while we were in Vegas. I look forward to finding out.

"Mikey, I think it would be great for you to come if you are able. The service is at 5pm, day after tomorrow."

"I'll check out some flights," he says and then pauses a minute. "You're going to be fine. You know that right?"

"Thanks, Mikey. I believe I am. I'm finally learning how to open up and let people help me. Thanks for being such a good friend." I share.

"Anytime."

I smile. I suppose there was something good that I left in Las Vegas. Mikey is a real friend. I need to do a better job keeping up with people. "I look forward to seeing you."

"Me, too. I'll get the details figured out and let you know when my flight is."

"Sounds good. I'll talk to you soon."

Chapter 39

Take Me Home

ARIA

I don't know what to wear. I didn't bring many clothes. I figured I'd only be gone a couple days. I had no idea I would be attending a funeral. I stand in front of Leana's closet with a very daunting task.

"I don't think you should wear black." Leana advises.

"It's traditional." I argue. "I don't know if I'm even all that upset by all of this. Wearing something flamboyant is not going to help my guilt about that."

"That is the reason to wear something that stands out. I'm not saying arrive there with a floral sundress like it is another day on the beach. But something not black."

"Well, it's kind of up to you anyway," I shrug. "I didn't exactly pack for a funeral."

"In that case I have a couple of thoughts." Leana dives into her closet and comes out with two options. First she holds up a wine red maxi dress with a low cut v neck and a slit up the front to my mid thigh.

"That's gorgeous. It'd be great if I were going to a show." I exclaim.

"That is why I got it. I wore it when I saw *Hamilton* up in Charlotte last fall."

"That sounds fantastic. I don't want to sully that memory with my mother's funeral."

Leana rolls her eyes and holds up the next option. The navy blue sleeveless high-low maxi stuns me. There is a silver broach at the waistline where the v neck meets it and a sheer layer on top of the navy undercoat that flows even on the hanger.

"I thought this would be the one." Leana says to my reaction.

"It's beautiful," I reach out to touch it affectionately. "It's elegant, yet soft. This is perfect. It makes a statement without overpowering the moment."

"This is a ceremony to let go of the past and step into the future. You deserve to look beautiful and dignified."

"Thanks, Leana."

"It's what I'm here for. My wardrobe is here to serve." Leana leaves me to get ready.

I take a deep breath. This will all be over soon.

The last twenty-four hours have felt like limbo. It's been the only day in a week where there wasn't some sort of emotional upheaval. Instead, everything started falling into place. Mikey's plane landed late last night. He's in a local hotel for a couple nights. The funeral home called to confirm my mother's ashes were successfully stored and ready for the memorial.

We picked up a local paper with the obituary in it. The article was short and sweet. It covered when and how Marilyn Dalton died, that I was the last living relation and details about the memorial.

I still don't know why we are bothering with a service at all. Leana believes it will be important for people to have a chance to come. Roman agrees that it needs to happen so I can get closure and be able to move forward with more confidence.

It makes sense. I am learning to let them in to help me. They are the only reason I am getting into a very pretty dress to say goodbye to my mother one final time.

Yesterday we spent some time out at my house. We

opened all the windows to let a breeze come through. It took out a lot of the stuffiness. I got the electric and water turned back on and we were able to make some small improvements. We swept the entire house. So much dust flew up I had a coughing fit. We wiped down the kitchen and bathrooms. It took half a day to take inventory of what needed to be fixed up or tossed out. We also made like of items that needed repairing or replacing.

It was a fun time listening to beach music and feeling the ocean breeze through the windows on a beautiful day. We celebrated our achievements by spending the early evening on the beach. It was great to swim in the water and enjoy the salt breeze kiss my face. It was a happy day almost borrowed from time.

This entire week has felt almost otherworldly like an emotional roller coaster vacation I never asked for. I have learned a lot about myself and what I'm capable of. I've learned a lot about my mom and who she was. Though I don't completely agree with her choices, I understand that she did not have full control of herself. I don't know for how long or how much of it was her own doing. At the end of the day it is how it is and I can't change that.

No matter how much I struggle with her choices, I can't change them. I can learn from them and forgive her. She can't afflict anymore on me. I work to process what had happened and move past the bondage of my past.

I hear Roman coming toward the bedroom door, "Aria are you almost ready?"

He opens the door. "Wow," he staggers, "You are breathtaking."

"Thanks," I smile then frown, "Do you think it's too much for a funeral? Leana was determined I not wear black."

"I think it's perfect." He walks to me and sweeps me up

in a kiss. "Well, let's just say it's a good thing we need to leave or you wouldn't be wearing that for long."

I revel in his arms. Yes, the future looks very bright indeed.

"You don't look so bad yourself." I comment on his dark khakis and crisp button up.

"It turned out to be a good thing I came from work or I wouldn't have had anything to wear either."

"I'm sure Leana would have loaned you a dress." I tease.

"I wouldn't want to stretch out her pretty things. Besides, my butt would never look right in a dress like that. Yours, however, fills it out nicely." Roman reaches around to clutch my buttcheek causing me to laugh.

As our laughter subsides, he looks me over, "You ready?"

"Yeah. Are you sure we need to go?"

"Yes, I do. Leana says she's already gotten several calls about the service."

"I will have to thank her again for putting her number on that announcement. She's so much better at handling all of that. At least right now."

"She's a pro, I'll give her that. She has everything ready. We're just missing you."

"I'm ready." I say with a nod. Roman escorts me out of the bedroom through the apartment.

We meet Leana at the door. "You look great," she says.

"Thanks. You are sure it's not too much?"

"Nope. They aren't going to come to see your mother. You might as well make an impression," she states.

"So people are going to come?"

"Yes, Aria," Leana assures. "Do you know what you are going to say?"

"I've been contemplating it all day."

"You'll be great. You are a writer. The words will be there when you need them. They always are."

I hope she is right.

ROMAN

The funeral home was is bleak and foreboding as it was a couple of days ago. I suppose cheerful isn't an appropriate target but warm and comforting would be an improvement.

I can tell Aria is nervous. She keeps fidgeting with her dress and has put her hair up in a ponytail then pulled it out at least five times already. I sense she is ready for this to be over. I completely understand that.

I hope she knows that we are trying to look out for her to go through with this. It will be important to be able to move forward.

I take Aria's hand in mine to offer her comfort. We pass through the glass doors and see "Marilyn Dalton" on a sign with an arrow towards the small chapel.

Ralph, the funeral director, greets us at the door. "Everything is ready. The urn is set up on the altar and there is plenty of room for your guests. It is up to you if you want to greet people or if you want to remain in the chapel."

We look to Aria, but she seems frozen in place. Leana saves her, "I don't mind greeting people if you want to go sit."

I squeeze her hand to let her know that was fine and she answers, "Yes, that sounds good. Thanks, Leana."

"Of course," Leana hugs her, "You are going to be just fine."

We walk into the empty chapel and sit on the first row

right in front of the urn. As much as Aria doesn't want this ceremony, it is really short and sweet. After everyone gets here, Ralph will welcome everyone and introduce Aria. She is supposed to talk and then Leana wanted to sing a song. That's it, as simple as we could make it.

Her family is not religious, so there will be no sermon or anything. They allowed time afterward to visit with guests. Aria was so sure no one was going to come. I notice people already starting to file in slowly and sit down in the pews.

After some time I realize I recognize someone coming through the doors. Aria has her head down in thought. I lean over to her and whisper, "I'm going to be right back. You okay?"

"Mmhm," she acknowledges without looking up.

I leave my spot and go say hello to my mother and Gran.

"How's she doing?" Mom asks.

"Hard to tell. She's been handling it all well. She seems nervous today."

"That's understandable."

I nod in agreement. "She said that no one was going to come today. She was persistent that no one would want to see her mother even as ashes."

Gran looks around exaggeratedly, "I would say she is wrong about that."

"Yeah, me too. I don't think she realizes how many people care about what happens to her."

"She will learn the power of people's affection today. It will be good for her to receive their love." Gran declares.

"I hope so." I agree. "I got a chance to meet her mother. I understand why it is so hard for her to accept love from others. Her mother didn't exactly give her a good road map. She was a harsh woman. That is putting it nicely."

"It is good that they got some peace in the end." Mom confirms resting her hand on my shoulder. I'm glad they came.

"Yes, it was a powerful conversation. A hard one with a lot of impact."

"We won't keep you," Mom says. "Let's find our seats."

Before going back to sit with Aria, I head into the foyer to the bathroom. I watch Leana effortlessly talk to people as they come through the glass doors. They all seem to know her. I don't think Leana ever meets a stranger.

I recognize Mikey as he walks through the door. I head over to say hello. "Hey man," I reach out to shake his hand. "It's good to see you. I'm so glad you could come out."

"Hi. Roman, right?"

"Yeah." I confirm thankful he remembers me.

"I'm glad I could. She was there for me when my Dad died. I figured I could return the favor."

"That's really kind of you. I know Aria is glad you are here. She's inside preparing for her speech."

"Okay, I'll talk to her afterward. Thanks, Roman."

"I'll see you inside."

I walk away toward the restroom when I hear Leana's breathless voice, "You."

I turn to see Mikey stop in front of her with a dreamy look on his face. After an awkward beat, he holds out his hand to her, "Hi, I'm Mikey."

"I know."

"Right, we met at the bar when you were in Las Vegas."

"No," Leana stumbles, "I mean yes, we did. I remember that. I know you because I've seen you in my dreams. I didn't realize it was you, but now I can see."

"Really? I had a dream about a bird," he shakes his head like he is trying to make sense of it all.

"Aria told me." Leana nods. "Thanks for coming." She shakes his still outstretched hand. They hold on for a couple breaths longer than necessary.

"Can I save you a seat inside?" Mikey asks.

"If you sit near Aria, that'd be great." She smiles warmly and watches him go into the chapel.

I shake my head. It is significant that he came. I know Aria is excited to see him. After witnessing that interaction I would put money on something going on between Mikey and Leana. If it isn't already, it will be soon.

By the time I get back to the chapel, most everyone is seated. I escort Leana in on my arm as I head towards the front of the room. The place filled out nicely. Leana was right. People did come for Aria. When we reach the front, I wink at Mikey as Leana sits next to him in the pew behind Aria. I return to my seat next to her and realize her eyes are still closed.

"You okay there, Love?" I ask.

"Yeah, ready to get going." She replies.

"I think it's about time." I say and take her hand, giving it a small kiss. She looks up at me with a sweet look of love as Ralph climbs to the pulpit to welcome everyone.

He keeps it short and sweet. He knows his audience well. He gestures to Aria, welcoming her to the front. She gives me a nervous look but her eyes are bright. Her inner light is shining. She will be just fine.

She walks to the front and turns around. Even without the microphone on the podium in front of her I would have heard her gasp where I sat. "Wow," she says, "Don't you all have better things to do?"

A nervous laugh escapes the crowd.

"My mom must have annoyed more people than I

realized. If you're here to collect her debt, I'm sorry to say I can't pay. Think of it as a send off fund for Marilyn." She pauses then continues, "Maybe we'll call it the good riddance fund." The room laughs in earnest now.

I enjoy seeing Aria on stage. I know she is a good writer, but I didn't know she was a great speaker as well. I wonder if she realizes it.

"Most of you know that I didn't have a very good relationship with my mother. I don't know if she had a good relationship with anyone really. Maybe Jack Daniels, he knew her inside and out.

"My mother was a hard woman who didn't know how to take care of herself or much of anything else. I grew up wondering what was wrong with me that my mother didn't love me. I learned at a very young age the best way to avoid any disagreements was to leave. I ran as far as I could. I ended up in Nevada and it still wasn't far enough." She pauses with a contemplative look, "I still wasn't free."

"I never questioned my mother's sanity. In hindsight it makes sense that my mother suffered from mental illness. It doesn't excuse her behavior but it does help me understand it.

"Just before my mother died, she sobered up long enough for the doctors to help her with some medication to counter her mental illness. I was ready for a battle of wills when I finally decided to talk to her. I was surprised to have a real conversation. One where neither one of us yelled.

"I was shocked but thankful. It was in that moment I knew I would forgive her. It was the first time she'd told me she loved me since I was a kid. I always thought she regretted having me, but that wasn't the case. She didn't know what to do with me. But she loved me. That changed everything. It was a transformational exchange.

"It is amazing the power of love. I am only now

beginning to understand what it can mean. Changing my habit of running has been hard to break. I was searching for home. I lived in a wonderful house. But it often felt empty and full of conflict, especially after my grandmother died. All I wanted was to feel safe and loved. I didn't grow up with a place like that.

"I loved spending time with my best friend Leana. Thankfully Mrs. Grace practically adopted me as her own. Still, I eventually had to leave. I spent as much time as I could at school or the library," I smile to those who knew me there. "Nowhere felt like home. It was an elusive concept for me. Home was wherever I could sit with a book and not worry about anything or anyone else.

"As soon as I was able, I ran to Las Vegas. I thought it was a place where I could finally break free and be my own person. I was wrong. I spent five years there but it never felt like home. I did make one great friend there and he flew all the way here to be with me today. I am grateful for that."

I look back to see Mikey give a thumbs up.

"I feel like I've been buying time. Waiting for something to live for. I finally found the missing piece in Roman. It surprised me how intensely and quickly we connected. I soon realized he represented everything I was searching for. He is my home. In him I found a place where I feel safe and loved."

I look up at Aria with my eyes shining and blow her a kiss. She looks out at me with such luminous affection my breath catches in my throat.

"Home is not a physical location. Though I am glad to be closer to the beach again. Home is a state of mind, a peace Roman held up for me to see. Now I can see the magic of love everywhere. I see it in my friends that care so much and I see it in all of you."

"Now that I found my home, I can release the resentment I help towards my mother who never provided that for me. I can now go toward my dreams because I know where I am safe and loved. No matter what happens out there, I can come home and know everything is going to be okay.

"My mother's last gift to me was forcing me to confront her and realize how strong I am. I can forgive her now that I understand more about her. It helps to know that after it all, she really did love me. Believing that has allowed me to be free. I hope in the end my love allowed the same for her.

"After that one enlightening conversation with my mother, her heart failed. Even the doctor said that it seemed like she just let go. With the information I have now, I realize that my mother was very troubled. I hope now that she is finally at peace. That we can both find our own wings to fly.

"When we set up this service, I wondered why we should bother. I didn't think anyone would come. Hell, I wasn't sure I wanted to come. Now I look out at all of you and I am so very thankful I listened to my best friend and did this. My cup runs over. Thank you so much for coming and sharing this moment of love and loss with me."

I look around and notice many eyes glistening throughout the room including my own.

"My best friend, Leana Davis, would like to sing." Aria introduces and waits as Leana comes up to hug her. Aria sits next to me while Leana moves to the piano bench.

"That was beautiful." I whisper.

"Thanks," she blushes. I wrap my arm around her shoulders, pulling her close. A place to feel safe and loved. What a meaningful way to describe home. It also describes my love for her. I kiss her cheek as Leana begins to play.

The melody of "Home" by Philip Phillips becomes a

powerful ballad as Leana belts out the chorus. The song is perfect. It's like they planned it though I don't know when. Of course, they speak the same language. I'm learning that these things tend to happen when you hang around these two.

By the time the song is over, I hear a constant sniffling throughout the chapel. I reach for a tissue box handing one to Aria then taking one for myself.

The last note vibrates through the air as Aria stands, clapping for her friend. I stand and join her. Before we know it, the entire congregation is on their feet.

Leana steps away from the piano and Aria jumps out of her seat to embrace her friend. They stand together for a few moments. Aria walks back to the microphone, "I want to thank you all again for coming and for showing me that home is a place where you can always be found. We are able to stay in this room for about an hour. If you are able, I would really like to thank each of you for showing me so much love." She turns to the urn, "Goodbye Mom. It's time for us to be free."

I go to Aria as soon as she puts down the microphone. "You did it my love."

"I'm glad I did. How is it you two know what I need so much better than I do?"

"Because we love you." Leana answers.

"Well, that's true."

Aria seems surprised but also pleased by all the people who came out. Over the next hour I meet lots of people from Aria's past. She introduces me to a few of her teachers, including the drama club director and the librarian. Her mother's salon owner is there along with Mr. Carter and his wife. There are many more people from around the town that all became a blurry memory of names and handshakes.

I meet Leana's brother, Caleb. I see Alicia again and meet her boyfriend as well.

The most exciting meeting is between Leana and Gran. There were squeals from three very happy ladies. "It's so good to meet you, Gran," Leana embraces her.

"You, too, my dear. I feel like I already know you." Gran leans into her hug.

"It's because you speak our language, too." Aria clarifies.

The three of them chat like they've known each other forever. Mom leans over to me, "I think your grandmother has found her people."

I laugh at that, "I think you're right."

By the time our hour is up, most of the visitors have made their way home. Leana's mom invites us all over for dinner including Mom and Gran as well as Mikey. It feels good to see my family grow. Especially when I walk out with Aria in step beside me.

"You seem lighter, do you feel the weight lifted now?" I ask.

"I do. It feels good to finally be home."

Epilogue

Always and Forever

ARIA

The warm wind caresses my hair tickling my shoulders. The sun is still warm as the water laps over my feet this autumn afternoon. My new favorite beach smells of salt and sunscreen, the most perfect smell there is.

I lean back with my eyes closed taking in the beautiful moment. I try to ignore the feeling like I'm waiting for an alarm to go off and wake me from this dream.

Instead of the squeal of a clock, I hear the low rumble of a deep voice asking if I want more lemonade.

"Yes, please." I smile meeting sapphire blue eyes before he reaches into the cooler parked next to us. As I watch him lean over, I fall in love with him all over again. I admire his kindness, bravery, diligence and yes, his body, too.

He hands me my cup and accept the kiss that comes with it before he settles into his chair.

"What are you thinking about?" he asks.

"That this is all a dream."

"Then it is a very good dream."

"Yes, that's true." I laugh. "I used to dream of sitting on the beach just like this when I lived in Las Vegas. I didn't believe I could come back here."

"Are you glad you did?"

"Very glad. I don't have enough imagination to dream you up. I like reality better."

He laughs at that then adds, "I've read your manuscript. I think you have plenty of imagination."

"I suppose I do have my moments." I laugh.

I think of the day I finally finished my novel. It still needs work, but it is complete. I shared it with Roman, Leana, Gran and Ms. Grace. I haven't gotten much feedback yet. When Roman finished it, he came over to my chair and kissed me. He said, "Your mind is magic. I loved getting transported to another time and place." It felt like high praise.

Now I have to do some final revisions and learn how to publish a book.

That is a problem for another day. For now I am enjoying a beautiful afternoon sitting on the beach with the man I love.

I reach out for Roman's hand. "You have helped me so much. You believed in me and encouraged me to chase my dreams. You helped me face my mother and have done so much for me. Thank you."

He smiles at me "Well you are very welcome. You have done so much for me, too. You helped me remember what it means to dream. You have opened my eyes and my heart for love in a way that I didn't even realized was possible. How do you make it all look so easy?"

"That's easy," I answer, "You just have to take a leap of faith."

"Marry me."

"Roman?" I ask laughing.

"I'm serious." He turns around to get something out of his backpack tucked behind his chair.

He moves in front of my chair and gets down on one knee holding up a cushioned box containing a simple band with three embedded diamonds.

"Aria, I love you. I have since that first moment I

experience your fiery spirit on the streets of Vegas. You brought me to life. I want to spend forever and always with you. You are my dream. Aria, will you do me this honor? Will you share your light, your fire, your life with me? Will you marry me?"

My heart overflows with joy. I want to say I'm not good enough but I know that is not the case anymore. It is because of Roman that I believe in my strength. The power he held up for me to see.

I look into his eyes and see his love. His genuine affection and desire for me. I look and I am mesmerized by hope. I see something worth living for. Someone worth living for. I can see myself, my best self, through his eyes. I want that. I want all of it. I want all of him.

I think of Gran's words, "Don't be surprised if he pops the question before Christmas." It seems he couldn't wait that long. We still have four months to go. I'm glad he didn't wait. I am ready for his love, and support. I look forward to the family we will build together. He is my home, the place I feel safe and loved. I can't imagine being anywhere but here with him.

I close my eyes and I grip his hand like my life depends on it. In this moment, it does.

I look into his eyes, holding the biggest question, and I take a leap of faith.

"Yes. Yes, Roman. Yes, I will marry you. I love you."

He smiles broadly as he puts the ring on my finger. His arms wrap around me and his lips are on mine. I am in heaven.

It takes a few moments for us to hear the applause and cheers on the beach from the good natured people around us who have witnessed his proposal. We both started laughing. I do a little curtsy and the people fade away.

I look back to this man, the one who means everything

to me. I am very thankful for this love we share. Life is hard and painful and anything but fair. Sometimes a little piece of good finds you and that makes all the difference.

Everyone said I was brave for moving across the country with a guy I barely knew, for coming back home and facing my mother and for making a new life. I never felt brave. I was searching. I am glad for the home I found.

My life changed and it wasn't solely because of any of those things. It was all of it put together. My life changed because of a leap of faith. One so small and yet so big. Letting someone in. Having someone to care for and feel their love in return. Love has made all the difference.

The End

Acknowledgements

Thank you for reading my debut novel, "Leap of Faith." Publishing this novel is a dream come true. I have learned and grown so much through this process. I am glad to finally be able to share this story.

I want to give big hugs and kisses to my husband, Stephen, and daughter, Zoey. I appreciate your patience through my writing mood swings. Thank you for all of your never-ending love and support.

I thank my parents, Billy and Delores Gurganus, who have always supported me and encouraged me to go towards my dream. I would not be the woman I am today without their all-encompassing love.

I send a huge shout out to my best friend, Dana Torgersen, who was with me when I got the inspiration for this story. Thank you so much for believing in me and cheering me on.

I am proud of this publishing achievement, but I could not do it alone. I want to thank my beta readers: Dee Gurganus, Dana Torgersen, Kat Stiwinter, Paige Ingle, Kevin Hicks, Shannon Moore and Catrina Guglietta. You all really helped me put the finishing touches on this story. Thank you to Jenny MacLeod for helping me get organized and motivated to start this project. Thank you to Trina Krieger for an amazing book cover design.

Thank you to all of my friends and family that have been encouraging me and cheering me on. I could not have accomplished this without your amazing support.

"Leap of Faith" has been a joy to write. I have challenged myself and proved that persistence pays off. Thank you, reader, for sharing in my journey.

About the Author

    Amanda McCusker is the owner of Balancing Tree Press, a publishing company that encourages you to embrace your story. She graduated from Clemson University with a B.A. in English. Amanda has been published in newspapers and magazines, including "Legacy." *Leap of Faith* is her first published novel. Amanda lives in Seattle, WA, with her husband, daughter and cat.

www.balancingtreepress.com

Made in the USA
Columbia, SC
11 January 2020

86526675R00257